S.A. ALBA

King's Preparatory and the Stolen Power

Cover designed by Miblart

First edition

ISBN: 979-8-9858360-2-8

This book was professionally typeset on Reedsy.
Find out more at reedsy.com

Contents

Prologue

Rose lay on the floor. Shuddering, sweating, stuck with the constant urge to quench her thirst with the potent, harsh taste of alcohol. Except, for her, that flavor would be warm, soothing, and delicious. A sense of freedom overwhelmed her as the liquid touched her lips, and she would be restored with a small amount of happiness as the drink hit her stomach.

"I'm so sorry, darling, but there is no other way," the tall, bulky man said. He bent over to raise Rose Connors the Seventh off the ground slightly and kissed her cheek. Lifting one of his hands, he grazed a finger across her face but bolted upright as the knob clicked and the door pushed open. After resting her back on the floor, he rushed around the corner and listened.

The light footsteps of a child entered the room, and Rosie's young voice sounded.

"Rosie," he breathed and continued to listen.

"Mom? Mommy?" Rosie asked as she neared her mother's fallen body. Suddenly, panic erupted in her voice. "Mom!" she screamed.

"Shit," the man muttered to himself, and, for only a second, he debated whether to step forward.

"Mr. Zimmers," Rosie gasped, "it's my mom! She's… She's not moving. Please, her lips are blue."

A muffled voice, from one end of a phone, spoke to Rosie. *I have to get out of here.*

The man crept from around the corner, ensuring his face was distorted in case Rosie noticed him. He couldn't let her realize his true identity or be able to describe his appearance. She set the phone down and began to kneel by her mother, but her head turned as the man knocked a glass over to the ground. Shards split off in every direction, but Rosie's attention remained fixed on him.

She stared at the man, forgetting for a moment that her mother was dying in front of her. He tilted his head, taking in her appearance. He memorized her eyes, nose, hair, and then he stepped towards her, placing his hands on both sides of her head. Her eyes lit up blue, and when his hands left her cheeks, her attention immediately returned to her mother.

He closed the door and walked away, leaving the only two people he had ever loved in his long life to be miserable for the rest of theirs.

Chapter One

Rosie dove for cover as shards of rock splintered through the air and rained down on her.

"Ah!" she yelled as a piece sliced her shoulder. Her shirt began to soak with crimson blood. Ducking behind a boulder, she surveyed the damage.

Not too bad, she thought and whispered, "Tostiek," while holding her hand over the gash. Her face scrunched as the separated skin sealed, and she inspected her healed skin.

"Okay, what next?" she murmured to herself as she sat in the dirt contemplating her options.

She lifted her head. The world went still, and silence befell her. No, the world was silent, but the distinct crunching of dirt from footsteps approaching grew louder. She peered around the boulder, unable to locate her attacker, but somehow, she knew they were closing in on her.

Before she could decide if she should use a masking spell to slip away or fight with an attack curse, scraping nails sounded from the other side of the boulder.

Rosie jumped from behind the rock and yelled, "Britenium!" Blinding light shot from her palm, and her counter flew backwards. Rosie ran to the culprit and positioned her foot on the person's chest and held one hand forward to the person's face while her other hand clasped her necklace.

"I yield," Professor Walker said, gently tapping Rosie's foot.

Rosie lifted her hiking boot and assisted Professor Walker up.

Dusting herself off she eyed Rosie.

"That wasn't too bad, but can I ask why you used the Britenium curse?" Professor Walker asked, now attempting to remove the boot print that stained her shirt.

"I wanted to disarm you, not hurt you."

The two started to walk through the desert mountainside, Rosie wondering what she had done wrong in this lesson.

"Rosie, if you truly want to be ready for when Egil returns, then you must give me your all. I can handle it."

Rosie thought of Egil and his ghastly appearance, demeanor, and actions. "*If* he returns," Rosie said, kicking a rock.

Professor Walker lifted an eyebrow, and Rosie continued, "I mean, it's been months since he attacked me and disappeared. There haven't been any random killings in one singular area that fit the same pattern. For all we know, he got himself into trouble elsewhere and we'll never see him again." She kicked another stone but then looked up at the sky. She logically knew her hopes were just that.

Professor Walker paused and placed a soft hand on Rosie's shoulder.

"When," Professor Walker explained, "or if, either way, you need to be ready for any threat. You learned a lot this summer and you are a natural witch, but you need to unleash your power. Stop restraining yourself." Giving Rosie one more glance, she turned away and started walking back towards the front entrance of King's Preparatory, leaving Rosie alone on the lakeside.

Plopping down in the sand, Rosie gazed across the glistening lake. Schools of streaper fish splashed up, screeching as they breached, and Rosie's mind transported her back to the beginning of summer.

After saying goodbye to Riley, Rosie spent every day with Professor Walker, training, and learning all that she could about her new power. Staring at her hands, Rosie started to circle them above the sand, causing the small flecks to rise and dance.

Riley will be here tomorrow.

Over summer break, Rosie talked to Riley every day. He told her about home and seeing all their old friends Well, his old friends. And she told him about the new spells she had learned. He would describe the events his mother, Rosie's unofficial guardian, Glenda Zimmers, would force him to attend, and she would talk about what crazy situation Professor Manger had set up for her to escape. He would tell her about his summer assignments that Professor Shay had sent out to all the students to work on, and she would tell him about her one-on-one lessons with Shay, where she learned more about the history of magic. Finally, he would tell her how her mom was doing, and Rosie would change the subject. As far as she knew, her mother didn't care she was in another state, much less alive. Rosie even had Glenda, instead of her mother, noted as her emergency contact.

"Rosie!"

"Hey," Rosie said as she watched her cheeks turn red in the small box on her phone screen. Riley's sparkling smile grew, and his piercing eyes bore into hers.

"I can't wait to see you tomorrow. You'll have to show me all the cool tricks you learned," Riley said, his glistening, white smile gleaming through the phone.

Rosie flicked her hand up and snapped her fingers. One small flame sat on the tip of her index finger, and she laughed but Riley groaned.

"I can't actually see what you are doing," Riley argued, staring at her dancing finger. "The phone alters it. It just looks like you are snapping."

Rosie giggled and gave a hearty laugh before blowing the flame out. She then turned the camera, so it was facing the lake and pointed the phone to the mountainside.

"Are you excited to see this in person?" The phone reflected the various colors that illuminated the sky. Hints of baby pink, lavender, peach, and gold were painted above her, and she watched Riley's face for a reaction.

"Yeah, but mostly so I can kiss you under it."

Rosie teased the rectangular locket that Riley had given her the previous year. The horizontal bar sat just below her Valtic pendant. She grazed her fingers up and then clutched the Valtic ruby.

Almost one year ago, Rosie had arrived at King's Preparatory and tested into the school. She learned that supernatural creatures existed, and throughout the school year, she learned she was actually a witch. When she was admitted, she was forced to choose between the four different teams. Valtic, Astive, Haply, and Surgent. She remembered Professor Shay's hand swaying the four different necklaces in front of her. The ruby, holding a hot fire within it, drew her towards it.

She released the jewel and turned the phone camera back

on herself and started to stand.

"I need to get going, but when do you get in tomorrow?"

"I land around nine, so ten-thirty?"

A smile spread across Rosie's face. "Perfect. I'll see you then."

"See you then."

Rosie ended the call and took one last glance at the descending sun before heading up to the King's Preparatory lobby.

Entering the school, which sat in the rocky Sonoran desert mountainside, Rosie slowly made her way first through the grand foyer and then walked into the school's main lobby. She peered up at the high glass ceiling as she maneuvered through the pieces of fine Victorian furniture. The setting sun lit up the room, but as it continued to set, the lights in the room automatically turned on. She smiled at the magical automation and continued, making her way past the lobby desk to the second waiting room.

Shifting the ornate rug over, she lifted the trap door up from the ground, displaying the long, dark, hidden staircase.

Stepping down, Rosie walked past the many suits of armor, portraits, and murals that in one way or another, held secrets whether they told a story of the school's past or were hidden passageways to other parts of the school. Her fingertips glided along the rough stone walls, and she guided herself to the dining hall.

The soon-to-be-filled room sat below the great lake, the glass ceiling displaying schools of fish and soon, the school's mermaid population.

She passed the many long wooden tables with cushioned high-back chairs and entered the Valtic Library. Rosie inhaled her favorite scent of old books and bounded up the stairs, passing thousands of texts. Finding the hidden button on one of the shelves, she opened her secret study room.

She clicked the bookshelf door behind her closed, sat down in the candlelit room, and pulled open *Being*, studying the spells she left off on.

"Taking one's power is no easy feat," Rosie read aloud, processing Christion Flare's words, "and doing so can become detrimental to the taker's physical and mental state."

Just as Rosie was about to continue reading, her ruby stone began to vibrate.

Once Rosie clasped her hand around it, Professor Walker's voice filled her head.

"Rosie, please meet me in my office in twenty minutes."

"Really?" she muttered, shutting the book and storing it away. "She couldn't have talked to me an hour ago?" Rosie walked to exit the room, and before leaving, she swished her hand. A mild *whooshing* of wind soared through the room, and the flicker of candles ended, leaving the room in a state of dark stillness.

Retracing her steps, Rosie entered the small waiting room again, and then entered the never-ending hallway, finding Professor Walker's door.

Entering Professor Walker's office, Rosie couldn't help but think of its previous occupant: Doctor Witam—or better to say Egil Vidar Ruud. Rosie looked around the office as she entered and noticed that it had, thankfully, been transformed to meet Professor Walker's needs and the needs of the students who were affected by Egil's deception.

A fresh coat of dark navy paint covered the room, and a blush velvet sofa sat where the leather sofa once did. A glass desk replaced the wooden one, and a pristine, clear gold clock sat on the wall. Professor Walker had changed the office to match her style, but the memories Rosie had with Doctor Witam still haunted the room.

"Hi, Rosie. Thank you for seeing us," Professor Walker said.

She turned to look at the sofa where Professor Shay sat, one leg behind the other, her hands placed delicately in her lap.

"Um, sure," Rosie replied. Her eyebrows furrowed together, and she remained standing.

"Please," Professor Walker said, gesturing towards the glass chair across the desk.

As Rosie sat, Professor Shay examined her nails and spoke, "As you are aware, almost a year ago, you came to this campus and tested to gain admittance." Professor Shay lowered her hand and then stood. "Professor Walker and I have seen a lot of improvement from you this summer, and we think it would be beneficial if you acted as a student liaison to the intellect candidates."

"I will be needed elsewhere, so I will need you to take my spot," Professor Walker clarified, then raised an eyebrow.

"Like, call back students and take them from each exam or interview?" Rosie asked.

"Yes, and like I did last year, proctor their first exam and check their answers. You'll know if they are correct."

Rosie grinned, "Okay, yeah. I can help."

"Perfect," Professor Walker said with a smile and added, "We will also have you be a part of the transformation performance. You will do this alongside Liam, Marina, and Owen."

Rosie thought about the other sophomores. Liam, a vampire in Surgent, Marina, a mermaid in Astive, and Owen, a werewolf in Haply. Rosie thought back to her interviews and remembered how each team had a person representing them so their personalities could be displayed to her. If a candidate made it that far in the testing, Rosie told herself she would try to display her true self for them.

"How many candidates are expected?" Rosie asked.

"Around two hundred invitations were sent out," Professor Shay said, "and only fifty-three replied. Of those fifty-three, twelve are intellect candidates and the rest are protector candidates."

Rosie nodded and noted Professor Shay's demeanor. After last year, Professor Shay displayed a newfound respect for Rosie. Rosie suspected this was only because she developed her witch powers, but she did show a bit more compassion towards the natural students when she spoke of them.

"Now," Professor Walker explained, "we will need you in the front lobby at ten sharp, but report to my office tomorrow at nine forty-five so you can review the list. Remember, some may go home before even taking the written exam depending on how they handle getting to the school."

A flash of lightning pierced Rosie's mind as she recalled that first test. Finding the hidden school, hiking up the mountainside toward the school or at least she had hoped she was going towards the school. She had been dropped off and only told to *follow the lightning*. She also had to face a rattlesnake to make it to the lakeside where the entrance sat, and she had to be on school property before noon. Her lips lifted a little as that's when she realized her life had started.

"There are fewer candidates this year so we are starting

earlier and will hopefully be done earlier as well," Professor Walker said.

Rosie nodded, and that's when she remembered Riley.

He'll have to wait, she thought with a twinge of sadness.

"Okay, I'll be here tomorrow morning," she confirmed.

"Perfect. Also, similar to last year, you will be interacting with Professor Manger if candidates make it to the next stage of examination."

Ugh. While Manger had lightened up on Rosie since being forced to teach her over the summer, the man still thought less of her and the other naturals. Honestly, the majority of students. Why he ever became a teacher confused Rosie.

Rosie nodded.

"Great," Professor Walker said, now standing and indicating for Rosie to do the same. "That's all for now."

Rosie nodded once more and left the office, pausing for a moment in the hallway. Pulling out her phone, she found Riley's name and sent him a quick message.

Can't meet tomorrow until after dinner, sorry!

She continued to hold her phone up with the message displayed. Three bubbles in the text screen popped up, indicating Riley was formulating his reply but then they disappeared.

Come on, Riley... Try to understand.

She shook her head and dropped her phone into her back pocket before starting back to her dorm room.

The witches' dorm was much larger than the naturals' dorm she had stayed in last year, and it had been upgraded more over the years since more students lived there.

While the floor delegations were essentially the same, the size of the floors were much larger, including the lobby.

Multiple couches and rectangular tables sat scattered there. The kitchenette and study rooms on the next level were also far superior to the natural dorms as they were three times the size and were complete with new appliances, furniture, and projectors.

Placing her hand on a mirror in the lobby, Rosie felt the glass turn from cold and hard to warm and mushy. Slowly, she entered the mirror and appeared on her dorm floor. She walked the long hallway and entered her single bedroom.

It was almost an exact replica of her and Eleanor's room, but it was cut in half. In the room, her body began to numb, and her magic dulled. If she was honest with herself, the feeling started as soon as she entered the dorm.

When it first happened, she wanted to see if anyone else could feel their powers being dulled, especially since the sensation grew stronger as summer continued, but there wasn't anyone else on campus besides her and her teachers.

It's just a safety precaution, she reasoned but honestly didn't know if there were such protocols in place.

She wiggled her arms and jumped in the air. Warm tingles began to surge throughout again, and Rosie practiced lighting flames on each finger. Relieved to see the small dancing flames, she giggled and climbed into bed.

I wonder if any intellects will get in tomorrow, she thought, thinking about how she would act and what she would say when she met the candidates. Rosie's mind became entangled with what her day would look like, starting with testing the potential new students and ending with being with Riley. She thought of his every feature and quirky trait until she fell into a deep slumber.

* * *

Rosie sat in the cave where Egil Vidar Ruud and Justin Fent had taken her. They stood, conspiring in the corner, perfecting their potion of immortality. Egil turned to Rosie, his terrifying true self revealed, and he glided towards her. Rosie's hands shot up and streaks of lightning flew from them. Electricity crackled throughout the cave with a shock so intense it shook Rosie to the bone.

Egil and Justin were gone, and Rosie wasn't in the cave. She sat in her bed, surrounded by sparks of electricity igniting throughout the air.

"Ceasarsio!" she yelled, attempting to put the small sparks out, but they only grew in size. "Ceasarsio!" she screamed again but the same effect occurred.

A smashing of glass sounded from the opposite side of the room, beyond the sparks. Emerging from a portal, made from Rosie's full-length mirror, Professor Walker entered the room and waved her hands. As she did so, small shocks and sparks erupted along her own body, but soon after, the remaining electrical current dissipated.

Standing up, Rosie moved carefully around her bed. She searched the room in astonishment as she breathed fast and hard.

"What happened?" Professor Walker asked, her eyes wide and mouth remaining open.

"I-I," Rosie started as she shook her head.

"Were you trying a new spell?" she asked, moving around the room. "Were you trying to set the dorm on fire?"

"No," Rosie replied, wondering why Professor Walker

seemed more unnerved than angry. "I was just sleeping, and I woke up, and then there was all this electricity around me. Professor Walker, what happened?"

"I don't know." Professor Walker searched the room and called for any hidden curses to be revealed but none came forward. Finally, she sat in Rosie's desk chair.

"Could this have been Egil?" Rosie asked, thinking about the man who tried to kill her last year.

Professor Walker's eyes connected with Rosie's. "Maybe," she responded. "I will make sure Professor Shay knows you were targeted, and we will put up extra protection layers around campus. Even have Premier Kingsley send Superiority security to patrol the campus." Professor Walker tapered off and sat in silence, staring at the floor. Her eyes moved back and forth, and Rosie could tell her mind was racing.

"Thank you, Professor Walker."

Bringing her eyes back up to meet Rosie's, Professor Walker nodded and stood. "You should start getting ready, and I will see you in a couple of hours."

Rosie's mentor exited the room and Rosie stood, inspecting her hands. They sat raw and burned, scorch marks starting to disappear from them.

This wasn't Egil. I did this.

Chapter Two

With her hands firmly shoved inside her jean pockets, Rosie dredged to Professor Walker's office. Fear swarmed her, but she shifted her focus towards testing the new candidates.

I'll revisit Being *and see if dream magic happens. It must. I can't be the first person to manifest magic from a dream. It's just like last year. When I was drowning in blood and then coughed some up when I woke. It's okay. It's just a heightened environment. There is nothing wrong.*

"Connors!"

The growl hit Rosie's ears, and she turned to greet Professor Manger.

"Hi, Professor."

Without returning her greeting, the giant, bulky, surly Professor Manger spoke, "Professor Walker said to give you this." He handed her a clipboard with the potential students who were to be tested further.

"I was just heading to her office now to go over everything once more."

"No need. She is on a call with the Superiority. Something about a witch causing more problems at the school."

Professor Manger's smirk made heat rise to her cheeks.

She dipped her head down and focused on the clipboard. Out of the thirteen intellect candidates, nine were crossed off.

"Only four?"

"I'm happy you can count." Professor Manger chuckled and then stalked off towards the lobby.

Rosie followed him and listened to the same speech Professor Manger had given her and the other candidates last year. First, he dismissed the students who had failed the first test—finding the school—and then he called back the potential protectors. A total of fifteen trailed him through the left-side lobby door, which led to one of the never-ending hallways.

Rosie inspected each candidate who followed Manger through the door. Each was built wide and seemed athletic enough to perform any physical task thrown their way, but the most noticeable was a boy who had to have been over six feet tall and was at least two hundred pounds of pure muscle. Aside from his ashy brown hair sculpted perfectly on his head, he could've been a miniature Manger. Well, not miniature, but a younger replica. The kid smirked as he passed Rosie, and she narrowed her eyes at the candidate before he exited the hall.

Refocusing on her clipboard and then scanning the room, she noted the four students staring at her. Three were green in the face and visibly shaking, but the fourth, a girl, sat smiling. Chuckling almost. As if the other students' nerves calmed her.

"Nikki Ceadie, Hank Needine, Richard Satra, and Dana Randolph, please follow me." The first three scuttled their feet quickly to Rosie while the last, Dana Randolph, smirked and took her time. The smirk, she noticed, matched perfectly with the mini-Manger protector candidate.

They must be siblings, she thought.

Leading the potential students into the smaller waiting room, Rosie paused and said, "Nikki Ceadie, please follow me. Everyone else, please find a seat." Rosie spied the others who began sitting down, and then she led Nikki to the second never-ending hallway.

Once in the first room, which remained the same as when Rosie had taken her test last year—cold, sterile, intimidating—and after Nikki sat down, Rosie began, "You will have twenty minutes to complete the exam in front of you. If you answer every question correctly, you will move on to the next task. You may start now."

Nikki fervently turned over the exam and began to read. She passed the first question and the second and the third.

Rosie tried not to judge, but she couldn't help thinking that Nikki was not King's Preparatory material.

The twenty minutes passed, and Rosie picked up and studied the paper. Only eight questions were answered. Rosie smiled at Nikki.

"Nikki, I'm sorry but you will not be moving on. Please follow me." Nikki stood up, water wetting her eyes. Opening the door, Rosie found Doctor Geller, the school's in-house doctor.

"Miss Ceadie," Doctor Geller started, smiling down at the girl, "I want to thank you for attending King's Preparatory. I will escort you to a vehicle, which will take you back home."

Tears now streamed down Nikki's cheeks, and she sniffled loudly. Nikki nodded and started to move past Doctor Geller, but as she did, he raised his hands to both sides of Nikki's head. A blue glow emanated from all sides of Nikki's skull, and she turned back to Rosie.

"Thank you so much for the opportunity," the young girl said, the tears now gone. Nikki slurred and stumbled as Doctor Geller led her away. He turned to wink at Rosie, and she walked back into the exam room. With the flick of her wrist, another exam flew to the table, the pencil sharpened itself, and she moved back to the lobby.

Alright. Next candidate.

The next two candidates left King's Preparatory as Nikki had. Stupidly happy, with no indication of how they got to the school. Only with the memory that they hadn't passed their test and went back home.

For a moment, Rosie examined the clipboard, already knowing the name of the final candidate but still waiting.

"Dana Randolph," Rosie called. She studied the confident girl. Her ashy brown hair was cut in a bob, and she stood at five-foot-ten or eleven. She bounded forward, her mouth set in a horizontal grin while her eyes squinted.

"Ready when you are," Dana said as she side-stepped Rosie, staring down at her, and walked through the door first.

Rosie stepped back but found her footing again and then carried herself forward. She slid past Dana, who gave her barely any room to squeeze by, to the first door in the hallway. Rosie opened the door and Dana brushed past and took a seat.

Still put off by the actions of the candidate, Rosie stayed in the doorway, stunned.

"Well?" Dana asked, now holding the pencil ready.

Rosie stepped into the room and then relayed the same instructions she had previously. Before Rosie finished speaking, Dana started scribbling across the page. With only the sound of scratching graphite on paper, Rosie leaned up against the wall and crossed her arms. Five minutes went by. Then ten.

Rosie stared at her watch but jerked her head up when the pencil noises ceased.

"Done," Dana stated after thirteen minutes with the test. Rosie raised her eyebrows and moved towards the table. Lifting the paper, Rosie read each answer.

She answered everything correctly.

"Um, follow me, please," Rosie said, attempting to hide her surprise. She turned her back and recomposed herself. When she entered the hallway, she searched both directions in case Doctor Geller was there, but he wasn't.

"Is this where I'm following you to?" Dana asked, snark dripping off every word. "Or is there an actual place I am supposed to go?"

Rosie spun towards the girl, her eyes narrowing. "Excuse me?"

All Dana did to answer the questions was shrug with a smirk and then gesture her hands forward for Rosie to keep moving.

Heat rose to Rosie's cheeks but rather than allow her emotions to overwhelm not just her, but also her magic, she moved down to the next door in the hallway, entering the stairwell and then opening the door to the grassy field.

Professor Manger stood waiting, the candidates he called back surely with Professor Shay now.

"Professor Manger," Rosie started, "may I introduce you to Dana-"

"Randolph. Dana Randolph," Dana said abruptly and

brushed Rosie to the side.

Professor Manger smirked at Rosie and turned around. "Follow me this way."

Shaking her head as the rude professor escorted the candidate to the next test, Rosie sat on the grass and then closed her eyes, allowing the heat from the sun to warm her after being in the chilly school. Laying her head back, she ran her fingers through the grass and concentrated.

"Talisen Grothem," she whispered and the grass around her hand grew. She sat up, ensuring her spell worked. Smiling at the outcome, she then whispered, "Cutamenti," and she pursed her lips and blew air on the grass. The wind sliced the grass back to its normal height. She continued to practice, attempting to now grow the grass in designs.

Ten minutes went by, then twenty, but Rosie had too much fun practicing. Suddenly, a big, dark shadow engulfed Rosie's body and a low growl sounded behind her.

Rising from the ground and brushing her hands on her pants, Rosie stared up at Professor Manger's glare. She then looked around Manger to Dana, who smiled and stared at Rosie's hands.

She couldn't have seen, Rosie thought, as it wasn't until Manger stepped aside that Dana had a full view of Rosie.

"Take her to Professor Walker," Professor Manger grumbled, his ears red and his eyes set as slits.

Rosie nodded and hurried up the steps with Dana in tow.

"Hm," Dana cawed as the two bounded back up the stairs, and Rosie was happy her back was to Dana as her cheeks stayed reddened and her eyes rolled.

Opening the door to the hallway, Rosie paused and let Dana pass her, allowing Professor Walker to formally greet the intellect candidate.

"Hello, Dana."

"Oh, hi," Dana said, her confident demeanor falling for a second making Rosie smile.

"Thank you, Rosie," Professor Walker said, "Please join the others for now."

Rosie nodded and made eye contact with Dana once more. Dana spied Rosie's hands again and then winked before she entered the room. The door clicked closed, and Rosie shook her head and kicked her toe into the ground.

"Ugh," she grunted, before heading down the hallway.

Rosie, locked in her thoughts, entered the room which resembled a teacher's lounge.

I should've been more careful. I shouldn't have been practicing.

"Hey, Rosie," Owen said, forcing her attention up to the three classmates seated at a table.

"Hey," Rosie said, shifting her feet before spying two untouched lunch trays. "One for me?"

"Yep, you choose, and whichever is left can go to whoever is about to get in," Marina added, pushing both trays in her direction.

Rosie studied the trays. A chicken salad sandwich sat on one with orange slices and a bag of chips, and the other had a steak wrap with the same sides.

"Steak wrap it is," Rosie said, scooching the chair in and digging her teeth into the wrap.

"So, what have you been up to?" Liam asked just as Rosie ripped off her first bite.

"Uh," she muttered as she chewed and swallowed. "I've just been hanging out here. Nothing crazy."

"Nothing crazy? Yeah, right. How's your training been?"

Marina asked.

"No, really. I've just been learning about my magic." She started to take another bite but caught all three staring at her with anticipation. "What?" she asked, now running her tongue across her teeth, hoping there wasn't anything stuck to them.

"It's just," Maria continued, "This never happens. Someone developing their powers so late. You're sure your parents aren't witches?"

Rosie set her wrap down, realizing she wouldn't be eating lunch anytime soon, and wiped her hands before propping one under her chin.

"Well, no. I don't remember my mom displaying any crazy powers."

"What about your dad?" Liam asked.

Rosie grimaced. "Never met him."

"Has to be your dad then," Marina said. "It's too bad you weren't trained before you were attacked last year. You totally would have killed Justin and Witam then."

Rosie's eyes grew. *Kill?*

"Um, why don't you show us something you learned," Owen asked, being the only one who noticed the color in Rosie's face fading. Rosie turned to him, and he nodded his head encouragingly. Happy to oblige as it changed the subject away from killing Justin, Rosie snapped her fingers. The lights in the room all went out.

"Okay," Liam said, "that's it?"

Smirking, Rosie cupped her hands around her mouth and blew. Light began to fill the room but not from the bulbs. Rather, orbs of swooshing light floated, creating a relaxing atmosphere.

"Okay, that's pretty awesome," Liam said, reaching to touch one. As his fingertip grazed the edge of the orb, he pulled it back fast. Smoke rose from the tip and the burned flesh began to heal itself. "Cool to look at, but don't touch," he added with a laugh.

The others laughed too, but not Rosie. Instead, she stood and examined the orb, putting her fingers out to touch it. Her finger sizzled, and she drew her hand back to her chest.

"Didn't I just say they were hot?" Liam asked, laughing.

Rosie stared at the three who were giggling and enjoying the spell. Rosie let out a measly laugh in return and sat back down.

She examined her finger, a fresh, red burn mark sitting on the pad of her fingertip. *Those shouldn't be hot at all*, she thought, and then with a wave of her hand, the orbs floated through the air and returned to the lights.

"So cool," Owen said, grabbing Rosie's shoulder and squeezing.

"Did you learn any attack spells?" Liam eagerly asked as he leaned closer.

Rosie raised an eyebrow. "You'll have to wait to see what I can do in combat training," she joked.

The group laughed but quieted as Professor Walker opened the door. The group turned and stood.

"Students," Professor Walker stated, "this is Drew and Dana Randolph." She ushered the potential students into the room and allowed each student to study the candidates.

Dana stood next to the "mini" Manger, both tall and confident. "So nice to meet you all," she said, her smile oozing fakery but it was only noticeable to Rosie.

"Nice to meet you," Liam said, Marina and Owen also

sharing pleasantries.

"Oh, I see you were only expecting one student," Professor Walker said, noting the one tray. "Why don't you all sit to talk, and I'll go fetch another tray."

"Professor Walker," Dana started before anyone was able to move, "you must be so busy. Please, allow me to go get my own lunch. Plus, I am a vegetarian so I can be a bit picky."

"I do have a lot on my plate," Professor Walker muttered under her breath. Her eyes then met Rosie's, and Rosie nodded her head.

"Dana," Rosie said, "I'll go ahead and grab you something. Why don't you take my seat and you and your brother can relax? I'll be back soon with your meal."

Smiling, Professor Walker left, and Rosie started to follow.

"Oh, Rosie," Dana said, causing Rosie to pause. She turned, expecting the girl to thank her, but instead, Dana just added, "Remember, vegetarian." She smirked and turned back to the table with her brother, pulling out a chair and starting up a conversation.

Rosie took her leave, a hatred forming for the girl. As she closed the door, she peered back at the group. Sure enough, Dana sat in her seat and Drew side-eyed her as they laughed at a joke Owen told.

"Ugh," Rosie grunted as she clicked the door shut and found Professor Walker in the hall.

"What do you think?" Professor Walker asked, crossing her arms.

"Oh, well—"

"Won't it be great to have two more naturals at the school?" she asked. "It's important that the enhanced students learn more about the outside world."

"Why?" Rosie asked, stepping back from confusion.

From Rosie's knowledge, once they graduated from the school, they would find a place within the supernatural community, not the normal world.

"Because," Professor Shay's voice sounded as she approached the two, "Premier Kingsley is working to integrate us further into human society."

"What?" Shock rippled through Rosie. *The man who Egil said wanted to take over the human race now wants to become entwined with them?* "How does he want to integrate?"

Professor Shay wrinkled her nose at Rosie but continued, "It's not really any of your business."

"She should know," Professor Walker spoke up. "She will probably be one of the selected."

"Selected? What?" Rosie said, but Professor Shay spoke over her.

"Fine. Premier Kingsley had the brilliant idea of stationing qualified individuals within certain departments within the human government." Professor Shay then positioned herself next to Professor Walker and opened her mouth to speak again but turned back to Rosie, who still stood in the hallway. "Do you need something else?"

Rosie, of course, wanted to ask more questions. Get more of an idea of what James Kingsley was up to, but instead, she shook her head. "Oh um, no. I'm just getting one of the candidates a lunch."

"Well, hurry along then," Professor Shay said, turning back to Professor Walker. The two spoke in hushed tones, and Rosie moved away, heading for the dining hall.

Integrating supernaturals into the human government. Would the President know? Would any human? Or just Premier

Kingsley? Rosie's mind raced at the possibility of James Kingsley not only being the leader of the Superiority but also pulling strings within the United States government. *There's no way he would expose us.*

Rosie moved to the dining hall and grabbed a tray, inspecting it to ensure it was, in fact, a vegetarian meal before returning to the others. As she entered the room, she studied the group of teens all laughing.

She put a smile on her face and set the tray of food in front of Dana as the others continued conversing.

"Um, I don't think this is vegetarian," Dana said, inspecting the salad.

"I double-checked that it was," Rosie responded, the corners of her mouth now beginning to pull down.

"That's okay. I'm not that hungry anyway." Dana pushed the tray away with a look of disgust and then turned back to Liam.

Rosie stood, as there wasn't a chair for her. Her brows pulled down and her arms crossed at Dana's attitude, but instead of saying anything, she observed and listened in on the conversation.

"You guys have been going here since you were five?" Drew asked.

"Yep. Well, all except Rosie. She tested and was accepted last year," Owen said, staring at her with admiration.

"I mean, it's not that hard," Dana piped up. "That test was a joke. I could have finished my first test faster if my pencil wasn't so dull." As she said this, she stared at Rosie and then turned back to the group and let out a giggle. The others began to laugh as well.

Rosie gave a huff and stepped forward, but as she did, the

door opened and Professor Walker entered.

"Dana, Drew, I hope you enjoyed speaking with the students."

The group sat up straighter at her appearance.

"We have," Dana said, pulling her hands together.

"Great. Now," Professor Walker said, turning to the students, "If you four would now go to where you're supposed to be."

The group nodded, and Rosie, Owen, Liam, and Marina all exited and entered a room down the hall. The four stood in the dark, silent and focused. Within a few minutes, lights blared on over the group and Professor Walker's voice came over the speaker system.

"Students, please begin."

Liam started first, his fangs protruded and eyes blared red. He took Marina's wrist and bit into it.

Marina allowed Liam a single gulp but pushed him back with webbed hands and all-black eyes. Her legs came together, and scales began to pop out.

The tear of Owen's shoes splitting apart and his bones popping out of place sounded as he began his transformation. Thick hair covered his arms and his canine teeth enlarged.

It was Rosie's turn. Clasping her hand around her ruby pendant she began to whisper, "Hovitee lowstrum." Her feet lost contact with the ground, and when she opened her eyes, they emitted a blue glow. She chanted again and snapped her finger to turn out the light. At the click of her index finger and thumb rubbing together, the light bulb burst and sent the students into darkness.

There was a screech across the speaker, and the group returned to their normal state.

"Woah, Rosie," Marina started, "Watch the glass next time."

"Sorry," Rosie grumbled as she opened the door to let some light in. The three passed her and entered the hallway, but she stayed, examining the shattered glass on the floor. She shook her head and followed the others.

Rosie thought about Dana and Drew and how they would be giving Professor Walker their true reaction to supernatural creatures existing. It would be the final determination if they would be admitted into the school.

Catching up to Marina, Rosie stopped her. "Hold on," she said and lifted a final piece of the broken bulb from her hair. "Sorry, again. I meant to only turn out the light, not burst it."

"It happens, Rosie. Don't stress about it," Owen said, smiling. Rosie returned it and the four continued down to the dining hall.

"Think they made it in?" Marina asked.

"Oh, yeah," Liam replied, "They don't seem the type to freak out over something like this."

The four entered the dining hall where the rest of the high school students were already seated, chatting before Professor Shay began speaking to the freshman class. Rosie's eyes peered over the group, and she found the ones she desired.

Riley. Her heartbeat sped up, and it took everything in her not to run to him. Instead, she glided towards the sophomore table, her eyes trained on him, and she slid into the open seat at his side. His eyes dropped down and came back up.

"Damn, I missed you," he said, leaning over to kiss her.

Her face warmed as his soft lips brushed hers. She pursed her lips back, welcoming him.

"Ah-em," Eleanor proclaimed.

Rosie withdrew her lips and turned to her friend across the table. Eleanor reached her hands across, and Rosie pressed her palms into her best friend's.

"I missed you so much," Rosie said, staring at the beautiful blonde.

"Missed you more, sister," Eleanor replied, winking.

"Um, hey, what about me?" Garrett said, pushing Eleanor's hands out of Rosie's and into his. "I missed you most." He winked and the four laughed.

"Garrett, what are you doing here?" Rosie laughed, noticing an empty seat at the junior table.

"Babe, I sit wherever I want, whenever I want." The four friends laughed again, and a small warmth built inside Rosie, easing her mind. She was with her friends. Her best friends. Her family.

"How are the candidates?" Riley asked as the group settled down.

"Well, there's two that made it to the big reveal. A protector and an intellect, and they're twins."

"Cool. I bet they feed off of each other," Garrett said.

"Excuse me, what?" Eleanor asked in disgust.

"The small number of magic protectors and intellects normally have is probably enhanced, sicko," Garrett responded, laughing and then continued to explain, "Sometimes siblings who both have enhanced abilities can feed off of each other's power and make themselves stronger. More so with twins, triplets, and so on."

"Did you know about that?" Riley turned to Rosie.

"I read something about siphoning in *Being* when I unlocked the book, but that information disappeared after Egil vanished."

Rosie had discovered that *Being* returned to its normal self soon after her battle with Egil and heart-to-heart with James Kingsley at the end of the last school year. When James Kingsley had asked Rosie where the book disappeared to, she mentioned she didn't know, but she held onto it, understanding the knowledge within would assist her should Egil return.

The specific knowledge, including the immortality spell that revealed itself once to Rosie after her blood dripped on the pages, had dissolved back within. Over the summer, she had tried to bring the information back to the pages, but no matter how many times she pricked her finger and dripped blood upon the leathery pages made of human skin, the words stayed hidden.

"So, can they steal my abilities?" Eleanor asked, her eyebrows furrowing together.

"No, they aren't witches. Don't worry," Garrett replied to his girlfriend, pulling her closer.

"Owen, Liam, Marina, and Rosie, please come forward," Professor Shay said. Though the statement wasn't an announcement, as Professor Shay said Rosie's name, the room quieted, and eyes darted over to her.

After last year's attempt on her life and her miraculous outing as a witch, Rosie was treated differently. Not as a celebrity, but more so as a science experiment that had gone wrong. She hesitantly stood up and then walked towards the stage. With a whip of her hand, Professor Shay held a crystal ball.

"Is that the same one from last year?" Liam asked with a smirk, eyeing Rosie.

"As a matter of fact, yes," Rosie declared. Over the summer

she had worked with Professor Shay to heal the ball and put it back to its original state after she had broken it last year with her indecision to select a team to join.

Clearing her throat, Professor Shay continued, "One by one, you will each place your hand on the ball, and it will then see what you have experienced today with the candidates." She eyed Liam and then nodded her head, indicating to start. One by one, each sophomore placed their hands on the ball and then left to sit until it was Rosie's turn. Rosie reached her hand out, but Professor Shay pulled the ball back.

"Please, don't break it this time." A teasing grin played at Professor Shay's lips, and Rosie smiled, placing her hand on the ball.

Instantly, Rosie transported to the same plane as the ball, and a mystical voice spoke to her.

"Rosie, allow me to see."

Nodding, Rosie took a deep breath and opened her mind. The day's events flooded from her and formed into swirling clouds of wind. The strands and puffs played in front of her, and then they all converged into a tangled ball. A light grew from within the tangled memories and a flash burst through. Rosie blinked her eyes open, and relief flooded her. The ball hadn't cracked again.

"You may take your seat," Professor Shay said, turning around.

Rosie nodded and then found herself next to Riley who grasped her hand, his thumb rubbing hers.

"So, should we take a stroll after dinner or—" Riley started, but before he could finish the dining hall door opened, and his eyes widened.

Rosie spun her head forward expecting to see the candidates, but entering the dining hall and walking towards Rosie was Justin Fent.

Chapter Three

The boy who joined as the other intellect last year, alongside Rosie, and who had been involved with Egil Vidar Ruud's evil plan to attack various supernatural beings in order to become immortal, was back at King's Preparatory.

"What's he doing here?" Riley said as he crushed Rosie's hand.

"Ow," she muttered, pulling it away and massaging it, all while not removing her eyes from the boy.

Whispers scattered throughout but ceased as the boy neared the clusters of students. His head stayed down until he reached the table, where he reluctantly lifted his head and searched for an empty chair. At the head of the table on the far side, with at least six feet between the other students, Justin finally sat down. His eyes studied his hands for the first few seconds, then his gaze pulled up. His eyes connected immediately with Rosie's, but it was only a glance. Their eyes met, and Rosie recognized pain in his but in a blink, he brought his attention back to his lap.

"How could they let him back?" Eleanor asked.

"Did you know he was going to return?" Riley asked Rosie.

"No. I mean I knew he was being *deprogrammed* and

received help from the Superiority for falling under Egil's manipulation, but I didn't know he would be back here." Rosie turned back towards Justin and studied him once more. Dark circles fell under his eyes, and his skin was paler than normal. His dark hair had a few streaks of silver, and his hands had grown rough calluses. Before Rosie could inspect her old friend further, the door to the dining hall opened again.

"That better not be a sasquatch," Garrett said, turning towards the door, ready for anything.

Now entering the room were Dana and Drew Randolph.

"They passed the last test," Rosie grumbled under her breath and watched as they took a seat at the freshman table.

Once seated and ready, Professor Shay stood at the front of the platform where all the teachers posed themselves in grandiose, plush chairs, situated in an arch.

"Welcome old students and welcome new," Professor Shay started. Her speech and Premier Kingsley's hologram speech were almost the same as the prior year's. Rosie surveyed the Freshman class. Last year it seemed almost all of the students who had been attending the school since kindergarten had an air of confidence surrounding them, but this year's class seemed to be made up of shaking legs, bitten nails, and nervous ticks, which vibrated the room.

"Garrett, why are they so nervous?" Rosie asked, still spying the other underclassmen.

"What do you mean? This is how every freshman looks before the crystal exam. Your class last year almost shattered the glass ceiling and flooded the dining hall." Rosie tilted her head up and stared at the ceiling where, on the other side, lay the lake that sat in front of the school.

Who knew building a school under a body of water could be so dangerous, she joked with herself.

"No way," Eleanor said. "We totally rocked our tryouts."

"Darling," Garrett started, "You and the other humans almost crapped yourself when our resident lake monster swam by."

Riley held a chuckle, and the four turned back to Professor Shay.

"Now, teams, please display your talents."

Every sophomore, junior, and senior stood and separated into their respective teams. Riley kissed Rosie on the forehead and walked to the other Surgents.

"You two are too cute," Eleanor whispered, bumping her shoulder into Rosie's as they walked to the Valtic corner. Attempting to hide a blush, Rosie quickened forward, and they joined the Valtic team.

"Think it'll be capture the flag again?" Rosie asked, looking around.

"Not a chance," Katherine said with a giggle. Katherine, a Valtic vampire, hugged Rosie.

"How have you been?" Rosie asked, her smile from ear to ear.

"I'm good! Happy to be back. What about you? You get your powers sorted?"

"For the most part." Rosie winked and turned back towards Professor Shay who called their attention.

"Whichever team can solve this riddle first will be excused from homework for the first week of classes." She began to move her hands, and words formed in the air.

Students read the riddle out loud to themselves and started to deliberate.

"I end in 'S' when I'm alone but end in 'T' when I'm well-known. I contain water yet I rarely drink any. If you try to steal it, your pain will be many. Come too close and you may die. I should only be touched with the sight of your eye."

Rosie read the riddle once more and turned to see what the other teams were doing. The Astive team stood silent, each member attempting to solve the riddle on their own. The Haply team went around in a circle each giving a guess. Finally, the Surgent team broke out into small groups. The groups Rosie noticed had each type of creature, and they gave guesses based on their background. Rosie turned back to her team.

"Well, that's a poor rhyming attempt," Garrett laughed. "So, Rosie, what is it?"

Almost every Valtic member bore their eyes into her.

"Um, well I assume it is school related. So, if we start there, can anyone think of anything around the school that contains water and causes pain?"

"The lake?" Eleanor guessed.

"Professor Shay if you fail to turn in your work on time?" Garrett said, causing laughs throughout the group.

"It's a cactus," a rough, quiet voice said.

"What?" Rosie said, peering over the group to see who answered.

Sitting in a chair, separated a few feet from the group, was Justin.

"A cactus. A cactus is the answer," he spoke again.

No one replied to Justin. The group was still and even more so when Justin stood and made his way to Professor Shay. At his separation from the group, the other teams paused to watch him as well.

Professor Shay stared at the boy with indifference as he approached her.

"Does your team know the answer, Mr. Fent?" she asked.

"A cactus," he muttered out in a small voice.

"What's that?" she asked, turning her head slightly so her ear faced him.

Clearing his throat he spoke up, "The answer is 'cactus'."

"Well, that's correct," Professor Shay said. She opened her mouth to continue but paused and stared at Justin. "Please return to your seat, Mr. Fent." Justin gave a curt nod and started walking to the back of the table again. As he did, Professor Shay finally spoke, "Congratulations to the Valtic team!"

The Valtic team should've cheered. They should've been laughing and clapping each other on the back, but all were still shocked as to Justin answering the riddle on their behalf.

"All teams, please resume your seats," Professor Shay continued as the students shuffled around the room.

Rosie sat back down and stared at Justin, whose eyes were fixated on his shoes.

"You okay Rosie?" Riley asked, sitting beside her.

"Yeah, I'm fine. I just wasn't expecting to hear Justin talk or participate with the team again so soon."

"Or to see him at all?" Eleanor whispered.

Rosie nodded, breaking her gaze from the boy and focusing on her hands. She clasped them in front of her and rested them, but Riley pulled them apart, taking one into his own.

"I'll make sure he stays away from you. You shouldn't have to deal with him."

One side of Rosie's mouth turned but only to show Riley she acknowledged his comment.

"I hope he doesn't think we all forgive him just because he got us out of homework for the first week," Eleanor said.

"No one thinks that, babe," Garrett replied, glaring at Justin.

"Freshmen, it is time to find out which team you will be a part of!" Professor Shay announced.

One by one, each freshman presented themself in front of the other high school students and the crystal ball to learn which team would be their family for the next four years.

A surprising number of students didn't need to try out further and found their place easily within one of the four teams. The exception to this, however, was Dana Randolph.

"Ms. Randolph, you have been given the opportunity to try out for both the Astive team and the Surgent team."

Dana smiled at Professor Shay as she spoke, and then twisted her head to her brother who donned a gold ring with a diamond.

"Four students in this room will find a jewel in their hand. If you are one of the students, do not say. You, Ms. Randolph, must decipher which student holds a jewel before five minutes is up. The orb will be studying you, so ensure you show your true self."

Dana nodded and studied the group of students.

She smiled, and after walking across the tables to study each, she stated, "Dana says stand up."

"We're playing Simon says?" Garrett responded, laughing as he stood.

"More like Dana says," Eleanor joked.

Kids laughed, but the majority obeyed the girl. She stared at the handful from each table who remained seated, but continued, "Dana says, touch your toes."

Again, everyone participated.

So, this is how she is going to find the jewels, Rosie thought.

"Dana says, raise your arms up high."

Giving the students one more glance, she peered back at Professor Shay. "Okay, I know where the jewels are."

"Show me," Professor Shay said skeptically, raising an eyebrow.

Dana walked between the junior and senior table. Two students sitting across from one another remained sitting during the game.

"You two," Dana said, proffering her hand so they would open their fists. Their hands unclenched and each held a jewel. One sapphire and one emerald. She collected the stones and started to hand them to Professor Shay.

"If you find them, they are yours," Professor Shay stated.

Dana smirked and placed the stones in her pocket. She glided back down the aisle and then up to Rosie. Rosie lifted an eyebrow at her approach, but her eyes widened when Dana stopped next to Riley.

"Your jewel?" Dana requested from Riley. With a sly smile he opened his hand, and Dana's fingers grazed Riley's palm as she lifted the jewel from him. She winked and continued down the aisle. Whispers began to sound from the students as amazement filled them.

"Dang, boy," Garrett said, "You kept that secret well."

Riley smirked, and when Rosie tried to meet his eyes, he had already turned around to follow Dana.

Dana strutted up the aisle, a devilish grin spread across her face. She pretended to point out students, then shook her head laughing. Finally, at the back of the room, all the way down the aisle, she paused at Justin. She raised an inquisitive eyebrow at the depressed boy who hadn't participated in the game and simply held out her hand. He dropped the ruby jewel into her palm without so much as blinking.

She pocketed the last jewel and walked straight up to the crystal ball. Placing the entirety of her hand around the orb, Dana's eyes closed, and she was transported to speak with it. A smile spread across her face, and she removed her hand. The ball liquified and at its base was a gold necklace with a diamond pendant.

"Surgent!" Professor Shay announced as she placed the necklace around Dana's neck. Surgent members cheered as Dana clasped her new necklace.

Rosie turned to Riley who clapped fervently, and she raised an eyebrow.

"What? We need an intellect," he said, smirking.

Dana stared down at her pendant as she walked back to resume her seat next to her brother, and her smile turned down. Rosie spied the diamond pendant and noticed what concerned Dana.

The diamond pendant, which was normally crystal clear, was clouded.

That's odd, Rosie thought. She tried to get a better look at Drew's ring to see if it had the same clarity, but as she peered over Eleanor's shoulder Professor Shay spoke.

"Teams, move to your respective tables and get acquainted with your new members."

Rosie kept trying to look but bodies swarmed and shuffled about the room.

"See you later tonight?" Riley asked, pulling her attention.

"Oh, yeah, definitely," Rosie said then smiled as he gave her a quick kiss.

Rosie, Eleanor, and Garrett all walked over to the last table and joined the other Valtic team members.

"Hey, man," said Reese, a cardinal shifter, clapping a hand on Garrett's shoulder, "I hear congratulations are in order."

Eleanor lifted an eyebrow, and Rosie furrowed her eyebrows together.

"Yeah, thanks," Garrett called as Reese strode off.

"Congrats?" Eleanor asked.

"Yeah, um, I'm kind of the new Valtic Illumination Team captain," Garret murmured, rubbing the back of his head.

"What? That's amazing! Congrats, babe!" Eleanor swung her body into Garrett's, enveloping him in a kiss. Rosie smiled and waited until the two parted, but that wasn't happening, so she spoke anyway.

"Seriously, Garrett, that's awesome," Rosie said. "Why didn't you tell us?"

Garrett peeled his lips from Eleanor's and caught his breath before answering. "Ha, because I wanted to play it cool and watch from afar. Check out everyone's skills then pick the team. I guess now that the word's out, though, I'll have to have proper tryouts."

"You can do whatever you want," Eleanor said, then added, "as long as I make the team." She giggled and hung onto his arm and batted her eyes. A huge sigh erupted from the werewolf and Eleanor said, "Don't worry. I'm kidding."

"Yes, Garrett, as captain, do what you need to do in order to select the best team. We'll support you," Rosie said, grinning.

"Thanks, Rosie," Garrett said sheepishly.

"Do you have any thoughts on who you want on the team?" Eleanor asked. Garrett huffed and Eleanor said, "I'm not fishing to see if I'm on it. I'm just trying to help."

Rosie studied Garrett. He bowed his head, and his grip

loosened around Eleanor. Rosie understood that Garrett saw himself as a goofball, the class clown, the funny guy. This leadership role he was nominated for and agreed to created an insecurity within him.

"Hey, what do you think of the new freshmen?"

Garrett lifted his head a little and smiled at Rosie.

"Some seem cool," he said, acknowledging the new freshmen on their team.

"I wonder if I'll get moved to a single room this year," Eleanor said, realizing that it would just be herself and Dana on their floor in the natural dorm.

"It's more likely you'll room with the new girl," Garrett said and nodded his head in her direction.

Eleanor looked over Rosie's shoulder, and Rosie turned around. The two girls stared at Dana, who seemed to be telling a very interesting story. Even Riley seemed enthralled with the tale.

A sour churn swirled in Rosie's stomach, and she turned back around.

"Hey," Eleanor said, "Even if we are rooming together, no one can replace my girl." Eleanor let go of Garrett's hand and held Rosie's.

Rosie smiled and winked at her bestie, but her face dropped when, out of the corner of her eye, someone stood next to her.

"Ros—" Justin started, but before the rest of her name could leave his lips, Garrett lunged across the table and swooped in front of Rosie, standing between the two.

Eleanor was on her feet as well, her eyes in slits, shooting darts at Justin.

"You need to leave," Garrett said, staring Justin down.

"I just want to apologize. To Rosie and to both of you." He started to reach out, but Garrett glared.

"It's not accepted. Now go."

Rosie turned her head to find Riley, but he was smiling, talking to Drew. The spell that hushed the students' conversations so they could only hear their own team's discussions was still in effect.

The Valtic team quieted at the interaction, though, and Rosie turned her head to Professor Shay.

Professor Shay had thankfully seen what was transpiring and lifted her hands. As she did so the room burst in volume and the students then quieted.

"Students," Professor Shay said, "let us feast."

Out of the back wall, plates, silverware, cups, and trays soared in front of the students and food plopped down.

Justin and Garrett still stood, but Justin surrendered and maneuvered around the flying dinnerware, finding his secluded seat at the back of the table. Rosie continued to watch him, study him.

"We won't let him get near you," Garrett whispered to her before walking back around the table to his seat.

Rosie gave a small smile but continued to watch Justin. His eyes remained down on his food, and he shuffled it around, not taking a single bite. While she hadn't forgiven Justin for his actions from last year, she realized he had been skillfully manipulated by Egil, and a small pang of guilt overcame her.

"Rosie, come on, eat," Garrett said. "You don't have to worry about him."

"Yeah, we'll make sure he doesn't bother you," Eleanor added.

Rosie mustered a smile, but like Justin, her appetite didn't exist.

Sitting on the edge, she listened to Eleanor and Garrett talk about their summers and they asked way too many questions about her and her training.

"Did you hear anything about Witam? I, uh, mean Egil? Ugh, that's still so weird to me," Eleanor said.

"El, don't," Garrett warned, but Rosie shook her head.

"No. I know the Premier was out searching for him, but I don't think he'll be back anytime soon."

"Plus, he knows you can blast his ass back to the 18th century," Eleanor giggled.

Rosie smirked as the plates cleared themselves and again, her eyes swept across Justin, who was staring at her. She halted on his eyes before startling back.

"Ready, Rosie?" Eleanor asked, standing up.

"Yeah, but I think I'm going to head to bed instead. I'm pretty tired."

"Okay, well, split-second decision but I decided to have tryouts tomorrow," Garrett announced.

"Really?" Eleanor asked, bouncing.

"Yes, but El, you know I'm not giving you preferential treatment."

"No, of course not. I wouldn't expect any!" She leaned on him, kissing his cheek.

"Okay, good," Garrett said, laughing, "Now can you go spread the word?"

Eleanor nodded her head vigorously and bounced off.

"What changed your mind?" Rosie asked as they walked through the Valtic library.

Garrett sighed. "Since everyone knows, they'll expect it, and if I just choose the team without a tryout where everyone can participate if they want, then they'll think I'm being unfair. But you don't need to try out, Rosie."

"What? Of course I do. Just like Eleanor, I shouldn't get preferential treatment."

A coy smile spread on Garrett's face. "Co-captains don't need to try out."

"Wait, co-captain?" Rosie asked, with a smile she was unable to hide.

Garrett gave a nod and wink. Rosie's stomach flipped with joy, and she squeezed her friend's arm.

"Are you sure?"

"A badass intellect witch? Hell yeah, I'm sure."

A chuckle left Rosie's lips as the two entered the Valtic living room.

"Well, then I accept." She laughed.

"I wouldn't have let you decline."

She smirked. "What do you need from me?" she asked her captain.

"Just help me put together the best Illumination Team Valtic has ever seen."

"Done," Rosie said before he nodded stoutly and then stepped away from her side and found Eleanor's waist.

She watched as he slid a hand around her and pulled her close. Rosie smiled and then she did a slow spin around the room. She surveyed everyone and her mind began to make calculations on who would fit best on the team.

As she gazed at the members in the room, her eyes again halted. Justin stared, pleading with her. She shook her head down and clenched her hands. Her nails split the skin on her palms open, and she closed her eyes, allowing the pain to distract her.

"Ah," she heard a small gasp.

She looked back up at Justin, who now inspected the palms of his hands and the tiny crescent gashes in them. Rosie unclenched her fists, and his eyes spied her own bleeding palms. Widening her eyes, she turned and stepped out through the portrait to the witch dorm.

Did I do that? Rosie thought, staring at her palms. Her magic had been under control at the beginning of summer, but over time, she hadn't been able to have it completely surrendered to her.

Heading through her dorm lobby towards her room she studied her hands and then brought her palm around her Valtic pendant. As she walked through, a shoulder pushed into hers, knocking her back.

Her eyes refocused on the person who hit her, and her stomach dropped.

Olive.

Olive's eyes narrowed, and her teeth clenched together. This was one interaction Rosie had dreaded with school starting up again. Living in the same dorm as her tormentor from the previous year.

"Thanks a lot," Olive gritted out, smoothing her skirt down as if Rosie had wrinkled it.

Not this year, Rosie thought before speaking. "What do you mean?" Rosie asked, planting her feet and staring Olive down.

"I don't get to room with Tabitha now because of you."

"Wait, what?" Rosie tried to say, but Olive continued to rant.

"You just had to ruin everything for me. I was supposed to be able to chill in my room with my best friend since childhood and not worry about the *amazing* Rosie Connors and her newly developed gifts, but now I have to babysit you."

"Babysit?" Rosie cocked her head to the side.

"Jeez, and they say you're an intellect." Olive pushed past Rosie and continued through the lobby, entering a door that Rosie assumed led to the Surgent living room.

Rosie stood for a few seconds, her mind swirling. She shifted her feet and made her way to her dorm room, and of course, the door wouldn't unlock.

"Oh no," she said, her forehead resting on her old door as realization hit her. She turned around and across the hall, Rosie read the names on the door.

Olive was scrawled in beautiful gold lettering while a piece of paper hung next to it with Rosie's name on it.

"No, no, no, no, no," Rosie kept repeating, her head now resting back against the wall. Boring a hole in her name, she took a step forward and unlocked the door.

All her belongings had been moved into the left side of the room and on the right were all of Olive's things.

Rosie shuffled to her bed and found a decorative note with Professor Walker's curvy handwriting.

Rosie, I thought it would be best if you shared a room with a trained witch now that school is in session. Olive is one of the brightest witches in your grade, and she may be able to assist you in learning more about your new powers.

Rosie paused.

Does Professor Walker know I don't have full control?

She refocused and continued reading.

Meet me at my office tomorrow around 3.

Rosie set the note down on her desk and crawled into bed.

Putting her phone up to her face, she read the messages she had missed.

OMGOMGOMG! Garrett just told me you're co-captain! Congrats girl! I'm so happy for you!

Rosie giggled at Eleanor's text and continued to the next from Garrett.

Hey, tryouts tomorrow morning at 9. Starting at the field, and then we'll move to the new obstacle course.

Rosie nodded as she read, thinking about the new obstacle course. She had helped design and build it and agreed that it would be a good, challenging task for the Valtic members trying out. She responded, telling Garrett she would see him at breakfast, and they could talk more about the day's events.

She clicked open the next message.

Babe, are you able to meet tonight? 11? I need to see you.

Rosie perked up at the message.

Was something wrong? Her fingers flew across the screen, and Riley replied not even a minute later.

Everything's fine... I just miss you, beautiful.

A rush of heat covered her face, and she relaxed back into her pillow.

Of course, I'll be there. Meet outside your dorm?

Yep. See you then, gorgeous.

Rosie set her phone down and stared at the ceiling. While her new roommate situation sucked, she had Riley. A vibrating pulsed in her hand, and she rushed to see what Riley had also added, but an unknown number popped up attached to the message.

She opened the text and instantly knew who it was.

Rosie, I'm so sorry. For everything. For trying to talk to you today. For everything that happened last year. And for being an awful friend. I understand if you don't respond to this. I just needed you to know that I still care about you, and I hope one day you can forgive me. I'm sorry.

Rosie read the message over and over. At least one hundred times. *Justin.* She held her phone against her chest and thought about him. He had betrayed her. Turned evil. But that was due to Egil. If Egil had never been in his life, he would've never done any of the horrible deeds Egil demanded. But still, his mind must have wanted the power Egil searched for or else he wouldn't have been manipulated so easily. Yet again, Egil had a lot of time to mold Justin to be his assistant. His minion.

Conflicting thoughts tangled in her mind, but she snapped out of it when her phone buzzed again.

Where are you?

"Oh, shoot," Rosie said. It was eleven-oh-four. Time always flew by whenever she fell into her own mind.

Swinging her feet out of bed, she jumped down and slipped on her shoes. She rushed to the door, and as she pulled it open, she ran right into Olive.

"Ugh, watch it," Olive said, shaking her head and rolling her eyes.

"Sorry," Rosie muttered as she slipped past her.

Rosie hustled up and out of the dorm and breathed in the warm, sticky air when she exited onto the mountainside. She lightly jogged, hopping over rocks and bushes. One could easily get lost in the desert, but not her. It was her home. She made her way around a tall boulder, but her feet stopped before the rest of her body could. She flew forward and tumbled.

"Rosie," Riley called, rushing to her side. "You okay?"

"Yeah," she replied. She brushed the dust off her thighs and her eyes met the person who caused her to fall.

Dana.

Chapter Four

"Run much?" Dana asked, chuckling.

Rosie didn't respond to Dana, but instead looked around Dana and saw Drew, Gunner, Flynn, Eleanor, and Garrett.

"What's going on?" Rosie asked Riley.

"Well, I just thought, you know, since Dana and Drew are new, they could continue to get to know everyone."

"Oh," Rosie said, staring at her scraped hands rather than at Riley.

"Riley has been such a sweetheart," Dana added, lightly touching his arm.

Rosie's pulse quickened and rage filled her, but she forced it back with every ounce of might.

"Yeah, he's pretty wonderful," Rosie said, stepping up to his side, thankful that he leaned down and kissed her. Rosie's fingers slipped seamlessly into his hand, and she led Riley away from Dana and towards Eleanor.

"Hey co-captain!" Eleanor yelled, sipping a red cup.

"Okay, that's enough juice for you," Garrett laughed, taking the cup.

"Humph," Eleanor said, pretending to pout.

"Um, was there a little something extra in the loose juice

this evening?" Rosie asked, studying Eleanor's drunken state.

"Just a little something more," Eleanor whispered, her nose now touching Rosie's.

"You should go get some sleep, babe," Garrett said, gingerly wrapping her arms around his shoulders. "You'll need all your energy if you want to make the Illumination Team tomorrow."

"Oh poo. You're right." Eleanor turned away, her arms drooping and swaying at her side. She fumbled with a rock shard that she thought was the opening to the natural dorm.

Dana slipped by Rosie and gently grabbed onto Eleanor. "Don't worry, I'll get her to bed," Dana said to Garrett.

"Roomie!" Eleanor yelled, hugging Dana.

Dana assisted Eleanor inside and every one of the guys thanked her for the rescue.

"So, Eleanor and Dana *are* rooming together," Rosie stated as the door closed.

"Yep," Garrett confirmed, then added in a jittered voice, "I think I'm gonna get some rest, too. Big day tomorrow." He smiled at Rosie and headed off to his dorm.

"Wanna go for a walk?" Riley asked, but before Rosie could answer, Drew, Gunner, and Flynn popped by his side.

"Hey, bro," Drew said.

Rosie noticed how deep and relaxed his voice already was with Riley. *Must've really gotten to know one another with the other Surgents*, Rosie thought, staring at the massive figure. "We're heading in. I wanna be ready for tryouts."

"Yeah, Riley, you should think about coming back too," Gunner added. "You're not a shoo-in just because you were on the team last year."

Riley nodded. "I'll be back in the room in a sec."

Gunner gave a small nod at Rosie and as he walked away, she glanced at his leg. A missing chunk of muscle had been carved out last year as part of Egil's immortality ritual, but all that was there now was a long scar. Rosie raised her eyes back up, and Drew stared at her, wearing a smirk. He continued walking next to Gunner and Flynn and spoke.

"Can't believe I got stuck with the nut job. Let me know if either of you wants to switch rooms," he joked.

Well, that's something Justin and I have in common, Rosie thought. *We both must be babysat.* The door closed, and Rosie turned to Riley.

"Hi," he said, his forehead leaning down and touching hers. Rosie closed her eyes and inhaled his sweet yet musky scent.

"Hi," she whispered back, opening her eyes and staring into his.

She kissed him lightly but then fell into him, deepening the kiss. After a moment she pulled away and led him to a rock near the entrance.

"How was your night?" Riley asked, running his fingers up and down her outer arm as she rested on his shoulder.

She chuckled. "Well, Olive is my new roommate, so the night could've gone better."

"Shoot, really? I'll talk to her and make sure she doesn't mess with you."

"That's sweet, but I got it handled," Rosie said.

"You sure?"

"Yeah, just tell me about your night."

Riley smiled. "It was fun. I got to know the twins better, and they're cool. They have some crazy stories." Riley paused and laughed to himself. "They're from a little town not that far away from campus. Drew is super chill. He doesn't panic or get nervous about anything, and Dana is super smart. Well, obviously."

Rosie gritted her teeth and forced a smile. "Good. I'm happy you're able to make them feel at ease here." As the words left Rosie's mouth, she knew she didn't mean them. Something was off with the twins, and she couldn't tell if they were just rude or if it was something more.

"Yeah, but I'm nervous about tomorrow. I don't think I'll make the team again."

"Don't say that!" Rosie gripped his hand and continued, "They need you. You think differently than a lot of the supernatural students that go here."

"True, but so does Gunner and Flynn and now D."

"Oh it's D, now?" Rosie playfully said.

"Shush it," Riley replied, bumping her arm with his.

Rosie smiled and cupped Riley's chin. "You got this," she said, and she pulled him down, and her lips met his.

* * *

"Okay, so I have the tests regarding the physical tasks for the tryout figured out," Garrett said, pushing his full plate of breakfast away as he conversed with Rosie. "What I need help with is the intelligence part of it. Now, we can do a trivia match like we did last year."

Rosie stared into Garrett's worried eyes. Never had she seen the cool, calm, collected werewolf a mess. "What if," she suggested, "instead, we quiz them as they are doing physical tasks. We throw them curve balls and see how they do under pressure?"

"Yes!" Garrett yelled then grabbed her shoulders, shaking them. "This is exactly why you're my co-captain."

Rosie chuckled, and the two put their heads together and continued to brainstorm.

As Rosie tossed around the idea of having Garrett shift mid-obstacle course and seeing what the other students would do, Eleanor plopped down next to Garrett.

She lowered her head down into her arms on the table, and her eyes remained closed.

"Hey, Eleanor," Rosie said, a small smile playing at the corners of her mouth.

Garrett's hand gently rubbed her back. "Babe?"

Eleanor raised her head and stared back and forth at the two. "Hot tip of the day, don't mix loose juice with other substances." Her head fell back down, and Garrett and Rosie stared at each other before bursting out in laughter.

"Shhh, that hurts my head," Eleanor said, sitting up and covering her ears.

"Why were you even drinking that concoction? Where did you get it to begin with?" Rosie asked, still chuckling but in a lowered voice.

"Dana had made me the drink and we were just toasting to being new roomies, and just trust me. Don't mix the two."

Garrett started to chuckle again and pulled Eleanor into a hug. Rosie sat, pensive.

Dana?

"Hey, Eleanor?"

"Yeah," she said, her blonde head of hair resting on Garrett's shoulders.

"Did Dana drink any?"

"I think so? I don't know. Why?"

"Just curious." Rosie peered around the room and found Dana sitting with her brother and a handful of other Surgents. She certainly didn't seem sluggish. Rather, she seemed to glow. Silky smooth hair cascaded down and the sun-kissed skin covering her legs caught the attention of many boys around her.

Rosie fixed back on Eleanor.

"Are you ready for today?" she asked her friend.

"Ugh, I guess," Eleanor responded, adjusting her head so it sat in her hands, blocking all light from hitting her eyes.

Garrett eyed Rosie, a worrying look covering his face. "Alright, we're going to go set up. We'll see you on the field in a few," Garrett said and then kissed Eleanor on the top of her head.

A grunt came from the slumped blonde as Garrett and Rosie walked away and out to the field.

"Think she'll make it?" Garrett asked Rosie, a twinge of hope coated in the question.

"She doesn't look very good, huh?" Rosie responded.

"I can't believe I'm going to have to cut her from the team. She's going to be so pissed."

"Hey! Maybe she'll turn it around?" Rosie raised an eyebrow and Garrett tilted his head.

"Yeah."

The two stepped out of the school building. Valtic team members who wanted to try out and be a part of the Illumination Team were already scattered across the grassy field. Garrett directed Rosie that he would lead the tryout while she would mark who would make good members on the team. She held a clipboard and put on her sunglasses so not even the bright Arizona sun could block her vision from studying each participant.

"Alright everyone, gather around!" Garrett yelled.

As the Valtic students formed a clump of bodies in front of Rosie and Garrett, another small group of students exited the building and then plopped down on the grassy hill.

Gunner, Flynn, Drew, and Dana sat down.

"Hey, closed session guys!" Garrett yelled at the group, but the Surgents merely glanced at him and then continued talking.

Garrett shook his head and started towards them, but Rosie put a hand on his shoulder.

"I got it," she said. "Go ahead and get everyone started, and I'll rejoin you."

"Thanks, Rosie."

"I'm here!" She heard Eleanor shout behind her, and she shook her head laughing.

Rosie headed towards the group as Garrett began to shout instructions. Moving feet sounded behind her, but her attention lay solely on the intruding group.

"Hey, Rosie, what's going on?" Flynn asked as she walked up.

"Hey guys, sorry to do this, but this is a closed tryout, so we really need you to take off."

The four Surgents stared at Rosie, and Gunner and Flynn began to stand. When their eyes caught Dana and Drew still sitting though, they sat back down. Frustration grew within Rosie. As her mouth opened to ask them to leave again, a warm hand touched the lower middle of her back.

"You guys ready?" Riley asked the sitting group.

Dana bounced to her feet. "Definitely," she chimed and

spun to walk off, the other three boys following.

"Coming to my rescue?" Rosie said, turning to Riley and lightly kissing his cheek.

"Always." He smiled and lifted her chin so their lips touched.

Rosie, red-faced, stepped back. "I need to go back to tryouts, but thanks."

"I have to go too. See you later tonight?" he asked, hope gleaming in his eyes.

"Of course. I'll see you tonight." Riley began to walk off and Rosie yelled to him, "Good luck. I know you're going to kill it!"

Riley turned his head back and winked, joining the other Surgents and disappearing towards the front of the school.

Rosie made her way back to the group of Valtic members who were now in a circle doing warm-up exercises.

"Thanks for that," Garrett said as Rosie stood at his side.

"No problem."

"Want to start heading over to the obstacle course?"

"Yeah, give me five minutes and then surprise them by heading over there. I want to see who makes it first and how they do it. Once they start the course, I'll randomly ask each person a question or send them to do a different task."

"Perfect. This should give us the best team Valtic has ever had."

Rosie winked and grabbed Garrett's upper arm in excitement and began to walk off. As she did so, she spied her bestie. Eleanor was staring back at Rosie, but rather than smile she sneered and then continued her warm-up.

What did I do? Rosie thought to herself but reasoned that Eleanor had the sun in her eyes and she continued on to the next tryout station.

* * *

Garrett and Rosie dismissed the Valtic members who tried out for the Illumination Team and sat on the bank of the lake discussing which eight members would join the team with them.

"Yeah, but Reese was on the team last year, so he has the experience," Garrett argued, his eyes poring over the detailed notes Rosie had taken throughout the day.

"I know, but if you see the scoring system, Ellie overall did better."

"And we can't use the argument that he can fly, huh?"

Rosie glumly shook her head. Ellie Reed, a sophomore, could shift into a bat.

"Okay. I guess if he takes any issue, I'll sit down with him and explain why he didn't make it this year. Can he be an alternate?"

"We can only have one alternate and we already listed someone. Now, if you want to pick a different alternate—"

"No," Garrett moaned. "We can't."

"She'll understand, Garrett," Rosie said, placing a hand on his shoulder reassuringly and looking down at Eleanor's name by the alternate title.

"She didn't do great today, did she?" Garrett asked Rosie.

Rosie shook her head. "No. She didn't try out at her normal performance level. I'm sure it's just because she had a little too much fun last night."

"That shouldn't be an excuse though," Garrett said, sitting up a little straighter. "I think we need to take her off."

"Really?"

"Yeah. If I'm to be objective and make this team as if Eleanor wasn't my girlfriend, I wouldn't even have her listed as alternate." The two grimaced and Garrett continued, "Ugh, she is going to be so pissed at me."

"Throw me under the bus," Rosie piped up.

"What?"

"Tell Eleanor that she didn't make the team based on the scoring system that *I* created. Then the blowback will be evenly distributed between the both of us."

"You sure? I don't mind taking the brunt of it."

"Oh, you'll still get it bad."

"Ha, okay then. Who's on our winning team?"

Rosie peered back down at her list. "So, we have you, a werewolf; me, an amazing witch slash intellect; Frederick, a wizard; Cameron, a vampire; Alec, a werewolf; Katherine, a vampire; Pine, a fairy; Aquamarine, a mermaid; Ellie, bat shifter; and Madeline, wildcat shifter."

"And Reese as an alternate?"

"Yep, Reese as an alternate," Rosie repeated to Garrett. He clumped sand in his fists and repeated the soothing technique.

"Okay," he said, and stood. "Let's go break some hearts."

CHAPTER FOUR

Chapter Five

As predicted, Eleanor didn't talk to Garrett or Rosie the entire evening after finding out who made the Illumination Team.

"Babe," Garrett called, but Rosie stopped him.

"Give her time. This is a huge blow to her ego. She really wanted this."

"Then she should've been more prepared," Garrett reasoned, a hint of annoyance in his words.

"I'm sure, along with being mad at us, she is also pissed at herself. Let's just give her some time."

Garrett nodded and walked off. Rosie found an open seat and, sinking into a cushy chair in the Valtic living room, she pulled her phone out of her pocket and typed.

Can you meet? she wrote to Riley.

Three small dots appeared and then disappeared. Disappointment washed over her.

He must still be at tryouts or doing something with the Surgent team.

She tucked her phone away and left to enter her secret space. As she neared her hidden study room in the Valtic library, she heard voices coming from inside.

The bookcase popped inward, and Justin walked about the room, talking to himself. No, talking on the phone. Rosie's eyes widened, and she stepped back as Justin turned towards her.

"Mom, can I call you back later? No? Okay, next week then." Justin slid his phone back into his pocket and gathered his things. "Sorry, I didn't know you were still using this room."

Rosie stood, lips pressed together, as he packed papers and books into his backpack. He slung it over one shoulder and made eye contact with her.

"I'll just…" He pointed past her shoulder, to the Valtic library, but Rosie didn't move, forcing him to step around her.

Processing the run-in and unfreezing, she turned towards Justin, who was already halfway down the hall and moving swiftly to the stairs.

"I forgive you," she called out, not expecting the words to leave her. She stepped back in surprise, and Justin halted. Keeping his body forward, he turned his neck back. He gave a small nod and continued on his way.

Rosie watched him descend into the library before she entered the room and shut the door. She searched the space and found everything in its place then pulled a book off a small shelf in the room and began to read. As she read, she made configurations with her hands and whispered spells.

"Occularti Visizim Farssi Nosium," she said, staring out a small window that she had conjured. Immediately, the spell took over and her vision zoomed in on an owl, perched atop a saguaro miles away. She leaned forward slightly and listened as it *wooed* into the night. Three smaller heads popped up and Rosie smiled at the babies by their mother.

Her own mother's face popped into her mind. She reached for her cell phone to send a "I'm doing fine" text to her mother when shrill snickers sounded. Rosie twirled in a circle, but the laughter came from outside, not in the library. Her attention zeroed in on the noise, and her eyes found the culprit. Dana. She walked with her brother and a few other Surgents.

Riley? Her boyfriend trailed along Dana's side, and Rosie immediately put her phone screen in front of her face and typed.

Hey, what are you up to?

Rosie turned back to the group, the spell allowing her to refocus on them. Riley took his phone out and read her message and then shoved it hard back into his pocket.

What? Why? Is he mad?

She continued to stare at the group and turned her head so her ear would get closer to the conversation.

"Riley, don't worry about it. I'm sure you'll make the team," Gunner said reassuringly.

"I shouldn't have fumbled that last task," he replied, shaking his head. "Ugh, it would suck not to make the team and have to listen to Rosie talk all about it." Rosie took a step back.

I shouldn't be listening to this. She tousled her hair over her ears as if that would block the noise as she walked back to the book to end the spell, but then Dana spoke.

"Just tell her to shut it," the girl said. "If you don't make it, just ignore her when she talks about it. I honestly don't know what you see in her."

Rosie's blood began to boil, and heat flooded her face. She rushed back to the window, her hands gripping the pane.

Gritting her teeth together, she tried to hear what else the girl had to say.

"Like, she was so rude to me yesterday."

I was not! Rosie had now heard enough. Rage continued to fill her, and as she turned to end the spell, she heard Riley and Dana shout at the same time.

Dana writhed on the ground, yelping in pain. Riley ran and knelt next to her side, followed by Gunner, Flynn, and Drew.

"What's wrong?" he asked.

Rosie zoomed back in and studied the girl. Her skin was bright red, and she had pools of sweat dripping down her face.

"My body—it's so hot!" she cried out. Rosie's eyes widened and she read the pages in the spell book. Repeating the words backwards, she ended the spell and hoped it was enough to stop Dana's own blood from actually boiling.

* * *

Rosie ran back to her room, which was difficult seeing that her hands were clamped shut together in front of her.

"Hey, Rosie," someone called out to her in the Valtic living room, but her head remained down as she dodged through bodies. As she neared the entrance to her dorm, she accidentally rammed her shoulder into someone.

"Sorry," she muttered before trying to move forward.

"Rosie, stop," Eleanor said.

Rosie raised her head and stared at her best friend, whose

eyes were rimmed red.

"I'm sorry, Eleanor, but I need to go," Rosie said, her eyes shifting to her hands.

"No, not until we talk about tryouts."

"I really can't." Rosie tried to move past, but Eleanor stepped in her way.

"We are talking," Eleanor started, but Rosie stopped her.

"ELEANOR, MOVE." Her voice reverberated around the room. All heads whipped in their direction, and Rosie saw her opportunity. As Eleanor stood, mouth agape, Rosie hurried to her room.

Shutting the door and resting on it as it closed, Rosie closed her eyes and let out a breath of relief.

"What are you doing?" Olive asked.

Rosie peeled open her eyes and stared at her roommate. "N-nothing," Rosie said, shaking her head and walking to her desk.

"Ugh, whatever," Olive said, shifting her head back to a book she'd been reading.

Rosie sat down, and the task that presented itself sent waves of nausea throughout her.

"Hey, Olive? Can I ask you something?"

"Ugh, what?" Olive responded, putting down her book and rolling her eyes.

"Has your magic been..." Rosie attempted to find the correct words. "Um..."

"Oh my gosh, has my magic been what?" Olive asked, but as she said it, the lights in their room flickered angrily.

Both girls studied the room, and Olive's eyes grew wide.

"Never mind. Question answered," Rosie said, her hands still tightly shut.

"What do you mean?" Olive asked, sitting up. "I don't know what happened."

"You do, and it's been happening to me as well."

"So, your magic?" Olive began to ask.

Rosie nodded her head. "It's been acting weird, too. A lot more since everyone arrived. Is there anyone else you've noticed this happening to?"

Olive's mouth opened, but she snapped it shut, narrowing her eyes, and hopped out of her bed.

"Say anything about this, and I'll tell Professor Walker you don't have control of your magic." She stomped from the room, leaving Rosie wondering who else had trouble controlling their power.

* * *

"How have you been feeling, Garrett?" Rosie asked her friend as she noticed bags under his eyes and poorly hidden scratch marks on his wrists.

"Oh, um, I'm fine. Little sleep. Plus, Eleanor."

Garrett tugged his sleeves down further, the bruising and rubbing on his wrists now completely out of sight.

Rosie lifted her eyes. "Is she still mad?"

"Not as much as yesterday but she hasn't gotten over it yet. Have you talked to her?"

"No. I am this morning though." As she said it, Eleanor entered the dining hall. Rosie stood and approached the girl, but her strides halted as a paper butterfly landed on her shoulder. She opened the note, and in beautiful writing it said:

Rosie, please meet me in my office. I want to discuss your schedule and a few other items with you before the school year starts. -Professor Walker.

Realization dawned on Rosie as she remembered she was supposed to meet Professor Walker yesterday afternoon. Rosie searched for Eleanor, but she was already seated next to Garrett, and Dana had taken up residence in Rosie's seat.

Leaving the hall, Rosie promised herself that she would talk to Eleanor by the end of the day, no matter what.

Entering Professor Walker's office, Rosie sat in one of the chairs situated by the desk.

"I'm sorry I missed our meeting, Professor Walker. I got held up at tryouts and totally forgot."

"That's alright, Rosie." Professor Walker paused and gave Rosie an intense, concerned stare but continued, "I wanted to give you your schedule before the craziness of the day begins, and to give you enough time to process it."

"What do you mean?" Rosie raised an eyebrow, and her heart quickened.

"Well, similar to last year, you will be in various advanced classes, and like last year, a handful of them will just be you and Mr. Fent."

"Oh, okay," Rosie responded, taking a piece of paper from Professor Walker which detailed her first-semester schedule.

"On the plus side," Professor Walker continued, "Dana will also join the two of you, so if you need a buffer, she will be in the room as well. You will also have a few classes with only the other witches and wizards in your year."

Rosie studied the schedule and nodded her head.

"Do you have any questions or concerns?" Professor

Walker asked, lifting a curious eyebrow.

Bringing her eyes to meet Professor Walker's, Rosie shook her head. "No, I think I'm good."

"Are you sure? Mr. Fent's return was probably shocking—"

"Really, I'm fine."

Professor Walker nodded her head. "Okay, excellent. Now that that's taken care of, how are your powers fairing with everyone returning to campus? Sometimes they work in overdrive as your magic is surrounded by others who have similar power or even stronger magic."

At Professor Walker's words, the muscles throughout Rosie relaxed as relief flooded her.

"Oh, my magic is great," she said, understanding the mishaps had to have been just because students were returning.

"Great. Well, if you need anything, I'm here."

Rosie smiled and nodded, then left the room, but shock brought her body to a halt as she took in who just exited the hallway for the lobby.

"Mom?"

Chapter Six

Rosie ran into the school's lobby.

That was her, Rosie thought, and she ran out the front doors to the lakeside. Still nothing. Then her heart leapt. Re-entering the building, she jumped up onto Francie's desk—who was only there one day a year for the interviews—and plunged through the gigantic portrait of James Kingsley to enter his office.

"Rosie!" James Kingsley announced as he assisted Rosie's mother into one of the chairs. Her mom was on her feet again.

"What's going on?" Rosie asked, unable to stop herself, and evaluated the situation further. There, in the hidden office in the magical school, stood her mother. She scanned her over. She stood in a disparaged pair of jeans and tattered shirt, but other than the clothing, she was whole. Her skin was brighter, and her eyes were clearer. She didn't twitch or avoid eye contact, and best of all, she smelled like honeydew and fresh linen. Not her normal brand of vodka.

"Why don't you have a seat next to your mom?" Kingsley asked, sliding another seat out.

Rosie's mom stared into her eyes. Tears filled them.

"Rosie, honey, I'm so sorry," she said, tears starting to fall. She reached out a hand, attempting to grasp Rosie's, but Rosie stepped back.

"Sorry? What the hell is going on?" Confused at her mother's affection towards her, Rosie turned to Kingsley.

"Please, both of you take a seat. All of this will be explained."

Rosie tentatively took the seat next to her mother's and stared directly at Kingsley.

"Rosie," he began, "your mother has been under the influence—"

Rosie snorted and swung her head back with a chuckle. "You could say that." Her eyes met her mother's, and Rosie bit her tongue at the sight.

Is that remorse in her eyes? Rosie thought.

"Sorry," Rosie said, turning back to Kingsley, attempting to hide her disgust and anger.

"As I was saying, your mother was under the influence of dark magic."

"What? When? How?" Rosie sputtered, sitting on the edge of her seat and turning her head from one body to the other.

Kingsley held up a hand and continued, "After your powers developed last year, I thought it best to visit your mother and get a better idea of your past and family line. I also suspected that Egil could have found your mother and enacted his revenge on you through her."

A warm, soft hand cupped Rosie's. Her mother's. She stared down at her fingers intertwining with her mother's, and her heart leaped.

"When I found your mother," Kingsley continued, "she seemed to have no clue where you were. Only that you were at a school in another state. Now, while I have seen a parent's disinterest in their child, I knew something wasn't right when she still maintained a photo of the two of you. Specifically, it seemed that she clutched the photo at all times, or it was always on her in some way. I continued to visit her until she allowed me to *read* her."

"I thought he was a psychic," Ms. Connors piped up, "but there is so much more to the world—your world, my love." As she said *love,* her hand gripped Rosie's harder.

Kingsley shot her one of his award-winning grins and continued, "I sorted her mind and stumbled upon a well-concealed memory. Someone who I do not know as he was disguised, had altered her state. To purposefully fail you as a mother, to force her to not allow you to realize your powers, to hopefully prevent you from ever coming to King's Preparatory."

"What?" Rosie shook her head and looked up at her mom. "Mom?" Tears fell down Rosie's cheeks, and she stared into her mother's eyes.

"It's me, baby," her mom said, then she pulled Rosie into an embrace. "I'm so sorry, my love. I never meant to hurt you as bad as I did."

"You-you remember?"

Rose the Seventh nodded glumly and pulled away. "I remember. I'm back, and no one will ever hurt us again."

Rosie fell into her mother's warm, loving arms, and she allowed a sob to escape her. The two sat for a moment in each other's embrace.

"Honey, there's more," Ms. Connors stated, gently pulling away.

Drying her eyes and attempting to compose herself the best she could, Rosie turned back to Kingsley.

"I learned more about your magic, Rosie, and why it didn't appear until last year," said Kingsley. Rosie sat up again, leaning in. "Along with your mother's memory, I believe someone tried to suppress your power."

"But how? Wouldn't that take an extraordinary amount of magic to do?"

"It would, and they wouldn't be able to perform such a spell from afar."

"You mean?"

"Yes. I believe you participated in such a ritual when you were a child. Probably around the same time your mother's mind was altered. Your mind may have been altered as well."

Rosie turned to her mom, grabbing her hand.

"It's okay, honey." A comforting hand rubbed Rosie's back as she searched her mind.

How far back could she remember? she wondered. She closed her eyes and searched her memories. Meeting Riley, snuggling her mother, finding her mother near death due to alcohol, living with the Zimmers'.

"I don't know what made you change," Rosie said, shaking her head in disbelief. "I can't remember what happened before I found you that day."

"May I?" Kingsley asked, standing and nearing Rosie. He pulled his hands upwards, and Rosie nodded. As he placed his fingertips on the sides of her head, Rosie's vision blurred, and she was transported within her own mind.

Black smoke swirled and dissipated, revealing a memory which she didn't completely recognize. She hung up the phone after alerting Dan Zimmers, telling him her mom had passed out, and as she did so, a man with a blurred face stepped from a corner. Emotions flooded Rosie. Fear at the giant man standing in her home, worry that her mother was dead, and dread as the man put his own hands on her head like Kingsley was doing.

Rosie snapped out of the memory, her heart racing.

"Sweetie, slow breaths," her mother whispered as she pulled Rosie into her chest.

"The man," Kingsley said, "he altered his appearance physically and within your memory. I am unable to restore it so his identity is revealed, but can you remember anything about him that could help us find him?"

The last thing Rosie wanted to do was pull that memory back into light, but she tried.

Kingsley lifted his hands again and after shutting her eyes the vision of the man came back into view. She visualized the man's face, but it was still a blur, so she focused on his other aspects. He was broad, muscular, and tall. His hair, the same auburn color as Rosie's. When he touched her skull, it was with care rather than malice, and from his movement after the spell, he reached out to brush the hair off her mother's face, and then his hand cupped her cheek before finally leaving the room.

Rosie spun back into the present, and she stared at her mother.

"Mom, you've never talked to me about him, and I swore to you I'd never ask, but who's my dad?"

Ms. Connors leaned backwards shocked but began to speak, "Well, he-he was… hmmm, I can't remember."

"Interesting," Kingsley muttered under his breath. Rosie faced him and nodded.

"You also think the person who altered our memories is my father, don't you?" Rosie asked, her heart racing.

"It seems that way, and it makes sense," Kingsley agreed. "Your father possesses a great deal of power; yours must have come from him and from what I have observed, he must be able to cover his tracks skillfully."

"Shouldn't you have some idea of who he is?" Rosie asked, exasperated.

"Rosie, I can't keep track of *every* supernatural being known to man. The Superiority has records, but some people slip through the cracks. Some people decide to learn from home rather than at King's Preparatory. Some people appear to be gone when, really, they are very much around." He raised an eyebrow and Rosie knew he was referring to Egil. She nodded, and he continued. "It is why I am trying to partner with specific groups. So, we can identify and track potentially dangerous individuals within our community and prevent any wrongdoings from occurring."

Rosie lowered her head and looked at her mother. "You don't remember him? How you met? His name? Anything?"

"I remember the idea of us being together. Being in love with him. And he with me. Nothing more."

"Can you bring back her memory?" Rosie asked Kingsley.

"I can try." Kingsley moved over to Ms. Connors and placed his hands on her head, and Rosie watched as her mother transported. She held her mom's hand, and when her mother transported, so did she, and she watched the memory as if it was her own.

The man's face was blurred, but the same auburn hair sat on his head.

"Rose," the man muttered, drawing close to her face as the two lay in bed. "I am forever yours and you mine. There won't be a day that passes where I will not think of you. I have to put a few things in order, but I'll return, and we can start our lives together."

"Oh, C-"

The memory ended, and everyone gazed at each other, back in the present.

"What happened?" Rosie asked frantically.

"He seems to have snipped the memory apart and taken it. There is no way to recover anything else." At this, Kingsley walked back behind his desk and sat.

"Ms. Connors, I think after exhausting our efforts, it is best to move forward now that you are better."

Her eyes lightened, and she nodded in agreement and turned to Rosie.

"My love," Ms. Connors started, "Mr. Kingsley has been gracious enough to provide me with a place to stay not far from campus and a job with the Superiority."

Rosie's cheeks hurt from how far her smile spread.

Ms. Connors continued before Rosie could speak though, "But I told him I would have to check with you before I took it. I've hurt you so much, and the thought of doing so kills me, so I will leave it up to you if you want me to stay."

Hope filled her mother's eyes, and Rosie had only one answer. "I need you here, Mom."

Both embraced one another again and then stood. The two Roses turned, hand-in-hand, and walked out of the office and into the lobby.

"I have an associate setting up your housing. They will be in contact with you to learn more about your background, so you are put in a position that fits best within the Superiority."

"Thank you again, Mr. Kingsley," Ms. Connors said.

"Mom, it's Premier," Rosie added, acknowledging the

respect James Kingsley deserved.

"I'm sorry, Premier," Ms. Connors corrected, tilting her head down in his direction.

"It's no trouble at all. Now, I have set up a car to take you into Kingstown. Here is an advance in pay so you can get what you need until you start work and can have your belongings shipped."

Rose the Seventh stared at the envelope in awe, her hands remaining at her sides. Without hesitation, Rosie took it from Premier Kingsley's hand.

He nodded at Rosie and then turned to a chair which had been occupied by a person the entire time they stood in the lobby yet had gone unnoticed by Rosie.

"Mr. Fent," Premier Kingsley said to the boy waiting to meet with him.

"Hello, Premier," Justin said, standing. He stood for a second and stared at Rosie, who was also staring back. Justin broke eye contact and entered the Premier's office.

"Ladies," Premier Kingsley said and entered behind Justin.

"Rosie," her mother whispered into her ear, "Is that a friend of yours?"

Rosie didn't answer her mother. Instead she smiled, held her hand, and the two walked out to the car waiting for them.

* * *

In a small apartment above the tailor shop that Ms. Peiler owned, Rosie's mother had set up her new life. She was still unsure of what her position with the Superiority would be, but Rosie was over the moon to have her mother back and to have her so close to her.

"I can't believe your mom is here," Riley said, "and I can't believe what happened to you guys."

Rosie clutched Riley's hand and squeezed it. "Me either," she said. The two sat shifting their food around their plates.

"Does she know about you, your magic, about us?"

"She knows about the Superiority and this world but, no, she doesn't know you're here, and we're together."

"Can I tell my parents? So they know she's here and not missing?"

"Yeah, of course. I want Glenda and Dan to know." Rosie's mouth formed a small smile, and she thought about how much love Glenda and Dan had given her and that she hoped they knew how much Rosie loved them and appreciated all that they had done for her.

"Hey, guys," Garrett said, plopping down next to Riley. Rosie stared at him and then was shocked when she felt a warm presence next to her.

"Rosie," Eleanor said. Rosie lifted her head and stared at her best friend. "I heard what happened."

Rosie whipped her head to Garrett, and he nodded. *How fast can news travel in the supernatural community?* Rosie thought.

"How?" Rosie asked.

"People noticed Kingsley was in town and wondered why and then they saw you with a woman and people talked, and I don't know, the rumors just started to fly. Are you okay? Is your mom okay?"

Eleanor placed a soft hand on top of Rosie's, and Rosie allowed her eyes to fill with tears. "Yeah, she's okay. We're okay."

Eleanor enveloped Rosie in a hug, and the two lightly laughed. As they separated, Garrett and Riley shook their heads but smiled.

As the girls were breaking apart, Riley asked, "So when are you going to see your mom again?"

"Probably this weekend. She has her new place set up, and she should be getting her assignment from the Superiority this week, but I'll talk to her later."

"Yeah, let her know how classes go."

"She's already asking how she can help me." Rosie smirked and then a chime sounded, indicating classes were going to start in ten minutes.

The group stood and made their way down to the high school and college floor, each dispersing into their respective classrooms.

"Hey," Riley said, holding Rosie's hand and pulling her closer just as she was about to enter her first class. "You going to be okay?" He nodded in the direction of Justin sitting in the front left corner by Professor Walker's desk.

"Yeah, I'll—"

"Oh, she'll be just dandy, Ri," Dana answered for Rosie, brushing by her and entering the room. She took a seat in the front, on the opposite side of Justin, and turned and winked at the pair. Well, winked at Riley.

Rosie turned and stared up at Riley. Giving her a grin and kiss on the forehead, he walked away, leaving Rosie to enter the icy room.

Professor Walker had taken up residence in Professor Witam's—Egil's—old classroom. Rosie sat in the front center of the class, and her mind took a swan dive into the cave opening behind the glass wall. She tumbled down the dark corridor and images of being carried over Justin's shoulder to her death flashed through her mind. She jumped from her seat, the chair tipping over and the desk skidding across the floor.

"Are you alright, Rosie?" Professor Walker asked, turning from the lesson she was reviewing.

"Um," Rosie's eyes shifted to Justin then to the cave then back to her desk. As she put her desk back into place and sat down in her seat, she nodded her head and Professor Walker turned her attention back to her lesson plan. Out of one eye, Rosie spied Justin, guilt riddling him, and he stood to leave.

"Mr. Fent, where exactly do you think you're going?" Professor Walker proclaimed, one hand hitting a popped-out hip.

"The library? Independent study?" Justin answered, pausing by the door and shifting between legs uncomfortably.

"Sit back down, now."

Justin lowered his head and walked back to his seat. Rosie kept her eyes forward but realized Dana watched the interaction closely. Turning her head completely to her audience, Rosie observed Dana's features. Her eyes were set on Rosie's and half of her mouth turned up into a smirk while one eyebrow lifted. A small scoff left her, and she returned her attention to Professor Walker.

Rosie also faced Professor Walker and the three students sat in silence for the remainder of the class.

* * *

The majority of Rosie's classes went the same way. Her, Justin, and Dana would sit, listen, take notes, only speak to the teacher when requested, pack up, and shuffle to the next class. It wasn't until Rosie went up a floor in the school that she found a moment of peace. Up to the floor where supernatural students practiced their specific set of magic, Rosie escaped the thick tension. Her mind swirled with the new spells, mixed potions, and rituals she would be learning about.

Rosie entered the hallway to the supernatural classrooms. Her lessons over the summer with Professor Walker took place outside, so her shock at entering the hall was genuine. The stark contrast between the level below, which was light, airy, and warm, as one half of the walls were windows to the outside desert, couldn't have been more of the opposite on this floor. Dark stone covered every inch of the hallway besides where the doors were and the artwork hung. A dewy dampness overwhelmed Rosie as she moved down the hallway to her next class. Roars echoed behind one door. Sounds of shifters learning about their abilities. A whipping noise sounded from another classroom. The sounds of speeding vampires attempting to stop themselves without slowing down from their freakishly fast speed. Rosie read her schedule and the directions which she needed to use to access her next class with her other magical peers.

She held her palm to the center of a door down the hallway and closed her eyes while her other hand grasped her pendant. She smirked as her mind spoke the entrance words.

Open Sesame.

The door split down the middle, and each side slid over

to create an opening. She entered the room and noticed it was only filled with light by floating candles and a chandelier which hung from the tall ceiling. Eyes of the other witches and wizards followed her as she sat at a table, and Olive growled as she plopped down in the only empty seat, next to her.

Rosie turned and raised an inquisitive eyebrow.

"We're the only other witches from our grade in this class, and Professor Shay wants me to help you," Olive barked before turning back to her textbook.

Rosie studied the other students. Some were only a year older while some were at the college level. Her eyes found the interior of her backpack and she began to pull out a notebook when a knock came from the door.

Everyone turned to see if a student would enter, but more knocking came. Rosie stood to open it, but Olive shook her head.

"If they can't get in, then they shouldn't be here."

Rosie sat back down, but the mysterious knocking died as the door opened again. Professor Shay strutted in and behind her was Dana.

Olive's eyes grew, and a smile spread on her face as Dana moved over to their table and slid a chair up to the side.

"What are you doing here?" Olive asked excitedly.

"I wanted to audit a few creature courses and Professor Shay said I could sit in on her class." Her eyes shifted to Rosie. "She's been ever so accommodating."

Rosie's head bobbed, and her gaze fell to her class materials.

"Students," Professor Shay started, and the hum of the class died as their attention shifted to their teacher, "Today we will be learning, and throughout the semester hopefully mastering, the difficult skill of disguise."

Quiet snickers broke out, but Rosie lifted her head to find Professor Shay's. Rosie had been trying to understand and learn about Egil's master trickery. How he disguised himself as Professor Witam with little effort and truly made others believe he was a completely different person.

"Now, there are many ways to disguise oneself. Who can name a few?"

"A glamor charm?" one of the older girls said.

"Yes," Professor Shay turned to the wall, and she slowly waved her hand across one of the stone walls. Immediately, a blackboard appeared to be hanging. "A glamor charm can be effective in hiding one or two physical attributes, like a pimple or scar, but it is a small charm. While that can be handy in everyday life, it won't be as useful if you become an agent for the Superiority." Professor Shay whipped her hand around and a piece of chalk sat between her fingers. She wrote *Glamor Charm* on the board and continued. "What else?"

The students looked from one to another and Olive squeaked, "There's the, um, altering elixir."

"Yes, and what are the results of such an elixir?"

Olive cleared her voice. "Ahem. Well, depending on the choice of disguise, hair color, eye color, and even the sound of someone's voice can be changed."

Chalk scratched across the blackboard spelling out *Altering Elixir.*

"Good. Can anyone else think of a way to disguise oneself?"

"A mask from the general store?" a boy laughed.

"Yes," Professor Shay scoffed, "but I was thinking more of a magical way to hide one's identity."

"Faculty charm!" someone else called out.

"Ah yes, where you charm one person to see you in a way while remaining the same to everyone else."

"Engorgement spell!"

"Plastic surgery without the surgery. Or the more complicated engorgement ritual where effects will be permanent rather than temporary. Come on, there's still a big one no one has guessed yet." Professor Shay's eyes found Rosie's.

Rosie opened her mouth and spoke.

"Power."

"Power?" Olive asked, confused. She turned to her, along with the rest of the class.

"Pure, unrendered, intense power. Power that can be wielded to act in any capacity one wishes. Power that can be used to hide oneself with zero effort."

Power appeared on the board in large print.

"Yes, and can anyone perform such magic?"

"Only with a great amount of time, skill, and harnessing a magnitude of magic can such an act be performed," Rosie continued.

"Correct! Can anyone think of someone who possesses such power?"

The room murmured and Rosie spoke up, "Egil."

The silence of the room and eyes on Rosie caused a rush of blood to her cheeks.

Professor Shay paused as well before lightening the mood. "I was referring to Premier Kingsley." She waved her hand, causing the chalk to vanish, and addressed the room again, "Everyone, you will each work throughout the semester to master one form of disguise. Any type of magic can be used to perform this task, but if you fail, you will have to repeat the course. Also, please do not attempt anything that is outside your power range. Doing so can and will lead to destruction and possibly death. Now please read pages four through fifty for homework and make a transformation potion. Something small, like hiding bad breath or dry skin. I will grade these next period. You may use the rest of class to work independently."

Pages flipping filled the class, and Rosie looked around. Everyone's noses were gulping up the words except Dana's.

"So, who is this Doctor Witam that I've heard so much about?" Dana asked, tilting her head.

"Well," Olive said, leaning in closer to Dana, "he was the school psychologist and then he attacked some people—" Olive stopped, being abruptly cut off by Rosie.

"He was a bad man. A sick, twisted man. That's all you need to know. That, and he is still running loose."

Rosie turned away from Olive and Dana's whispers and played with her magic. First turning her fingernails, a different shade of blue, then red, then purple.

"This isn't a new subject for you?" Professor Shay asked, coming around the table.

Rosie shook her head.

Professor Shay nodded her head. "Then I guess you will need more homework on new topics then. Anything you want to learn about?"

Rosie smirked, and a few subjects floated through her mind. "Yeah, I can think of a few."

"Good, make a list and we can review them next class. I still expect you to complete this assignment, however."

"I wouldn't expect anything less." Rosie smiled.

Professor Shay walked off and Rosie fell back into practicing disguise magic. She attempted to change the color of her skin on her hand. Her eyes focused, and she clasped her pendant with her right hand. Her left hand began to lighten in color and freckles popped up on the surface. Her lips curled up, but she clenched her teeth in pain as the freckles became scratches. She let go of the pendant and the flow of magic stopped, but the damage was done. Holding up her hand, Rosie watched as the blood dripped down to her wrist, staining her white button-up. With the cut hand, she clasped the pendant once more, and using her other hand wrapped it around the bloody marks.

"Tostiek," she whispered, and she pulled both hands away. The cuts were gone, but the evidence of her out of control magic still remained as scars formed.

"Tostiek," she said again, but the scars weren't erased.

She peered her eyes around the classroom but only one person had watched the hiccup in magic. Dana.

Chapter Seven

"Rosie?"

Garrett's eyes seared Rosie as she looked up from the tiny scars that covered her hand.

"Focus, *co-captain*," he spouted, his words dripping with annoyance. He turned back to the rest of the Valtic Illumination Team, attempting his first team pep talk before their first match against Surgent tomorrow.

Rosie tried to focus, but she couldn't help but examine Garrett, as his tone wasn't lost on her. Over the last month, Rosie had noticed his personality changing ever so slightly. A growl of anger here where a motivational quip would normally be, or a scoff of disdain in place of encouraging mentoring with a teammate.

Stress, she told herself. It had to be the stress of being captain, but he wasn't the only one with a different attitude. A different personality. Her peers were changing. Mermaids ditched class to be in their true form more; werewolves stopped shifting as often and were more aggressive and irritable; vampires went through the blood bags on campus so fast that extra supplies had to be called in.

No one else seemed to notice what was going on except

her. She shook her head, and the thoughts left her mind as her focus turned back to the clues in front of the team.

A key, a jagged piece of wood that was the size of Rosie's hand, and a small note with the words *don't fear darkness for it will go, unless you're wrong then fright you'll know.*

"The wood could be a sample of a specific plant we need to search for," Madeline, a senior wildcat shifter, suggested. "Pine, are you able to identify it?"

The senior fairy, who was on the team last year with Rosie, examined the wood. His hands stroked the smooth surface, and he twisted the piece in the light. Twinkles bounced off the item, and Rosie realized the clue wasn't a piece of wood but a rock.

"Petrified wood," Pine said, his eyes evaluating every inch of the stone. "I think it's safe to say that we will be taken to the petrified forest."

Rosie closed her eyes and rocky, hard ridges and hills filled her mind, and petrified wood surrounded her. Rocks that were once plants transfixed Rosie, and she reached out to feel the mineral in the desert night. As she turned her palm up to examine the slab of rock further, a weight sat in her palm. When her eyes opened, the petrified wood sat in her hands.

"Do you also think we will be taken to the petrified forest?" Garrett asked Rosie.

"Yes, and Pine correct me if I'm wrong, but a lot of pieces of petrified wood are shards or broken off bigger pieces?"

"Most of the time. It depends if the specimen was broken off a tree and then petrified or if it was petrified as a whole and then erosion caused a break in the rock. If you look closer at the shard, specifically the inner surfaces, what do you see?"

The tips of Rosie's fingers grazed the inner surface of the rock. The edges were rigid, but each individual ridge was flat.

"It was broken after it was petrified," Rosie said.

"How do you know?" Garrett asked.

"Petrified wood is essentially quartz. It doesn't break neatly across its crystal faces. The edges of the piece resemble the breaking of quartz rather than a separation of wood. But I also think there is more use for this piece than figuring out where the games are taking place."

"Like what?"

"I think it's a puzzle piece."

"Seriously?" Pine asked, examining the piece in her hand.

"Yeah, Rosie, that would be almost an impossible puzzle to solve. If we are taken to the petrified forest, how would we figure out where that shard belongs?" Garrett reasoned.

"Almost impossible," Rosie repeated. "These are the Illumination Games, right?" She stood from her seat and strutted around the table. "The Games aren't easy. They are supposed to test our skills to the extreme. I think there will be a puzzle to solve with this rock. No, I know there will be."

The team looked at each other then back at Rosie, and Garrett grinned.

"Alright, Connors," he jokingly said. "What else do you got?"

She studied the other clues and the right side of her mouth turned upwards.

* * *

"Do you know why we are all meeting in the dining hall?" Rosie whispered to Garrett as she eyed the Surgent Illumination Team. Dana was leaning over a table, whispering to Riley, and both pulled their lips up in coy grins and side-eyed the Valtic team. Riley, noticing Rosie watching them, turned fully, putting a hand in the air and waving it.

Rosie cocked an eyebrow up and pulled one side of her mouth upward and turned back to Garrett. Riley, Dana, and Drew had all made the Surgent team, to everyone's surprise.

"I think we are going to need to use the key here. In the school. I don't think we are going to be taken anywhere," Garrett said in a barely audible tone, so any members on the Surgent team with heightened hearing wouldn't know their strategy.

Rosie motioned her hands in a rainbow above her head, setting a silencing bubble around the group. "You think one of the doors or passageways will transport us to the petrified forest?" Rosie countered at a normal volume.

"Exactly.Does anyone have any idea what door could be the one that takes us where we need?"

The group spied one another, searching for any indication that one of them knew where to go.

"Ahem," Ellie said, waiting for everyone's attention to turn to her. "Last week, in detention with Manger, I, um, kind of stumbled on this room. I was supposed to be oiling all the suits of armor because I skipped class to go fly instead, because in my bones I needed to be in my shifted form, and Manger really didn't like that, so he gave me detention and-"

"Ellie," Garrett whisper-yelled.

"Ha, right, sorry. Anyway, the room, uh, it had a sort of pond in it, and when I looked into it, I couldn't see the bottom.

I bent closer, and on the other side were helictites, drapes of flowing wavestone, moist air, and thousands of bats. I stepped in the pond. I didn't know why, but I just did, and there wasn't a bottom. I mean, I went into the pond, and it wasn't a pond, but a hole disguised as a pond, and I went through it and was home. Not home but bat home."

Everyone in the group had their eyebrows pulled together and were staring at Ellie quizzically.

"So," Garrett started, "You're saying somewhere in the school there's a magical pond that will take us to a cave?"

Rosie's features relaxed and she let out a small giggle. "No, Garrett. I think Ellie is trying to say there is a place in the school that is an *any-hole.*"

"A what hole?" Frederick, a senior wizard, gasped laughing.

"Shut up," Rosie said with a smile and nudged Garrett who was also cracking up. "I'm not sure what else to call it. The portrait holes take us to specific places. It sounds like this pond, as you describe it Ellie, can take us to any place we imagine."

Ellie nodded enthusiastically before her gaze drifted off.

"Okay, so to get in the room, we need this key," Garrett began, holding up the small, golden item, "then we enter the pond to get to the petrified forest, then use the shard to solve the puzzle and then in the dark, find the finish line?"

"I guess," Rosie agreed. "Let's just take it one step at a time."

"Alright teams!" Professor Shay shouted as she entered the dining hall. Rosie lifted the bubble and both teams shifted around and faced the designer of the games. "If you don't know why you are here then you are in for a long night."

Rosie smirked and turned her head, finding Riley staring back at her with a similar expression.

"Well, what are you waiting for?"

Both teams scrambled at the surprise start, and Rosie noticed that while she and the rest of the Valtic team were leaving the dining hall and making their way into the school hallways, the Surgent team entered their library.

The group entered the main staircase, and just before descending, Garrett halted. "Wait!"

The group's feet planted while their upper halves jolted forward.

"What are you doing?" Fredrick balked.

Rosie glared at him then turned to Garrett. "What's wrong?"

"I want to know where the Surgents are going. I want to know if they know something we don't," Garrett whispered to Rosie while the rest of the team turned to Ellie and inquired how they should get to the any-hole.

Rosie studied Garrett. Sweat dripped past his temple, his eye twitched ever so slightly, and a small tremble surged through his body. "Garrett," Rosie said, placing both her hands on his arms. "You got this. We have a plan. Let's focus on that. Not the Surgent team."

Garrett stared at Rosie and lifted his head and faced the group again.

"Okay, Ellie, tell me where we need to go."

With Garrett in the lead, Ellie gave turn-by-turn directions, sending the group further into the winding passages and dark corners of the school. Areas most members on the team had never seen.

"Here," Ellie announced abruptly after the group traveled in silence.

The door Ellie faced head-on was dark, ornate, and held

an elegant design of rocky mountains and high desert, but when studied at an angle, rough, splintered edges rose from the frame and a jutting piece fell out of place.

"We aren't going to the petrified forest," Rosie said under her breath, as she retrieved the petrified wood piece from Pine. Her fingertips gently grazed the edges around the void in the door and she matched the rock to its corresponding ridges.

As the rock sat back in its place, the door boomed, sending everyone a step back. Dust plumed from around the ridges and the door creaked inward, exposing a bare room made up of only petrified wood. In the center of the room, a raised pond sat, with one side having a flowing waterfall feature. The waterfall originated from a rock connecting to and opening at the ceiling. From the opening, the moon fell through and trained its rays upon the settled pond.

Ellie moved forward and grazed her fingertips along the top of the water, sending not only a ripple across the surface but a rumble in the room. Dust and small rocks fell from above and Rosie clasped onto Garrett's arm and he hers for balance.

"Rosie?" Garrett asked, still holding her and surveying the room.

Rosie shook her head and turned to the group all circling around her. "Okay, we obviously aren't going to go to the petrified forest anymore, and if we disrupt the water, we are going to disrupt the structure of the room."

"Everyone, circle around the pond," Garrett ordered, turning back and finding a place next to the water.

The others followed suit and soon the ten Valtic members stared into the water, into a bottomless void.

"Imagine being at the next stage of the Games. Not the finish, not your bedroom, the next phase," Rosie announced, ensuring her teammates understood the request. The group stepped up, each balancing on the edge of the pond. They stood, squished but stable, making sure no one fell before or after the whole of the group.

"Okay, on three," Garrett started, closing his eyes and clasping one hand with Rosie and the other with Ellie. The team gathered their hands and closed their eyes. "One, two, three!"

As Rosie's feet hit the water and her body passed through the threshold, a wave of fuzzy warmth flew through her. Once her head passed the opening, her feet hit solid rock.

The sudden landing sent the entire team to the ground and Rosie let go of Garrett's hand to catch herself. Her hand hit sharp jags, and her eyes shot open in pain. She held her hand, wanting to observe how bad the cut was, but blackness consumed the team.

"Is everyone here? Sound off! One!" Garrett yelled in the dark cave, initiating the roll call of the team.

"Two," Rosie yelled, and the numbers continued until Alec Quay, the other werewolf on the team, finished the sequence.

"Okay, good. We're all here," Garrett said, relieved. "Can anyone see anything?"

"Can't you?" Rosie asked, hoping the wolf's nighttime eyesight could penetrate the darkness."

"Nothing. Can you, Frederick, Katherine, or Pine make a light or fire?"

Rosie held her palm out and willed a ball of fire to form but nothing happened.

"I can't," she said. "There has to be some way-"

"I can see," Rosie heard Aquamarine say and she turned to the exclamation.

"You can?"

"Yes, I transformed a bit, and am dying of thirst but it's like swimming in deep water, where no light exists. Here." She grabbed Rosie's hand and led her across the cave. "Rosie, you're in front of a table now. I checked and there aren't any openings, but on the table, there are a bunch of items. Talismans, potions, keys-"

"Wait, keys?"

"Yes."

"Let me handle this, Rosie," Frederick said, his shoulder sharply jutting against her. "Aqua, hand me the potion."

"Fredrick, what do you think you are doing?" Rosie asked, stepping back.

"Which one?" Aqua asked. "There are three. A blue one, a bubbling green one, and a hissing purple one."

"The purple one," Frederick demanded.

"No!" Rosie protested, but she heard the shuffling feet around her.

"The potion gives sight. If I drink it, I can see, and then I can help Aqua find the door and use the key to get us out."

"Fredrick," Aqua began, "I don't know about this."

"I'll be fine!"

"Um, okay."

"Wait, Frederick, this isn't a good idea."

"Rosie, relax. I got this." Rosie heard a chug and silence fell across the room. Anticipation knotted Rosie's stomach.

"Fredrick?" Garrett called, but only muffled sounds echoed through the room. They were panicked and loud. "Aqua, what's happening?"

"He, his, um, his mouth. It's gone."

"Ugh, okay. Frederick, calm down. You'll get fixed up after the games," Garrett said, his voice relaxing. "Rosie, you're up, unless anyone else has any ideas?"

Rosie held the key and guided her hand across the table's surface. Near the back ledge, her hands felt the different key shapes.

"Aqua," Rosie started, "are there any keys that don't look complete? That could snap into the one we have?"

Tinkering at the table sounded and after a minute, Aqua finally answered.

"Here, I got it," she said. Her hands caressed the key out of Rosie's hands and a small snap sounded. "Okay the key is together."

"Wait, I see something," Madeline said.

"Me too," answered Katherine.

"MMMEEEOOOO," Frederick muffled.

Sure enough, with each blink, Rosie could make out the dark room as her eyes adjusted. It wasn't much, but it wasn't the total blackhole she was in a few moments earlier.

"Okay, everyone, find a keyhole!" Garrett ordered, and the bodies moved carefully through the room, using the walls to guide them.

"Here!" Cameron answered, and Rosie watched Aqua move to him. She forced the key into the opening, but it jammed.

"Something is blocking the way," she said, removing the key.

Rosie stepped forward and held her hand up near the hole. Blood from her previous scrape had dried, but as her palm rested on the rocky wall, sharp pinching ran over her flesh and the wound popped open again.

"Mmmm," Rosie heard Cameron hum as he took a deep inhale.

"Back off, Cam," Garrett whispered, now at Rosie's side.

Cameron opened his eyes and his cheeks reddened at his lack of self-control.

"Sorry," he muttered as Rosie's attention turned back to the keyhole.

Holding one hand up and the other hand holding the key, Rosie blasted the blocking rock which was jammed in the hole and fitted the key in. At its entrance, the wall of the cave shuddered, and rock fell backwards. Katherine swiftly lifted Rosie and moved her back, away from the rock crumbling before the group.

As the dust settled, the Sonoran Desert expanded in front of them, the starry sky and full moon lighting their path.

"I hear the rest of the school," Katherine said, stepping forward and into the desert. "Surgent hasn't won yet!" She laughed, and Rosie turned to Garrett with a smile.

"Well? What are all of you waiting for?" Garrett said. "Let's go!"

The group ran out of the cave and onto the mountainside, following Katherine as she led the team.

The path narrowed so only two at a time could occupy it.

"Here!" Katherine yelled at the peak of the trail. She faced the group and light from the school reflected from her face. Rosie made it to her side, and she peered below.

"We're only about half a mile away—" Rock shards flew, and the force of blasted air caused Rosie to tumble to the ground.

"Rosie!" she heard Riley call. Her right hand slipped around the back of her head, and she massaged the bump that was already forming beneath her hair. Using the support of her arm, she slowly lifted herself up and found Riley attempting to rush to her side, but Drew held him back. Her legs wobbled as she moved her body upward and her eyes met Riley's. She had to tell him she was okay. She put one foot forward in his direction, but a giant wolf tackled the two Surgent members. It was Alec.

Taking a step back, Rosie stood, shocked at the brawl ensuing. Valtics on Surgents and Surgents on Valtics. Her peers in their supernatural form, attacking one another.

"Wait." She started moving to Riley, but the form of someone moving away from the group shifted in her peripheral vision.

Turning her head, she spotted Dana sprinting down the mountain and to the finish line. Rosie took one last look at the group before she bolted forward and shifted her hands behind her, utilizing the wind to pick up her speed.

Dana peered back and spotted Rosie closing in. Rosie watched as Dana's feet quickened and the gap between them grew.

Rosie stopped and searched around, finding a medium rock to fall and block the trail so Dana couldn't move past.

With her hands angled at the top of the mountain at the boulder, she allowed the magic to flow through her veins. Her eyes shone bright blue and her feet lifted from the ground.

"Mortrivisium notrioutios ibubi!" she screamed, as her power hit the rock.

The mountain shook, and the boulder tipped and rolled down the mountainside toward the path, but that wasn't all. Following the intended rock, a massive, protruding boulder which was fused to the mountainside popped out of place and soared through the air, rumbling the ground with each huge bounce it took.

"Watch out!" Rosie screamed at Dana as the boulder took its final tumble.

Dana halted as the medium boulder blocked her path, and then she turned to the rock and stared at it as it plowed her down.

Chapter Eight

"No!" Rosie yelled—or tried to, but the words stayed lodged in her throat.

Dana's eyes shot out of her head, and she threw her arms up in front of her face. Rosie planted her feet as she watched the poor girl freeze in terror.

"Shapini!" Rosie yelled, positioning herself toward the boulder. Just as it approached Dana, it exploded and both Rosie and Dana were blasted backwards.

Black spots clouded Rosie's vision as she blinked her eyes open after feeling the weight of a body on her, slapping her awake.

"Dana," Rosie grunted, but the Surgent girl held Rosie down and wrapped her fingers around her throat. "Da..na.." Rosie wheezed. As the pressure increased, Rosie's eyes bulged and her mouth dried. Grasping the ground, her hands search for something, anything to remove the tight constriction. Her hand wrapped around sharp pricks, but not caring about the cactus spikes penetrating her skin, she smashed the piece of jumping cholla into Dana's face.

With Dana now feet away, screaming as she clawed the cactus off, Rosie gasped and coughed, feeling the rush of oxygen inflate her shriveled lungs. Rolling over to her hands and knees, Rosie focused on a flat rock as she gained her strength back. Before taking her next breath though, a foot jammed itself into her gut.

Forced onto her back, she gripped her stomach as jagged pain and throbs riddled her ribs. Rosie looked up at Dana, whose shoe was about to stomp directly on her nose.

Rosie peered up at the sole which had small rocks stuck in the grooves, and swiftly rolled out from under it as it met the ground with a quaking force. On her feet, Rosie positioned herself for the fight Dana wanted.

Without another thought, Dana ran forward throwing jabs, punches, and kicks. Rosie blocked each while trying to explain to Dana that the tumbling boulder and the explosion were both accidents.

"Listen! I didn't mean to—" but a hard fist landed across Rosie's cheek. Her eye and the surrounding area began to swell.

Fine, Rosie thought. *If you aren't going to listen...*

Rosie advanced on Dana, and the two drew closer to the edge of the mountainside. A sharp, vertical drop presented itself beside the path. Rosie watched Dana stumble and her foot slip by the edge. Rosie stopped and turned away.

"This is over, Dana."

Rosie began to walk away.

"Didn't think you were such a coward. What does Riley see in you? You're pathetic."

Rosie turned to the girl, who wore an amused smirk.

"You know nothing about me," Rosie countered, taking a step closer to her tormentor.

"Riley told me about your year last year. How poor little

Rosie got all wrapped up with big, evil Witam… or I should say Egil, right?"

At Egil's name, Rosie flinched. Snippets of her fighting with him in the caves crossed her mind. Fear of how she thought she had lost Justin, and the betrayal of him helping Egil gutted her.

"You should have let him kill you. Then Riley would be happier, and you wouldn't be forcing him to pine and worry and give everything he has to you rather than his own future."

Rosie lifted her eyebrows, understanding just how much he and Dana had talked and spent time with one another.

"You're jealous?" Rosie asked, then cocked her head.

"No, I just know when someone would be better off dead."

At the last word, Rosie swiftly pulled her arm back and shot it forward, making direct contact with Dana's nose. Dana slouched down with a small grin as she brought the back of her hand up and wiped the blood that dripped. Suddenly, Dana's amusement faded, and she allowed fear to sweep up across her face. She reached out for Rosie's hand and allowed her footing to fall.

Rosie fell to her stomach, and she held Dana's hand as the girl dangled on the side of the cliff.

"Dana! Rosie!" Riley yelled and Rosie looked back to see both Illumination Teams running towards the two girls.

Rosie stared back down at Dana, who was once again smiling.

"Let's see if Boy Wonder still thinks you're so great after he learns you tried to kill me." Dana dug her nails into Rosie's arm forcing her to release her other hand. Rosie watched in horror as she fell, but a small ledge poked out of the cliff and Dana made her landing. She smiled up at Rosie and then dropped to the ground and began to scream in fake wails of pain.

"Oh my gosh, Dana!" Riley yelled as he made it to Rosie's side.

"She's fine!" Rosie exclaimed, passing the other students as they too rushed to the edge. "She's not even hurt!" No one listened to Rosie though.

Drew jumped down to his sister's side and yelled up to everyone, "She's in shock! We need to get her to Dr. Geller!"

"Rosie," Riley said, turning to her, "you have to levitate her, take her to the hospital wing!"

"Riley, she isn't hurt!"

"There's blood!" Rosie could hear Drew call up to the group. "Lots! Please, someone help!"

Riley turned from Rosie and went to a Surgent team member. The older boy's eyes gleamed blue, and he raised Dana from the cliffside, and the group rushed to the finish line.

"Rosie," Garrett said, "what did you do?"

She stared at him in disbelief and opened her mouth to explain, but dryness filled it, and no words came out.

Garrett shook his head and raced behind the rest of the group.

She shuffled along far behind the group, and watched from a distance as Professors Shay and Walker stepped forward from the surrounding students waiting to see who won.

Horrified faces formed on her classmates as Professor Shay transported Dana back to the school. Rosie searched the crowd, and her eyes met Professor Walker's. Disdain and disappointment glistened in them, but what was much worse were the eyes of the person who stood behind Professor

Walker. Rosie's mom stood in shock, but only for a moment. Then she ran forward to Rosie and embraced her.

Fullness filled Rosie, and she melted into her mom.

"Are you okay, honey?" her mom whispered into her ear.

Tears fell from Rosie's eyes, and she nodded her head onto her mom's shoulder. Rosie pulled back and another small hand rested on her shoulder.

"I'm sorry, Ms. Connors, but I need to escort Rosie back to school. I need to take in her accounts of the Games," Professor Walker said, avoiding eye contact with Rosie.

"Can I go with?" Ms. Connors asked, growing closer to Rosie. Protecting her.

Professor Walker stared at Rosie, who was snuggled under her mother's arm. "Of course."

* * *

"So, you didn't try to intentionally hurt Dana?" Professor Shay asked as she joined the small group in Professor Walker's office. Rosie sat, not at all shocked at hearing Dana's retelling of what happened on the mountainside.

"No. Well, we did fight, but she attacked me."

"She said you tried to kill her with a boulder," Professor Manger spat as he entered the room.

"I just tried to block her path, but with a smaller rock. I never meant for the larger boulder to fall."

"I think my daughter needs rest," Rosie's mom stated, now standing with a hand on Rosie's shoulder.

"I agree," Professor Walker said.

The two Roses nodded and left the room. Rosie tried listening as the three teachers discussed the event further, but her mother guided her swiftly out into the night.

Walking under the starry night sky back to her dorm, her mother asked, "Are you sure you don't want to spend the night with me? We can put on a movie and eat junk food and talk?"

Rosie's mouth turned down as she kept her eyes on the rocky path. "No, I better stay here." She lifted her eyes to meet her mom's. "Do some damage control. Talk to Riley."

The two reached the seemingly normal mountainside and Ms. Connors took Rosie into an embrace.

"Please, call. If you need anything I will be here in a heartbeat."

This renewed bond between the two of them not only reassured Rosie, but it comforted her. "I promise."

Rosie let go of her mom and whispered, "Revilio openiterium sanguine." A door-sized hole appeared in a saguaro and her mom laughed.

"I don't think I will ever be used to you doing magic." She kissed Rosie's cheek and turned to leave.

"You'll be okay?" Rosie called out to her mom.

"I'll call you when I get back home, deal?"

Rosie smiled and watched her mother's figure disappear over a small hill. She entered the saguaro and dropped down on the short slide which brought her into the witch and wizard dorm lobby.

The silence of the area overwhelmed Rosie, but she then fell into it. No one to pressure her about the events that happened. No one to shoot daggers at her.

"Ahem," a voice said from the darkest corner of the room.

Rosie's head whipped around, and her eyes landed on Olive.

"Olive? What are you doing awake?"

"Waiting for you, or I should say, being forced to wait for you."

"Why?"

"Let's just go to bed." Olive rolled her eyes so hard that Rosie thought she must've seen the inside of her head. The two made their way back to their dorm room but before unlocking the door, Olive turned on Rosie.

"Just stay on your side, and don't try anything."

"Excuse me?" Rosie asked, confused at the statement.

"You heard me." Olive crossed her arms and lifted an eyebrow.

That was it. The patience Rosie had carefully maintained, a trait she had curated and cultivated and practiced for years ran out, and she snapped.

"Olive, enough! Enough with the bitchy comments, enough with the superior attitude, enough with the clear annoyance with me! Tell me what your exact problem is!"

Olive took a step back, and her arms fell to her sides. Her narrow, scolding face turned into raised eyebrows and a gaping mouth. Rosie noted the surprise but didn't let it deter her.

"Now!"

"Um, well," Olive stared like a deer in headlights, attempting to regain her composure, "you attacked Dana! You wanted her dead all so you could win the stupid Games, and you think you're sooo special with being so smart and now getting your powers and, and, and-"

"I didn't try to kill Dana!"

Rosie turned away and entered the room, Olive close behind, and she ran her hands through her hair. She realized Olive wouldn't care or believe her. Dropping her arms, she picked the cuticles on her thumbs with her index fingers and her arms began to shake. Her weight shifted from foot to foot, and heat rushed through her body.

"AH!" Rosie suddenly screamed. As she did, with her eyes sealed shut, a brightness penetrated them, and a sharp yelp sounded from Olive.

Opening her eyes, Rosie saw nothing. Blackness consumed the room. She formed a small ball of fire in her palm. Shards of glass from the room's broken light scattered on the floor and crunched underneath her feet as she shifted.

"Olive?" she said in a small voice. She raised her hand and found Olive's face stunned in an expression of fright. "Are you okay?"

Olive remained still, and with the small light brightening the room she shot sideways to the door.

"Wait! Olive, I'm sorry!" Rosie called after her, but when Rosie had stepped under the harsh fluorescent light, Olive had already disappeared.

Rosie closed the door and climbed into her bed, not bothering to even change, and decided to lay and wait for Professor Shay to barge back in and reprimand her. But no one came. The room stayed dark. And Rosie was left alone.

* * *

"Rosie!" Professor Walker screamed while pounding on the

dorm door.

"Huh," Rosie said groggily as she pushed strands of her hair off her face. "What?" she murmured to herself as she sat up in bed and listened to the pleas.

"Rosie, I need you to open up, now!"

Rosie jumped from her bed and sped across the room. A light from the early morning rising sun created a dim room, but harshness burned her eyes as she opened the door for Professor Walker.

"Am I expelled? I didn't mean to, Professor Walker. I didn't attack Dana, and the Olive thing was an accident—"

"Rosie, stop," Professor Walker said as she made her way into Rosie and Olive's room and opened the curtains, allowing more light into the room.

"But if you just let me explain, please," Rosie said, before cutting her foot on some of the fallen light blub. "Ow!"

"Rosie. There was an attack last night."

The six simple words traveled across the room from Professor Walker's lips and entered Rosie's ears, and instantly Rosie's stomach lurched, and bile rose to the back of her throat. Flashes of last year's attacks moved before her eyes. Victims being maimed and killed at the hands of Egil... and Justin. A sudden thought disrupted her memory, though.

"Is my mom okay? She was hiking back to town after the games and Olive, Olive left. Who's hurt?"

"It's Justin, Rosie."

"What? Did Egil come back? Did he attack Justin?"

"No. Another student attacked him. A vampire did."

"Is he okay? Did the venom enter his system?"

"He will be okay, but he did lose a lot of blood." Relief washed over Rosie. Though Justin and her had a complicated past, she certainly didn't want him dead.

Professor Walker continued, "Thankfully Dr. Geller was able to provide a transfusion from the school's storage, but it could've been worse."

"Yeah, I, um. I'm happy he's okay."

Professor Walker let a grim, small smile appear and her eyebrows raised a little. "Rosie, have you been losing control of your powers? Have you sensed any irregular force upon you or taken from you?"

Rosie's eyes widened, and she turned her head down. She wasn't ready to admit she couldn't control her magic. "What about my mom?" Rosie said, trying to change the subject. "Did you make sure she's okay?"

Professor Walker lifted her arm and placed her palm on Rosie's shoulder. "We checked with the Kingstown mayor, and it seems everyone in town is accounted for and fine."

"And Olive?" Rosie raised her eyes and searched Olive's empty bed, hoping she would pop out from under the covers and make herself known.

"Olive is already in the dining hall eating breakfast. Everyone else is fine, with the exception of Mr. Fent."

Rosie nodded her head and made eye contact again with Professor Walker.

"Rosie, have you been able to control your magic?"

A thousand explanations ran across Rosie's mind that she could pair with her answer, but none of them would matter so she let the truth slip from her lips, "No."

Chapter Nine

"Well, what other reason can there be?" Professor Manger snarled.

Rosie listened as she sat on one of the stone steps in the descending staircase outside Professor Shay's private office, hearing Professor Manger trying to make a point that Rosie had just gained her power and that she somehow had to have been the reason for the attack. But all his points were baseless.

"Professor Manger," Rosie heard Professor Walker's calmer voice speak, "why don't we ask Rosie herself."

"Yes," Professor Shay stated. "Let's."

With a rattling, the two suits of armor who stood blocking the entrance into Professor Shay's office stepped to either side, and Rosie understood her cue to enter. Poking her head in the door, Rosie looked at Professor Walker, whose eyes held concern and worry, and then to Professor Manger, whose face was even more scrunched in anger than normal. Finally, Rosie glanced at Professor Shay, who was holding a piece of paper on her desk and motioned for Rosie to enter.

The grand office only had two seats facing Professor Shay, who was sitting behind her own desk. A crystal chandelier dangled above the group, sending shimmers across each of their faces. Crystals and gold covered the minimalist office, and Rosie moved down the clear path to one of the empty chairs, feeling the disdain from Manger and worry from Walker wash over her.

As Rosie sat, she asked, "Professor Shay, how are you?"

"Ha, well you could say not so good."

The small laugh thickened the tension rather than diffuse it, and Rosie heard creaking behind her as Manger's body shifted from foot to foot.

"I didn't try to kill Dana, and I was in my room the entire night."

"You have an alibi that can't be accounted for," Professor Manger sneered.

Rosie twisted in her seat and stared at the bulky build of a man, shooting him a glare.

"Rosie," Professor Shay started again, and Rosie turned back, "I just need to ask you a few questions."

"Okay," Rosie said, and she sat up a little straighter.

"Professor Walker said that you've had trouble controlling your powers. Is that correct?"

Rosie began to pick her nails and pulled back the top of one which peeled a little too low. A wince of pain shot through the tip of her finger, and she put both of her hands on her thighs.

"Yes, that's right."

"How long have you not had control? Was it always or did it start recently?"

"No, you can ask Professor Walker. I had control of it. Just recently, since the start of school, it's like something is missing, is shifted."

"Mmm, okay. What do you mean shifted?"

Rosie thought about the last few weeks at school. How her magic seemed to have a mind of its own. But it wasn't only her. Other witches and wizards in her classes also took longer to complete and master spells. Small explosions and melting of items practiced on occurred frequently. But it wasn't only that group.

The students who were werewolves and the more aggressive shifters seemed agitated and easily disturbed. Rosie took note of the mermaids who ditched class and stayed out in the lake full time. Vampires asked to leave class more often to visit the dining hall for an earlier lunch or extra blood snacks. As Rosie noted all the strange, uncontrollable urges and lack of self-control in her head, she grasped the pendant around her neck.

"My ruby," she said, peering down at it. The dark red stone sat in her hand, cold and dull. When she first selected the necklace, just over a year ago, the gem held a fire within and always sat warm around her neck. It provided comfort and strength but also a harness around her magic. An anchor so she could manipulate what power she had flowing throughout her. She dropped the pendant and a tiny smack sounded as it hit her skin. She glided both hands around her neck and unclasped the copper strand the pendant sat on and set the necklace on Professor Shay's desk.

"What are you doing, Rosie?" Professor Walker said, taking a step forward.

"They don't work."

"What do you mean they don't work?" Professor Manger snarled, and stepped closer and snatched the necklace from the desk. He held it up and inspected it.

"Rosie, every pendant, every strand, all crystal ball-made items are sourced from powerful stones," Professor Walker clarified.

"But is every gem connected somehow to a main stone? Like a power source?"

The room sat quiet, and from that hesitation, Rosie knew the answer.

"We have to check the main crystal," Rosie said, standing abruptly, skidding the chair she was in back.

Professor Shay also stood and splayed her hands on her desk. "Sit back down."

"But Professor, if the main crystal doesn't have its magic, then the rest of the pendants can't control the students, and if that happens then there's going to be chaos!" Rosie yelled, her mind swirling with the true impact of what life would soon be on the King's Preparatory campus.

"Professor Manger, please take Rosie back to her room," Professor Shay stated, smoothing out her skirt as she eyed Professor Walker.

"What?! No, I know what's happening. I can help!"

A firm grip tightened around her upper arm, and soon, she was being steered from the office. She turned her head back as Professor Shay and Walker spoke in hushed voices, and Rosie couldn't hear a word over Professor Manger dragging her from the office.

* * *

With clear instructions from Professor Manger not to leave

her dorm, Rosie immediately conjured a mirror portal in her room.

"Um, what are you doing?" Olive's disgusted voice sounded as she opened the dorm room door and entered.

Rosie got off the floor, where she hovered over her textbooks, and moved past Olive, sticking her head in the hallway. With no one in sight, Rosie closed the door and went back to the mirror.

"You can't go anywhere," Olive said in a nonchalant manner as she plopped down on her bed.

"What?" Rosie asked, turning away from the mirror.

"We're on lockdown. A vampire attacked someone last night."

Leave it to the King's Preparatory rumor mill to ensure everyone on campus would know the exact events of Justin's attack. "But the vampire was a student and Justin's fine."

"Whatever." Olive opened her phone and stared at her screen. "Do what you want."

Rosie moved to her own bed and took out her phone. Unread messages and missed calls from Riley, Eleanor, and Garrett populated the screen. She stared at the liquid-like surface of the mirror, and she stuffed her phone into her back pocket and passed through the portal.

"Whoa," Eleanor said as Rosie popped out of the human-sized desert mountain scenery painting and into the human dorm lobby. "How'd you do that?"

"Yeah," Riley said, stepping forward, "I thought different supernaturals couldn't access others' dorms?"

"Let's go meet Garrett. I'll explain outside," Rosie said, walking to the exit. Sure enough, Garrett stood there waiting.

"What the hell is happening?" Garrett asked, moving

towards Rosie, Eleanor, and Riley.

Once the four were in a group, they searched over their shoulders, ensuring they were alone.

"We should hurry," Eleanor said.

"Is this lockdown because of Justin?" Garrett asked.

"Ugh, that guy," Riley said, annoyed.

"Listen. Your pendants don't work. I don't have a lot of time to explain, but right now the jewels are just pretty pieces of jewelry. They won't protect you from anything-"

"What are you talking about? I just used mine earlier to enter our classrooms," Eleanor said, thumbing the jewel.

"They worked on the door because the pendant matches the keyhole. The keyhole changes around each pendant. Like a fingerprint scan. The door holds the magic, not you." Rosie didn't stop at that though, and she turned to Garrett. "They won't let you turn before a full moon and on the full moon, Garrett, you'll turn. With no control or awareness."

Garrett examined the ruby in his Valtic ring and stumbled backward.

"The light… it's out," he whispered.

Rosie nodded her head but noticed Eleanor and Riley giving each other a confused look.

"Riley, Eleanor, have you noticed getting angrier faster? Irritated and frustrated at meaningless things?" Rosie grabbed one of each of their hands. "Wanting to break something or fight?"

Eleanor looked past Rosie at Garrett then ran to hug him.

"So, when you tried to kill Dana last night, it was because your powers weren't in control?" Riley asked, cocking his head.

Rosie threw her head back and let out, "I didn't try to kill her!" She brought her head down and stared him in the eye. "I did a spell where a boulder was supposed to block her path. That spell was more powerful than I had intended." Rosie wanted to add that with Dana's pendant not controlling her mind, she formulated some psychotic plan to get rid of Rosie.

But for what reason? Rosie wondered.

Clinking of rocks sounded just over the ridge, and Drew's voice could be heard. Rosie pulled Riley behind a wide saguaro and Garrett swung Eleanor to the side of a boulder.

"What are we going to do if we are under lockdown?" Drew asked, edging closer to the group.

"I'm sure they'll let the humans continue class. They only need emotional support and aggression outlet lessons," Dana responded.

Rosie peered around the cactus and watched the two stop in front of the human dorm.

"We will be together soon. Let's just get through the next few days and we can move forward."

Drew nodded with a grin, and the two entered the dorm.

The four stepped out of their hiding spots and regrouped.

"Do you think they're right? We will be out in a few days?" Eleanor asked Rosie, but she did it while holding onto Garrett's arm and watching his every move.

Rosie mulled over the twins' words, as they were curious, and she wanted to ponder them over more, but she stopped and answered Eleanor, "Yeah, Dana has a point. I think with anger management lessons and meditation sessions you should be able to roam campus freely. That is if every other supernatural being is kept in lockdown."

"Garrett, are you okay?" Eleanor asked, as she studied Garrett's reaction to this news.

"I can't shift. This entire time I've been trying and while we were hiding, I forced it and I think I broke my leg." He grunted and limped forward.

"Oh my gosh," Eleanor whimpered, "are you okay?"

"Yeah, it's partially healed, but Rosie," he huffed, in pain but also worry, "if I turn, and I get loose, I'll attack whoever I see. I could kill someone. I could turn someone!"

Rosie put both her hands on Garrett's shoulders. "Garrett, breathe. Go back to your dorm. I'm sure Manger will be there soon and will give instructions for what will happen on the full moon. It's going to be okay."

The only sound was the panicked breaths of Garrett attempting to calm himself, and when unsuccessful, he turned and ran off.

"Let's get inside," Rosie said, and the three reentered the lobby. As they climbed through the door, they saw Justin enter the lobby from a separate entrance.

"Oh," Justin said as the portrait closed behind him.

"Justin," Rosie said, letting go of Riley and moving to him. "Are you okay?"

"Yeah, Dr. Geller fixed me up. Um, what are you doing here?"

"Can you tell me what happened?" Rosie moved closer and continued, "Did your ring buzz or send a protection enchantment? Did the vampire's stone glow or try to hold back the blood lust?"

"Um, what? No, Martha just attacked. Well, not just. I mean she played with me."

"Martha, played with you?" Eleanor chirped, joining Rosie.

Justin stared at the group before answering, "She, um, acted as predator and forced me to act as prey."

Riley snorted and everyone turned to him. "What?" he said at the confrontation. "It sounds silly." He crossed his arms.

"Vampires like the hunt," Rosie said, explaining.

"They like to play with their food," Justin added with a small laugh. He continued, "So the pendants don't work anymore, huh?"

"Nope," Rosie answered.

The four plopped down on the couches in the lobby.

"What now?" Justin asked Rosie.

Rosie stared at the boy. He sat in his own chair, still separated from the group, but Rosie couldn't worry about the dynamics of her friends at the moment. "You three stay in lockdown until it's safe to leave the dorm. Once out, I'll need you to send me every book on stone power you can find, on campus and in town, that is if it's also safe."

"You think you'll have to stay in lockdown?" Riley asked, reaching for her. She slid her hands away, caressing them.

"It's not safe. I'm not safe," she said, shaking her head.

"These crystals don't just lose their power. Their magic doesn't just dry up," Justin said, trying to change the subject. "Could someone steal the magic from the main power source of the pendants?"

"And keep the power themselves?" Rosie pushed her hands through her hair. Her mind raced through every day, every hour, every minute, every second since the start of school. Her eyes shifted back and forth and as she replayed every moment, Rosie heard her friends yelling her name. She couldn't respond though, and she couldn't move either.

Stopping her playback of the past, Rosie started to regain feeling and control of her body.

"Rosie!" Riley called at her as Justin lifted his hands from holding her by her side.

"What—" she stammered as she sat up with Riley and Justin supporting her.

"You were seizing," Justin said. "You can't overwork your brain like that. Without the crystal, you'll…"

"Implode?" Eleanor said in a breath as she relaxed backward from the exciting event.

"Ha," Rosie said, sitting up, Riley helping on one side and Justin on the other. "Okay, I'll act as every man's dream. Slow thinking and pretty." No one laughed and Rosie understood why, so she continued, "I promise. I won't think too fast. How about that?"

"Maybe take a break from learning?" Eleanor suggested.

"What?" Rosie said and stood.

"No," Justin chirped, "you can learn, just don't overwork your brain. Don't panic. If you start to feel your eyes wiggle, stop, and do a relaxing exercise." At his words, he gripped her arm, but quickly released it and stepped away.

Rosie nodded, and after Riley helped her up, she walked away from the group a few steps. "I should get back. And you three should get to your rooms. I'll call you when I learn more."

"Or we'll call you if we know more," Riley said, moving towards Rosie and grabbing her hands. She tried to pull them back, but he held on tight.

"You can't hurt me," he said.

She grinned and fell into him, allowing his arms to wrap around her body.

"You going to be okay?" he whispered as his nose nudged the top of her head.

She nodded into his chest, but her eyes found Justin's, and he knew what she was thinking.

No one is going to be okay...

Chapter Ten

"I need to get out of here!" Olive exclaimed as she fell back onto her bed with her arms spread.

Two weeks in lockdown. Two weeks of witch-specific training to learn how to use one's magic without it being harnessed. Two weeks alone with Olive.

Rosie sat at her desk while the TV situated on the far side of the room near the door had Professor Walker demonstrating power orbs.

"Now embrace the extra surge of magic and focus on flowing it out of the tip of each finger and into a ball."

The same lecture repeated every day, twice a day and still not one witch or wizard formed a power ball. The first day, determination took over Rosie and she tried her hardest to form the ball of magic, but the power would build in her fingertips and then sparks would explode from them. On her first attempt, she broke her desk lamp, on the second, Olive's ceramic pug statue, and on her third, Rosie shattered her standing mirror.

Olive, amused at Rosie's struggle, laughed and jeered but she herself tried only one attempt at harnessing her magic and ended up blasting a hole in their bedroom wall. Since then, only Rosie practiced and from the snide comments Olive made as she watched, Rosie was the only one trying to make the orb this far into the lockdown.

BAM! A streak of lightning whizzed from Rosie's index finger and hit the floor, starting a small fire. Olive nonchalantly took her eyes from her phone screen on her bed and manipulated the water in the glass on her desk over to the fire, extinguishing it.

Rosie grunted and fell face forward onto her bed. As she made impact, she allowed the fluffy white comforter to reshape and wrap around her. The closest she got to accomplishing the magic ball was making one the size of a pea. It lasted a whole second before bursting, which sent Rosie flying backwards.

If such a small amount of harnessed, pure magic could do that, what could a ball the size of a fist do?

Suddenly, she flipped to her back and sat up, realizing what Olive had just done.

"Olive, did you just control your magic? Have you made an orb? How did you do it?" Rosie was now standing at the side of Olive's bed, her head leaning over the lying girl.

"Um, back up, please," Olive said in disgust with a hint of annoyance. As Rosie took a step back Olive got up from her bed and did a small whirl of her pointer finger. Dust from the top of Olive's bookshelf collected and disposed of itself.

"How'd you do that?" Rosie asked eagerly.

"It's just small spells. Stuff you learn as a kid. No real power is behind them." Olive side-glanced at Rosie as she passed her, taking a seat at her desk.

"It is so a big deal." Rosie pulled her desk chair over to Olive's and plopped down. Olive lifted her eyes from her textbook and cocked an eyebrow as she stared at Rosie.

"How?" Rosie asked again, but Olive ignored her. "HOW?!" Rosie now yelled, spinning Olive's chair towards her.

"Ugh, okay!" Olive said. "Any form of magic being performed needs to be harnessed somehow. When I do these spells, there's a small tug at my fingertips and I get a dull pain in between my eyes but it goes away as soon as the spell is done."

"Did that happen when your pendant worked?"

Olive shook her head, and Rosie grabbed her hand.

"Olive, teach me everything you know."

* * *

Over the course of the next few weeks Olive, at first reluctantly, taught Rosie how she managed to control her magic. Starting with little spells, Rosie first learned the simple task of moving small objects from one place to another. After mastering a pencil simply rolling from one side of her desk to the next, Rosie moved on to making the pencil stand on its eraser, then spin on its tip, then levitate the pencil, make it fly across the room, make it fly fast and then stop suddenly. With each use of her untapped, uncontrolled magic, Rosie sensed an internal tug, a draw on her internal power source, and then a surge of pain pass through her as the magic traveled.

"Why can't you feel the pain?" Rosie asked Olive, as she practiced making her bed with only the flip of her wrist.

"I do. It's just normal to me now."

Rosie cocked her eyebrow and bowed her head in Olive's

direction.

"Just, here." Olive paced over to Rosie and demonstrated the movement of the curtain being pulled back. As the task was done, Rosie's eyes remained fixed on Olive.

"You hold your breath while you do it."

Olive took a small breath and nodded as she moved to her bed and sat.

"Doesn't holding your breath defeat the purpose of controlling your magic, though? If you don't endure the extent of the pain, aren't you limited in what you can do?"

Olive's eyes narrowed. "Fine. If you want to be in pain so be it." She flicked her wrists and the gauzy canopy that hung around her bed closed, concealing her.

Rosie rolled her eyes and put both hands out in front of her. Like she was conducting a symphony, she flicked her wrists inward to close the curtains. She held her breath and only a tiny twinge raced down her arm. She flicked her wrists outward but breathed out as she did so, and a sensation of sharp needles cutting her flesh sprang upon her skin until the magic stopped at her fingertips.

"That was too big," Rosie muttered, moving to her desk and sitting down.

She laid the pencil on the flat surface and tapped her fingertip to the table on one side. As she tapped, the pencil rolled to the other side and only a slight pinch where her fingertip pressed on the table emanated under her skin. With each tap, she increased her pressure and force. The pencil roll sped up, but the pain built up from a pinch to a cutting-like sensation on her palm. Rosie paused and massaged her hands.

There must be a way to use magic without feeling pain, she thought.

Rosie glanced up and eyed Olive's bed. The canopy still hid her roommate, and Rosie quickly opened the bottom drawer of her desk. Reaching down as inconspicuously as possible, she grabbed notebooks and spare parchment and moved it out of the drawer. With nothing left, she bit the inside of her cheeks and pressed her palm to the base. A flinch of magic flowed out, sending a wave of searing pain up her arm, but she had done it.

She had been barred from reading *Being* since the only way to access it was by using her magic. Over the weeks of practicing, of growing used to the pain of her magic, she decided to try to reveal the hidden book.

Staring down at the stitched-together text, *Being* by Christion Flare, waves of excitement rolled through her. She reached down, and as her hand wrapped around the cover made of different supernatural beings' skin and hide, a warmth spread up her aching arm. Tingles rushed through her, and her exhaustion was gone.

Is the book a power source? How?

Awake, refreshed, and strong again, she put everything back as it was and moved to her own bed, closing the canopy as she lay on the plush comforter.

She traced the stitching which connected each piece of hide and then opened the book. Flipping to the first page, Rosie bit her finger pad, drawing the smallest drop of blood. She pressed it to the page, and as the crimson smudge hit the paper, she waited anxiously to see if any words would surface. Nothing came forward though.

Groaning, she sat back and wondered why the book's knowledge remained hidden to her. Sitting back up, she had another idea. This time, instead of a finger prick, she grabbed tweezers from her vanity and hid herself again. Staring at the pages and then her palm, she called her magic and cut her hand with the sharp pointed edge of the tweezers at the same time. Pins and needles erupted under her skin, and the red blood turned into light. She smeared her hand on the page, and a sly grin slid across her face.

Crossing her legs, Rosie stared at the book in front of her. *It has to work*, she thought as she examined the pages. Nothing happened though. Bowing her head low, she set the opened book in front of her. Her heart began to race at the thought of the searing pain about to course through her. She closed her eyes and held both hands over the book and whispered, "Pressendio." As the magic swelled in her core, aching erupted in her lower back, and as the flow of magic surged out of her palms, her eyebrows furrowed together, and her jaw clenched. It was worth it though.

Opening her eyes, she looked down hopefully, but only a slight flutter of the corners lifted and fell. Raising an eyebrow, Rosie tried again, with the same pain and result. Lowering her hands, she inspected the thickness of the book and quickly thumbed through the pages. With her body aching again, and a pit in her stomach, she laid her hand down as tears stung her eyes.

"Please, Christion," she whispered. "Show me."

At her plea, a soothing sensation fluttered down her arms and her hands worked without her direction. The textured paper grazed her fingers and the pages flipped. As they did, small cuts sliced her skin and tiny droplets of blood sprinkled the edges as they passed. Rosie winced but allowed the book to continue its control. Finally, her hands stilled and wrapped around the edges.

Peering down, Rosie began to read. Passages she had no recollection of appeared and a wide grin spread on her face. The text was back. The full knowledge of Christion Flare was at her beck and call again. She clutched the book to her chest and kicked her feet up, silently cheering.

After finishing her celebration, she reopened the book and began to read.

The power of magic is one of the strongest forces in the universe, Rosie read. *Calling upon it can be detrimental to the body, mind, and soul. When harnessing your magic, Rosie...*

Rosie stopped and read her name over and over again. She knew she shouldn't be surprised since the book did call to her, but seeing her name plain as day written on the page solidifying that the book was hers, was still shocking.

When harnessing your magic, Rosie, it is imperative to first expel every ounce of magic within and endure it to its fullest extent. Even the pain associated with your power. The discomfort will be overwhelming and could lead to death, but it is the only way to gain full control.

Rosie set the book to the side and fell back onto her pillow. The idea of enduring that much pain terrified her, but more than anything, she missed her magic. When she learned she was a witch, it was as if a missing puzzle piece fell into place and now without it, she felt lost, alone.

Flicking her hand to move the canopy back, Rosie tried to spy Olive. The sharp throb that stabbed the middle of her palm as she fluttered Olive's canopy open to see her sent another reminder to Rosie of how much this experiment could harm her, but she didn't care.

Tomorrow, she thought, before curling into a ball and falling asleep.

* * *

"Rosie, I swear!" Olive's muffled objections sounded behind the locked and blocked closet door. "If you don't let me out of here you will regret ever coming to King's Prep!"

"Sorry, Olive!" Rosie shouted, sitting cross-legged, surrounded by a pillow fort and the *Being* book laid out on her side.

Along with the directions of expelling all magic from within and forcing blunt pain to her body, Christion also left a recipe for an elixir which would restore her power and heal her. She was to drink the potion before the expulsion to not delay being powerless.

She stared down at the clear glass containing the thick, brown, grainy drink. Holding her breath, she chugged the mixture of garlic, turmeric, chamomile, and various other herbs, attempting to inhibit her sense of taste.

With a churn of her stomach as the solution hit her center, she paused, feeling the liquid starting to make its way back up. She breathed and then swallowed and gasped, tasting everything.

"Ugh," she said, as she reached for her water and tried to chug the last bit off her tongue.

"Rosie!!!" she heard Olive call again.

With a twinge of pain she placed a silencing bubble around her.

She grabbed the book and ran her finger across the page.

"Okay," she started, shaking out her arms. "I need to force out every bit of magic I have." She reviewed the page again for another hint to see if there was a specific spell or charm she needed to say, but beyond what she had already read, the rest of the page was blank.

"Screw it," she uttered and tossed the book aside. The last few weeks of being unable to use her magic, the most wonderful surprise she had only just received a few months ago, of being separated from Riley and Eleanor, of being stuck with Olive, all of it, welled within and the power in her core grew astronomically fast, as did the sharp stabbing.

Screaming, she continued and brought her arms up, even though it seemed like a drauger was gripping her wrists and pushing them back down. Sweat dripped from her forehead and with the sensation of her fingernails being ripped off, a ball of magic formed between her palms.

Her yell grew and a dense hum hung in the air. With a final push, Rosie could feel the last of her magic flush from her body, and as it passed, searing burns formed across her skin. Her eyes focused on the now giant ball, and as soon as the last of her magic passed her fingertips, the ball sat in front of her.

She collapsed to her side but managed to pick herself up slightly. Leaning forward, a small, tired chuckle left her, and her mouth twitched as if it had been bitten. The tiny speck of magic glided from her mouth, and then hit the ball.

Rosie flew backward as the ball burst.

* * *

Rosie's head bobbed up and down, and sharp nails dug into her shoulder blades.

"You idiot! Wake up!"

Rosie blinked her eyes open and found Olive, wide eyed, staring down at her. Rosie glanced over at the closet. It had been ripped off its hinges.

Aw, she does care about me, Rosie thought, somehow believing that Olive broke down the door to help, but Rosie quickly scanned the room. The closet door had fallen in, not out. And as though a bomb went off, black ash and burn marks scorched the entirety of the dorm room.

"Rosie!" Olive yelled again, and what was a muffled scream before now could be heard by Rosie.

"Did it work?" she asked, staring at Olive.

"What are you talking about, you psycho?" Olive asked, dropping Rosie and standing up. "What did you do?"

Rosie sat back up and looked at her hands, and then examined the rest of her body. Her clothes had been burned and ripped, and her skin was covered in black marks, but other than her appearance, she felt totally fine. She bounced up and put her hand on her chest and closed her eyes.

"It's here," she murmured with a grin, allowing the smooth, sweet tickling sensation to flood her veins. She opened her eyes and found Olive with her arms crossed and cheeks flushed. Rosie then furrowed her eyebrows and cocked her head. "But did it work?"

With a small wave of her hand, Olive's closet door swung up and reattached itself back into place, without the slightest jab, stab, or twinge of pain. Only a gentle flow emitted from her.

"It worked!" Rosie yelped and jumped.

"What worked?" Olive said, exasperated. "What are you going on about?"

"This," Rosie said, grinning and grabbing Olive's wrist and pulling her closer. Once positioned, Rosie formed a ball of magic in her palm and cradled it up to her Valtic necklace. With great care, she pushed the magic into the pendant and as she did, the necklace glowed.

Still staring at the necklace, Olive sputtered, "H-how?"

"I'll teach you, but there's something I have to do first." And still covered in soot and in her tattered clothes, Rosie flashed her hand over her roommate's standing mirror that somehow was still intact. She stepped through the makeshift portal, leaving Olive in their destroyed room.

Chapter Eleven

Rosie jumped through the painting of the school's mountain range and landed on the lobby floor of the natural dorm with a thud.

She watched as the group of people sitting on the couch jumped up and stared at her. Then, Riley ran to her and she to him.

"Are you okay?" he asked, pulling her into his arms, then pushing her back, examining her tattered clothes and soot-covered body.

Resting her forehead on his chest, allowing him to nuzzle his nose into her hair, she sighed in relief, "Yeah. I'm okay."

Pulling away, she stared up into his eyes and then suddenly fell to the side as Eleanor tackled her.

"I'm so happy to see you right now!" she yelled, laughing and picking Rosie back up off the ground. On their feet, they embraced, and then Rosie headed for the couch, jumping into interrogation mode.

"How's campus? Are intellects and protectors still the only ones allowed out of quarantine?"

"Um, so far, but I think the fairies are close," Riley said. He continued to examine Rosie as he spoke, "They are allowed to come to class, but most of the time they are outside, in the sun."

"In human form?"

"No. As far as I know, no one has been able to control their power."

"Well, except for one person." Rosie raised her hand and held a ball of magic in it and grabbed Riley's hand. She brought his Surgent ring in front of her and pushed her magic into the stone. The diamond glowed and then set. Riley's body relaxed some and Rosie could see the vein in his forehead, which normally only protruded slightly when he was mad or stressed, settle back.

"Feel better?" she asked.

Riley began to laugh and picked her up and twirled her.

"You have no idea!" he responded.

"Do me! Do me!" Eleanor shouted, moving to Rosie's side.

Rosie produced the same-sized magic ball and pushed it into Eleanor's necklace. Like Riley, her shoulders dropped, her eyebrows relaxed, and she pulled her high and tight ponytail out and shook her hair.

"Hallelujah!" she yelled, hugging Rosie once more.

As she let Rosie go, Rosie stumbled back a little.

"Hey," Riley said, grabbing her arm and pulling her steady, "are you okay?"

Rosie lifted her hand and massaged her forehead.

"Yeah," she responded, "just a head rush. I think I need to sit down."

With Riley on one side and Eleanor on the other, they helped Rosie to the couch, and the three sat again.

"I guess I can't give away too much of my magic," Rosie said, a tiny, dull ache sitting in her stomach. "I'll have to see if I need to do anything to replenish my magic or if it will come back on its own," she muttered to herself.

"If you don't give it away, do you still get like this?" Riley asked.

"I'm not sure," Rosie said with a small chuckle. "I just got control over my power, like ten minutes ago. I haven't even practiced yet."

"What? How? How did you gain control?"

Rosie looked tentatively at Riley, unsure if he would approve of consulting Christion Flare, but before she could answer he read her face, and he sat back.

"That damn book," he said, shaking his head.

"Well, it worked, didn't it?" she said.

"But at what cost?"

A knot of anger but also guilt formed in Rosie's stomach, and as she opened her mouth to reply to Riley, to tell him she had no other way, a gruff voice sounded in a dark corner of the room.

"Do you feel any pain? When you use your magic, I mean?" Justin asked, standing and coming into the center of the room.

"Jeez, Justin," Eleanor started, "how long have you been here?"

"Was here before you two sat down. Don't worry," he said, noticing Eleanor's cocked eyebrow. "I only heard part of your call with Garrett and as soon as that started, I focused on my own work." He gestured back to the armchair littered with books and papers around it. "So, any pain?" he asked again, facing Rosie.

She shook her head and answered, "None."

Justin nodded and examined her, then walked towards the

threesome.

"Woah," Riley said, moving in front of Rosie with Eleanor shifting to his side.

"It's okay, guys. He isn't going to hurt me, or anyone, right Justin?"

"Never." Justin gave a small, apologetic nod to Riley, but Riley remained still, even though Eleanor moved back to Rosie's side.

"Riley," Rosie whispered. She caressed his arm and gently pulled him back to her other side.

Stepping backwards, Riley followed Rosie's touch, but his eyes remained trained on Justin. Justin stepped forward and sat on the couch.

"You say you're unsure on how to replenish your power? Do you feel drained?" Justin inquired, meeting Rosie's eyes.

She shifted around Riley and sat next to Justin. "Yeah. I'm tired and just want to crawl back into bed."

"I might be able to help."

"Tell us," Riley demanded, squishing into the tiny space between Rosie and the armrest.

Justin's eyes trained back to Rosie's and her eyebrows raised. "Well, there are a few options, but I think the right one will be in the *Being* book."

"What options?" Rosie asked, shifting closer to Justin.

"Like Egil," Justin started, and as the name escaped his lips a growl erupted from Riley, and he stood viciously.

Rosie jumped up and put her hand on his chest. Holding him back, she moved her hands from his racing heart to his shoulders and pushed him back to the couch.

"Do you need to leave?" she asked him, annoyed, the loss of her magic making her irritable.

He shook his head as he gritted his teeth, and Rosie sat down again and turned to Justin. "Tell me. What about Egil?"

Justin, who hadn't moved during the disruption, eyed Rosie again. "As an amalgam, he was powerful but also hindered by his abilities."

"Didn't his pendent keep him under control?" Eleanor asked, sitting forward.

"It wasn't a true crystal."

"Huh?" the three asked.

"Rosie, what kind of pendent did Egil have?"

"He had an onyx stone, set in a gold band," Rosie said, recalling the ring Witam always had on.

"It wasn't onyx."

"Then what the heck was it?" Eleanor asked, sitting back, flabbergasted.

"It was a corrupted diamond. As his true identity was always hidden, when he got to campus, the stone he was given by the crystal ball couldn't read his personality properly. The stone worked, but it also didn't."

"That doesn't make any sense," Riley announced, standing and pacing the space behind the couch. Rosie took note of his ring. The stone was completely dull again and his forehead vein popped.

"Riley, you need to go back to your dorm," Rosie said, moving around the couch and taking his hands in hers.

"What? No way!"

"You burned through the magic I gave you already. That should've lasted at least a week. You need to go relax before your aggression gets the better of you."

Riley looked around Rosie and stared down Justin. Rosie

heard the mashing of his teeth grinding together.

"You need to go," Rosie said again in a more forceful but motherly tone.

"I'll take him and come right back," Eleanor said. "Riley, I will be with Rosie, don't worry." She led Riley to the hidden entrance, but before they entered the stairwell, Riley turned. His eyes were filled with regret, and he bowed his head low.

Eleanor waited in the doorway, and as soon as she heard the door to Riley's floor click open and shut, she moved back to a chair opposite the couch. She picked up the pendant around her neck and turned her head.

"Why do I still have control?"

"Probably because you don't hate me as much as Riley does," Justin muttered, raising his hand and running it through his hair.

Eleanor shrugged and dropped the necklace. "Go on. About Egil."

"Right. Egil. Since his stone could only partially control his magic, he had to learn to harness it. His blood thirst was minimal due to the stone, but he learned over many years how to bend his magic to his will."

"What about his brains?" Eleanor asked.

"He was raging mad."

"Dr. Witam?" Eleanor scoffed. "The school psychiatrist? Ha!"

"How?" Rosie asked, pulling Justin back into her gaze.

Justin leaned forward. "He heard voices. His own multiplied and talking in a hundred different tones and spewed different theories. He would talk to himself. Have conversations out loud with them."

"So, he didn't have control over his intellect abilities."

"Absolutely none."

"How are you?"

"Um, I'm okay. I'm fine," Justin said as he sat up.

Rosie reached out and took his hand in hers. She tilted her head down and continued, "No voices? No manic states? Or depressed ones?"

Her grip tightened, and he stared back into her eyes. His attention shifted to Eleanor, and he let go of Rosie and put his hand around the back of his neck.

"Some. Voices I mean. The information I take in, it manifests and yearns to be deepened or problems must be solved." Justin studied Rosie's concerned face and added, "I've got it under control. Walker is meeting with me, twice a day and I have a journal— well, multiple—where everything is flushed out."

"Here," Rosie said, beginning to form another ball of magic to place in Justin's ring.

"No," he said definitively, grabbing both her hands before any magic could leave her. "You need it, and I'm okay. You, on the other hand, need to be replenished. Since Egil would draw on his inner magic rather than from a stone, he would siphon magic from students he was meeting or teaching."

"What?" Eleanor gasped.

"Yeah." Justin lowered his head, attempting to hide his reddening cheeks.

"Did anyone catch him?"

"Never. He was always discreet. Placing a hand on a shoulder or knee in session. Plus, he had me. I gave willingly to him."

"Justin, you were manipulated. If he didn't brainwash you, then you never would've been in that position," Rosie said, trying to reassure her former friend.

"Sure."

Rosie slid her hand across the couch and clasped his again. Their eyes met, and she could feel a warmth rise in his hand and then spread through hers. Suddenly, her tiredness faded, and her cheeks filled with color again. Her eyes widened and she let go of Justin.

"Did you just?" she asked.

"Give you a 'bump'? You needed it."

"Thanks," she whispered.

Eleanor, who had been still pondering Egil's sick siphoning, chimed back in, "Well, Rosie isn't going to go off stealing others' powers! Right, Rosie?"

"No. Not intentionally." Her cheeks brightened and she stood. "I need to get back. Check out the *Being* book and learn how to replenish my magic. There was an elixir I drank to replenish my magic after I expelled it, but I don't think it is to be drunk more than a few times. After I learn more, I'll find Walker and Shay and let them know I have control. I can help find a solution to this mess."

Rosie and Justin stood. He nodded in her direction, and she walked back to the painting she jumped out of.

Eleanor came up to her. "Let me know if you find a solution."

"You got it, El." Rosie took her friend in and when she pulled away, she held onto Eleanor. "Hey, don't tell anyone about this yet."

"Of course," Eleanor said before letting Rosie go.

"I'll see you then?" Justin asked as Rosie turned to him.

"Yeah, you'll see me." She waved her hand over the painting before stepping through it.

"There you are!" Olive's shrill voice sounded as soon as she stepped through the mirror and back into their dorm room. "Explain yourself! Now!"

Rosie stared at the destroyed room which Olive hadn't cleaned.

"Okay," Rosie said, and she raised her hand, simply thinking about what she wanted completed.

The scorch marks faded, the fallen chandelier reconnected to the ceiling, and the room was returned to how it was before Rosie had expelled all her magic.

"What?" Olive said, spinning in her spot, studying the cleanup and then Rosie. "Aren't you in pain?" she asked.

Rosie shook her head while smiling, and Olive's mouth dropped.

"Tell me," Olive demanded.

"It's a long story, but I need to do something first." Rosie eyed the *Being* book that had been set on her bed. She bounced over to it and shut herself behind the canopy. She opened it, but before she could find what she needed, she heard the tapping of nails on a phone.

Rosie poked her head out, and she leaped from the bed and grabbed Olive's phone.

"What are you doing?" Olive screeched, pawing Rosie for her phone.

"I can't have you tell anyone about this. Not yet." Rosie stared at the phone screen and sure enough Olive was sending out a message to every Surgent about what she had just witnessed.

Rosie set the phone on the floor and then sent a fireball at it. The phone burst and as it did, Rosie felt all of Olive push her to the ground.

"What is your problem?"

"Olive, get off!" Rosie sent her roommate up in the air and over to land on her bed. Olive began to move back to Rosie, but Rosie just said, "Do I need to lock you back in the closet?"

Olive stopped and eyed the closet door. Turning her attention back to Rosie, she grimaced and sat back on her bed.

Rosie stood and moved back to her own bed and closed the canopy again.

Turning to the page that detailed how to gain control, she searched for a magic-restoring elixir. Sure enough, the one she drank before she expelled her magic could only be used three times. She searched some more but she couldn't find another one. As she continued to scan and read the page, she landed on a sentence and her stomach knotted.

Siphoning. The best way to replenish one's power.

Seriously, Rosie thought before continuing.

While seen as corrupt and what some consider as thieving, siphoning is one of the easiest and fastest ways to bring yourself back to your fullest power.

Okay, it says 'one of', Rosie weighed. *There's got to be more.*

To siphon properly, one must draw on its prey's innermost power in a particular way using a particular sense. This sense depends on the creature one is. A vampire could siphon a witch's magic by biting the source directly and using its own inner strength to pull out that witch's magic. Once drunk, that vampire will hold that power and depending on how much is taken, the witch could be left feeling fine or depleted.

"A vampire could drink my magic?" Rosie muttered.

Pulling that power, though, comes at a cost. For one, it is difficult to tap into oneself. Second, it takes practice to perfect the siphoning process if trying to perform on unknowing or unwilling subjects. Many who attempt the act take too little, not gaining any power or too much, leaving their victim dead.

"Dead?" Rosie gasped and continued.

It is best to attempt this process on magical creatures that are considered nonbeings, who possess magic in a small amount and who won't be missed, such as humans with strong mental or physical power.

Rosie slammed the book closed. Her brain rattled with the idea of accidentally killing other intellects or protectors as a way to practice siphoning.

"There has to be another way," she whispered, reopening the book and scanning the page she was on.

Siphoning, siphoning, siphoning, she thought as she read, then her eyes flashed over the words. *Power Source Rituals.*

Rosie's heart hammered, and she hopefully read what Christion thought was another feasible way to gain power.

To perform the rituals properly, and not only replenish one's source of magic, but also never run out of it...

Rosie paused. She couldn't help wondering why anyone would siphon magic if they could retain their magic indefinitely by performing a ritual. Then she remembered Egil. The ritual he attempted resulted in kidnapping, brainwashing, and murdering. Rosie read on.

To perform the rituals properly, and not only replenish one's source of magic but also never run out of it, the individual attempting to gain power must complete each step without any error.

Rosie read the potion that had to be brewed, and her stomach churned. Like the immortality spell, blood would need to be shed, but not in such a drastic way, thankfully.

From each type of supernatural being, she would need a droplet of blood from willing participants as, per Christion Flare, *"those volunteering their blood, their livelihood, will make the potion more potent and easier to ingest."*

At least it's not whole body parts, Rosie thought and continued past the potion to what the rest of the ritual required.

After drinking the potion, which needed to brew for a full moon cycle, she needed to climb to the tallest peak and be in view of the sun, moon, and stars for a full twenty-four hours as the rays and light were absorbed. Her body must remain supine and unmoved for the entire duration, except for one turn, from stomach to back, on the exact second the twelve-hour mark hit. And she must be alone.

She would need to cover herself in a balm which would help absorb power from the surrounding elements, and in the last minute before the twenty-four-hour mark ended, she needed to repeat a spell to finalize the draw of magic.

Rosie reread the ritual, understanding the ease of siphoning in comparison. That, and she knew only a few people had access to the ritual in the first place to even attempt it.

Now understanding every aspect of the ritual, Rosie went back to the siphoning section. She had siphoned magic from Justin easily and with little knowledge. Grabbing her phone, she began to message him. Her thumb paused over the send button, but she needed to know. She needed to understand how she could siphon from him without hurting him.

Bubbles popped up to her *Can you talk?* text and his reply came swiftly.

Of course.

Can I call you?

Seconds after the message was delivered, his name popped

up on her phone, and it began to buzz.

Rosie peeked her head out of the canopy and stared at Olive. Olive looked up and glared back at Rosie. Starting the call, Rosie got out of her bed and slipped on her shoes.

"Give me a sec," she said, moving to the door and entering the small foyer that connected their bedroom to the bathroom and dorm hallway. She turned the knob, but the door wouldn't budge. Holding the knob, she closed her eyes and heard a small click. She opened the locked door, exiting her quarantine officially. She glided through the hallways of the dorm and found herself outside in the fresh air.

"Sorry. Needed to find some privacy."

"No problem. Are you somewhere safe at least?"

"I think so," Rosie responded, her confidence of probing Justin dwindling. A few moments passed and Justin broke the silence.

"So, what did you want to talk about?"

"Well, I just was curious, about, um," Rosie stammered. She, then spoke fast, spurting the words out, "How could I siphon magic from you without killing you?"

A small chuckle escaped Justin, and Rosie raised an eyebrow and stared at the phone, waiting for him to stop.

"What's so funny?" Rosie asked, her worry gone and annoyance taking its place.

"Nothing, it's just—I'm surprised you didn't figure it out."

She huffed and replied, "Well, I didn't, so do you mind sharing?"

"Of course, I'll tell you." Rosie could hear Justin recompose himself and he started again, "I was basically Egil's pet last year, right?"

A twinge of guilt caught in Rosie's stomach, but she let

Justin continue.

"He would siphon magic from others but if it came easily from a volunteer victim, he could take it without the worry of killing."

"Egil cared whether or not he killed someone?" Rosie snorted.

"Yeah, I know, but he couldn't be caught accidentally killing a student in a session. So when he was focused, he would take from others unknowingly, but when he was emotional, he asked to take from me, and well, I let him."

"He didn't hurt you?"

"At first, I was exhausted. I had little energy, and my mind was clouded, but over time, even though I was under his influence, there was a part of me that knew I had to put up a defense. To protect what magic I had. When I had access to the *Being* book, I read how to put up a wall around my power and only allow what I wanted to give out."

Justin finished, and there was silence from both ends of the call for a moment.

"I'm sorry, Justin. You went through more than I can imagine."

Justin laughed again. "Rosie, YOU went through more than I can imagine."

Shuffling her feet, she stared into the desert and listened to Justin speak again.

"Did you find a way to regain power to your liking?"

"Sort of. It's going to be hard, and I think I need to siphon in the meantime. Try on some mythical creatures and such." An uneasy laugh escaped Rosie.

"Siphon from me. I can give you power when you need it, and you won't have to worry about hurting me."

"No, Justin, I couldn't."

"Rosie," he stated firmly, "you can, and you will. And whatever you need, I'll help."

A small smile spread across her lips, and she said into the phone, "Thanks."

"Anytime."

"I better go."

"Yeah, I'll talk to you soon?" Justin asked.

And a very tiny but present sensation of butterflies danced in her core. "Definitely."

Chapter Twelve

Staring at herself in her mirror, Rosie adjusted the tie around her neck and smoothed out her plaid skirt. Then, she picked up her backpack, slung it over her shoulder, and moved to the door.

"I'll see you later," Rosie called to Olive's bed, but to her surprise, Olive came in through the dorm entryway in her own uniform. "What are you doing?"

"If you think I am just going to stay here while you gallivant to Professor Shay, saying you're cured, you're crazy."

"But I am cured, and you don't have control yet."

"I have enough."

Rosie's backpack slipped from her shoulder. "Olive, it's too dangerous. Without the power in your stone, your magic could go haywire. It can be amplified or be nonexistent if needed. You need to stay here."

"Bite me, Rosie. I have it in check."

Rosie sized up Olive and watched a small bead of sweat form on her forehead. "Are you trying to control your emotions with magic? I can see you're in pain, Olive."

But Olive brushed past Rosie, grabbing her own school bag. "Let's go," she said, side-stepping Rosie and exiting the room.

Rolling her eyes and lifting her backpack up, Rosie followed. Olive walked two steps ahead, and in the lobby of their dorm, Rosie noticed Olive walking to a portrait hole that supposedly led straight to the Surgent living room. Rosie continued in Olive's footsteps, and at the painting of lightning striking a tall peak, Olive turned sharply.

"What do you think you're doing?" she asked, crossing her arms.

"I'm not leaving you alone," Rosie answered simply.

The two stood still, staring each other down. Rosie broke the silence. "Are you going to open the door or not?"

"You can't enter the Surgent living room or go through our library," Olive pouted, crossing her arms.

"Watch me." Rosie cocked an eyebrow, and after another moment of reluctance, Olive huffed and turned back to the painting.

Raising both hands, Olive set them on the frame of the painting and muttered a few words under her breath, indistinguishable to Rosie. The painting popped open inward, and as Olive brought her hands together, she massaged her palms, and Rosie noted that they shook.

"Would it be easier to just walk to the main entrance?" Rosie asked, knowing Olive may have to perform more magic to get to the dining hall.

Throwing a look of disgust in Rosie's direction, Olive turned to the painting and stepped through it. Rosie followed, and once her feet planted on the marble white floor, she looked up and was taken aback by the vast room she had entered.

Unlike the Valtic living room, which was dark and cozy

with couches and chairs close together for group gatherings, the Surgent living room was open, airy, and ceiling-less. Or that's what it seemed like. The illusion created a clear blue sky above with a few small clouds floating across. As Rosie moved carefully around the white couches and linen poufs, she read the gold-framed quotes on the walls. As she stepped forward to make sure she read who said them correctly, James Kingsley, her hand slid across a couch back. Suddenly, the false sky started to fill with dark, heavy rain clouds and thunder boomed as lightning flashed.

"Move it!" Olive shouted, grabbing Rosie's hand as a bolt shot down and hit the spot she just was.

"What's happening?"

"The room's been enchanted!" Olive screamed over her shoulder, weaving Rosie around the many obstacles. "Anyone not in Surgent will be forced out!"

Rosie jumped over a glass coffee table and caught up to Olive's side.

"Where's the exit?" Rosie asked, dodging another lightning bolt. The splattering sound of giant raindrops hitting the floor sounded behind Rosie, and she turned her head. Close behind, the storm that erupted above, chased her.

"Here!" Olive shouted, running to a door. She lifted both arms and as she winced in pain, the door swung open. Olive dove through the opening first. Rosie took a final look behind her. As golf ball-sized chunks of hail hammered down, she hopped through the door and slammed it shut, an echoing boom of thunder erupting behind the closed door.

With her palms on the door, Rosie shut her eyes and caught her breath before spinning on her heels and finding herself face-to-face with Olive.

"Didn't want to give me a heads up?" Rosie asked, stepping closer to Olive.

Olive staggered a step back but recovered. As she opened her mouth to respond, Rosie's eyes left Olive's, and she stepped past her and took in the Surgent library. But it didn't look like a library.

There were chrome tables with matching chairs the length of the stark white room. Rosie walked towards them and with her fingers sprawled, she reached for the surface. Pausing just before she made contact with the table, she turned to Olive.

"Is it safe?" she asked, her fingers now pulled in, forming a loose fist.

Olive rolled her eyes and nodded.

She outstretched her hand again and touched the smooth surface and studied the room.

"Where are the books?" Rosie asked, attempting to see if there were any hidden enchantments or illusions set on the room.

Olive let out a small chuckle and strutted down towards the door at the end of the room, which Rosie presumed led to the dining hall.

"We typically study in big groups," Olive said, "and if we need to research something, we just ask the room."

"What do you mean, 'ask the room'?" Rosie said, coming up to Olive's side.

Olive rolled her eyes but not in annoyance. More playful at Rosie's interest in her team.

"You know how we order food most days? Grab a slip, write what we want, and then it comes out of the kitchen?"

"Um, yeah?"

"Basically, it's the same concept. Whatever you need information on, you go over to the information desk…" Olive swung her arm up to her shoulder and pointed with her thumb to a smaller chrome desk against the wall with small parchments of paper and a cup of quills behind her, "And write the topic and subtopic down along with your table and seat number. Then you slide it into a slot on the side of the desk and your books are there by the time you get back to your chair."

"What about when you're done with the books, or you didn't find what you needed?"

"There's a card in each book. You sign it if completed, then close the book and set it aside. It's then returned-"

"Returned where?" Rosie pressed.

"I don't know," Olive retorted, moving on to the next part of Rosie's original question. "If we need more information, then we return to the desk and request a different book with more information on what we are looking for."

"But what if you just want to browse? Doesn't this setting," Rosie gestured to the sterile-like room, "suppress creativity and further learning? Finding out about topics that you *might* be interested in?"

At the end of the room, Olive rolled her eyes again. "Listen, we work as a team, a unit. If someone doesn't understand something, we help them."

"You mean cheat?"

"No, Rosie. We don't cheat. We teach them. This room is for focused studies and learning. If someone wants to just browse books, they have the main library or they can go into town. Make sense?"

Rosie nodded her head, understanding the Surgent student's strategy in academia. She took one last look at the room and then placed her hand on the door handle. She turned back to the steel door and turned the handle. As she slowly pulled open the door to her, her heart quickened. She was going to be back in the dining hall with her friends. No more delivered meals, no more online lectures, no more uncontrollable magic, at least from her.

Rosie stepped through the doorway, and Olive followed. The few intellects and protectors who attended the school were scattered across two tables in the middle of the room and only Professor Shay and Professor Walker sat at the teacher's table.

Upon their entrance, every head turned their way, and both Shay and Walker stood abruptly, not caring that Professor Shay's chair clattered backwards.

Rosie searched the room and found Riley's eyes. Already standing, he jogged towards her and took her in his arms.

"I was wondering when you would show up," he said, a smirk pulling at the corner of his mouth. He kissed her forehead, and she nestled under his arm. Rosie turned back to make sure Olive was still at her side, but she had broken off and found a seat next to Dana, who was with her brother and Gunner.

Allowing Riley to guide her, Rosie moved towards Eleanor who was bubbling with glee, but before she reached her, Professor Shay and Walker intercepted her.

"What do you think you are doing? How did you get out of your room?" Professor Shay asked, swiftly strutting around the table, nearing Rosie.

"She's cured, teach," Riley joked, bringing Rosie closer in.

"What?" Professor Walker gasped, eyeing Rosie up and

down then spying her necklace. "Your pendant isn't glowing. There's no magic. You need to get back to your room. For your own safety, Rosie."

Rosie took a step away from Riley and held up her hands. She had planned this moment carefully. Ensuring no light glowed within her necklace, no magic tittered within so she could demonstrate her powers. Warmth spread from her center all the way to the tips of her fingers. A bright, yellow, mesmerizing ball of magic floated in between her hands.

"Woah," Reid whispered to Eleanor as he watched Rosie.

Proving her point, she began to disband the magic and reabsorbed the power back within her, but not before a small amount was placed into the ruby, charging it. Once done, she lowered her hands and smiled, but a wave of exhaustion hit her. As the magic she reabsorbed hit her core, the exhaustion waned, and her energy returned. She still hadn't figured out a quick fix to regaining her magic other than siphoning, and she needed to make sure her first day out of quarantine wasn't without magic. She could run into a blood thirsty classmate, or a fully changed, unaware of what they were doing, predator shifter.

"How?" Professor Shay asked, grabbing Rosie's wrists and studying her palms.

"I found a solution," Rosie muttered, pulling back her hands and staring at the two.

"And Olive?" Professor Walker asked, staring at Rosie's roommate.

Olive eyed Rosie, silently pleading to cover for her.

"She has some control. But not without causing herself pain. She needs to go back to our room. So she stays safe." As Rosie spoke, Olive pushed back, scraping the legs of her chair across the ground, causing a shivering scratch.

"Mutant!" Olive screamed, her hair falling in her face and her nails digging into the wooden table.

Rosie's eyes grew and she clenched her jaw together, but she didn't look over at her roommate. The term cut at Rosie's heart, and she forced herself to swallow the jab. Her nails dug into her palms and sticky blood coated them.

"Agh!" Olive yelled, and Rosie flew forwards to the ground. She heard a thud behind her.

"Are you okay?" Riley asked, picking her back up to her feet.

She rubbed her knee that she landed on, nodding as she turned and stared at Olive's unconscious body.

"She needs to go back to our room. She should be fine, just passed out from overexerting her magic on me, but Doctor Geller should probably look still," Rosie said.

Professor Shay assessed Olive, checking that Rosie's deduction of the incident was accurate, then she levitated Olive in the air before sending her through a portrait on the other side of the room. Rosie peered into the portrait, which now looked like her dorm room, before turning back to a painting of dense wood covered in snow.

"Not sure if I should refer to you as a mutant or a snitch," Dana said, as Professor Walker and Shay were huddled near each other, talking low.

"Excuse me?" Rosie asked, turning and stepping towards her.

"You heard me," Dana retorted before walking away towards her brother, a grin covering her mouth as she leaned into him and Gunner. The trio laughed as they stared back at Rosie.

Rosie stepped towards the group, but a firm hand wrapped around her upper arm.

"Are you okay?" Riley asked, facing her towards him instead and examining her knee that had a smudge of blood on it.

"Oh," she murmured, before licking her thumb and wiping the blood off. "Yeah, I'm good."

"Want me to take Olive down next time I see her?" Eleanor quipped, pulling Rosie over to a chair.

Rosie gave a small chuckle. "No, she'll settle down as soon as I teach her how to use her magic without falling into a coma."

"Speaking of using one's magic without pain," Professor Shay announced, swaying back to Rosie, Professor Walker on her heels. "How did you manage it?"

The remaining students fell silent, listening in, and Rosie paused, determining how she could best explain herself.

Not wanting to reveal to all the source of her knowledge, the *Being* book, she told half-truths, "When practicing your assignments Professor Walker, I couldn't shake the stabbing pain that erupted whenever I tried to use my magic. I thought, if I try to shoot out as much magic as possible to overcome the pain, I could then control it. It worked."

"Not before you blew up your dorm room though," Dana said, her cronies laughing.

Rosie shook her head, realizing Olive must have gotten a new phone somehow. Rosie stared at her two professors and silence sat between the group until Professor Walker spoke.

"Can you teach us?" she asked, admitting she too felt the sting of magic whenever she used her power.

"Of course." Rosie smiled, nodding enthusiastically.

"Great," Professor Walker said, turning back to the head table and grabbing a notebook. She pulled out a pen from the binding and began writing. "First the teachers. You can show us how to draw from our own magic. Is it just witches and wizards you can help?"

Rosie pulled the pages of the *Being* book to the forefront of her mind, reading the process of how to gain control of one's magic for each type of supernatural being.

"No, I think I can help everyone. But it's probably better if I teach one person from each group first."

"Me!" Rosie heard the voice coming from Eleanor's phone. "I'll be the werewolf volunteer!" Rosie stared at Garrett's face on Eleanor's phone screen. Large, dark bags sat under his eyes and a fresh scratch, the length of his face, fell over his left eye.

Rosie wished she could muster a smile, but his appearance clutched her heart. She nodded. "I'll make sure you can control yourself, Garrett. I promise." Garrett's demeanor relaxed and his smile grew before he ended the call.

"Okay, everyone return back to your dorm. You have the day off," Professor Shay announced. She strutted to Professor Walker and examined the notes she took.

"We can go to one of the safe rooms to practice this method," Professor Walker said, starting for the main staircase.

"Yes, Rosie come with—" Professor Shay started but a loud, piercing, cracking sound above them stopped everyone in their tracks. The noise rattled from the top of the room down to the group and Rosie peered up at the glass ceiling.

A drip of water fell from a small crack and hit Rosie's cheek, sliding down and grazing her lips. The crack split off and grew a foot, then split off in another direction, growing more.

"Run!" Justin shouted, as the glass continued to crack, faster now, and rushes of water spilled into the dining hall. Up above, a louder crack sounded, almost like the crunching of an empty plastic water bottle, and then shards of glass hit the floor. Rosie's feet swept out from under her as the gush of water spilled into the middle of the room.

"Everyone! Get to the walls and grab something anchored!" Professor Shay commanded. Rosie released her grip on Riley's hand and used both of hers to hang on to a wall sconce.

She peered around at everyone else who was doing as Professor Shay said, except for Dana, who wasn't in the room anymore. Trying to find her and make sure she wasn't trapped under the now waist-deep water, Rosie spotted a portrait shifting back to its normal state, Dana's figure, fading in the background.

Rosie looked to Drew, who was frantically searching for Dana as well.

"She's safe," Rosie called across the room to him. He stared back at her, relief flooding his eyes, and he nodded back, grasping onto a divot in the wall.

Suddenly, the remaining glass fell into the water and the room was now part of the lake.

Chapter Thirteen

As to not feel the full force of the ceiling and lake falling upon her head, Rosie dove under the water as the crash of waves hit the surface. The contact pushed her up against the wall, and her head hit against the stone. At the wall, she grasped the sconce again, now searching the room, counting everyone who seemed relatively unharmed. She loosened her grip, and pushing off the floor, she shot herself upwards towards the surface of the lake.

Turning back, she found everyone else followed, and as they passed the opening of where the ceiling once was, Rosie heard singing in the distance.

Her eyes widened, and she floated in her spot, spinning around, searching for her mer-classmates, hoping they had some control over their primal siren desires.

Finding Professor Walker's wide eyes, she nodded and the two attempted to usher their group up faster. That didn't seem to be an issue, though, as almost everyone was clawing their way up for air.

Riley grabbed Rosie's hand, and they kicked up to the surface together.

Breaking the surface, Rosie gasped for air, her lungs

burning as they inflated. She spewed out water as she caught her breath.

"Are we missing anyone?" Professor Shay shouted, turning and counting the heads bobbing on the surface.

"I think everyone is here—" Justin shouted. Rosie looked at him, only a few feet away, but he was abruptly cut off and shot down.

"Get to the shore!" Rosie yelled before diving down to search for him.

The mer-students caught up to the group, two directly beneath them, their eyes completely black, and their tails shimmering in hypnotic patterns. Rosie peeled her eyes off the two boys' tails and saw they were pulling Justin further down back towards the dining hall. A small handful of mermaids were waiting at a table, their sharp teeth set in a wide smile.

Rosie swam to Justin and began to pull on her magic. A hand grasped around her waist and pulled her back, though, breaking her connection with her power and sending her mind into a swirl of panic.

Breaking the surface of the water again, she turned to Riley.

"What are you doing?" she yelled, trying to get back to Justin.

"We need to get to shore. If we don't, we'll drown!" Riley yelled back, dragging her through the water.

Rosie ripped her arm away and sent him a glare. "I'm not leaving him. You can help me or go to shore, but don't try to stop me again."

She dove back down, the water stinging her eyes as she searched for Justin. Floating in her spot, the water stilling around her, she turned. In the distance, more bodies with tails swam her way. Her heart quickened and eyes popped as the approaching sirens swam closer.

A muffled scream in the distance sent bubbles up and past her, and she looked down.

In the dining room, with three mermen holding him down, was Justin on a table. Rosie burst to the surface, and took a deep breath in, filling every inch in her lungs.

She darted down, her hands in front, a fireball forming underwater and causing the water touching it to send boiling bubbles up. She pushed the ball forward, hoping it would reach the table in time for Justin to break free and breathe. She stared back down at him, her fuzzy vision only making out his body and the fireball hurling towards the group.

Come on, Rosie thought, watching the ball, which would normally fly at a fast speed in the air, trudge through the water.

A merman's arm stretched towards her, and the rest of the group moved outward. Suddenly, they all swam in different directions as the fireball reached Justin, and it exploded next to the table.

Rosie grew closer to the table, which now was empty. She searched for Justin, fire burning in her chest as she yearned for air. She shook her head vigorously, trying to find him. A hand reached out from under the table and he swam upward towards her. She pushed herself closer to him and outstretched her hand. He grasped it, and she pulled him up as she swam to the surface.

She turned back, his weight growing, and his face starting to turn a light purple. She kicked her legs faster as his body became heavy with unconsciousness.

She continued ahead, kicking her legs with all the force

she had in her body, and she stared, determined, at the sun glinting on the swishing water at the surface of the lake.

So close. Just a little further, Rosie thought, pushing herself to overcome the burning sensation in her lungs, and the desire to breathe in.

With her primal instincts taking over, a blackness began to seep in at the corners of her eyes, she breathed, her nostrils taking in the lake water. Stopping mid-stroke, she gagged and seized, the blackness taking over. She stretched out her hand searching for the break, her fingertips growing cold as fierce wind brushed through them.

She kicked once more, knowing life was inches away. She broke the surface, and the smooth water slid down her face as she bobbed up. Water spewed from her mouth and coughing erupted from her and from the boy beside her.

"Are you okay?" Rosie asked between deep breaths. She swam closer to Justin, who threw up water. He met her halfway and studied her.

"Yeah," he said, coughing, "I think so. Are you?" He grabbed her hand and motioned to put her arm over his shoulders.

"I'm okay. I can swim back."

"You must be exhausted. Let me take you."

Rosie was about to object, but exhaustion filled her muscles. She nodded, moving closer.

"Yeah, okay—" But before securing her grip around him, a slimy, webbed hand wrapped around her ankle and pulled down.

"Rosie!" Justin called, diving below to catch her.

She outstretched her arms and reached for him, but she was being pulled down faster than he was able to swim to her.

Staring down at the mermaid who snatched her, she kicked feverishly and caught her in the nose. The mermaid lost her grip and grabbed her nose, blood trickling out and floating in the water around her.

A loud, vibrating groan echoed around them, and Rosie noticed all the mer-students dash away. All except the mermaid she kicked, who was now being shunned by the others.

She swam quickly in the opposite direction, and another loud growl sounded.

Rosie spun in a circle, trying to see what was making the sound, but the water was clear around her. Justin reached under Rosie's arm and pulled her up top.

"Did you hear that?" she gasped as they swam at the surface.

"We need to get out of here. I thought they would've been trapped still, but they're out."

Justin began to swim rapidly to the shore, the tiny specks on the sand motioning them to return to land fast.

"Wait, what was that sound?" Rosie called, following Justin.

But Justin didn't respond. He kept swimming, turning every few strokes to make sure Rosie was still by him. She moved up to his side, and she stared at his urgency.

"Come on, Justin—" she started, but watched his eyes widen as he stared behind. "What?" she asked, turning. Shocked in place, the screams and shouts from the group on shore dwindled as she focused on the creature heading towards them.

Poking out of the top of the water was a long, ridged, lime-green fin heading towards her. She poked her head under the water and saw a monstrous creature cutting through the water effortlessly. It was the size of a school bus with a long nose and long, sharp, jagged teeth. The creature dove below and began to snap its powerful jaws through a tall seaweed garden. Rosie could see the injured mermaid from earlier dodging the snapping razor-sharp teeth of the creature, but she couldn't leave the field, and the monster had no intention of giving up its meal.

Rosie stilled and watched the struggle continue. The long, wide creature tucked its legs into its sides, and with a *swoosh* of its shark-like tail, it dove right into the middle of the tall, thick seaweed forest.

The mermaid sank further down and pressed herself onto the sandy bottom as the beast rooted up the stalks one by one, clearing the area of any obstruction.

Rosie knew she could help, use her magic somehow to fight off the creature and save the mermaid. Even help her to safety. But she hesitated.

She pondered the idea of leaving her. She had tried to drown her, to hurt her. She hit the surface and gasped for air and spun, looking for Justin, but he wasn't there. She poked her head back underwater, and she watched Justin speed towards the mermaid.

With her mind made up for her, she followed him fast, and made it to Justin's side. While the creature snapped its jaws, blind to its surroundings outside of the kelp, they snatched the girl and swam to the surface.

The closer they got, though, the mermaid struggled to be freed from their grasp. Rosie turned, gripping her harder out of annoyance, but she pushed off Rosie. Rosie turned to grasp the mermaid again but paused. The mermaid stayed in place and shook her head, her eyes wide with fright at the sight of the oxygen-filled air above the water.

She turned back to where the creature was, now tangled within the long strands of kelp, and she pointed to where Rosie thought shore was. Then she held out both her hands, and Justin without hesitation grasped it.

Justin nodded at Rosie and looked at her hand and then the outstretched one of the mermaid's. Rosie placed her fingers in her palm and immediately she grasped them and swished her tail, zooming through the water.

A roar behind them sounded, and Rosie turned to see the creature free and his sharp menacing eyes catching up to them. With her free hand, she willed her magic, and as the creature drew open its wide mouth, she sent another fireball into it. The ball of flames hit its snout and the creature flew back, erupting in howls of pain.

The mermaid didn't stop to see the creature falling behind and retreating. She instead continued to swim as fast as she could to the shore.

Once near enough, she released the two and smiled before returning into the depths of the lake.

Rosie and Justin stood up in the shallow bank, catching their breath.

"Are you okay?" Riley asked, sloshing into the water, trying to help her out of the thick sand which pulled her backwards.

"Get off," she muttered, pushing past, falling and catching onto Justin, whom she didn't let go of.

Riley eyed her grip on Justin and with his face turning red, he barged away from the group, Drew, Flynn, and Gunner following him.

"Here," Justin said, helping her to the sandy ground. "You need to siphon."

The two sat next to each other, and Eleanor squatted down

by Rosie, observing her.

"You okay?" she asked, offering her own hand.

"Yeah," Rosie answered, and she gripped one hand around Justin's and the other around Eleanor's. As they volunteered themselves to allow Rosie to draw on their magic, a rush of power tingled up Rosie's arms, and she released them both after a few seconds.

Justin raised an eyebrow, his hand still out. "You sure you don't need more?" he asked.

Rosie softly shook her head and stood, pacing towards Professor Shay and Walker. The two teachers gave her a quick once-over and then did the same to Justin, ensuring neither was seriously injured.

Breathing a sigh of relief, Professor Shay spoke while untangling a twig from her hair. "How about we all get washed up, and we meet back in my office to practice our control? Say six o'clock?"

Rosie nodded her head and the two teachers headed back through the main entrance to the school.

Rosie turned back to Justin, Eleanor, and Reid, all of whom were now at her side.

"Want to get ready at my place?" Eleanor asked. "I can kick Dana out of our room?"

A sly smile spread across Rosie's face as she remembered the intellect girl disappearing, leaving them all to potentially die, just before the break of the dining room ceiling.

"I'd love to."

CHAPTER THIRTEEN

Chapter Fourteen

Justin trailed by Rosie's side as the four traversed back to the human dorm.

"Are you sure you're okay?" Justin asked Rosie as they reached the stone handle and pulled open the door to expose the dorm lobby.

Rosie grinned. "Yeah. I promise I'm fine." She grasped his hand as he helped her through the threshold, and then he released her and closed the door. The room dimmed and the four awkwardly stood, still damp in the room.

"Do you two need any magic?" Rosie asked, her own power source growing further with the assistance of Justin and Eleanor's power. "Reid, how are you?"

Reid's hand ruffled the hair on the back of his head. "I'm okay. Been tough staying in a good mindset, but I'm fine."

"You've been the most focused out of all of us," Eleanor chimed in. "I haven't seen you get overly aggressive like the others." She placed a hand on his wrist, and his cheeks reddened. Rosie grabbed his other hand, and a finger hit his inner wrist, grazing a raised line.

Her eyebrows furrowed and her eyes met his. He tried to pull back his hand, but her strong grip remained. Pulling up his sleeve, she inspected the length of his arm. Old and new cuts covered him, and Rosie inspected the other arm as Eleanor raised that sleeve, showing a similar chaotic pattern.

"Reid," Eleanor said, grazing her fingertips over the marks.

"I'm okay, I swear. I just need an outlet, and I don't want to hurt anyone else." His head bowed and Eleanor drew him in. Rosie wrapped her arms around him, too, while her eyes focused on Justin.

As if communicating telepathically, Justin nodded and moved to the staircase.

Rosie peeled back, and with a forceful but caring tone, she spoke, "Reid, you're going to start rooming with Justin. You aren't allowed to be alone, and he can help you. He knows what you're going through."

"No, I can't—" Reid started, but he realized there was no point in arguing further after staring into Rosie's set expression. He gave a small nod, and Rosie grasped his hand again.

"Tostiek," she whispered, pushing magic from her into him. The scars on his arms started to heal, and Reid's shoulders loosened.

"What are you doing?" he asked, mesmerized at the healing process.

"Giving you a boost," she replied, beginning to feel depleted herself. As the scars disappeared, she stared back at Reid. "Better?"

His once-furrowed forehead was now relaxed, and rather than a face of seriousness he grinned. "Loads. Thank you."

"If you ever get that urge, you need to find me or Eleanor or talk to Justin. You don't need to be embarrassed to ask for help, Reid." He nodded again, and stared at Justin, who came back into the room.

"Come on, man. We better get cleaned up." Justin tilted his head to the staircase as he walked to Rosie, immediately putting his hand in hers and pushing a bit of power back to her.

"Is it that obvious?" she asked with a laugh.

Justin chuckled and shrugged then led Reid down to their room.

"Sooooo," Eleanor said, her voice full of mischief, "what's going on there?"

Rosie whipped her head up, her eyes widening, and she grasped the wall as the two entered the staircase and moved down to their dorm hallway.

"Nothing," Rosie muttered, her gaze refixing on the wall as they moved to her old dorm door.

Eleanor gave a small giggle and opened the door to the bedroom.

Rosie's eyes fell on Dana laying in her bed. Dana sat straight up and jumped.

"What's she doing here?" she posed to Eleanor before turning on Rosie. "You can't be here."

Before Rosie could respond, Eleanor pushed herself between the two. "I want her here, so she can stay. Leave if you can't deal." Eleanor stared down at Dana, her arms crossed and her body shielding Rosie.

"Ugh," Dana sounded before stomping around Eleanor, grabbing her coat and staring at Rosie, searching her up and down.

"But before you do," Eleanor continued, mirroring Dana so she couldn't leave just yet. "How the hell did you manage to get out of the dining hall before the ceiling crashed in?"

Dana smirked and placed a hand on her hip, ready to answer, as if she was anticipating the question.

"I saw the shit-show that was about to happen and ran."

"Didn't want to help anyone else? Not even your brother?" Rosie asked.

"He can handle himself. Plus, I thought you all knew what was going to happen and got out too. Not my fault you didn't cut and run." She flipped her hair over her shoulder and moved past Rosie.

As she did so, Rosie noticed the pendant which hung around Dana's neck. Rather than wearing her Surgent necklace, she had on a nearly identical one, but the stone sitting on her chest wasn't a diamond.

"Cool moonstone," Rosie said, her eyes darting to the necklace.

Dana gasped then grasped the pendant in her hand before stomping to the door, whipping it open, and slamming it shut. The chandelier clinked at the echo, and Rosie stared at Eleanor before the two burst out laughing.

"What is she? Five?" Rosie asked, jumping on Eleanor's bed.

"She's a different breed, I'll tell you that."

"Do you know why she has a moonstone on?"

"To be honest, I didn't even notice. Does that protect her from something?"

"It could, but maybe it's just a necklace. It's interesting, though." Rosie racked her memory to see if she was wearing the Surgent pendant elsewhere.

"Do you want to shower first?" Eleanor asked, inspecting a crusted hair strand of her own and using her other hand to wipe sand from her arm.

"Yeah, let me hop in really fast," Rosie said, moving to the bathroom. "I need to get to Shay and Walker. Help them get their power under control."

As Rosie showered, her mind swirled, pondering whether or not she could help everyone restore their control, restore their true magic, and restore order to the school.

Slipping on some of Eleanor's shorts and a long-sleeve tee, Rosie waited for Eleanor to return to see if she could get a little boost before making it up to Professor Walker's office. She examined her hands and started to pick at a nail when a blood-curdling scream reverberated throughout the dorm room.

The chandelier above her shook, the glass pieces clinking against one another. The force of the scream even caused a few to shatter. Rosie jumped to her feet and rushed to the bathroom to check on Eleanor.

The two ran into each other, both thinking it was the other that was hurt. Another scream sounded, and Rosie grasped Eleanor's hand.

"Sorry, El," she said before pulling a small dose of power from her then shoving her back into her room. "Stay here! Lock the door!"

"Like hell!" Eleanor said, busting the door open and falling into step next to Rosie.

The two ran up the stairs, and as they exited into the lobby, they ran straight into Justin and Riley.

"What's happening?" Rosie asked, slipping through the two and around Drew, nearing the door.

Riley grabbed her hand and pulled her back.

"What are you—" she started to ask, but he placed a hand over her mouth. She nodded her head, indicating she wouldn't speak, and he lifted it, pointing to the door where she could see out into the mountainside. The sun was falling fast and, already rising behind a mountain peak, was a great, round, full moon.

A howl echoed through the trees and another scream vibrated the desert trees and cactus surrounding the entry. Small rocks jumped as a barely visible flash ran by the entrance. The group hopped back in surprise but jumped even higher when a monstrous grey and black wolf pounced and landed right in front of the door.

A snarl rippled from its jaw, its long, sharp teeth barred. It snapped at the door, as if knowing what lay within the so-called boulder. It slowly stepped forward, snapping a bark this time.

"What do we do?" Drew asked in a barely audible whisper.

Just as Rosie opened her mouth to speak, the flash was back, and it ripped by the werewolf, knocking it sideways. Only on the ground for a second, the wolf jumped up and sprinted after the vampire.

"This isn't good," Rosie whispered, peering around at Riley. "They're out. They've escaped."

At the words, the group scurried through the nearest portrait hole, entering the Valtic living room.

"Are we safe here?" Gunner asked, spying the room, ensuring no other beast was going to attack.

"I don't know," Rosie said, also surveying her surroundings.

"Should we go to the hidden room?" Justin suggested. "We should be safe there, and we can see what's happening on the grounds."

Rosie and Eleanor nodded, moving the group towards the Valtic library entry point when a flash of wind whipped up

Rosie's hair and ends of her shirt. Before her was Katherine, blocking the exit.

Rosie gulped, and Katherine swiftly turned her head only an inch to spy Rosie.

Her eyes were bright red, and her teeth were elongated into fangs. Her mouth and cheeks were smeared with blood, as were her hands. Blood had dripped down her neck and also covered her chest. Rosie realized that it wasn't her own.

"Katherine," Rosie pled quietly, stepping towards her.

"You brought outsiders into our room, Rosie. Tsk, tsk," she said, her eyes bouncing from Gunner, to Flynn, to Riley, to Drew, and then to Reid. Then she fixated them back on Rosie. "We need to fix that."

Before Rosie could utter a word, Katherine bolted past her and grabbed Flynn, sinking her fangs into his neck. Blood spurted and gushed from the bite mark, and Katherine held her position, drinking as much as she could.

Flynn's scream echoed throughout the room, and Rosie stood still. Flashes of Egil doing the same thing to her crossed her mind—his cold, scaly hands pinning her as he sank his jagged teeth into her, sucking her dry.

"Rosie! Rosie!" she heard Riley call out, and she refocused on Flynn.

Drew knocked Katherine and Flynn back. Katherine released Flynn, and Reid and Gunner snatched him and followed Eleanor through the portrait to the Valtic library.

"Come on," Riley said, pulling her hand while Drew and Justin had Katherine cornered.

"Go!" Rosie said, moving in between Drew and Justin while forming a ball of bright yellow light between her hands.

Katherine hissed at Rosie, but Rosie continued to grow the

ball, as if creating a small version of the sun.

"Back off, Katherine," Rosie yelled, continuing her concentration on the light.

Smoke began to rise from Katherine's skin that was directly exposed to the light, and the harsh smell of burnt hair and melted skin filled the room. Rosie looked behind her, seeing only Riley was still in the room, and she herded Katherine to the opposite corner, allowing Riley to exit before she lifted her palm, and brought the miniature sun to the middle of the room.

"When I leave, Katherine," Rosie shouted, backing towards the exit, "the ball will begin to shrink. Please. I know you're in there. I know you can fight this. Go back to your room. Stay there. Don't let the bloodlust control you." With a final look at her friend, Rosie closed the portrait hole shut. Spinning her head in every direction, she found the group already making it to the third level of the library with Justin leading the way.

Rosie and Riley ascended the steps, skipping two at a time.

"What happened?" Riley asked as they bounded up.

"Somehow the vampires and the werewolves got out. Or…" she started.

"Or what?" he asked.

"Or they were let out."

Riley's eyes widened but before he could question her, Eleanor's voice yelled at the end of the bookshelves.

"Garrett," Eleanor said, forcing Rosie to run faster, "you can fight this."

"Eleanor," he said in a whine, "leave, please, before I hurt you."

Rosie halted next to Eleanor at the hidden room's entrance.

Garrett sat in what was no longer a study room but what now looked like a dungeon.

The bare, now-windowless room held only Garrett behind a row of bars that were erected across the middle of the room. He had shackled his wrists and feet to chains which hung on the wall. His eyes gleamed yellow, and his canines were lengthening.

"Garrett," Rosie said, moving closer, "how did you get out?"

His eyes remained trained on Eleanor, but he answered, his voice quivering. "Someone unlocked all the prison gates. Every full moon, we've locked ourselves up, trying to ensure we don't kill anyone or change anyone. But this afternoon, as we were all waiting to shift, the gates opened and wouldn't lock." His back cracked, and he groaned as his bones shattered and reformed in his spine. After catching his breath, he continued, "We tried to race back to our dorm rooms. To at least lock ourselves up there, but the moon began to rise, and everyone started to shift. I knew I could wish this room to be something that would restrain me—" He stopped abruptly, his scapula cracking outward and a painful grunt escaping him. "You need to go. I don't know if this cage will hold me. With each full moon, with each full uncontrollable shift, I've been—all the wolves—have lost our sense of human self once in wolf form. We can't control ourselves. We're dangerous."

"Yeah, you and the vampires," Gunner snorted under his breath, moving back down the bookshelf.

"Where are you going?" Rosie heard Riley ask. Her and Eleanor's eyes remained trained on Garrett, but Rosie heard Gunner's answer.

"I'm going to our library. A place where there aren't

vampires or werewolves."

"How do you know there aren't any, idiot?" Riley called. "We probably have the most vampire students in Surgent. Really want to chance running into them?"

"Yeah," Flynn spoke up. "At least there, I don't have a chance of running into Garrett in his shifted form. No offense, man!"

"None… taken," Garrett grunted as, one by one, his fingers cracked and broke. The room went still, and all heads faced Garrett. His nails grew into claws, fur sprouted around his face, and through all the bone cracking, he muttered, "Run."

Without hesitation, Rosie pulled Eleanor back as Garrett allowed the full transformation to take hold of his body.

"Run!" Rosie echoed, sprinting to the middle of the group as they ran back down through the library. Gunner ran back to them, joining as they each tried to make their way out of the space.

"Watch out!" called Justin as he grasped Rosie and Riley by the arms and pulled them through a stack of shelves. Another werewolf bounded into the room. The group scattered, and Rosie crouched next to Justin and peered through the small opening of the bottom bookshelf. Giant paws tapped the tile floor as the creature moved through the room. Rosie's eyes met Eleanor's, who was across the library with the others. Rosie tilted her head, indicating to move back towards the Valtic living room portrait.

Snorts and sniffs from the wolf in the room sounded, and small growls emanated as if this wolf knew he wasn't alone.

Rosie got off her knees and to the balls of her feet, still in a crouched position. Each step she took away from the wolf, just on the other side of the bookcase, was made with the greatest of care. Justin was on her side and Riley right behind her. Across the way, Eleanor led the other group. Only a tiny, almost inaudible shuffling of feet sounded.

Almost there, Rosie thought, growing closer to the end of the row.

A loud squeak reverberated throughout the room. Rosie spun her head and eyed Riley and then his sneaker. Out of the corner of her eye, the huge beastly wolf stepped around the back corner of the long bookshelf and growled at the three.

"Go!" Eleanor called from the other side, forcing the wolf to whip its head in her direction.

Making the second count, Rosie burst up and sprinted to the end of the row. The wolf bolted towards them after their first movement. Rosie's only goal was to get out of there without anyone getting hurt. Her, her group, or the wolves. Her feet skidded to a halt, though, when at the end of the far wall, another wolf jumped forward.

Justin and Riley collided with Rosie, and they dove through the bookcase to the center of the room. The wolves ran into each other as the three dove out of the way, each landing on its back. They met the others and turned to run to the opposite corner of the room.

"What do we do?" Flynn yelled, his pale skin and sluggish movement, worrying Rosie, but the snapping jaws of the wolves refocused her.

"We go up!" Drew yelled, jumping up the bookcase and making it to the top in three swift movements. Riley, Drew, Flynn, Gunner, Reid, and Eleanor followed.

"Here!" Justin said, his eyes trained on Rosie's as he put his hands out as a step for her to jump up.

"Rosie! Hurry!" Riley said, his arm extended out from the

top.

Rosie nodded at Justin and ran, swiftly jumping into his hand as he threw her upward. She slipped her hand into Riley's, and he pulled her up.

Now on her stomach, she reached over the side, one arm extended to Justin, the other bracing the surface for leverage to pull him up.

"They're coming!" Eleanor screamed, helping Gunner up and running to the other end of the bookcase. Rosie stared at the two wolves clumsily hitting one another as they tried to bound towards Justin.

"Come on, Justin!" Rosie yelled, reaching out further.

He stepped back and ran forward, climbing up a few shelves, reaching her.

"Grab on!" Riley said, now leaning over the side next to Rosie. Both hoisted him from under his arms, and as his foot made contact with the top of the case, a snapping jaw caught the edge, splintering the wood.

The three ran to the rest of the group, the wolves waiting on the ground for them to make their next move. They paced back and forth, waiting for their prey to make a single mistake that would lead to them having a feast.

"Do we wait until morning? When will they shift back?" Drew asked Rosie, staring between her and the wolves. The wolves below tracked them, jumping and snapping at the group, trying their best to reach them.

Rosie looked back up. "We could—" she started, but a howl erupted in the library and two more wolves appeared.

"How are they getting in?" Gunner asked as he ran his hands across his face.

"There!" Justin said as he pointed to an open portrait

leading to the mountain-side.

"When did that get there?" Eleanor asked, staring up to the room which held Garrett. Bangs and clattering chains hitting walls sounded above, and the blood drained from Eleanor's face.

"He's going to be okay," Rosie said, gripping her hand.

"But we won't be," Gunner said, his eyes fixated on the open portrait as Martha Ash entered the library.

"Can't you do any magic?" Drew asked Rosie, his eyes wide with fear.

"She has to conserve it until we absolutely need it," Justin said, planting himself between Rosie and Drew.

Drew huffed but gave a small nod and turned his attention back to the current threats blocking them from safety.

"We could jump across," Riley whispered to Rosie. "Get to that far bookcase and bolt out the same portrait hole and close the wolves in."

"And what about me?" Martha's chilly voice asked at the end of the same bookshelf.

Her eyes, like Katherine's, were bright red and she, too, was covered in blood.

"I think this might be a good time for your magic," Drew said as he and the rest of the group backed up towards the edge.

With Martha closing in on top of the bookshelf and the wolves following them from below, Rosie spun, trying to find a way out.

"Let's see if amalgams really do taste the best," Martha said, giving a hearty laugh as she made towards Rosie.

A loud crash of crumbling brick sounded, and a deafening howl made everyone and every creature halt in place.

Bounding over the railing from the second floor was Garrett in wolf form, and before he could reach Martha, she had already sprinted out of the room.

Garrett landed in front of the other wolves below the group, and they growled at each other. Garrett gave a sharp bark at the four wolves, stepping forward at them. All backed away and bowed. His head shifted up, and his eyes connected with Eleanor's, and then he broke away, bounding out the door, the other wolves following.

The force of the exit blew the portrait shut and the room was still as wolf howls and vampire cackles echoed between the mountain peaks.

Chapter Fifteen

As the warm yellow sun broke the horizon, Valtic werewolves, vampires, and even shifters began to file back into the library. Hidden still up on the top of the back bookcase, Rosie watched the disoriented students while the rest of her group began to climb back down.

"You coming?" Riley asked her, his eyes bloodshot and a tired frown hanging from his lips.

"I need to find Professor Walker."

He nodded and jumped to the ground. He waited for her to descend, but she wasn't ready to leave, to exit to the grounds and see the carnage and hell that laid waste to the school. Shaking her head and closing her eyes, she thought of Garrett who had saved them, Katherine who tried to kill them, and the innocent who might be dead.

Taking in a deep breath and finding her will, she climbed down and grabbed Riley's hand. He squeezed it and walked her to the open painting with the desert landscape on the other side.

"Do you want me to go with you? Walk you at least?" he asked her, pulling her into a hug.

She nuzzled against his chest and shook her head.

"I'm going to see if Shay and Walker still want to harness their power. Otherwise, I'll help clean up whatever mess lays out there. I'll call you if I need you."

"You don't always need me?" Riley asked, a tone of seriousness hiding his silly question.

"You know what I mean." She smiled and pulled herself back, looking up into his eyes. He kissed her forehead and released her so he could follow Eleanor back to the natural dorms.

"I'll talk to you later," she said as she hopped out, closing the passage behind her.

She started toward the front entrance, surveying the destruction of the night before shown on the wrecked mountainside.

Saguaros lay snapped in half, and deep cracks in the ground edged towards the cliffside where chunks of rock had fallen to the valley below. Rosie raised her hand to block the bright rising sun from her face, only to realize a boulder that would have normally blocked the hot rays was now in crumbling pieces. Stepping over a tree that had been ripped from the ground, Rosie took in the drag marks, the tufts of fur, and the blood stains.

Horror of the events that must have ensued under the moon flashed before her eyes, and it wasn't until glints and shimmers of light moving out of the corner of her eye brought her back to the moment.

Through the still-standing trees, in a semi-hidden meadow, fairies danced from flower to flower, and a quiet, serene hum filled the air, sending a sense of calm in the chaos which wrapped around Rosie like a warm hug.

She stepped towards the playing fairies, their relaxed,

happy energy reviving Rosie and her faith in the goodness of creatures.

"Let's get inside," she heard Professor Shay's voice say, breaking her from the trance.

Swiftly, but stealthily, Rosie moved towards the voice, and paused behind a boulder. She peered around it and watched a group of teachers enter the school.

As they moved up and through the entryway, Rosie jumped down from behind the boulder, down to the bank of the lake. Climbing the stairs two at a time, she entered the front entrance of the school, suspecting the teachers had already made it into the main lobby.

Standing in the foyer, she listened in, wanting to gain any knowledge of the night before that she could.

"And were there any dead?" Professor Shay asked, her voice carrying through the hall behind the closed doors.

"Only a lone shifter, traveling from New Mexico," Professor Manger responded.

Rosie's eyes widened, and she pressed her ear up against the door even more.

"And all the students who escaped are accounted for?"

"Yes, all are back in their dorms," Rosie heard Professor Walker say.

"You might want to check on the fairies," Rosie said, entering the room and shutting the tall foyer door behind her.

Rosie studied the three teachers grouped together as she walked towards them. All had bloodshot eyes, shaking hands, and yesterday's clothes on.

Did they get all the students together using magic? Forcing themselves to endure that pain?

Before she could ask about the extent of the night's events, a different voice perked up.

"And what are the fairies up to?" the voice said in a chair off to the right. Rosie's head turned sharply, and rising from his seat, was James Kingsley.

Standing in a black suit and tie, James Kingsley stared at Rosie, a smirk about his mouth.

"Um," she continued, "they were out in the meadow, just west of here."

"They should be fine," Professor Shay murmured, turning back to Professor Manger, measuring a gash he had on his arm.

"Well," Rosie started again, her eyes still on James Kingsley's, "they were dancing, and it's hard to explain, but they were emitting this sound and—" Before she could finish Kingsley cut her off.

"Manger, collect the fairies. Make sure they are secured in their dorm before anyone else is hurt."

Manger pulled his arm away from Professor Shay's hands and made his way back through the long hall towards the lake. As he pulled the door open, Kingsley shouted at him again.

"Oh, and Manger, don't forget to plug your ears."

Manger nodded in response and left.

"So, I take it's a good thing I didn't enter the meadow when I first saw the fairies?" Rosie asked Kingsley, who was now gesturing for her to join himself, Professor Walker, and Professor Shay.

"Not unless you don't mind being taunted, scratched, pulled, and potentially tied down."

Rosie nodded, her suspicions of all supernatural creatures

regressing to a primal stage becoming true.

"Are you okay, Rosie?" Professor Walker asked, an inquisitive look scanning Rosie.

"I'm okay. A few of us-"

"Witches? Wizards?" Kingsley asked.

"No, um, naturals—intellects and protectors," Rosie corrected, "we were in the natural dorm and saw what had happened."

"What were you doing there?" Professor Shay asked with a raised eyebrow.

"I decided to get ready at my old dorm. I was...oh my..." Rosie said, then her mind raced.

"What is it?" Professor Shay asked, stepping closer.

"Um, Eleanor's roommate, Dana, she wasn't with us last night. She left the room before this all started, during the day, and we didn't see her throughout the night."

"She may have just been with her brother," Professor Walker said.

"No, Drew was with us." Fear washed through Rosie. Was the blood stain she saw this morning Dana's? Had she driven her from her own room and caused her death? "We need to find her. Make sure she's okay."

"We'll locate her," Professor Walker said, eyeing Professor Shay and pulling her phone out.

Rosie did the same, and sent a quick message to Eleanor to see if Dana made it back to her room.

No, she isn't back, Eleanor's reply read.

Without responding, she messaged Riley.

Maybe she was with her brother now, she thought as her fingers flew across the phone screen.

No, she isn't here, but I'll check the rest of the dorm, Riley replied.

The pounding of Rosie's heart quickened, and she dialed her mom's number, putting the phone up to her ear.

"Hi, sweetie, are you okay?"

"I'm okay, but Mom, are you okay? Things got crazy here last night."

"Crazy? What do you mean?"

"Just, are you okay? How's town?"

"Everything is fine here, hon, but what happened? I'm getting worried. Is Riley alright?"

"I'm okay, we're okay. Just there were students, supernaturals, who were out last night, and they weren't themselves. They—"

"Ms. Connors," Rosie heard a voice say in the background.

"Mom?"

"Oh, hold on sweetie.

Please, you don't even have to ask, Dana. Help yourself. There's also coffee brewing."

"Mom?"

"Sorry, honey. What were you saying? What happened at the school?"

"Mom, who's there? Is-is Dana there? A girl from my school?"

"Yes! Sweetest girl! She was in town, crying around dusk, and I went to check on her. She said she went to school with you and that she got in a fight with her roommate and didn't want to make the trek back, so I offered her the bed in your room here."

Rosie's heart sank to her stomach. "My room?"

"Yes. Oh, here, Dana wants to say 'hi.'"

"Wait, Mom."

"Hey, Rosie," Dana started into the phone. "Your mom is the best! So kind, so sweet, so innocent." Dana's voice lowered to a whisper, and Rosie jammed the phone against her head, not wanting to miss a single word or threat. "How was campus last night? Have lots of fun with your classmates?"

"Did you release them? Did you cause this? The danger you put us all through?"

The line went dead. Rosie called back, but the attempt was fruitless as the call went straight to voicemail.

"Dana is with my mom," Rosie blurted. Kingsley, Shay, and Walker turned to stare at Rosie, relief in their eyes, but Rosie couldn't hide what she learned. "Dana let everyone out of their rooms last night."

"What?" Professor Shay said, stepping forward.

"Rosie, she wouldn't know how," Professor Walker started, moving towards her. "There are wards, protections, too many obstacles that even an intellect wouldn't be able to get past to remove the boundary."

"She basically admitted it to me," Rosie said, her voice growing firm.

"Did she say she let the students out?" James Kingsley asked.

"Well, no, but she insinuated."

"Okay, then," Professor Shay said. She turned back, pulling Professor Walker closer, and they started talking again.

Rosie turned to Kingsley. "I know she did this."

He stepped towards her and put a gentle hand on her shoulder. "I'm sure your suspicion is warranted, but it might not be for this."

Rosie raised an eyebrow in confusion and watched him speak with the two professors. *Did he mean he also thought*

Dana was guilty of something, just not this? she wondered. Then, she thought of Egil. *Has Kingsley been able to locate him?*

"Premier—" she started as he was leaving, but Professor Walker cut her off and brought her attention back to the current issue.

"Okay, Rosie, let's go," Professor Walker said, meeting her at her shoulder and guiding her through the second waiting room and to the never-ending hallway.

"Wait. I need to make sure my mom is okay." Fear clutched her heart and worry knotted her stomach as she wondered if she was about to lose her mom after just getting her back.

"I just sent a representative from town to grab Dana and bring her back. She is meeting your mother now. She's fine."

"Okay. Well, aren't Professor Shay and Premier Kingsley going to join us?"

"Premier Kingsley is heading back to the Superiority office, and Professor Shay has parents to address."

"What about her power—"

"You and I," Professor Walker stated louder, "are going to address how to fix the issue at hand. You obviously know how to get your power under control and how to replenish it without a fixed source. I need you to break me away from the pain. I need you to help me first, then we can help the rest of the school."

Rosie nodded and felt her own magic swirl within her.

"Professor, why don't you have your own power source? Why aren't the other creatures taught to truly harness their power?"

Professor Walker shook her head and moved behind her desk, grasping the back of her chair with her hands, leaning into it.

"We're supposed to." She moved around the chair and sat down, sighing. "Over the years, when a student entered the next phase of their power at the age of fourteen or fifteen, and the bulk of their magic was quote-unquote 'unlocked', said students were supposed to have gone through training and lessons on how to secure such power before accessing it."

A small laugh escaped Rosie, and she turned it into a cough. "Sorry, Professor."

"As time has gone on, the curriculum has become, well, in a nice way, relaxed, and in a plainer way, nonexistent. We've relied on the team pendants to harness everyone's power and keep students and teachers in check."

"Why hasn't the town been affected by all of this?"

"There is another source for the town."

"How many sources are there?"

"Only a handful."

"But there are two here?"

"Yes. This is the most populated area of supernatural beings in the world."

"Even considering places like Transylvania, Siberia, and the Amazon?"

Professor Walker let a smile flash across her face. "Rosie, your time here has been limited to campus, Kingstown, and the desert surrounding us, but we are ingrained here. In Arizona. I know you feel the spark in the air, the magical current. It is natural for us to be here, and more will come if their beacons give out."

"But what if they don't?"

"Then I expect a mass exodus and the closing of King's

Preparatory if we can't gain our control back, through the stones and through ourselves."

Rosie nodded and then stood. "Okay, Professor. Ready to gain complete control?"

Chapter Sixteen

In the field by the school, Rosie guided both Professor Walker and then Professor Shay, who joined later, through expelling their magic to gain it back. Professor Shay, though skeptical, took to the method easily, only needing three attempts before fully draining herself and allowing her true power to come in. Professor Walker needed seven attempts, but finally released everything and gained it back.

While they performed the ritual, the natural students, those who volunteered, as well as some of the other teachers, stood by. As soon as the ritual was completed, Manger and Justin allowed Shay to siphon off them, and Riley and Eleanor allowed Walker to do the same.

The week moved forward, and as they now had better control and access to volunteers to siphon, Professor Shay and Professor Walker were able to teach the natural students. The protectors, now with accessible magic for their pendants and better training, were able to gain better control on their aggression with more meditation and relaxation classes.

"All I'm saying is it's weird," Riley chuckled, his hand interlaced with Rosie's as they ate on the sandy lakeside.

"Yoga isn't weird, it's calming," Rosie replied, closing her eyes and humming.

"It is also hilarious. I mean, picture Manger doing a headstand and Flynn toppling into him."

Rosie laughed and the two laid back, staring up into the blue sky. Since the inner replenishment of magic, Riley had gone back to being his fun goofy self, and his mood swings had lessened. On top of his daily yoga and meditation classes, he and the other protectors also had to keep journals, practice calming exercises, and have daily group therapy as well as weekly individual sessions.

"What's the plan for everyone else?" Riley asked, his hand tangling in Rosie's hair, his fingers combing through it.

Rosie settled closer to him, her mind reviewing what was to happen next. After starting with Professor Walker and Professor Shay, they moved on to the other witch and wizard professors, including Doctor Geller and his staff. Then they worked with the protectors, then the intellects, who had a similar treatment to the protectors, even though both Justin and Dana had a handle on their gifts.

"Manger is going to lead the shifters next. They should acclimate to controlling their shift a bit easier than the wolves, but after that, that's where the real fun for them begins."

"What do you mean?"

"Crazy, but shifters have the capacity to shift into other animals if they practice, even other humans."

"What? Seriously?"

Rosie sat up and rolled to her stomach and stared at Riley while he was still on his back.

"Yeah, Manger is able to shift into at least ten other animals."

"I had no idea."

"I don't think anyone did."

"Well, maybe except for Professor Shay," Riley said, a mischievous grin playing at the sides of his lips.

"She may have," Rosie replied, giggling and laying her head on his chest.

"Are you helping? With the shifters, I mean?"

Rosie read the *Being* book and Christion Flare's notes on supernatural power control and accessing the full capacity of one's magic.

"Yeah. I mean, Manger is going to lead but I'll assist, even if he doesn't want me there."

"Maybe you shouldn't be there,"

"What?" Rosie asked, perking up.

Riley also sat up and continued, "I just mean, these are shifters—big, small, mean, nice, predators, prey, unpredictable. You saw how things were when the campus went full-blown psycho with creatures crawling about. Garrett even said they were starting to lose sense of their human selves once in animal form."

"I'm sure everything will be okay."

"Rosie, they have been locked up just like the other creatures. They aren't themselves."

"And I don't believe that."

"Just be careful. Talk to Manger about starting with the smaller, less dangerous shifters and then move onto the other students. The predators can be with the wolves."

Rosie chewed her lips, mulling the idea over.

"Ha, you like it, don't you?"

"Shhh," Rosie said laughing, lightly hitting his arm before standing up.

"Wait," Riley started, grabbing her hand to stay. "Where are you going?"

"To tell Professor Manger your brilliant idea."

"And let you take all the credit?" Riley joked, now on his feet by her side. "Onward, Rosie! To relay such genius thoughts to such a thick-headed man!" He pulled her forward and through the front entrance, laughter echoing through the hall.

"Rosie?" Premier Kingsley said, halting both Rosie and Riley.

"Oh, hello, Premier," Rosie said.

Floating down from his portrait office, he landed before the two. "Having a fun afternoon?"

"Yes, um, we were just about to talk to Professor Manger. See if we should be starting with the less aggressive shifters tomorrow rather than teach everyone at once."

James Kingsley stared at her then chuckled. Rosie and Riley looked at each other in confusion.

"No need to tell him. I had the same thought myself and only the prey-like shifters will be taught tomorrow."

"Great," Rosie said, unsure what to do next in the Premier's presence.

"You should go meet with Professor Walker. I think she may need some assistance in sorting out the wizard and witch strategy."

Rosie nodded and moved aside, allowing Kingsley to move towards the exit and out to the lakeside.

"That guy," Riley said, shaking his head.

"What?" Rosie said, her eyes still on the front door before drawing them back to meet Riley's.

"He just gives me the heebie-jeebies."

Rosie snorted and pulled his hand. "Come on. I need to find Professor Walker and you should finish your report on your dream analysis."

"Nooooo," Riley whined. "Why does it matter?"

"Dreams are super important!" Rosie encouraged. "You remember all those dreams I had last year about my ancestor reaching out to me."

"Yeah, because you were a hidden witch! I don't see how vampire Eleanor chasing me through campus is helpful to anyone."

Rosie rolled her eyes and tried to walk away, but he pulled her back close to his chest. Lifting her chin up with his hand, he kissed her nose then her lips. Rosie's heart raced, and she slowly backed away, nibbling her lower lip, a smile she was unable to hide playing on her face.

"Come on, killer," Rosie said, "we should go."

But as they entered the smaller waiting room, the glass ceiling in the lobby shattered and a loud thud erupted.

The two whipped around and ran to the man who lay sprawled on the ground. Limbs were turned in opposite directions, his head sat perpendicular from his neck, and blood pooled around him.

"Premier Kingsley!" Rosie shouted, her hands hovering over the wrecked body, unsure what to do. She leaned closer but both jumped back.

The bones before them began to pop back into place, and the blood that surrounded him absorbed back into his body through the open wounds.

Stepping closer to study the immortality curse further, Rosie watched as Kingsley's skin reformed together and bones reset. Finally, Kingsley's neck cracked back to the front, and giving a shake on the ground, he jumped up.

Eyeing him from head to toe, Rosie thought the only evidence he was ever hurt would be the tears in his clothes, the ruffling of his hair, and the glass shards that surrounded him.

"Premier," Riley said, "are you okay? What happened?"

"I believe," Kingsley started, pausing to stare up at the human-sized hole in the glass ceiling, "someone just tried to kill me." He ruffled the smaller pieces of glass off the crevices of his sleeves and ran his hand through his hair, attempting to put it back in place.

"I'll call the Superiority," Rosie said, pulling out her phone.

A laugh from Kingsley caught Rosie off-guard and she held the phone in place. "No, it's nothing to fret over. This happens every once in a while."

"You die?" Riley asked, cocking his head and eyebrow.

"I can't die, but every so often, someone likes to try."

"Shouldn't we do something?" Rosie asked, searching around to see if a culprit could be seen.

"I'll handle it. You two carry on with your day."

Riley moved back to Rosie's side, and the two hesitantly walked back out of the room, leaving Kingsley to motion his hands to the glass on the ground and seal the ceiling as if nothing had ever happened.

"Well, that was shocking," Riley said.

"Can you imagine? Dying but not dying?"

"No, but I will say that whole immortality thing is useful. I should consider becoming a vampire. You know? Close to immortal and indestructible but still able to go if I wanted. What do you think?"

"You're kidding, right?"

"No. I mean, yes. I mean, I don't know Rosie. It would be cool."

"Cool? You saw what Katherine and Martha were like when they had no control. You saw the damage Gyle did to me last year when he didn't have his blood thirst under control." Rosie thought about the vampire from last year, and how he had zero control until seized by the Superiority and kept prisoner in the school's dungeons.

"But if everything was back to normal, and I didn't have some thirst for blood, it would be awesome. Being super strong, being super-fast, being more than a natural, being more than just a step above human."

Rosie gripped his arm and pulled him into her. "I think you're perfect just the way you are."

"You're the perfect one," Riley teased, pulling her closer.

"Ah-em."

Both teenagers turned in surprise, stepping back. Peeking her head out of her office door was Professor Walker. Her arms were crossed, and she tapped her foot.

"Professor Walker," Rosie said, "I was just looking for you."

"Funny. You didn't knock on my door." She opened the door further and gestured for Rosie to enter.

Rosie squeezed Riley's hand and moved into the office, giving him a small wave before Professor Walker blocked her view of him.

"Mr. Zimmers, I suggest you make your way to the dining hall."

"Dining hall? Are we doing water therapy or something?" He twisted his lips and gave a small laugh.

"The dining hall has been repaired. Your classmates are meeting there for a lesson on managing others. It is time the protectors see their importance in our society."

"Which would be?" he asked, switching feet and stepping back.

Professor Walker raised a concerned eyebrow and stepped forward, placing a hand on Riley's shoulder. "Protectors need to be able to handle, without strength and speed, each supernatural creature. That means skillfully de-escalating situations and understanding the thought process behind different creatures."

"So, we're going to be like psychologists?"

"Riley, protectors are the main reason there are so few attacks on normal humans by our kind. You are our first line of defense."

Sticking his nose in the air proudly and nodding happily, he responded, "Yeah, okay, I like that," and he moved down the hall, finding a different passageway to get to the dining hall.

"Is all that true?" Rosie asked as Professor Walker closed her door and sat behind her desk.

"Of course. After graduation, Riley and the other protectors will most likely be assigned as guards or agents for the Superiority. They are our contact to the human world and know how to best protect them from us, us from each other, and most importantly, us from them."

"Cool," Rosie said, sitting in front of the desk. "So, who are we freeing tomorrow?"

Professor Walker scanned her notebook on her desk and then flipped through a stack of files before pulling one out of the stack and handing it to Rosie.

"Really?" Rosie asked skeptically, opening the file and reading the analysis.

"I think she's ready. After all, she is your roommate."

Rosie stared down at Olive's school photo. Olive had been watching Rosie practice in their room, trying to follow her movements. Though she had been unsuccessful, Rosie could tell the level of pain she endured with each attempt and admired her determination.

"Okay, we start the wizard and witch round with Olive. Anyone else?"

Professor Walker rested her hand on the rest of the stack and slid it over to Rosie, smiling.

"Got it. What about the other students? Professor Manger is working with less combative shifters tomorrow. What about the littles?"

"Unfortunately, Premier Kingsley and Professor Shay agreed that all elementary school aged students should return home. Get training directly from their packs, cults, finagles, you know? Be surrounded by others who have control without beacons and become disciplined from a young age."

"That's probably for the best."

"Yes, just sad we aren't able to figure out why our source is drained."

"Can I take a look at it?"

Professor Walker paused for a moment before replying, "Possibly, but let's focus on this first. Remember, you may be a witch, but first, you were an intellect."

Rosie nodded, pulling her own notebook from her bag and writing down each class of supernatural being.

This week, the small shifters, the witches and wizards, the fairies, and mer-students would face their challenges and hopefully be successful. If they were, then they could move forward with siphon training and just needed to perform a few rituals to maintain their control. Then, once no weak student was left unprotected, the vampires, werewolves, and deadly shifters could train.

"You found all of this consulting the prior class's course work?"

Rosie nodded. She had researched what was supposed to be taught to each being in order to maintain control through their supposedly mandatory but apparently not mandatory curriculum. She also sprinkled in her own research from *Being*.

"Yep, shouldn't be too bad, but the fairies and mer-students will need to collect their own pyrite and quartz. Supposedly, when they start their search, one will show itself to them and that will be their crystal after they go through the shifting process."

"Doctor Geller will be there during each transformation as will his staff."

"They have to endure it."

"I know," Professor Walker clipped, returning to the notes on her desk. The most difficult thing for her to grasp was how much pain everyone would have to experience to become self-reliant. Witches and wizards basically had to explode, vampires had to drain themselves essentially, and werewolves, shifters, fairies, and the mer-students had to shift on repeat without help or a break until they felt no pain from the process.

"You know," Rosie started, changing the subject, "someone tried to kill Premier."

"What? When?" she burst out, her eyes wide in shock.

"Just this afternoon, before I came to see you. He didn't say much. Just fell through the ceiling in the grand room, put himself back together then fixed the ceiling. He said it's happened before?"

Sitting back in her chair, Professor Walker responded, "Yes, there are those in the supernatural community who feel overlooked by the Premier."

"Overlooked? Do they see what he's done? He made an oasis for supernaturals."

"For most, yes, but there are others who haven't been as welcome."

"What?" Rosie racked her mind trying to think of who wasn't as protected.

"Sasquatches, banshees, spirits, dark watchers, and more. They're all protected by being in close proximity to the school and town, but otherwise are left to defend themselves."

"And these other species, they want to join the community? Come to the school?"

"Yes, and the Premier has offered, on multiple occasions attempting to fix the relations, but the grudge runs deep with them and supposedly, they are trying to make their own beacon and safe haven."

"What?"

Professor Walker nodded, turning a page in a different file and marking down a few sentences.

"Really? That's it? That's all you're going to tell me?"

Professor Walker set her pen down. "What else are you expecting?"

"I don't know. Maybe we are investigating these creatures as they may be the ones who took the power from our beacon for theirs?"

Professor Walker looked back down at her notes. "That's highly improbable."

Rosie sat up and scooted closer to the edge of her seat. "But still probable."

"But not likely," Professor Walker said in a tone of finality.

"Ugh, Professor!" Rosie said, causing Professor Walker to jump. "Give me a straight answer. Could they be behind this? Is there a way to get back the magic?"

Professor Walker pressed her palms into her desk. "It wouldn't matter anyway. We have a new system in place where we wouldn't need that source."

"But you must agree that the extra magic would be nice. We wouldn't have to siphon off of others or worry about constantly having protection spells cast around ourselves and our minds. We can relax."

"Rosie, we will restore the power and we will deal with these other creatures, but please focus. Do not obsess. Help the Premier by helping the school."

Rosie thought about the culprit now, the idea of someone, some other creature or creatures, being behind the chaos. She studied Professor Walker, wanting to know more, but her teacher's angled eyebrows and reddened cheeks allowed Rosie to know this wasn't the time to inquire further.

Rosie nodded as she packed up her things. "I should go prep Olive for tomorrow. Let me know where else you need my help." She got up to leave.

"I will," Professor Walker said, and Rosie left the room, which was filled with pen scribbles and meditation breathing.

Chapter Seventeen

"You have to try harder," Rosie said, sitting with Olive in their room.

"Do you not see that I am trying?" Olive shook out her arms, which were covered in little scratches.

"Here, let me heal you," Rosie said, reaching out, her magic already at her fingertips.

"No, I'll do it when I have full access," Olive said as she pulled her arms in towards her.

Rosie nodded and took a step back as Olive faced her palms towards one another and focused her energy towards making a sun.

"AH!" she screamed, a gash opening on each palm.

Blood splattered onto the carpet as Olive persisted.

"Olive, stop!" Rosie yelled, a deafening high-pitched tone of magic invisibly cascading through the air.

"I! CAN! DO! THIS!" she replied as her skin began to tear and scars formed and then reopened and continued to do so. "AH!"

At the last second, Rosie threw a protection bubble around Olive and a muffled bang erupted under it. Gold and silver gas that looked like liquid smearing across the bubble now made it visible.

Rosie lowered the shield, and as the silver, sparkly smoke cleared, Rosie found Olive passed out on the ground. A dark scorch mark surrounded her body and a lasting small purple flame sat alight on her shoulder.

Leaning over Olive, Rosie covered the flame, putting it out, and tilted her head to see if she could hear any breathing. No audible sound came from Olive. She pressed her fingers to Olive's throat, frantically searching for a pulse, but no faint beat pressed back.

Holding her hands above Olive's chest, Rosie started to press down, applying CPR, but then she thought about how hospitals would restart patients' hearts with defibrillators. She lifted her hands and set the palms an inch before her chest. Closing her eyes, she willed her magic to transform into energy and shot tiny lightning bolts against Olive's chest.

With Olive's center lifting from the ground as the electric current raced through her veins in the attempt to restart her heart, Rosie paused. She sent another bolt through her, and as her chest raised again her eyes shot open, and she panted heavily on the ground.

Rosie sat back on her heels, her arms slack by her side as she watched Olive calm her breath and sit up.

"Are you okay?" Rosie asked, Olive staring at her hands.

"Let's find out," she responded and snapped her fingers. The black marks dissolved from the ground, the tears in Olive's clothes sewed themselves together, and the color of her green shirt brightened. Her hair fell back smoothly into a sleek ponytail and the room cleared of any lasting smell of fire. It was as if time turned backward and put everything back to the way it was.

"I assume by your smile you're not in pain?" Rosie asked with a hint of sarcasm in her voice.

"I've never felt this good in my entire life!" Olive exclaimed, jumping up and spinning around then engulfing Rosie in a hug.

"Oh," Rosie said, embracing Olive in return before releasing her and inspecting her once more.

"What?" Olive said, annoyance in her voice.

"Thank goodness, you're still you,' Rosie said, rolling her eyes but fixating them back on Olive.

"Okay, what, Rosie?"

"I mean, you died."

"But I'm fine, and now I have my magic."

"But you died," Rosie reiterated. "I can't have anyone else try this. It's too dangerous."

"Rosie, I'm fine! Everyone else will be fine! You can't just let everyone else suffer."

Rosie stared at her phone, punching in Professor Walker's number to tell her what had happened, but Olive ripped the phone away.

"Olive, stop. This isn't a game. This is life and death. I had to bring you back. I can't put everyone else in this dorm through that."

"But you won't. It would be their choice."

"But—"

"No, Rosie," Olive asserted now. "You can't tell them no. If anything, they will try to expel their magic themselves and if they do that and you aren't around, then they will die."

"They don't even know what to do."

"Well, they do know. Now at least."

"What? How?"

"I did a live performance for the school. And…" She moved over to her phone, picking it up and blowing a kiss to the camera before dropping the phone to her side. "Looks like the majority of the school saw."

Rosie's mouth dropped. "Why would you do that?"

"Someone has to be the poster boy, or in this case girl, for the school and show that it's on its way to being back to normal." She pulled the phone back up and swiped through the comments, giggling.

Rosie shook her head in disbelief, snatching her phone back from Olive's desk and calling Professor Walker. The phone didn't even ring before Professor Walker's voice picked up on the other end.

"I saw, Rosie."

"What do we do?" she asked, unsure at this point if the students should be risking their lives for magic.

"For the students of age, we will have them decide if they want to try this method. For everyone else, we will get parents' permission." Professor Walker said.

Rosie sat in thought as she heard paper fluttering and the scribbling of a pen on the other end of the phone.

"Why don't you come to my office, and we can speak more?"

As Professor Walker asked, Rosie turned to see her mirror rippling and become translucent so Professor Walker's figure behind her desk sat just on the other side.

Stepping through the portal, Rosie watched Professor Walker grab a new piece of stationery, and as she set her pen to write for her, she turned to Rosie.

"In our world and the natural world, Olive has gone, what's the word? Viral?"

"What?" Rosie gasped, moving to a chair in front of the desk. "I knew the entire school saw the post, but I thought we couldn't post outside the school boundaries, or if we did, then the picture or video or whatever would be distorted or changed."

"Thankfully, to natural eyes, what they saw was Olive doing a magic trick, a sleight of hand. Basically, her concentrating, going into smoke and then coming out covered in tattered clothing. We've leaked in comments and swayed minds by saying she used a smoke bomb."

"Okay, good."

"But—"

"But?"

"There's the issue of the intellects and protectors who haven't yet been made aware of their abilities. They swear that what is happening in the video is real, and it's causing more trouble than expected."

"Do we need to conduct mind alteration?"

"No, we've decided to test them early." Professor Walker grabbed another piece of paper and scanned her eyes over it before setting it down and picking up another.

"Wow, do you need me to help?"

"No, Rosie. All you need to know is that the group will be brought to the Superiority."

"The Superiority? Why?"

Professor Walker paused, staring at Rosie, but continued, "Do you really think we should be testing them here?"

"Well, I mean, I guess not."

"It's still too dangerous."

"Well, what's going to happen if any of them pass?"

"Rosie, please. You don't need to concern yourself—"

"Professor, please."

"Okay. Anyone who passes will start initial training at Superiority headquarters, and I will also go and start teaching them the basics of our community."

"But we need you here," Rosie pleaded. "You have to stay. Can't another teacher go?"

Professor Walker smiled and focused entirely on Rosie. "Unfortunately, it must be me. I will administer the crystal exam and teach them proper meditation techniques and then, hopefully by the time they are done with basic training, we will have this figured out and our beacon restored."

"And if we don't?"

"Then the students will still come to campus, under tight security just in case, and be paired with a student mentor. They will protect them."

"So, the protectors will get some real-world experience, huh?" Rosie thought about Riley and how much he would love that, but her stomach churned with worry. She wasn't sure if he was ready to take on a natural threat, much less a supernatural one.

"They will be okay, Rosie," Professor Walker said, sensing her hesitation. "They are ready for this responsibility."

Rosie nodded and stood. "I guess I'll research stronger protection spells and see if I can find any other focusing charms."

"Please do and let me know if you find anything else out."

Rosie left the office, but rather than return to her room, she left for the library, having a sudden urge to sit in the musty yet floral fresh library-greenhouse hybrid.

"Hello, Rosie," Ms. Pamfet, the librarian, said as Rosie entered the stunning oasis.

The near-empty room had thousands of books, lit up by golden rays of light bursting through the greenhouse dome. Sliding a smile across her lips, she greeted Ms. Pamfet and walked up the stairs to the second level where a balcony ledge sat. At the top, she stared over the railing and noticed in a far corner table surrounded by various exotic plants was Justin.

Deep in his own thoughts and consumed by the texts in front of him, Rosie understood the transportation to another world and let him be. She turned back and grabbed a book on stone magic, natural remedies for focusing, and the history of each supernatural territory, and sat in a small, almost undetectable nook.

Once situated, she put the other books aside, and from her bag, she pulled out *Being*. Flipping through the pages, she found the one which detailed how exactly each supernatural being could harness their own control without a beacon.

Protectors and intellects are easy, Rosie thought. *They must practice relaxation and meditation daily if not hourly.* Rosie thought about Riley and laughed. She covered her mouth at the thought of him taking five minutes every hour to find his inner peace. *Well, he's going to have to if he wants to become as strong as possible.*

She continued to read and take notes, consulting the other texts and grabbing new books when needed.

Shifters should transform over and over until they no longer can feel the pain of their shift under their lunar or solar preference. Werewolves need to drink the old moon elixir which will allow transformation without the full moon, and then transform over and over until they can't feel the pain from shifting. Then, they need to wear a sunstone that has been charged by the sun at dawn after a full moon night to stay grounded. The vampires must drain their own bodies of blood and starve for a full twelve hours under a full moon, then wear citrine bathed in moonlight during the day to allow sun walking. Mermaids need to shift on land during a full moon over and over, then wear quartz charged in moon water to help with breathing and hydration while on land. Witches and wizards, I know, just need to force out all magic in order to unlock their true given power. And fairies need to shift under the sun until they can't feel the pain of their shift and wear earth charged pyrite.

Rosie scribbled as she hunched over her notes and studied the texts on where she could find each item. She would need to collect enough for those students who would try to find further control of their power.

"Interesting," Justin said behind Rosie, and as he said it, she jumped in her seat and placed a hand over her racing heart. Chuckling a little, he strolled and sat beside her.

"You scared me," she said with quickened breath, handing him the sheet and allowing him a chance to read it over.

"So, we know how to help everyone?" he asked, handing it back.

"Sort of. Did you see Olive's post?"

"No?" Justin said with confusion, pulling his phone out and finding the recording.

"What," he began to say but as he made eye contact with Rosie, she placed a finger up to her lips and tilted her head in the direction of a bookcase.

On the other side of the dense case, Rosie heard Dana's muffled, low voice.

"I need you to buck up and find a way to stop her," Dana said in an annoyed voice.

"She's actually cool. If you just gave her a chance." Rosie

recognized Drew, his voice pleading and caring.

"We aren't here to make friends, remember? We have one job, and she is ruining it. End her, or I'll make sure you're banished when we return home."

Heels clicking away sounded, followed by slow shuffling.

When both siblings had left, Rosie began again, "I knew they were up to something. I knew they were somehow involved in this mess."

"You also think they drained the stone?" Justin asked.

Rosie sat back, stunned.

"Uh, yes. Yes, I do."

"Remember, I learned a lot last year and even more this year. As a pariah, I've been able to observe, see, and listen to more than you know."

Justin cocked one side of his lips up and Rosie shook her head with her own smile and replied, "Well, have you learned anything more about the twins? I can't figure out their motive or how they could be doing this."

Justin sat back in his seat, studying Rosie before leaning back forward, and in a hushed tone, speaking again.

"Premier Kingsley and I met a few months back. He wanted to have a check-in on how I was doing and if there was anything else I needed. When the niceties were over, he asked me to keep an eye on them."

"Really? But why?" Rosie asked, shaking her head.

"Ever since they've arrived, I always felt off around them. Like they didn't truly belong here or at least weren't meant to be here."

Rosie nodded, agreeing with the statement. She, too, had always felt the two were different somehow.

Justin continued on, "Anyways, before the beacon was

drained, I studied up on the other creatures who are technically humanoid, like vampires and werewolves, but don't go to the school."

"Yes," Rosie exclaimed, searching the table for a book, finding it beneath a tall pile. She scooted closer to Justin and flipped the book open. A colony of banshees gathered in a stone hedge garden. She flipped to a different page where sasquatches transformed from beast to human. "Premier Kingsley mentioned that he is in negotiations with these other species. That they are mad they are seen as lesser than us. Or at least they think that."

"Yep, and it's kind of scary. I mean—" Justin started his cheeks flushing at the admittance of being scared.

She grabbed his hand and gave it a light squeeze. "It's okay."

His face returned to its normal shade, and he pulled his hand back. "I just meant that there are a lot more supernatural creatures, different types of creatures, outside of the school than in it."

"So do you think an outside creature figured out a way to take the power?"

"I think Dana and Drew took it. I don't think they are solely intellect and protector but are another type of being."

Rosie paused, letting out a long breath.

"Think about it," Justin continued as Rosie weighed his theory. "Both have seemed unaffected by the loss of control. Like they always knew how to keep control to begin with. And then I got to thinking, what if they aren't who they say they are? I did some research." Justin pulled his backpack off his chair and took out a tattered notebook.

Rosie leaned in and grasped both of his hands. "Justin, have you been overthinking, obsessing?" she asked, worry consuming her.

"No, I just dropped my notebook before heading up here." He squeezed her hand and smiled. "I promise. No craziness here." He laughed and opened a marked page.

Rosie huddled closer over the notebook and read dates, times, and locations.

"When the Premier asked me to keep an eye on the two, I decided to track them first. It was all normal comings and goings, but right after our pendants stopped working and everyone was quarantined, they started to venture off campus more."

"Where were they going?"

"I don't know. I would be right behind them, but every time they passed through the school's protections and wards, they would disappear."

"Did they exit the same way every time?"

"Yeah, how'd you know?"

"Okay, what if they didn't just leave campus? What if they crossed another barrier? One you need to know about to see or know the spell to in order to cross into a different territory?"

"Of course!" Justin exclaimed. He pulled out a rolled-up parchment. "I made this map last year. It's the school map, but I included the surrounding areas and noted which creatures dwelled where. Here." He pointed to a thick pine forest growing far off.

"Sasquatches?" Rosie asked.

"Sasquatches," Justin replied.

Chapter Eighteen

"Well, they weren't technically lying when they said they're from a nearby town, huh?" Eleanor said with a chuckle as she, Rosie, Justin, and Riley walked through town, ice cream in hand.

"Are we sure they are who we think they are?" Riley asked, raising an eyebrow as he eyed Justin and then focused on Rosie.

"I would like to know for sure myself," Eleanor added, taking another lick from the dripping cone.

"We'll have to draw out their transformation somehow. Make them show themselves," Justin said.

"How?" Rosie asked. "Obviously near-death experiences won't affect them. Dana hurt herself during the first Games, and still she didn't show any signs of being a sasquatch."

"Do you think anyone here is something else? Some other kind of creature?" Eleanor whispered, searching over her shoulder for passing groups.

"It's possible," Justin answered, doing the same.

"But guys, how do we prove they aren't who they say they are? How would they get an invite to the school? How would they secure entry at all?" Riley spouted, tossing his uneaten cone.

Rosie paused. She had thought about the skillful deception and magic that would need to be done to be accepted into King's Preparatory, but only fantastical theories floated through her mind.

"Hey, honey!" Rosie's mom shouted, causing her deep thoughts on the matter to melt away. She ran to her mom, who engulfed her in a bear hug.

"Mom! How are you?" Rosie asked, pulling back and taking her mother's appearance in. The months adjusting to her new life in Arizona suited her. Gone were the heavy bags beneath her eyes, wrinkle marks around her mouth, and pale, haunted skin. Her eyes were bright, her posture straight, and her once frail body had filled out to a stunning athletic figure.

"I'm good, sunshine. How are you? I got a letter from Professor Walker about finding control of your, you know. Um, your," and lowering her voice she whispered, "magic."

Rosie laughed and stood by her mom's side as her friends approached.

"Riley! It's so good to see you!" Rosie's mom said, giving him a hug. "And you must be Eleanor and Justin!" She shook each of their hands and put one arm around Rosie's shoulder and started to lead the group over to the general store.

"Mom, how's work been?" Rosie asked, slyly looking over to Justin. She and he had discussed the possibility of Rosie's mom learning about the other creatures' advances on the Superiority and James Kingsley's establishments.

"Work's been great. I've been reviewing records of every person registered as a, um, supernatural." She whispered the word again just like she had for magic.

"Mom, you can speak normally. Rarely does Kingstown

get tourists."

"I know, but I just like being safe."

Rosie laughed but let her mom continue as they entered the general store and grabbed a cart.

"Anyways, I've been ensuring everyone is now not only listed as what they are, but sending training and resources to people who don't live near a beacon or who are affected by the drained one here."

"Has there been anyone who has needed the help?"

"Honestly, no. The groups who live far from beacons either have full control of themselves or derive their control from a different source. The only people affected so far by the drained beacon is the school—"

A crash of splitting wood cracked, and Rosie whipped her head in the direction of the entrance. Clawing its way towards them was a bear, foaming at the mouth and eyes trained directly on them.

Screams erupted from the store and customers slipped behind the bear to exit the building, but the screaming didn't stop.

"That's Robert," Ms. Connors whispered, moving back as the bear knocked shelves out of its way, clearing a path. "He lives in my building and works for the Superiority. Security."

"Mm, wonder why he was selected for that role," Riley replied sarcastically as the beast grew closer.

"We need to get out of here," Justin said, eyeing an exit to the right.

"There's got to be more transformed creatures out there. The town's beacon is drained now," Rosie said, grasping one of her mother's hands and Riley's with the other.

"How do you know?" Riley asked.

"Can't you feel it?" Justin asked, eyeing Rosie. "It's gone."

"We need to get back to my place," Ms. Connors said, also eyeing the door. "Okay, kids, follow me and stick together. If anything happens to me—"

"Mom, I'm not going to let anything happen to you. To any of us." Rosie brought her palms together and then pulled them apart. A ball of near invisible purple energy surrounded the group and as they walked sideways the ball kept around them.

"Let's get out of here," Riley said, stepping closer to the exit.

"On three," Rosie said. "One, two—"

Suddenly, the group wobbled. A pack of coyotes burst into the store, followed by a red-eyed vampire, and Eleanor screamed, "THREE!"

The group burst from their spot, sprinting towards the door, but with their sudden movement, Robert jolted forward, barreling into stands and products in his attempt to reach the group.

Riley reached the door first and swung it open, ushering everyone out before slamming the door closed behind them. A booming thump rattled the wall.

"This way!" Ms. Connors yelled, leading the group down the dirt alleyway and behind the storefronts. Dust lingered in the air and faint screams from the center of the town echoed in between the parallel stores.

Close to the wall, Ms. Connors tip-toed to the edge of the building and poked her head around the corner, checking that the alley was clear.

From the snarls and sounds of tearing from the edge, Rosie knew it wasn't.

"Back up," Ms. Connors whispered, and the group moved back. The tall black and blue creatures glided around the corner and a blood-stained smile spread across the tallest's ghoulish face.

"What is that?" Eleanor asked, her voice shaking with each word.

"A drauger," Justin said. The zombie beast stunk of rotting flesh, and its skin peeled and had missing chunks. "Whatever you do," Justin started again, "don't let it bite you. Now, RUN!"

The group ran back towards the door they used as their escape from the shifters, but they had already made a massive hole in the wall.

"To the desert!" Rosie said, but before she could turn, a bulky, tall man jumped from the top of the building.

Fear froze her as she stared at the dark-haired, muscular man. He eyed Rosie and then her mom before stepping forward.

Riley jumped out, threw his arm back, and thrust it forward. The punch landed across the newcomer's face, but the man didn't even flinch.

"Back off, Zimmers. I'm here to help." The man raised his face, and Rosie gasped, stepping back.

"I know you," Rosie said, regaining her footing and moving forward again.

"I knew you would, kid," and after saying so, he lunged towards the drauger, tackling it down. Swiftly palming a basketball-sized boulder, he smashed it down against the beast's head. The body stopped squirming. Without even a moment of hesitation, the man jumped up from the ground and launched himself into midair with the bear lunging from the other side.

He swung himself around its neck and landed on its back. As the bear bucked and stood and shook, the man remained, his hands searching the bear's spine. Seeming happy with a position, he pressed down, and the bear let out a small whine before slumping down to the ground.

The furry, brown bear breathed slowly as it slept on the dirt ground.

"There," the man said, before stepping away.

"There?" Rosie asked. "Is he okay?"

"He's alive. Just asleep. He will wake in an hour or so. Now, how about we go back to your place, Rose."

He moved closer to Rosie and her mom and grasped one of each of their hands.

Rosie stared down at her hand and then up and into his eyes."

"Dad?" Rosie asked, staring up at the man.

He nodded and squeezed her hand before turning his head over to Ms. Connors, who could only whisper one word, "Christion?"

Chapter Nineteen

The silence in the Connors' home was deafening as the group sat nervously. Riley, Eleanor, and Justin continued to shift their eyes between Rosie, her mom, and Christion Flare, while Rosie and her mom stared at Christion, who returned their looks with apologies.

"So," Ms. Connors started, turning towards a cabinet and pulling down six mugs by their handles, "why now?"

Ms. Connors' tone of voice wasn't hysterical or even mad. The question instead brought authority and power, and a tinge of pride swelled in Rosie. She poured coffee and passed the mugs out, waiting for a reply.

"I had to protect you both," Christion began, moving closer to the two. Both leaned back on the counter, unable to step away. Christion paused and backed up again, turning to Riley, Eleanor, and Justin, hoping for some sort of help. They all averted their eyes at his gaze.

He started again, "I had to protect you."

"From?" Rosie asked, a hint of disgust covering the word as she spoke it.

"I have been alive for a very long time and have made my fair share of enemies over the years. I went into hiding, and

I never knew I would meet someone like you, Rose." He turned to her, and his eyes softened further. "The first time I saw you, I knew you were the only person for me. I know you felt the same way." He paused, staring at Ms. Connors. She stared back at him but averted her eyes and spoke.

"You ruined my life. My daughter's life."

"And I will do everything in my power for the rest of *my* life to apologize for that and to prove how much I love both of you."

"What happened?" Rosie asked, standing up straight, crossing her arms.

He turned to her now. "When you were little, I was located by a powerful demon."

"Demon?" Justin asked, and Rosie shot him a glare to zip it until later.

Christion refocused on Rosie. "Yes, demon. There are more creatures in this world, unknown to even the Premier. This demon is one of the most dangerous of his kind. I knew that if he found out about you both, then he would torture or even kill you to get to me. I couldn't risk losing you."

"But why put Mom through that pain? Do you know what you did to her?"

Grimacing, Christion spoke, "I needed you to fall under another's protection in case your mother was found. We had been seen together multiple times, but I was never seen with you. If you went to stay with another family, you'd have a chance of surviving."

"But mom—" Rosie began but her mother jumped in.

"No, honey, he did the right thing. I don't know what I would do if anything ever happened to you. It was the safest option for you."

Rosie wanted to protest, heat rising to her ears, but she stopped. Her mom took a step forward and reached out.

Rosie gripped her hand but widened her eyes as her mother drew her closer to Christion. Holding herself back, Rosie stared at her mother in confusion, but as her mom cocked her head and raised her eyebrows in hopefulness, Rosie allowed her to control her body.

With her other free hand, Ms. Connors grasped Christion's as she stepped towards him, and at her touch, the man stood taller and widened his mouth into a smile.

"Let us start fresh," Ms. Connors said, bringing Rosie's and Christion's hands together. As Rosie's hand slipped into Christion's, her magic came close to the surface without her forcing it, and a surge of power melded with her own and coursed through her. Then sudden flashes flipped through her mind.

She was four and held Christion's hand as they walked through a park. Then she was with him and her mom, and they were reading in a meadow. Next, it was her birthday, and Christion dabbed her nose with frosting. A fog in her memory cleared completely, and her mind sharpened.

"Did you?" Rosie started to ask, tears forming.

"I had to make sure neither of you remembered me. I had to strip any memory you had of me."

She stared in shock at Christion as the memories continued to flood her. Squeezing her hand, he came forward and kissed her forehead, and her anger seeped back as she remembered that kiss from before. As she remembered her dad.

Parting from her, he turned to her mother and embraced her, their hug sending tears down Ms. Connors' cheeks.

Giving her a similar kiss to the forehead, then placing his forehead against her mothers, Rosie watched in amazement at her parents' reunion.

A hand slipped into hers and Rosie turned to see Riley now at her side. He, too, kissed her on the head and then began to clear his throat.

The noise in the bliss pulled Ms. Connors and Christion away from each other and they turned back to the group.

"I don't want to dampen this reunion and all," Riley started, "but we really should discuss what's been going on."

Christion nodded in agreement before speaking, "Smart guy," and winking at Riley. Christion moved to the couch, Ms. Connors' hand in his. Rosie couldn't help but notice how the two moved as one.

Rosie and Riley followed. Sitting next to Eleanor, Rosie allowed her to embrace her and whispered into her ear, "I'm so happy for you, Rosie."

Rosie pulled away, smiling, still unsure about the event and the story Christion told but allowed herself to refocus on her father.

"So the attacks? The loss of power? What's going on Chri—" Rosie started before she corrected herself, "Dad?"

"Ha," he said, "call me whatever you want, whatever you are comfortable with. But I would be honored if it was dad." He smiled at her and continued, "I thought at first the area was simply being naturally drained of its power. It's been known to happen when too many beings have lived in one area, drawing on power for too long. But then I inspected the beacons and became one with the natural force. I determined the magic is nowhere near being gone. Rather, the supply to the beacons has been cut off. Redirected."

"Redirected? Like someone else is using it?" Eleanor asked.

"Exactly. Someone else is funneling all the power from the school and from town for their own use."

"But why?" Justin asked. "I mean, if they're able to take the power for themselves, then they must be in the area and somehow be affected by the chaos ensuing."

"Are you sure about that?" Christion asked, an eyebrow raised.

The group turned and stared at each other, confusion covering each expression.

"Think about it," Christion said. "Who would benefit from harnessing their power? Who has been vying for access to the beacons? To town? To the school?"

"The other creatures!" Rosie exclaimed, sitting up. "The sasquatches, the banshees, the other outcast creatures."

Smiling, Christion nodded. "They don't live in town, they don't attend the school, they live in the area but are hidden from the destruction they are causing."

"Why would they do such a thing?" Ms. Connors asked, gripping her hands together.

"They've come to think they have no other choice."

"But the negotiations," Rosie said. "Premier Kingsley was meeting with senior leadership. Trying to come to an agreement with the groups. Trying to tell them that they can join our community."

Christion laughed and then stared at Rosie. "Dear, from my source within the community, and it is a very good source, he hasn't made a single serious offer. The leaders have reached out, attempted to come to a resolution, but Kingsley has offended them with every counter. He'd rather they stay within their community but still fall under the Superiority."

"Wouldn't being under the Superiority be a good thing?"

"Not when they aren't being educated, protected, or accepted. That's why I think they've decided to take matters into their own hands and, at the same time give Kingsley a little taste of his own medicine."

Rosie sat back against the sofa, allowing the plush cushions to engulf her.

"What do we do?" Justin asked. "Should we tell the Premier that the other species are behind this?"

"Chances are, he already knows, but isn't sure how to mend the situation," Christion replied.

"I mean, it seems simple to me," Eleanor stated.

"Yeah, I see it too," Riley agreed. "Just let the other species join our community. No more of this high school 'you can't sit with us' crap, and everyone sings Kumbaya."

Snorting then calming his voice to a more serious tone, Christion replied, "If only it were that simple. Now that things have escalated this far, I fear war will start and many will die because of each side's bullishness."

"Well, we just can't let that happen," Rosie started, now standing up.

"What are you thinking?" Riley asked, standing by her side.

"I think I need to have a little chat with the twins." Rosie cocked an eyebrow and stared back at her dad, who stared back with his own raised eyebrow and sideways smirk.

* * *

The door to Eleanor and Dana's room slammed against the

wall as it was forced open and shook the above chandelier while Rosie strutted in to face Dana.

Dana wasn't there, though. None of her things were there. In fact, her side of the room sat completely bare, as if no one had ever taken over Rosie's side when she moved out.

"Where is she?" Eleanor asked, standing at Rosie's side.

"I don't know, but I know who would." Turning and running back through the hallway and up the stairs, Rosie found Drew sitting with Riley and Justin.

"Your sister?"

"What about my sister?" Drew spat from the couch, glaring at Rosie and eyeing the two boys who flanked him, knowing he couldn't escape.

"Where is she?"

"How would I know? And if I did know, why would I tell you?"

"Drew, we know why you two are here. We know what you are."

"W-What? I mean, I don't know what you're talking about."

"You're just a protector? Nothing else? Not special?"

"Hey!" Eleanor and Riley shouted at the same time.

Rosie shot them pointed eyes, and they refocused, understanding now what she was doing. "Just a protector. You have no special abilities. Just strong and dumb."

"No, I'm not!"

A smirk slid across Rosie's face, and she continued. "Not what? Just strong and dumb or not just a protector?"

The room sat in silence as Drew and Rosie continued their stare down.

"Drew," Riley started, putting a hand on the boy's shoulder, causing him to jump first at the touch but then surprisingly allowing the hand to stay rested. Riley continued, "We aren't going to be mad. Hell, we aren't even going to do anything about it. We just need your help. I know this isn't exactly what you signed up for. I know you weren't a part of Dana's plans to set loose the other creatures. We just want to make sure everyone stays safe."

"You don't mean everyone," Drew said, now shrugging off Riley's hand.

Riley sat down next to the bulky boys and with sincerity said, "We mean *everyone.*"

Drew sat still, his eyes shifting between Riley and Rosie. "I-I don't know where she is, really. We came together to see what the school was like. To report back on the Premier's movements, but that's it, I swear."

Rosie stepped forward. "Who sent you?"

Another pause lingered but Drew replied, "Our clan."

"Sasquatches?"

"Sasquatches, banshees, dwarves, elves, ogres, goblins, harpies, cyclops, giants—"

"What?" Rosie's head spun. All these creatures she knew about but didn't know about.

"We've been gathering for a while. We're just tired of being treated as second-class citizens. We want to join the school, join the Superiority."

"Why don't you? What's stopped you?" Eleanor asked.

"The Premier."

"That can't be," Rosie said. "I talked to him, and he said he tried to negotiate with your group. Wanted you to join us."

"Maybe he does, but what I'm told from within is that the members of the Superiority are ignorant and hateful. They want no part of our kind within. Thinking less of us."

"I promise that's not true," Rosie spoke up, but a deep voice thundered behind her.

"Rosie, there are some who do think that. On both sides. Thinking each other aren't as gifted or strong or powerful," Christion said, moving closer to Drew.

"But—" Rosie started but Christion stopped her.

"Now isn't the time to discuss the politics of it but rather find out how to stop the bloodshed before it occurs." Christion turned back towards Drew. "Now, what do you know of their plans to dissolve the Superiority? Will there be an attack?"

"I swear I don't know much. My sister and I were just sent as scouts."

"Are there more of you at the school?"

Drew shook his head no.

"What about within the Superiority itself?"

Hesitation sat on Drew's lips before blurting, "No."

"Boy," Christion said, his tone becoming firmer, "do you want your loved ones to die over a miscommunication?"

Drew paused but spoke. "Yes, there are a few in the Superiority."

"We need to find the Premier," Rosie said. "He could be in danger."

"He will be fine. What we need to do is bridge the two groups together now. Without anyone dying. Drew, do you think you could arrange a meeting with your leader?"

"I don't have his ear. Plus, I never really did any of the communicating. That was all Dana."

"Then we need to find Dana."

"Did she have a meeting point or way to get messages back to the clan?" Rosie interjected.

"Yeah, but I didn't know where."

"Didn't she trust you?" Rosie asked.

"We decided that it would be better if we split duties and knowledge. That way, if we were ever caught, we wouldn't have all the information."

"What about where the rest of the group is located? Would she return there?" Christion asked.

"The group is split up by the different species, and we move a lot to not get caught. But I know where the sasquatch horde was last week. They might still be there."

"Tell us where. We need to get there. Talk to someone," Rosie said.

"Hold on, kid," Christion replied. "You are still needed here, and so am I. We need to help get the school under control and then we can go work with the others."

"Staying here isn't as important as stopping a war."

"War hasn't started yet, and it won't until the clan knows the Superiority is weak enough to strike, and it isn't."

"Okay so what do we do until then?" Justin asked.

"I will help with getting the other student's abilities under control and harnessed. You will do the same, Rosie."

Slight annoyance caused a small roll of Rosie's eyes, but she nodded her head.

"How are you going to convince Professor Shay to let you stay?"

"Well, for one, none of you are to divulge who I really am. As for my cover identity, you'll find out soon enough."

Christion walked over to Rosie and kissed her head. "Kiddo, I meant what I said. You are safe until I tell you. Don't go looking for the clan. It's too dangerous." Rosie wanted to ignore her father's plea, but his next words hit her heart. "Promise me you won't. I can't lose you after I just got you back."

Nodding her head, she whispered to him, "I promise. Feel better now?"

"I do. I know your mother will as well. Now," he said, turning to the group, heading for the exit to the mountainside, "I have a meeting with the headmistress." With a smirk and skip, he hopped out the door and disappeared towards the lake.

"So, what now?" Eleanor asked, turning to Rosie and then eyeing Drew.

"We do what he says," Riley said, putting a hand out to help Drew up. "And we learn as much about these other creatures as we can. Think you'll be able to help us, Drew?"

Drew stood and smiled. "I never wanted a fight. We just wanted to be welcomed. If I can help ensure a battle doesn't break out, then I will tell you all I can."

"Great," Rosie said, and sat on one of the poofs by the couch. "Let's start with what you are, your abilities, your weaknesses, your strengths, Dana's abilities, and what happened to the power source."

The room grew silent, and Drew stared at Rosie, whose standoff disposition was clearly demonstrated.

"Um," Drew started, looking back at Riley.

"Rosie," Riley started, "we can give the guy a break. He has been upfront with us so far."

"Yeah," Eleanor agreed, "what if we start a little slower?"

"No," Drew said, finding his voice, "it's okay."

Rosie nodded for him to sit back down, and Justin, Eleanor, and Riley found their own seats.

"So, you're a sasquatch?" Rosie started.

"That's right. My sister and I both are."

"How do you look like that?" Eleanor asked. "I mean, sorry, that was rude, I just meant that every picture I've seen, and the folklore is sasquatches are giant, hairy, and well, have big feet." Her cheeks flushed red, and she furrowed her eyebrows together in apology.

A small laugh escaped Drew and he continued, "We are able to transform the same way wolves and shifters do. But while wolves and shifters are mostly in human form, we like to be in our squatch form."

"How do you communicate?"

"Telepathically."

"So just like wolves and shifters?" Justin chimed in.

"Yep."

"Isn't that annoying? Garrett said it sucked having other wolves in his head, knowing all his thoughts," Eleanor said.

"We learn how to shut out others and keep our own mind shielded so our every thought isn't on display."

"Mm, interesting," Justin said. "And what if you are closed off, but someone is trying to talk to you?"

"We can regulate it so it's just like having a normal speaking conversation. Keep out others' deepest thoughts but when called we will hear it and can communicate."

"And—" Justin went to ask but Rosie stopped him.

"Justin, trust me, I am just as interested in learning more about Drew and his abilities, but we need to find Dana."

Justin nodded but was brought to his feet along with the rest of the group, when a roar of animals brawling erupted outside. Everyone ran to the door to the mountainside to see what the commotion was.

Running by the human dorm were three shifters and a

werewolf in their forms, all being led by an unnaturally giant black bear. The werewolf turned his head knowingly to the group hidden behind the guise of the dorm which from the outside, looked like mountainside.

"Garrett," Eleanor whispered, her hand flying to the handle. Rosie gripped it before she could pull the door open though.

"Wait."

"Why? He knows I'm here. He has control."

"Barely," Drew pipped.

"Rosie, please."

"Whatever he's doing, there's a purpose. We can't distract him if that group is restoring their control. Did you even notice that he was shifted, and it's daytime? Let him be for now. I'm sure he'll be able to join us soon."

Eleanor nodded, tears sitting in her eyes as she watched the group run off.

"I recognized Garrett and Natasha, but who were the others?" Riley asked, staring at the group, who were now small figures in the distance, round a corner towards the lakeside and probably to the open field.

"The horse, I think, was from Astive; the cardinal was Reese; and the bear, I'm pretty sure was Manger," Justin said.

"Manger? He's the size of a van!" Eleanor quipped, shocked that she had never seen her professor in one of his many shifted forms.

"He must be teaching the top students who have the most control, so they can go teach the others," Rosie determined, then turned to Drew. "You and your sister should be helping. If you really don't want a fight, if you want peace, help us."

"I will, but I can't make the same promise for Dana."

"Then I'll make her."

"If you haven't noticed, no one can make Dana do anything. She will return to our group and follow orders."

"Then we better get our group ready. If she wants a fight, then she'll have a fight." Rosie gritted her teeth and grimaced, knowing if no solution between the groups was to be had, then everyone at school needed to start training. Training to defend, training to fight, training to kill.

Chapter Twenty

Under the rising, bright moon, Rosie whispered to her dad, "Are you sure this is a good idea?"

They both stood in front of the school's vampire population. Each student wore chains upon their wrists and ankles, which in turn were attached to one another and the ground. If one vampire made a move to attack Rosie or Christion, they wouldn't make it one inch before falling on their faces. Sure, Rosie contemplated the chances of them somehow strategically working together to rip her throat out, but from the hostile glances they threw at each other, she figured the possibility of that occurring was slim to none.

"Trust me. We will take it slow now and continue into the night, when their blood lust will be at its peak."

"And then tomorrow?"

"We will see after tonight who will be strong enough to undergo the ritual. Hopefully they all will."

Rosie eyed the group and found Katherine. Her eyes permanently glowed blood-red and her teeth sat as long, jagged fangs. Through her viciousness, her eyebrows came together and upward, concern riddling her mind as she stared from her classmates to Rosie.

"And they only want me?" Rosie asked Christion, turning back towards him.

"It's your blood that they smell, as I am a fellow vampire," he stated. This was his cover. What he told Professor Shay. Christion Flare's identity was now Christion Flame. The oldest and most knowledgeable vampire in the world, his story corroborated by stories in history books, which were really about a close friend of his.

With this story, he would be able to assist the vampires, fairies, and mermaids in gaining control. This was also, Christion explained to Rosie, a disguise he mastered through his years being immortal. And as an immortal, his blood was almost indistinguishable from a vampire's. At least novice vamps or other untrained supernatural creatures, like the ones at the school, wouldn't be able to sniff out what he really was.

"I said, I, a fellow vampire," Christion stated loudly, ensuring the uncomfortable group that sat chained before them paid some attention, "cannot tempt your classmates. What they need to learn is how I act. Each of you possesses the power and control to remain innocent. To not kill through your bloodlust. We will practice that now."

Christion walked towards Martha and pulled a key from his pocket. Gripping the chain that held her wrists together, he pulled her up, so she was standing.

"Martha, I'm going to unlock the shackles."

Really? He had to start with the homicidal psycho vamp who hates my guts?

Rosie continued listening to Christion's instructions. "When I unlock the shackles, you are to remain where you stand. You will take a deep breath in and immerse yourself with Ms. Connors' scent. You will listen to her heart race as blood pumps through her body. And you will keep your eyes on her neck, watching her pulse." He now turned to Rosie. "Rosie, you will not make any movement. Keep your heart under control. If it quickens, the vampire's natural tendencies of hunting its prey may assert themselves. Do you understand?"

Rosie hesitantly nodded her head and returned her focus on Martha. To Rosie's surprise, Martha wore the same face as Katherine. Concern and worry crossed over her features, and Rosie eased as she realized Martha wanted control.

"Okay, I'm unlocking you, Martha." The distinctive click of the key turning in the lock sounded, and the heavy chain clattered on the ground. As soon as freedom from the cuffs sounded, Martha raced in a blur to Rosie's side.

"Ms. Ash!" Christion started, but Rosie shook her head ever so slightly as Martha just stood at her side. She ducked her head down next to Rosie's neck, nudging her hair out of the way with her nose and leaning in closer. Inhaling deep, Martha's body shuddered in pleasure at Rosie's scent, and a light press of her lips hit Rosie's pulse. For a second they sat, but as quickly as she got to Rosie's side, she ran back to her place next to Christion.

"Very good, Ms. Ash. I'm going to re-shackle you now." She nodded, staring at Christion as she raised her wrists.

When the last clip was in place, Martha sat on the ground, and Christion gave her a small vial of blood. At the speed of light, she popped the cork and drained the thick liquid, tonguing whatever she could get from the skinny tube. As the class watched, they hissed and tried to near the vial, glaring down at it with hungry anticipation.

As Christion walked to Rosie's side, she whispered softly, still knowing her question would be heard by her classmates, "They fed before this right?"

Christion gave a small chuckle and a shrug before moving to the next vampire in the chained line to test him.

Stiffening, Rosie called her magic to the surface. Martha being able to show that type of restraint was one thing, but she wasn't about to trust the rest of her classmates, even Katherine, to show the same control.

As electricity bubbled near the top of her skin, she quietly heard the pop of the shackles and the whooshing of the next vampire rushing her. His cold hands reached out, grasping her shoulder, but as he pulled her in, mouth opened and teeth bared, she sent a ripple of fire out and into him.

Yelping backwards, Christion grabbed him by the wrists and re-shackled him and slammed him into the ground.

"Mr. Cruz," Christion stated to the freshman, who to Rosie's surprise, showed remorse with his hands covering his face, "you will try again after everyone else goes. Until then, watch and learn."

The class continued, and true to Christion's word, the moon rose, and as if he willed the clouds to separate, the moon blasted light upon the group. As the light hit the students, stirring roused them, and Rosie noted that they each loosened their grip on their humanity. Snarls sounded and a few even bit in Rosie's direction, cutting their own lips in the process.

"Enough!" Christion boomed. "Focus. Don't let the setting of the sun control who you are."

At the words, everyone forced themselves back to a full sitting position, some sitting on their hands or clawing at their own skin to distract from the aching want of blood.

"Each of you," Christion stated as he paced in front of the group, ensuring their eyes left Rosie and followed him, "has the ability to find inner peace. To find the strength to not feed. To not kill. Do not let the moon take your strength away, suck your power away." The gnawing and scratching stopped, and all seemed transfixed on their teacher. Smiling, he turned to Rosie. "Rosie, congratulate your classmates. They all will take part in tomorrow's control ritual."

Rosie smiled deeply, expecting the room to erupt in cheers, but every vampire sat on edge and nervously jerked their gazes around the room. The ritual either was going to work and give the students the control to rejoin their supernatural society, or it was going to kill them all.

* * *

"Do you have the citrine crystals?" Christion asked Rosie as the group of vampires sat in the dusk light, awaiting the full moon to rise above them. On the highest peak of the surrounding mountains, the group laid shaking, awaiting the trial they were about to endure.

"I-I don't know if I can do this," Rosie overheard one of the junior vamps from Astive mutter to her friend.

"Lightlark, we got this. You did great yesterday," her friend replied.

As the two passed the group, Rosie nodded and pulled a bag of clinking gems from her backpack and handed them to her dad. The vampires stared at the pulsating witch who passed, but they all remained still. At an altar, Christion laid out each crystal and awaited the moon to charge them for the end of the ritual.

Turning to the rising full moon making its way higher into the sky, Rosie couldn't help but notice the stirring group. Christion's gaze also found the round, bright yellow moon, and he quickened towards the group.

"It's time," he announced. "Pick up the silver daggers at your sides and let out your blood."

Rosie's stomach churned, and a lump formed in her throat. The students hesitated and stared at the daggers in each hand.

"When in Rome!" Katherine yelled before gliding one dagger across the opposite wrist and doing the same with the other. Then she sat on the ground and sliced similar cuts into her thighs. Setting the daggers back, she laid down and watched the moon as it grew higher.

Her classmates followed, and soon, each lay beneath the star-filled sky as the blood slowly drained from their bodies.

"Do you need anything else?" Rosie asked Christion, hoping he would so she could talk to him more about the growing threat of the other species, but to her dismay, he replied no.

"Why don't you head back to campus? You can meet me back here in the morning and we can continue with the fairy lessons and get the mermaids prepped for tomorrow night?"

Rosie sighed but responded, "Sounds good."

"And you know who to bring with you right?"

"Only volunteers. I know. There's five of us signed up already, but I'm trying to get the other protectors to help."

Christion nodded and then turned back to the group. As the moon grew higher in the sky and remained brightly trained on the swimsuit-clad vampires, their bodies began to jerk and twist. "Rosie, go. Make sure the wolves are secure and nothing interferes here."

Nodding, she raced down the mountainside, screams of agony and pain sounding from behind.

Hurtling bushes and dodging boulders, Rosie made a list in her head of her tasks for the rest of the night.

One, check that the wolves are secure. Two, check that the shifters are secure. Three, get more volunteers for the vampires. Four, prep for the fairy ritual. Five, prep for the mermaid ritual. Six, find Dana and get her to spill her guts. Seven, ask Premier Kingsley if he has heard of any disturbances or updates regarding the clan. Eight, call mom. Nine, find out the status of Manger's work with the shifters and werewo-

As the tail end of Rosie's thought formed, a wolf tackled her to the ground. Thankfully, flipping somehow firmly against the wolf's body, only shock pulsed through her. Finally stopping, she landed on her back and stared up at the snarling wolf growling in her face. It took a moment to register, but as soon as she did, she whispered, "Garrett, no."

His jaws snapped forward, and she turned with her eyes closed, ready to let her friend take her. Instead, a coarse, wet tongue slid across her face.

Opening her eyes and seeing the wolf stepping back and pouncing with his tongue lolled out of his mouth, Rosie laughed and raised her arm to wipe off the slobber.

"Garrett, as much as I love that you are you, how do you think Eleanor is going to react to you dog-kissing me?"

"I don't care at all!" Eleanor yelled, laughing as she bounded from behind a boulder and hugged Garrett around his neck. Nuzzling into his soft fur, she whispered, "Show her what you can do now."

Turning to Eleanor, Garrett licked her face and pranced to the boulder Eleanor had just jumped out of. In a split second, Garrett, in his human form, walked out in a pair of shorts and a too-small shirt.

"Hon, I think I grabbed one of your shirts," Garrett said, laughing as he tried to tug the bottom edge over his belly button.

"What? How?" Rosie asked, moving forward towards him.

With his big goofy grin, Garrett wrapped his arms around Rosie and swung her in a circle. She grasped him back, and when they stopped spinning Eleanor ran into them, engulfing them both.

When they pulled apart, Garrett stared up at the moon, closed his eyes, and breathed in deeply.

"You can thank Manger," he said, opening his eyes, staring back at Rosie.

"When he took you and the others out the other night? He trained you for your rituals?"

"Yep, the four of us showed the most control while shifted. We could control ourselves enough to not fall into our primal state. Manger took that to mean we would survive our rituals and then could, in turn, teach the rest of our kind. Me, the wolves; Natasha and the horse shifter, Duke, the predator and larger shifters; and Reese, the prey shifters."

"When do you think you'll have them ready? How did you break through so fast? You needed to shift under a full moon, over and over and over until the pain was bearable, and you didn't rely on the moon."

"I transformed about two times and that was it. Ended my trial thirty minutes ago. I'm cured, baby!" He picked up Eleanor and kissed her deeply and spun her as he did so. Rosie laughed, and when the two broke apart, he wrapped one arm around Eleanor's shoulder and the other around Rosie's.

"So, what now?" he asked Rosie, lifting an eyebrow. "Who's fighting ready? When are we going to take down these jack-offs messing with the school?"

"Garrett! Shhh! How do you even know about all of this?" Rosie asked, then peered her neck around Garrett and spied a blushing Eleanor.

"What? I filled him in on what's happening! Now that he's better, he will be in our strategy sessions on what we are going to do to stop the next supernatural civil war."

Rolling her eyes, Rosie trained her attention back to Garrett. "We're getting the students back to normal first. Getting everyone in tip-top shape. Then we're going to restore power to the beacon."

"We as in you and your dad?"

"Wow, Eleanor. You really covered everything didn't you?"

The group chuckled as they walked down the mountain-side.

As they neared the lake, Rosie continued. "Yes, Christion and I have been researching, and he found a way to restore the beacon's power."

"Won't that take it away from the clan?"

"Yes, but he is hoping that when that happens, they will be willing to join the Superiority, the community, and even enroll in the school."

"And if they're just pissed?"

"Then we will have the control and the extra power from the beacon to draw on."

Garrett nodded, and the three dragged their feet through the sand on the bank. "Well, what do you need now?"

"Now? Well, right now I need to know that all the wolves and shifters are locked up."

"Excuse me?" Garrett asked indignantly.

"Not locked up. Sorry. Secured," Rosie corrected.

Chuckling at the fix, Garrett responded, "Yes, the wolves are secured, but I think Natasha, Duke, and Reese are working on a few shifters. One-on-one, of course."

"Okay, that should be fine." Rosie thought of the vampires enduring the ritual on the mountaintop and guilt of the pain they were facing knotted her stomach.

"Anything else?"

"Well, I need more volunteers for tomorrow morning."

"What for?"

Rosie eyed Eleanor with a lifted brow and Eleanor stepped back raising her hands. Of course, her best friend left it to her to tell *her* boyfriend that the vampires need fresh blood in the morning to rejuvenate after the sun rises and their charms are secured.

"Um, so the vampires are all doing their trial tonight and need fresh blood in the morning."

"So, you need help carrying up blood bags? Done."

"Not exactly. They need fresh, from-the-tap, blood. You know? Straight from the vein?"

"Ha! I'd rather—" Garrett started but Rosie held out a hand to stop him.

"Garrett, please. I know werewolf blood will make vampires stronger, especially yours since you are technically royalty in the wolf world, but if anyone needs that kind of power now, it's them."

"My dad would go nuts if he ever found out!"

"But the relationship between the wolves and the vampires could also strengthen. You know, friendliness between your two groups only extends to the grounds of the school. The ties out there are weak, and this could technically help." Rosie widened her eyes and batted her eyelashes. She then clasped her hands together and brought them under her chin before saying, "Please?"

Silence filled the air before Garrett started, "I'm sorry, Rosie I just can't—" but a scream echoed through the mountainside. "Katherine?" Garrett asked, turning to see if he could pinpoint where the scream came from.

"Yes, Katherine, Garrett. Your friend."

Heaving a heavy sigh, he said, "I'll do it. And I'll get the trained shifters as well. What time?"

Rosie pointed to the mountaintop before saying, "Six-thirty, up there."

Garrett nodded in agreement and turned back towards the main entrance of the school.

"Don't look so glum, GarBear," Eleanor said, kissing his cheek. "It's a good thing you're doing."

"Yeah, yeah."

The two girls laughed at the moody boy, and Rosie pulled the heavy door open but didn't see right away that someone was walking out on the other side.

Running directly into James Kingsley, Rosie fell backwards and landed on her butt.

"Oh, Rosie, I'm so sorry," he said, assisting her back up.

Once on her feet, Eleanor and Garrett walked inside and turned to Rosie.

"Go ahead, guys. I have a quick question for the Premier,"

she said before turning to Kingsley. "I mean, if you have time?"

"I have a moment." He gestured to her to follow him, and Rosie smiled. Letting the door close behind her, the two walked back down the stairs to the moonlit bank. "So, what can I do for you?"

"I was wondering if you knew where a student was. Dana Randolph?"

Kingsley raised an eyebrow. "The intellect? Have you talked to her brother?"

"Yes. He isn't sure of her whereabouts either. I just want to make sure she is still around."

"And not with her clan?"

Rosie's eyes widened. "You know? Of course, you know," she exclaimed.

"I've known for some time. I also made sure her father, one of the clan leaders, knew I knew and that she and her brother would remain safe in our care."

"Did it ease tensions at all? Do they still want to fight?"

"Unfortunately, I believe that while Mr. Randolph is more inclined to be reasonable, I can't say the same for his colleagues. Ms. Randolph is back home, but I am trying to see if she would consider returning to help her brother teach the shifters and wolves self-mind care."

"That would be great," Rosie said, not necessarily thrilled at the idea of seeing Dana again, but if they were able to demonstrate cooperation between the two groups then the clan would relinquish the power back, join the Superiority, and share in the beacon's force.

"Anything else, Rosie?"

Shaking her head, she stepped away and up the steps.

"Rosie?"

She turned back, and Kingsley stared at the mountaintop.

"Premier?"

"Do tell Christion Flare I would like to have a discussion with him. Soon."

Then looking over the vast lake, Kingsley walked away, leaving Rosie speechless.

Chapter Twenty-One

"He was bound to find out sooner or later, Rosie," Christion said as Rosie healed the bite marks on her wrist that one of the vampires had just drunk from.

Rosie peered around at the volunteers she gathered who were all feeding their fellow classmates. A small smile played on her lips at the sign of togetherness but then she brought her attention back to Christion.

"How are you going to approach him?" she asked.

A laugh escaped him, and he placed a soft hand on her shoulder. "With the truth."

"All of the truth?"

"With what he needs to know."

"He's bound to feel a little threatened. He thought he was the only immortal until now."

"And I will tell him that I have no desire to reveal my true identity. I am just here to make amends with my love and my daughter."

Giving her a soft squeeze, he moved towards a few of the vampires who were still recovering from the long twelve hours they just had.

"Everything okay with you two?" Riley asked, gripping his

blood-dripping bite marks.

Holding his hand in hers, she ran her thumb over the marks, closing them instantly.

"Oh! Do mine please!" Olive said, rushing over. "I do not need this scarring."

After healing the wound, Olive flipped her hair and walked down the mountainside.

"How did you even get her here?" Riley asked, eyeing the flippant girl as she left.

"Simple. Blackmail." Rosie turned, raising a mischievous eyebrow before laughing.

"What?" Riley asked, his eyes widening as they watched Rosie stalk off, giggling.

She and the rest of the volunteers started back toward the dorm as Christion gathered the vampires in a group and gave a speech on the importance of control and respecting their power.

"I can't believe what the vamps had to go through," Riley said, catching up to Rosie. He shook his head.

"What do you mean?" Rosie asked, studying the concern on Riley's face.

"One of the guys who fed from me, he just described the experience. Really freaked me out."

"I mean, of course, draining themselves had to be hard."

"He said it was like he was killing himself. He could feel his body become colder, icier as it grew empty, and not even the warmth of his own blood that pooled around him helped. Once he was drained, he landed on a plane of death or subconsciousness or somewhere else. Said he spoke to the dead."

Rosie contemplated the idea of such a feeling. A wave

of nausea flowed through her at the feeling she knew well. She thought back to when Gyle attacked her and Egil. The coldness of blood loss. But at least in her scenario she blacked out rather than traveled to some realm.

"All while that was happening, he also felt his body start to decay. It just sounded awful."

"I bet." Suddenly Rosie stopped. "Do you know if anyone else was transported to a 'plane of death,' as you put it."

"Not me. The vamp boy. But I don't know. Why?"

"I'm just wondering if being that close to death puts you somewhere in the afterlife. I mean, Christion mentioned demons, and I can only assume there is an afterlife after my premonitions and dreams last year."

"Yeah, so?"

"There was just a time where I considered tapping into it. The afterlife, heaven, hell, purgatory, who knows."

"Why would you want to do that, Rosie?" His already furrowed brows moved closer together.

"I just wanted to learn more. About me, my family, my power."

"You have all the information you need. Promise you won't attempt to reach the other side."

She nodded her head and faced forward.

The two continued in silence until Riley asked, "So do you know what's on your books the rest of the day? Think there will be some time for just us?"

"Just us?" Rosie gasped dramatically. "I must ask, kind sir, what are your intentions?"

She chuckled, but Riley stopped and pulled her in close. "To make sure you remember I'm yours and you're mine." He pressed his lips to hers and butterflies soared throughout.

Deepening the kiss, she wrapped her arms around his waist but pulled back as a small cough interrupted them.

"I'm sorry," Justin said, awkwardly shifting from foot to foot. "It's just Christion, Rosie. He asked me to tell you to meet in the meadow in an hour."

"Yeah, no problem. Thanks, Justin," Rosie said, giving him a smile. She turned back to Riley, who kicked a rock near his foot down the mountain, no doubt picturing it was Justin. "Hey, I'll let you know when I'm free, but we will see more of each other today."

Pecking him on his cheek, she moved across the mountain rather than down, to the sunny meadow where the fairy students were meeting her and Christion.

As she walked further, she heard Riley behind her, "Seriously dude, you couldn't give me like one more minute?"

Smirking that Justin had caused the frustration, and that she left him wanting more, Rosie couldn't help but feel a little proud.

She continued to think of Riley and wondered if he would put something romantic together for them to do or if they would fall into their normal routine of meeting their friends and just hanging out. She thought it would probably be the latter, as Garrett was now free.

She leapt over a dried fallen log, and just as the sun rose over the mountaintop and the rays hit the grassy meadow, tiny fairies fluttered up and basked in the sunlight.

Smiling, Rosie stepped forward, and the fairies stirred more at the vibrations from her nearing. They fluttered higher, and then they rushed to the other side.

Cocking a curious eyebrow, Rosie moved in more to see where they were going. They knew to meet her and Christion here this morning, so why were they leaving?

But they weren't leaving. Just seeing who the newcomer was.

Stepping through the foliage on the other side was Sunnie Lightstrom. Her classmates twirled and danced gleefully, landing in her hands and on her shoulders, and she walked forward. She spoke softly to them, her bronzed skin glowing more in their presence.

"Rosie!" she yelled, waving her arm in the air, sending the flurry of sparkling specks back to their normal activities.

The fairy students had thankfully taken to their control practice more easily than the other groups. Only a few instances of wry, mischievous, devilish actions occurred since first losing the beacon, but other than that and just wanting to stay in their natural form, the fairies didn't cause too much trouble.

"Hi, Sunnie. How are you? I didn't know you would be here." Since last year's incident, where Egil viciously stripped Sunnie of her wings, she remained in her human state, unable to transform.

"Yeah, Mr. Flame called my dad and thought that being back at school and working with my classmates, I might be able to harness some sort of power again."

"Really?" This was the first Rosie had heard that her father had contacted the Lightstroms. As far as she was aware, when Sunnie's wings were sliced out, so was her magic.

"Yeah, plus being in a cabin in the woods by myself while everyone I love is either here or out working for the community just doesn't sit right with me. I want to feel whole again. You know?"

More than anything, Rosie did.

"Ah, Ms. Lightstrom!" Rosie heard her dad yell across the clearing as he entered the field. "Ready to tap into some power?"

"Yes!" Smiling, Sunnie walked back and sat in the tall grass, resuming conversation with the small pupils as they awaited the start of the ritual.

"I didn't think it was possible to perform magic after being stripped like Sunnie was," Rosie said to Christion, hoping for some answers.

"Truth is, she might not be able to access any, but I've seen some pretty extraordinary fairies in my time. One who lost their fairy state but could still practice simple magic. With her bloodline, I think Ms. Lightstrom has a good chance of being able to manipulate the earth and make healing elixirs from nature. She has a shot to still be a part of society, even if her father doesn't think so."

"Why wouldn't he want her to be normal? Feel normal?"

"It took some convincing, but Mr. Lightstrom just worries for his daughter. I mean, after hearing what you went through last year, I know I needed to be near you. Make sure you stay safe. He just wants the same, even if he doesn't realize that may not be what's best for her."

Christion smiled and walked towards Sunnie and the bright, almost blinding glow of the cluster of fairy students.

"Alright, everyone. If you want to complete the ritual, I need each of you to make your way out of your natural state and into your human form."

Small, high-pitched groans sounded but, one by one, they flew to a separate area in the meadow, and through winced faces and uncomfortable lengthening of bodies, each sat before them.

Rosie eyed Pine and gave him a small wave. He paused, massaging the back of his neck, and smiled brightly back.

"From your transformation, I noticed that each of you felt some sort of discomfort. What did you feel?" Christion asked the group.

The students looked from one to the other before a Haply member spoke up, "Well, we've been practicing a little bit every day since you came and spoke to us. At first, the transformation was unbearable. Like shards of glass prickling at the surface of our skin when we grew and shrank. And when our wings would pop in or out, it was like our scapulas were breaking to make room or adjust for them."

"And now?" Christion asked, pacing in front of the group.

"Now, it just feels like growing pains. Like each joint is inflamed and hot as they pop and grow."

"I have a salve that could potentially help with that," Sunnie said, smiling up at Christion.

"How does it work?" Rosie asked, stepping forward.

"Yeah!" a few in the group exclaimed.

Sunnie stared at Christion, who nodded his head reassuringly.

"It eases pain."

"How?" Christion questioned.

"When my wings were taken, I still felt them. It was like they were still there but torn and broken." Barely audible gasps escaped horrified faces. "It was some of the worst pain I'd ever been in, but I took to nature. I foraged for healing herbs and searched for sparkle water."

Gasps of awe sounded, but no one interrupted Sunnie from continuing.

Lifting an eyebrow at the foreign term, though, Rosie made

a mental note to ask Christion about sparkle water later.

"I concocted under the waning moon an elixir or salve of sorts. I applied it to my shoulder blades, and I haven't felt the pain since."

"Do you have any?" the girl from Haply asked. "Can we try it now?"

Murmurs of agreement burst out, but Christion brought everyone's attention back to him with a loud, head-splitting whistle.

"While a short-cut would be nice, you have to transform till the pain is unnoticeable. No salve can help you here."

Groans escaped a few students, but at the discouraging statement, Pine sat up and stared at his classmates.

"Well, what are we waiting for?" Pine asked, searching the meadow for support. "The faster we get this done, the faster we can rejoin the rest of the school." After the statement, a full-sized wing popped out of his left shoulder blade then the next, and suddenly he was the size of Rosie's palm. Fluttering in the air for only a second, he landed on the ground, and transformed back into his human state.

The rest of the group followed his lead, all except for Sunnie who followed Christion over to the edge of the meadow.

A concerned expression washed over his face, and soon after Sunnie wore a matching one. Tears began to fill her eyes and one fell down her sun-kissed cheek. Wrapping a supportive arm around her, Christion left her at the edge to work on pulling natural magic from the earth.

"Everything okay?" Rosie asked.

"Everything is fine. That salve she created. It didn't ease her pain but stole it."

"Stole it? What do you mean? Isn't that good?"

"The water she used-"

"Sparkle water? What even is that?"

"Um, have you heard of the fountain of youth?"

Rosie snorted and rolled her eyes then noticed the serious expression on Christion's face.

"I mean, yeah, in storybooks."

"Well, many stories arise from real life."

"You're saying the fountain of youth is real?"

"There is more than one. And it isn't a fountain. They are tiny water sources, typically found in caves or caverns, which were formed from dark magic. The use of it is highly illegal as it could kill you. Drinking that water or, in Sunnie's case, applying it, will steal pain and transfer it to the closest person nearby. Or age if you are attempting to stay young. Thankfully, she just applied the water with a mixture of other ingredients. When ingested, the water acts as a life source to the drinker. You can live immortally but only if you continue to drink the water daily."

Rosie looked over at Sunnie, who was now grinning at the tangle of flowers blooming in her hands, and then asked, "Why would she go after something that was considered dark magic? That doesn't sound like her."

"Sparkle water is rare and virtually unknown, but still known by few in the fairy world. Myths claim that near sparkle water star-dust can be found, which is coveted by fairies. Heck, it's why members of their community are put in such high positions within the Superiority. Fairies will search out star dust and sell it to the Superiority. It can be used in its natural form for a myriad of medicines and spells, but it is also the basis of fairy dust, which Mr. Lightstrom controls the export of."

"Like Peter Pan fairy dust? Can fairy dust make me fly?" Rosie asked skeptically.

"Not fly. But transport yourself from one place to the next, seamlessly. No complex spell work, no hidden doors. Just a pinch of dust, and you're where you need to be."

"Why haven't I heard of fairy dust or seen it?"

"As I said, Mr. Lightstrom and his family export the product to high bidders, but they are also the only producers of the substance. And since star-dust is already extremely rare, only a few pounds of fairy dust are produced every year. The supply that is bought by the Superiority is also heavily regulated. I'm sure only the Premier has unlimited access to it."

Rosie thought of Kingsley, how he happened to pop in and out of the school whenever he wanted. Then she remembered his request.

"Mr. Flame, I need to talk to you about the Premier," Rosie asked, ensuring Christion's identity remain hidden in case someone overheard.

Christion turned to her, interest jumping behind his eyes, but before she could continue, a splitting crack filled the air.

Rosie at first looked up to the sky, thinking lightning had struck, but the sky was clear. It wasn't until a painful scream sounded, and she found the source of the crack.

In his half-transformed state, a boy from Astive sat with one intact wing and the other crookedly placed, pointing out from his side.

Moving through the group that circled him, Christion kneeled by the boy's side and examined the damage.

"I'm going to count to three," he said to the wincing boy,

"and I'm going to reset your wing. Okay?"

Grimacing, the boy nodded and then, without uttering one number, Christion popped the wing back into place, sending another scream from the boy.

Kneeling on his other side, Rosie helped the boy to his feet.

"Rosie, get him to Doctor Geller. He should be able to mend that wing in no time."

"B-but w-what about the ritual," the boy spat out.

"Thankfully," Christion responded, "you don't have the same time restraints as some of your other classmates, and as soon as you get a clean bill of health you can resume transforming until it is painless, and then we can complete the ritual. Now go, get rest."

Wrapping a small blanket around his waist, the boy allowed Rosie to help him. As she ushered the boy down the mountainside, Rosie thought about her dad and when and if she would have the opportunity to find out what he knows and what Kingsley knows about the impending collision of the two societies.

* * *

"You have exactly ten minutes before I need to meet my dad on the lakeside to assist with the mermaid ritual, so what do you want to do?" Rosie asked as she cozied up to Riley on a couch in the human lobby. She closed her eyes, and rested her head on his chest as he wrapped an arm around her side.

"Just rest. We can talk more after we get through this craziness." Stroking her hair back, he leaned down and

259

placed a light kiss on her head.

"Mmmm," she hummed, allowing herself to fall deeper into a sleep, but the door crashing open, and the grumbling of familiar voices brought her to a sitting position.

"I just don't understand why you can't delegate further now and have those you taught teach the others."

"It doesn't work like that, Eleanor," Garrett said, walking closer.

"You're the leader. It works however you want. Oh, hey guys," Eleanor said before plopping down on the couch opposite.

Rubbing her eyes, Rosie sat forward. "What's going on?"

"Garrett is working with the older wolves tonight and the younger ones tomorrow. He's hoping he is able to cure everyone in this one full moon span, but I told him to take it slow."

"Are they ready?" Rosie asked Garrett.

"The older ones? Definitely. The younger ones, I think, just need tonight to settle further. To try to gain control while transformed."

"Then do it."

"Rosie!" Eleanor exclaimed, sitting up. "If they aren't ready, then they will kill themselves."

"Or just become overly exhausted and can try during the next full moon," Garrett corrected.

"We can't be used as leverage against the Superiority. We need everyone to regain control. Speaking of which," Rosie said, checking her watch. "I need to head down. I'll see you later." She kissed Riley then stood.

"Good luck," Garrett called.

"You too."

Rosie stepped out of the natural dorm and ran down towards the ritual area. Tightening her jacket collar around her neck, Rosie let the slight chill in the air nip at her nose as she watched the subtle rippling of the lake.

"Hey, Rosie," Justin said, meeting her at her side.

"Hey." She hadn't spoken a lot to Justin over the last few days, but she was happy he was here tonight. "Christion call for more reinforcements?"

He let out a small laugh and brushed a hand through his brown, wispy hair. "Yeah, something like that."

"Any clue how we're going to get the mer-students corralled to even participate?"

As she asked the question, bubbling erupted on the surface of the water a few meters from the shore.

"Good, they came!" Christion boasted as he stepped down from the entrance steps and waded a few feet into the water with a bucket.

"Wait, do you want to be doing that?" Rosie asked, stepping forward.

"Stay back, Rosie. With the smell of blood in the air and soon to be hitting the water, you two shouldn't be any closer." Christion reached a hand into the bucket, and with a gardening shovel, he hoisted bloodied chum into the area surrounding him.

"What are you doing?" Rosie gasped, stepping forward again, but Justin now clamped onto her upper arm.

"Getting them clustered, of course." He emptied the bucket and came back to shore as the bubbling water, which was now fiendish splashing, engulfed the dead fish. "Well, that should be all of them."

Picking up a fishing net, Christion cast it over the group,

successfully covering each of the mer-students.

High-pitched wailing escaped the water and Rosie and Justin clamped their hands over their ears.

"Why don't we reel them in?" Christion asked, laughing, now pulling in the haul.

"They won't be able to breathe! We can't take them out of the water."

"Mer-people, while most of the time highly intelligent, are also very stubborn and set in their ways. But they know, if they want to live, they will shift. Their will to survive is much more important to them than their desire to not be bested."

The flopping of tails and bodies being dragged up on the sand sent the three up the stairs.

Hissing began, and once it started the group laid on their stomachs and, in a formation, propped up on their elbows. Their black eyes rested on the three, anger and hatred pointed at them.

"Turn!" Christion bellowed.

Rosie searched the group, hoping one would cave in before running out of air, but their resolution remained solid.

"I said TURN!" Christion's voice thundered, and at the end, Rosie spotted Aquamarine and Cordelia screaming out as their tails were absorbed and legs formed.

"Justin, free them. Quickly!" Christion commanded.

Rosie followed to assist. One thing Rosie knew about mermaids was that if they didn't stick together, they would turn on each other instantly. Changing and falling out of rank, basically meant that Aquamarine and Cordelia deserted their peers.

Unwrapping the two and holding up the net, Justin and

Rosie pulled each out.

"Here," Rosie said, walking the two over to a stack of towels.

"Justin! Over here," she heard her dad yell.

Rushing back to his side, Justin grabbed a Surgent merman and handed him a towel.

One by one, each reluctantly turned to their human form, the last one passing out from waiting too long, but finally, all completed the transformation.

"He'll just need a moment," Christion explained. "Justin, go ahead and get started."

"Oh, um, okay." Justin turned to the frightened looking group who sat covered on the lakeside. "I'm sure you're each a bit confused and wanting to not necessarily remember the last few months." He cleared his throat and stepped forward, gaining confidence. "But, um, you should know that what was done is done, and no one holds you accountable for the actions of others. You were all forced into your primal state. Some of you even reverting to a deeper nature. Now that you are in your human state, your mind is clearer and a bit more rational. But you can't stay like this. If you want control over your gift, if you want to be accepted by the Superiority and not locked away, then you have to transform, again and again, until it is as easy as snapping your fingers."

He examined the group, their worn faces showing their young age. No one moved.

"I promise," Justin said to the unsure group, "we will help you the entire way and explain more afterwards." It was then that Cordelia stood and stepped forward, then sat closer to Justin, putting more distance between herself and the water. She laid the towel over her waist and legs.

A shout of agony escaped her, but her tail emerged from

beneath the towel, her fingers webbed, and gills emerged. Gasping for air she reached out to Justin.

Leaning down he grasped her hand and whispered, "I have you. Transform back."

His face winced as Cordelia's grip tightened as, once again, she reabsorbed the tail and other features.

Breathing heavily, Cordelia looked up at him and laughed. "How many more times?" she asked.

Justin laughed and after making sure she was okay, he stepped back. Others soon continued with the transformation.

Stepping back to Christion, Rosie couldn't help but ask, "That's why you had Justin help, isn't it? Because he's gone through something similar."

"He's a really great kid," Christion said to Rosie. "You're lucky he's your friend, and I know for a fact he is lucky you're his."

Blushing, Rosie grasped her jacket and tugged it in more then stepped down to see if any of the mer-students needed help.

The hours dragged on, but slowly, each student could transform in a matter of minutes, then seconds, then transform without showing an ounce of pain.

Cordelia, unsurprisingly, finished first, and when she went up to Justin to grab her moon water-charged crystal, she pressed her barely-covered body into him.

Strangely, Rosie's face grew hot at the sight. *She doesn't need to be that grateful,* Rosie thought, turning away to grab another necklace for a different student who was done.

I mean, I helped too.

"Wanna grab some breakfast after this?" Justin asked,

causing Rosie to jump and turn back to him.

"Oh, um. Yeah, that would be great," Rosie said, smiling up at him. The slight glow of the not-yet-risen sun shadowed Justin's features, and he smiled back at Rosie before picking up another necklace and walking back to another finished student.

"Thank you for assisting me, sweetie," Christion said, grasping his daughter around the shoulder. "I know we haven't had a lot of catch-up time, but how about dinner tonight? At your mom's place?"

"Yeah, that'd be great."

"Perfect. I'll let your mom know."

"Da- I mean, sir, what about Premier Kingsley?"

Christion looked around. "Think he is in his office?" Christion asked, staring up at the entrance to the school.

Rosie nodded, and the two looked over as the last student donned his necklace and headed inside.

"I suppose I'll go meet with him now." Grinning and winking at Rosie, he bounded up the steps and headed into the lobby.

Rosie was unsure if Kingsley was even on campus, but she had a feeling that Christion would make sure he had this conversation.

"Ready to go?" Justin asked at her side.

"Let's do it. Then we nap the rest of the day?" Rosie giggled.

"Definitely," Justin agreed as his hand found the small of her back.

The two moved through the empty lobby, passing scattered furniture and Francine's empty desk. Rosie then eyed the portrait above the desk and wondered what type of conversation was taking place within the hidden office.

"Have you seen the new dining hall yet? I heard Professor Shay revamped the ordering and delivery system."

"Really?" Rosie asked as she stepped sideways and watched Justin pull up the trap door to the hidden stairway. The two began to descend. Surprisingly, in between classes, training, teaching, and sleep, she had yet to see the new dining hall. Instead, she ordered all her food to her room and studied or ate with her dad or mom in town.

"Yeah, we can get a bit crazy with our orders and have a little celebratory brunch."

They moved through the hidden hallways nearing the dining hall.

"Celebrate, what?" Rosie asked as Justin found the door handle to the vast room and pulled the door open.

"Surprise!"

Shouts of laughter and joy reverberated off the tall walls, and Rosie stood shocked at the sight of the majority of her schoolmates sitting, waiting for her.

"What is happening?" Rosie asked, turning to Justin.

He stepped forward and led her to one of the tables where Riley, Eleanor, and Garrett sat, along with a big chunk of the Valtic team.

"We wanted to find some way to thank you."

Rosie laughed and walked next to Justin towards their seats as the applause continued.

Once she sat, the applause ceased, and Professor Shay stood to address the students.

"Everyone, welcome back to a somewhat normal restart of our school year."

"Professor Shay didn't get the memo," Justin whispered to Rosie, who chuckled softly.

"Now, I know the year thus far has been challenging, but now that everyone in this room has come to be in control of their power, the school year will resume as normal starting Monday."

There was a mixture of groans and cheers from the hall and Professor Shay continued on.

"New specialized schedules have been distributed to your rooms, and I expect each of you to raise any concern of your abilities to your advisors who are listed."

"Yeah!" Garrett yelled. "No ripping off of anyone's head!"

Scattered laughter sounded and Professor Shay sent a semiserious glare at Garrett but still grinned. "Anyway, in celebration of the majority of the school being back in tip-top learning shape, we are going to have quite the event tomorrow."

Rosie widened her eyes and stared at Eleanor, who scooted to the edge of her seat.

"Please say dance, please say dance," Eleanor whispered to herself.

Rosie turned her head back to Professor Shay.

"Tomorrow night, we will be doing a team-wide competition with each other. Surgent versus Haply versus Astive versus Valtic. Every team member will participate in a series of obstacles and challenges all culminating in a welcome back 'homecoming' dance."

"YES!" Eleanor shouted, shooting up from her seat. Her face flushed red, and she giggled as she sat back down.

"Yes, it's all very exciting! Now, the Illumination Team captains each have clues to the tasks at hand. I suggest you take today and tomorrow to work with your teams and see who will reach the finish first because whoever does not only gets to celebrate the night's fun but also will be exempt from the semester's finals!"

The hall vibrated with cheers at the announcement and didn't quiet down. Smiling at her pupils, Professor Shay waved her hands, and from thin air, a brunch feast filled each table, and the students began to eat.

The air was light and the tension and fear that once settled across the group months ago was gone.

Rosie filled up her plate, and as she ate, students from every grade, team, and kind came up and thanked her.

Not knowing how to react she smiled at each and gave a small nod, stuffing more food in her mouth or sipping her coffee.

"Hey, Rosie, after you take a nap and re-energize, let's regroup on strategy for tomorrow's games," Garrett said then slammed a huge slice of french toast in his mouth.

"Garrett, give the girl a day to recover. Since Mr. Flare showed—" Rosie shot a look at Eleanor who quickly corrected herself. "I mean Mr. Flame, she has been going nonstop trying to get the school back in order. At least let her chill."

"But—" Garrett protested, but Eleanor continued.

"No buts. She can catch up on the plan tomorrow morning. Until then, you have me and of course, Justin. Sorry, Riley." Eleanor smirked and took a sip of juice.

"No need to apologize. I have my own team to worry about."

"Hey, Rosie," a voice behind her seat said. Rosie turned and found Drew standing tall.

"Hey, Drew. Any news on your sister?"

"Actually, that's what I wanted to chat with you about.

Mind moving to a less populated area?" He jerked his head sideways and started moving away from the group.

"Sure." Rosie stood and slid her chair out, following the boy.

Walking to the far end of an empty table, the group sat and perched up, trying to hear anything they could.

"I've been trying to send out messages to her. Dana. I stupidly tried her cell but it had been deactivated, so I tried her old one—the one prior to being accepted—and it worked, but I know she knew it was me. It went to voicemail, and I left a message and texts but haven't heard anything back."

"Did you try anything else?"

"Of course. Next, I went to our old meeting spot where we would discuss the intel we learned. I left a scroll for her in a hollow saguaro. After sitting there for a few weeks, I decided to return to our last home."

"With all the other creatures in your clan?"

Drew nodded and continued, "I just missed them. The air was still filled with their scent, and the fires from the camps were still warm."

"So, another dead end?"

"That's what I thought, but I found a symbol traced on a tree trunk."

"What's that supposed to mean?" Rosie inquired.

"When we were kids, Dana and I made up a secret language. That way, even when transformed, and our minds were on display, no one knew what we were thinking. The symbol left was one of ours. She left me a message."

"What was it? What was the message?"

"Death."

"Death?" Rosie asked. "What else was there?"

"That's it. The only symbol she wrote was death."

"Do you have any idea what that means?"

"It could be someone in the clan passed, or they're moving on to richer land, or…"

"Or what?"

"Or they're preparing to move on the Superiority. They are preparing for a fight."

"We have to warn my dad," Rosie said, standing up.

"Premier Kingsley already knows. I made sure he was the first. He was with Christion when I told him and, as far as I know, they both are making plans. I even think your dad is on his way to track the clan and see if he can get a better read on the situation. Ease any tension."

"Drew, thank you. I know staying here and telling Premier Kingsley must have been difficult for you," Rosie said.

Standing up, he rubbed his arm. "Not like I had much of a choice. My family has shunned me for staying. As far as I'm concerned this is my new clan. This is my new family." He stalked off, and Rosie stood soon after.

"Where are you going?" Riley said as he joined her. She moved toward the staircase, to go up to Kingsley's office.

"I was going to—"

"You are going to bed. As far as I'm concerned, your dad and the Premier have it covered."

"You heard?"

"I was near you. Neither of you noticed. You should really be more observant." A cocky grin spread over his face and Rosie shook her head as he continued, "Plus, there might not even be a threat. It could be a misunderstanding on Drew's side. Even he wasn't sure what the message was."

"But—"

"No. Bed. Now. Or do I need to call Olive over here to escort you?"

Rosie grinned and threw her hands up in surrender.

"I got it, don't worry." She smiled and gave him a kiss before walking out of the room towards her dorm.

Joy filled her as she passed cured students gathering not only in the dining hall, but the library, team living room, and dorm lobby.

Honestly, the idea of her plush bed sounded like heaven, and as she walked, she wondered if she could reach her ancestor in the dream realm. Then she remembered her promise to Riley. Immediately, she shut the idea down. As she entered her room and closed the blinds, she realized that she hadn't yet learned to control her dreams. She wasn't an experienced lucid dreamer, and whoever decided to enter her subconscious could do so willingly.

She sat on the thought in bed only momentarily before she escaped into the deep slumber she desperately needed.

Chapter Twenty-Two

To Rosie's disappointment, her sleep was long, deep, and dreamless. As her eyes cracked open, Rosie sat up. The room was pitch-black, and Olive's restful breaths filled the silent air.

Finding her phone and reading the time displayed, Rosie hopped out of bed and quietly threw on her shoes and a sweatshirt.

Four in the morning. She had slept through the entire Friday and had missed strategizing for the night's games and dinner with her parents. Entering the bright hallway of the dorm, Rosie squinted her eyes, but kept moving even as they adjusted.

Reaching the lobby, she entered the mountainside and breathed the cool fresh air.

"Finally," she whispered, closing her eyes and taking in the sounds of crickets, birds singing, and the babbling of the nearby creek.

She headed up and over a small hill then carefully walked down the backside of the mountain towards Kingstown. More than anything she wanted to see her mom, especially after missing dinner. She checked her messages and sitting in her phone was a text from her mom saying she knew where she was and to get rest.

But now all Rosie wanted was to curl up on the couch with her mom and talk about the dance.

"Do you think you're going somewhere?" a clipped voice asked from behind her.

Spinning on her heels, she found Dana stood only a few feet away.

Rosie opened her mouth to speak but from behind, a long, thick, hairy arm reached around her and placed its giant hand with a palmed cloth over her mouth. As she tried to scream, she smelled a harsh scent and instantly her mind fogged and eyes closed.

* * *

"You're sure she's important to the Premier?" a gruff voice asked.

"Yes, he carries her file around with him and has gone to the school a lot more since she started." The second voice was a calm, even-toned woman's.

"Plus, she is an amalgam," Rosie heard Dana add.

As far as Rosie knew, she was taken by the clan. A black bag sat over her head and her feet and hands were bound to the chair she sat in.

"You don't have to ransom me or hurt me," she called from under the hood. "I want to help you if I can."

Movement in the room halted and a single pair of feet creaked the floorboards, growing closer to Rosie.

Unsure if speaking up was a good idea or bad one, she held her breath in case a blow was coming, but bright light hit her eyes and she squinted and closed them, spots swirling behind her eyelids.

"Good, you're awake. Now you can tell us what the Premier is planning to do about our group."

Blinking her eyes to adjust them to her surroundings, she took in the makeshift interrogation room she sat in. The room resembled an office, but on the desk a lamp pointed at her, making it difficult to see who stood behind it.

"Dana, I know you're here. Can we please stop with the theatrics?" Rosie asked, holding back an eye roll.

One of the figures nodded to another and they all stood up, which was strange because Rosie assumed they were already standing. That's when Rosie took in the high ceilings, large furniture, and huge bowls of food set out along a far table.

Stepping in front of the desk on both sides were ten foot tall, big handed and footed, hairy all over men. Widening her eyes at being in such close proximity to the sasquatches, Rosie couldn't help but study them. Her attention fell from them though as Dana stepped out behind the one on the right and a man and woman stepped out on the left.

"Hello, Rosie," the man said, moving closer to her. At average height and bald, Rosie wondered if he was in fact a sasquatch, or a different creature allied and traveling with the clan. His wire-rimmed glasses sat in the middle of his nose and his dark features made the whites of his eyes pop. He crossed his arms and stepped closer and as he did so, he placed his hand in his pocket and drew out a serrated knife.

"Um, woah, wait," Rosie stammered, and Dana belted out a laugh.

"Ms. Connors, please," the man said, and he cut the ties off her hands and feet.

Rosie caressed her wrists and as she did, she sized up the two guards again.

"Earth to Rosie," Dana said and snapped her fingers.

Rosie turned her head to meet Dana's and bubbling rage caused her to leap up and grab the girl.

A shriek erupted from Dana's throat but as soon as Rosie's hands grasped Dana's shoulders, Rosie had two sets of hands haul her back to the chair.

"Settle down now!" the man yelled, now glaring at the two girls.

"Do you know what you've put your brother through! He's been killing himself trying to find you, trying to make sure you're okay. What kind of sister does that to their sibling?"

Dana chuckled and simply replied, "Probably the same kind of person who would ditch their mom when things got a little rough."

Heat rose to Rosie's cheeks, and she attempted to stand again but two hands sat on her shoulders making it impossible to move.

"Dana. You are a distraction. Leave."

"But—"

"Now." The man gritted his teeth and Rosie realized the chance she once had to have a decent conversation was now gone.

"Raphael," the woman spoke, "let us move on." She wrapped a hand around his bicep, and he eased into her. Nodding gently, he refocused on Rosie and leaned against the desk.

"Rosie Connors, daughter of Christion Flare. Intellect, witch, and Premier Kingsley's pet."

"I have no idea where you got the idea that I am the Premier's *pet,* but your intel is sorely mistaken." Rosie eyed the woman and her eyes widened. This wasn't the first time the two had crossed paths. During last year's attacks, when the Superiority agents came to campus to investigate, she was there. She was a spy.

Raphael turned to the woman. "Jules?"

"She doesn't know."

He nodded and spoke to Rosie again.

"Ms. Connors, Christion has spoken highly of you. He used to travel with us, making sure our community remained safe and were treated decently. During our travels, as you know, our kind tend to be nomadic, although that isn't necessarily by choice. Christion talked about his lost love and daughter. How he would reunite with you. How he would unite the different species. How he would lead our world into a new coming. Ha. Well, I can't fault him for dreaming."

"It could happen," Rosie muttered under her breath.

"It could, could it?" Raphael eyed Jules and the two broke into a fit of laughter.

Shooting her head up Rosie continued, "The Premier wants peace. He wants you to join. It's your group that wants to fight. That is too stubborn to accept the Superiority's offer."

"Us? Refuse an offer? There has been no offer," Raphael spat. His voice grew hard, and his knuckles cracked as his hand formed a tight fist.

"The Premier has been lying to you, Rosie," the woman said, stepping forward. "I work at the Superiority, as you've deduced by now. I sit in on council meetings and strategy sessions, in which it is discussed how best to 'handle' our kind. If we should be designated to confined areas, exiled from cities where beacons are, or just eliminated completely. The only offers extended to us have been to leave. Find a new home. Keep traveling. Our kind wants to settle, but we can't without being a part of the Superiority, and they don't want us."

"No, you're wrong. That doesn't make any sense. You joining the Superiority would only strengthen it. More people to tax, more people to join services, a set of new skills to be utilized—"

"You don't get it. We are seen as lesser. Not the same as you. And after seeing the Premier's attitude towards us. We don't want to join the Superiority if he is in charge. But will if the right person is."

Rosie turned to Jules. "Has the Premier disclosed his disdain for your group? Say you are lesser? Not try to extend a helping hand?"

"Not directly but he's a political player. He lets others speak for him, so he doesn't get dirty himself."

"But that is just an assumption. The truth is you have no idea what he thinks. I'm sure during your time at the Superiority, trying to do anything of importance, something of this magnitude, needs not just discussion, but voting, lobbying, and backdoor deal-making. If you are insinuating that the Premier must step down or you will fight for him to do so, then you're crazy. He won't and no citizen under his reign will want him to. People will die for him and he can't, so your position is futile. We shouldn't even get that far. Just try speaking with him again. You have his ear clearly. Tell him who you are. He will help."

"The sixteen-year-old girl thinks she knows more than us,

Raphael." The two smirked and faced Rosie again.

"Can I leave? Or am I a prisoner?"

"You can leave whenever you want. But first, I need you to send a message back to your precious Premier. Tell him to let us in and to step down, or else blood will be shed."

Before Rosie could reply, a cloth similar to what she was covered with before doused her senses and she passed out.

* * *

"Rosie! Rosie!"

Coming to, Rosie blinked her eyes open and Premier Kingsley bent over her.

"Premier?"

"Oh, thank goodness you're okay. Whatever are you doing here?"

"Um?" she shot up on the plush couch she lay upon and spun her head around the room. The grand office sat in a circle coming to a point in the ceiling. A desk with a high-backed chair was placed in the middle of the room and a long table with chairs surrounding it was diagonally across from the desk. Painted on the desk was the entire state, and little figures stood in various locations.

"Rosie?"

"Am I at the Superiority offices?"

"Yes. In my office to be exact. Why are you here? How are you here?"

The events of the previous few hours came rushing back to her and she sprang up.

"Premier! The clan! I was taken by them. To give you a message. Jules, I mean I don't know what she calls herself here, but she's one of them and they said they're ready to fight if you don't step down and—"

"Rosie. Please come sit. Take a drink of water."

Rosie moved back to the couch and grabbed the glass of water that Kingsley extended. Drinking it all in only a few gulps, she caught her breath and started over.

"There are individuals in the Superiority who aren't technically a part of the Superiority."

"Okay? Care to elaborate further?"

"Sasquatches, banshees, elves, even spirits are working for the Superiority. Well, technically for but not actually for. They are collecting intel and distributing it back to the higher-ups in the clan. Raphael."

"You know who Raphael is?" Kingsley sat in his chair now, studying Rosie as she spoke.

"I met him. He, a woman named Jules, Dana, and two sasquatches grabbed me as I was heading to Kingstown to see my mom early this morning. Speaking of which, what time is it anyway?" She swiveled her head and found a grandfather clock. "It's three already!"

"Rosie, please. What else?"

Taking a breath, she calmed herself and continued, "Raphael, he said that you never offered or went to the group and asked them to join the Superiority. Is that true?"

"Rosie, it's complicated."

"What? They are ready to start a war! How complicated can it be to not get thousands of people killed."

"There's still a subset of people in our society. Those who believe they are truly superior."

"Mm, ironic. Superiority hiring superiors."

"The name isn't to reflect that we are better than anyone but rather to let people know that there needs to be a hierarchy in society. That to have order someone needs to be in charge."

"I know that, but it should also not dictate the lives of the minority. It should be present to serve all who fall under it. The Superiority, you Premier, serve at the pleasure of all supernatural creatures."

"That's very true, but I also need the various council members, who were elected by their own respective communities, to serve in *their* best interest, to sign off on new tax structuring, housing accommodations, jobs, wages, and a plethora of other details that go into forming a relationship with new species such as this. We can't just accept thousands in without a plan."

Rosie nodded. "But was an offer ever given? Was there any communication?"

"Of course there was. I extended the opportunity to join the Superiority when we had the capability and ability to do so."

"And we're no longer capable?"

"Unfortunately, no. But it is something which we are close to accomplishing again. In the view of Raphael though, that wasn't good enough. He wants immediacy and this is something we just aren't prepared for, but plan to be in the future."

"What are you going to do?"

"What else did he say? To be welcomed under a new regime basically?"

"He wants you to step down as Premier."

"Well, that isn't going to happen. I don't take kindly to

these types of threats." Kingsley stood up and paced, his hand resting on his chin. Looking up he walked towards the door. "Thank you for telling me, Rosie. Was there anything else you can remember?"

Yeah, they want Christion in charge.

"No, nothing else I can think of."

"Alright. Well, since I have you and in the spirit of full transparency, I know Christion Flare is your dad and I think it's spectacular that such a knowledgeable man has rejoined us after centuries in the background."

"Do you have a plan with how you're going to treat his presence?"

"We've discussed that. Right now, it might be best to keep his true identity from the Superiority. As of now, Christion Flame is a registered Vampire-Wizard Amalgam who has been assisting in foreign relationships and working deep undercover as a Superiority agent."

"So, he's safe? I mean, he has a place?"

"For a man who is an immortal wizard and who has founded multiple discoveries within our world, yes. He has a place."

"Okay, thank you. Will he stay around, you think?"

"For right now, his place is at my side for special missions and at the school, near you and your mother. I have a few assignments I could use his assistance on."

"Anything that could help dissolve tensions with Raphael?"

"I can't reveal the specifics."

"Use him."

"Really?" Kingsley cocked an eyebrow and continued, "You would give up spending time with your father?"

"If it kept Raphael from attacking anyone and could help

resolve the matter, then yes."

"Rosie, you continue to surprise me."

A small grin appeared on Rosie's face and as Kingsley stepped towards her, she stood.

"Why don't we get you back to campus?" He moved to a small, circular box on the corner of his desk and lifted the lid. It was filled to the top with black, sparkly sand which Rosie assumed could only be fairy dust. "Ready?"

"What do I do?"

"Just think about the entrance to the school. I'll throw this over you and when you open your eyes you'll be there." Rosie nodded and closed her eyes, visualizing the lakeside.

She heard the calm rippling of waves, the rustling of bushes as the wind blew, and the chatter of students in the distance.

Opening her eyes, just like Kingsley had said, she stood at the bottom step of the school's entrance. She stepped up and made her way to the Valtic library.

It was now close to four and Rosie still didn't know when the games were starting or what they would be doing.

Entering the room, filled with her Valtic teammates, she searched for Garrett.

"Where have you been?" he yelled across the room. "Never mind! Get over here! The games are in two hours, and we have a plan."

Rosie ran over to the forty or so huddled students and stared at the displayed white board. Scanning the scribbles, she could tell that the group would be divided into seven smaller teams, each tasked with a different challenge. She searched for her name and found it listed with Justin.

"Just us two?" she asked him, smiling as he walked to her side.

"Yep, just us. We are probably going to have to solve some impossible puzzle, according to Garrett. You been asleep this whole time?"

Rosie laughed and then lowered her voice. "It's a long story but I just left the Premier's office."

"What happened?" Justin asked, turning to her, furrowing his brows.

"It's okay, I'm okay. Just fill me in here. What happens when everyone finishes their tasks?"

Justin cocked an eyebrow but gave in. "If the task is completed successfully, then we'll be transported to wait and see who wins. If we win first, then we get to the dance first and no tests. Kind of a lame prize."

Rosie laughed and asked, "Do we play the games dressed up or do we just show up as we are?"

"Professor Shay instructed us to wear what we need in order to win, and the rest will be taken care of."

"Oh, Professor Shay, she is a sly one."

"That she is—"

"You guys!" Garrett yelled over the two chatting. "Do you know what kind of puzzle you'll be solving?"

Rosie and Justin looked at each other and then shook their heads.

"Then I suggest you start studying and figure out what Professor Shay and Professor Walker have in store for you."

Garrett turned away and continued from group to group, interrogating each. The two laughed at Garrett's stern expression as he did so but then focused. Together they wandered the library and searched for any clue that would indicate what they would be facing.

"Was there any other hint at what our challenge could be?"

"Included in the package Garrett got, there was basic instructions saying that all team members who were able, A-K-A had their powers in check, needed to be involved. Also, that the tasks would be like the games but since there were more players, then there would be more tasks, and that each task was supposed to be related to the next. Finally, like normal, there were a handful of different items—seven of them—that indicated what the tasks could be."

"And you guys have a good idea of each challenge?"

"Every one, except ours."

"Were there any leftover clues?"

"No, everything was deduced but we know there are eight challenges."

"So, seven tasks figured out, and ours is the only one we have no clue what it could be?"

"Yep!"

"Ha. Well, that's just great. What were the clues?"

"They were dolls."

"Dolls?"

"Of different creatures."

"But only seven?"

"Yeah, there was a vampire, werewolf, shifter, mermaid, fairy, witch, and protector."

"But no intellect?"

He shook his head and Rosie said, "We need the dolls." She paced back down the stairs to where the rest of the team was.

"What are you thinking, Rosie?"

Instead of answering she collected the dolls from the table and brought them to an empty one nearby.

"Hey, what's going on?" Garrett asked, moving towards the two.

"Rosie might have an idea of what our task is."

"Care to share, Rosie?"

"Just give me a sec," she responded as she lined up each doll in a row. She examined each with just her eyes, then one by one picked them up and tried to find anything out of the ordinary. Passing over them at first, everything seemed normal, but as she grasped the witch, she noticed an almost invisible seam around one of the hands. She pulled on it and the hand popped off. She moved to the next doll and another limb came off that one and it happened to the next, and the next.

"Woah, remind me not to let you ever get near my Madame Alexander collection," Eleanor said as she walked up to the table.

"What do you think it means? Do we need to reevaluate our plans?" Garrett asked.

"No," Rosie muttered. "This is for us. Justin, do you see anything."

Justin, who had also been examining each piece, moved forward. "Excuse me," he said, smiling at Rosie as she stepped aside.

Piece by piece, Justin laid out some pieces on the table in the middle and pushed others aside until what was left sent a shock wave through Rosie.

"Woah," Eleanor whispered, moving forward.

"Does that mean what I think it means?" Justin asked Rosie.

Nodding her head up and down she stared at Justin before staring back down.

The thing he created had one leg of a wolf, the other of a vampire, the torso of a fairy, an arm and hand of a mermaid, the other arm of a shifter, and finally, the hand of a witch.

"Where's the head?" Eleanor asked.

Rosie and Justin turned up to her and she realized what the challenge was.

"So," Justin started with a chuckle, "think I have what it takes to be a wizard?"

Chapter Twenty-Three

"A freaking amalgam," Garrett exclaimed. "How in the world does Shay expect one of you to become an amalgam in one freaking night!"

"Maybe that's not what it is at all," Eleanor said. "I mean, Rosie is already an amalgam. Just having her around will make the task complete."

"I don't think so," Rosie said, eyeing Justin with concern. "Justin, do you think you can handle this challenge? Missing exams isn't worth either of us dying."

"I'll be okay!" Justin reassured her.

"Garrett, give us a sec," Rosie said, and Eleanor and Garrett walked away leaving Rosie and Justin sitting in a far corner, away from the rest of the group. "How much have you been practicing?" she asked, her foot tapping.

"What?" he asked, rubbing his hand across the back of his neck.

"Justin, don't insult me."

"I know, I know," Justin said, wringing his hands together. "Since I was cured. I mean, a little bit before, with Egil. But I didn't touch magic again until I knew I could be in control. That I was stable enough to handle it."

"How far have you progressed?"

Justin snapped his fingers and a tiny spark appeared as the two fingers brushed together.

"I know it's not a lot but—"

Rosie widened her eyes. She knew one day it would be possible for Justin to channel enough of his mind and power into becoming a wizard, but she had no idea he had already reached that extent of power. "No, Justin, that's amazing. Incredible! You have no direct line or aren't a descendant of any witch or wizard?"

"From what I could find on my family, no."

"That means you learned how to harness magic without having any inclination towards it at all." A goofy grin spread across his face and his cheeks reddened. "Do you feel anything when you practice? Magic pulling you?"

"There's a warmth. A buildup of energy in my core whenever I try to use it."

"Any pain?"

"Not really. Just a pins and needles-type of feeling."

"Okay."

"Okay?"

"Yep, okay."

"Okay, what? What are you thinking, Rosie?"

"I'm thinking that tonight, you become a full-blown wizard."

"Rosie, what? How? We can't do that?"

"Of course we can. You're going to pull on that magic. You're going to bubble it all up to the surface and expel all that you can. Then siphon."

Justin nodded his head in agreement, then asked, "Is it going to hurt?"

"I'm hoping that since yours is just developing there isn't too much and it won't be crazy bad. But, honestly, I don't know."

Justin nodded and then looked up at the clock. "Well, we have thirty minutes to prepare as much as possible. Show me how to pull the magic forward."

Rosie smiled and grabbed his hands. His smooth, warm hands caressed hers and she examined his palms before resting hers in his.

"Okay, try to shock me."

Pulling his hand back, he exclaimed, "No! I said I wouldn't hurt you again."

"Justin," she said as she pulled his hand up from his lap and into hers. "I am giving you permission. You won't hurt me. I have a shield up. All I will feel is a very mild pinch. Now, shock me."

"Are you sure—"

"Shock me, Justin!"

At her command, Rosie watched a wave of magic surge through Justin's body. As it did so, his eyes clamped shut and he gritted his teeth while groaning. A pulse of energy left his palms and hit hers.

Whipping her hands back from the intense electricity still lingering around Justin, she shook them and grabbed his hands again, this time holding them.

"Justin?"

He opened his eyes and shook out his head and shoulders.

"Justin, are you okay?"

"Yeah, I think so."

"Okay. Well, the good news is you will be able to call up all your magic. The bad news is, it's going to hurt. A lot."

"Fantastic."

"You guys ready to get going?" Garrett asked, the rest of the Valtic team looking at them from the main table.

Both nodded and stood, following Garrett back to the group.

"Okay, everyone, split off into your groups."

For the first time, Rosie noticed that the teams were divided by creature type.

"They're going to have to demonstrate their control, huh?" Rosie asked Justin as the two stood closer together to create gaps on both sides to differentiate from each group.

"Yeah, I think Professor Shay just wants to make sure everyone who is back in class actually should be."

Rosie rolled her eyes and remained quiet as Garrett called for their attention.

"Okay everyone. One of the teachers will be here shortly to take us to the start. Break off as soon as you can to your respective testing points."

"How did you guys figure out where you each needed to go?" Rosie asked Justin, leaning a little closer.

Tilting his head down, his eyes no longer on Garrett but on Rosie, he replied, "We deduced they were the areas where each kind normally hangs out or goes. There was only one location for each that everyone in the species at the school had been."

"The places where they did their rituals."

"Exactly."

Just then, a door to the room opened, and Professor Walker entered.

"She's back," Rosie whispered, staring at her professor. *I wonder how the new protectors and intellects tested, if they're staying at the Superiority.*

"Hello, Valtics," Professor Walker said to the group.

Nods and greetings echoed in the library until silence overwhelmed the anxious bunch again.

"Everyone grab your doll, or what's left of it," Garrett said, a person from each subgroup grabbing their respective creature doll and shifting from foot to foot.

Rosie stared back down at the creature she held and stared up at Justin. He smirked and both turned to Professor Walker.

Professor Walker rubbed her palms together and then separated them wide and high over her head, and a shimmering gold mist fell over the group. As the magic hit Rosie, a tingling sensation swept through her but then her skin rose in goosebumps from a chill.

"When you arrive at your destination, your bodies will warm. When you've completed your assigned tasks, your bodies will return to normal and you'll be taken to the dance," Professor Walker instructed, and then she glanced at the watch on her wrist. "You may start."

Quick, shuffling feet scattered throughout the room as Valtic members left in all directions, hoping to reach their destination faster than the other teams. When everyone but Justin, Rosie, and Professor Walker had gone, Rosie stepped forward and turned to Justin.

"To the safe rooms?" she asked.

"To the safe rooms," Justin answered.

Rosie smiled at Professor Walker, but Professor Walker raised an eyebrow in confusion as the two headed to the classroom levels.

"We are supposed to go to the safe rooms, right?" Rosie

asked Justin as she stepped through the portrait and into the empty dining hall. Their footsteps echoed across the vast room and Justin slowed. The safe rooms had been created by the staff for the witch and wizard students to safely practice expelling and regaining their magic. It seemed the most logical place to go in order to assist Justin in becoming an amalgam.

"Yeah. I mean, where else would we go? The other wizards and witches will be in the lunar circle rather than the safe rooms so wouldn't we go there?"

"It's just the way Professor Walker watched us as we left. It seemed like she couldn't figure out what we were doing."

"Well, how do you feel? Are you warming up at all? I'm still cold."

"Same." The two halted as they entered the dim staircase.

"Should we try going down?" Justin asked, taking two steps down towards the rooms. He turned back to Rosie to see if she agreed but they met eye to eye, and Rosie stared into Justin's deep green eyes. A second passed and then a few more. Rosie leaned forward, Justin remaining still. Something had always drawn her to him. His intellect, their similarities, his plump lips. Riley popped into her mind, and as she stumbled back, he did too.

Landing on her butt a few stairs up, Rosie watched as Justin stumbled down a few more steps.

"Rosie—" Justin started, trying to help her up.

"No, I got it," she said, jumping to her feet and stepping back. She turned and looked up the staircase.

"Rosie, I think-" he started again, but she cut him off.

"Let's not discuss what just happened until later, huh?"

"Yeah, okay sure, but I was just going to say, either the

staircase has a mean draft, or we need to head up and not down."

"Oh." She whipped around to Justin who sent her a small grin and shrug. Unsure whether he was right or not she stepped down to the same stair he stood on and shuddered from a coldness sweeping through her. She then bounded up a few stairs and the chilliness subsided.

"Up we go," she said.

Leading the way and pushing up through the trap door, Rosie thought about where they would end up. As they crossed the threshold and closed the door, pulsating music reverberated throughout the room.

"Guess we found where the dance is," Justin said, and he stared at the thumping door.

Rosie neared it and grasped the doorknob, but she let go of it instantly as she cried in pain at the singeing of her skin.

"Ah," she grimaced, cupping her palm and staring at the ornate design now etched into her skin.

"Let me see," Justin said gently, grasping her palm, and pulling it up towards his face. Heat from Professor Walker's spell, her fresh burn, and Justin's proximity rushed to Rosie's cheeks.

"I think it will heal. The markings are already fading, but we can go see Doctor Geller if you want," Justin said, still holding onto Rosie.

"No, um. I'll be okay." Rosie grinned and examined her hand in Justin's. He was right. Sure enough, the marks were receding, and her palm was returning to its normal shade.

"Rosie?"

"Yes?" she asked, staring back up at Justin.

"I was curious if maybe…" Before he could finish, a loud

boom erupted as the trap door swung open and Garrett jumped through.

The two intellects parted fast and stared at Garrett followed by a handful of other Valtic werewolves hopping through the door, followed by the shifters.

"Awesome! Have any other groups made it back?"

"What?" Rosie asked.

"Um, no. Just us," Justin answered, moving towards Garrett.

"Okay. How was your trial?" Garrett asked in a lowered tone.

Justin turned to Rosie and then back to Garrett, shaking his head. "We didn't do it."

"What? I mean, do you still feel cold? Are you in the right place?"

"We both feel extremely, erm, hot," Rosie said, moving closer. "How do you feel? Is Professor Walker's spell still on you?"

"Yes. I mean, we are all hot too. What does that mean?"

"I know," Justin said, turning away before starting again. "The test was not to obsess. To move forward and not dwell on what the solution to the problem was but to just move on. To find the dance and enjoy it."

Justin raised his eyes and met Rosie's. Clear disappointment sat behind them, but he shook his head and widened his smile. "Hey, I don't think I hear anyone at the dance yet. No voices or footsteps. Just the music so we are still in the running to win."

As he said it, Eleanor popped through the trap door with the vampires and mermaids.

"Great!" Garrett yelled, and ran to pull Eleanor into a

kiss. As more Valtic members entered, the room began to get crowded and caused everyone to have flushed faces as the spell still stuck to them until the last of their team made it.

"Who's missing?" Eleanor asked, running to Rosie's side.

"The fairies and witches." But like magic, both groups appeared, entering the room through the never-ending hallway door.

"We're here!" Garrett yelled and Professor Walker appeared. The group quieted and stared at Professor Walker's serious face.

"What's going to happen?" Garrett asked, unsure if the challenge at hand had been completed.

Professor Walker grinned and held both hands high and waved them over the group as she had when the games started.

A refreshing coolness swept over Rosie, and Garrett ran to open the door to the lobby.

"Garrett, wait!" she called but to her relief, as he snatched the knob, he pulled the door open, and the thumping of music grew and extended to the room.

Placing an arm around Eleanor, he led the group into the room which had been completely transformed for all the students to dance, relax, and get back to enjoying their school year.

"Rosie!" Riley called, running across the room. Justin gave a small squeeze to her wrist and separated off.

As Riley approached, he eyed Justin but turned to Rosie, "You made it!"

"What? Only because we have more supernatural types on our team!"

"Whatever. You guys are the last! I mean, what were you doing? Dawdling?"

Riley laughed and his award-winning smile lit up his entire demeanor.

A small twinge of anger and annoyance fluttered in, but she shook it away and tried to smile as she searched the crowd. Every student on the other teams was dancing, laughing, drinking punch, or eating snacks.

"Who are you looking for?" Riley asked, attempting to follow her gaze.

She stared back up at him before turning back to the crowd and spotting Eleanor.

"There." She pointed and pulled him along towards the group.

The two maneuvered through the sea of students and Rosie looked overhead. The clear night sky showed through the glass ceiling and Rosie suddenly had the urge to lay out and stargaze.

"Rosie!" Eleanor yelled. "I can't believe we came in last!"

Rosie laughed and leaned in, "Right? It's just because we cared more about the overall goal of the challenge."

Eleanor snorted and rolled her eyes laughing. "Yeah, sure. Hey, Garrett mentioned that Justin didn't turn."

"Turn?" Riley interjected. "What do you mean?"

"Oh, he's an amalgam," Eleanor said then sauntered off.

"Um yeah," Rosie said, noticing a quick change in Riley's demeanor. Now stiff and stepping back with both eyebrows raised, Rosie thought she should continue, "He's a wizard. Well, will be once I work with him and he expels his magic."

"You can't be serious?"

"What?" Rosie stepped back and crossed her arms.

"Rosie, I can list over a hundred reasons why helping Justin fulfill his sick wizard dreams is a bad idea. How can you not see that?" Riley stepped back further, crossing his own arms, his face contorting with concern. "Are you going to help him?"

"I mean, yeah. I was going to. If he doesn't get his power under control, then he can hurt himself."

"Or he can just drop the magic thing, can't he? Stop before he progresses further and give it up."

"I guess, but why should he?"

"Why? Rosie, are you freaking kidding me?" Riley threw his hands up in the air and shook his head. "If you don't see anything wrong here then go. Help him. But don't come to me when everything goes sideways." He stalked off into the surrounding crowd.

Rosie stepped toward his direction but stopped, anger now filling her. She couldn't believe that after Justin had proved himself loyal, had changed, been back to normal, controlled his intellectual mind, that Riley could act this way.

Huffing a ragged breath, she moved in the opposite direction through the crowd. Bodies bumped into her as she weaved around them, and many others greeted her, but her focus was on one thing only and she spotted him.

She marched up to the seat he was in and bent down so he could hear her over the raging music.

"Want to do this or what?" She extended a hand to him, and he gripped it as he stood.

Justin stared down at Rosie, their bodies close together before he leaned down and whispered in her ear, "Lead the way."

Chapter Twenty-Four

Rosie led Justin by the hand as the two navigated through the lobby, pushed out the front doors, and jumped onto the lake bankside.

"Where are we going exactly?" Justin asked as he continued to be pulled by Rosie.

The two passed lingering groups and students who were sneaking off, much like them, but not to do what they were planning. Hopping through the surrounding desert and entering a shifted mountainside which now resembled forest rather than desert, Justin paused.

"Rosie, stop. What's wrong?"

Rosie stopped and paced a few feet ahead. Gaining her composure, she turned back. "I just think we need to get you to your fullest power."

"Oh, um, okay. Thanks." A hand shot to his hair and weaved through it, and he continued, "But I need to know… why now?"

She stepped towards him and in a firm voice said, "Because you are good. And like how my past doesn't define me, yours doesn't either."

Justin nodded before saying in a heartful tone, "Thank you,

Rosie. You don't even realize what that means to me."

Giving him a small grin she said, "Come on, we're going to get you to control your magic."

Before she could step forward, towards where a clearing would be in the forest, twigs snapped behind them.

She peered around Justin and running in their direction, at full speed, was Riley.

Ramming his body into Justin's, Riley threw Justin and himself into the trunk of a tree. Justin emitted a groan and Rosie searched Riley's eyes, but all Rosie saw was pure hatred.

"Riley, get off!" Justin yelled just before a punch landed on his jaw. Blood spurted from Justin's mouth, but the sight of red didn't stop Riley. Another blow landed in Justin's stomach and then a third across his face.

"Riley!" Rosie shouted, nearing the unhinged boy, but before she could reach his side Justin threw a protection bubble around them so she couldn't get in.

"Rosie," Justin said, his left eye swelling, "stay back—" Before he could finish his warning another punch landed.

Rosie ran to the invisible barrier, shouting to get Riley's attention. She looked at Justin who was staring back at her and she nodded.

With her approval, Justin thrust his head forward, hitting his forehead right on the bridge of Riley's nose. Stumbling back, Riley wiped the blood which trickled out of it and moved forward. Kicking a foot out, Justin landed a kick to Riley's chest, which sent him back to the invisible barrier.

"Riley, stop," Justin said, not advancing but rather lowering his hands to his side.

Riley ripped a growl from his throat and lunged forward. In two steps he was back in front of Justin, but with a quick jab, Justin punched Riley square in the face and Riley fell to the ground.

"Riley!" Rosie screamed again. As the barrier lifted, she stumbled forward and got to his side. Justin held his rib cage and leaned against a nearby tree.

"Rosie?" Riley asked, his eyes opening, staring at her.

"What were you thinking?" Rosie asked softly.

"You weren't safe."

"Riley. I will always be safe with Justin."

She heard the crunching of leaves and rocks and then a warm body knelt by her.

"Come on," Justin said, leaning down reaching towards Riley to help him up.

With Rosie's assistance the two managed to pull Riley to his feet.

"I don't need help," Riley snorted, but continued to lay his body weight on the two of them.

"You know what? No," Rosie said and began to shift the group towards a tree. "Riley, you are going to sit here and wait. Justin, let's go."

"I really think we should get him back, Rosie."

"Hey, I don't need you to try to help me," Riley said, stumbling away and leaning against the tree.

"Riley, please, freaking meditate. Calm down and when you have your head on straight again, we can talk," Rosie said, a hand raised to quiet him. Riley opened his mouth to speak but as Rosie raised an eyebrow, he clamped it shut and sat down. He massaged his side and took one last glance at Justin before shutting his eyes and taking deep breaths.

"Okay, let's get a little further away and then we can try this again," Rosie started but rustling at Riley's tree sounded, and he was up again rushing towards them.

"Riley!" Rosie shouted as he neared but to her surprise, he ran right past them and hurled into a gigantic, lanky, furry creature running their way.

Rosie's eyes widened at the sight of the sasquatch, but she didn't have time to think. Another body whirled through the clearing, this one a human.

"Dana?" Rosie asked.

A sly smile spread across Dana's face and then she bounded toward Rosie. With each stride, her body transformed, growing to near seven feet. Blonde tufts of fur sprouted all over and her eyes became a crystal blue.

"She can't use her magic in this form," Justin yelled to Rosie, nearing her side, but as he drew close a force threw him across the clearing. Thick, white smoke engulfed the forest and Rosie couldn't see past a foot in front of her.

Whipping bodies passing by sent her turning in every direction but still she couldn't make anyone out.

"Riley! Justin!" she shouted, but stopped and clamped her hands over her ears as a blood-curling, high-pitched scream shook the mountainside in the distance.

As the scream subsided Rosie could hear fighting nearby. Sprinting towards it, she ran directly into Riley, who lay on his back, his attacker, gone.

"Are you okay?" Rosie asked bending to help him up.

"I'm okay," he said as he caught his breath. "Are you?"

She nodded and the two stood searching for a way out of the fog. Another scream rang and both covered their ears and closed their eyes from the pain.

The scream clipped off though and as Rosie peeled her eyes open Justin had his hands spread wide and to his sides.

He sent the fog backward and cleared the forest. He then shot out a beam of light at the wounded banshee.

The banshee flew and flopped on the ground, then scurried to her feet before running back into the forest.

"He did it," Rosie whispered, staring at Justin in amazement.

"Did what?" Riley asked, scanning the boy.

"He's a wizard," she breathed, and studied Justin as he neared them.

"Rosie, Riley, are you guys okay?" Justin asked, running to their side, his hands dulling from yellow back to their normal shade.

"Yeah, but what just happened?" Riley asked.

Another banshee screeched, but Rosie knew where it was exactly. Screams of students by the school echoed before growls and blasts of magic were heard in the distance.

"War," Rosie muttered, before standing and running back to the school.

Riley and Justin both caught up and surpassed her, reaching the school first.

When she reached the lakeside, students were gathering, some pulling injured students off the ground, and others retreating back into the school lobby.

"What happened?" Professor Shay announced as she raced down the steps to assist a hurt student.

Rosie paced over to her. "We need to call Premier Kingsley. The clan. A group of sasquatches and banshees and other outcast creatures attacked."

Professor Shay nodded vigorously and leaned the injured student against Rosie and went back inside.

"Here, let me help," Justin said, taking over and carrying

the witch from Astive.

"Rosie!" Christion called, running across the bankside.

When he reached her, he pulled her up into a huge hug and then set her down. Justin nodded to her and left with the injured.

"I tried to get here in time to warn you. I called Kingsley but I couldn't reach him. Thank goodness you're okay."

"Dad, what happened? What's going on?"

Christion stared at his daughter and then Riley. Putting a hand on each of their shoulders he said, "Let's go find the Premier and we can discuss this further then."

"No. What's going on?" Riley asked.

"This isn't the best place to discuss such delicate matters," Christion replied, leading the two into the lobby.

The contrast of being under the nighttime stars and then entering the lobby, whose bright lights were on, stung Rosie's eyes for a moment. As the dark spots cleared from her vision, she studied the room.

They were the last three to enter and Rosie watched as the school left to go back to their dorms.

Clicking of heels neared them and Rosie spotted Professor Shay and Professor Walker.

"The Premier just arrived. He wants to see you," Professor Walker said to Christion.

Nodding his head he turned to Rosie. "I need you to go to your room. Don't leave. Don't try to visit Riley. Don't enter the main campus until one of us," he indicated to the other teachers, "says it's safe. Understand?"

"But—" Rosie began to protest but he stopped her.

"Understand, Rosie?"

Nodding, Christion grinned and then headed up to the

Premier's school office.

"Both of you," Professor Shay said, "off to your rooms. And no sneaking out."

The two stalked off back down the staircase and through the dining hall. Stopping before each could enter their team's respective libraries, Riley grabbed Rosie's hand.

"I'm sorry," he said. Then he squeezed it and left.

Rage rushed through her.

That's all he has to say? she thought, staring at the closing door to the Surgent library.

She shook her head and moved towards the Valtic door when a creaking on the other side of the hall sounded. She found Justin walking across the hall, staring at his hands.

"Hey," Rosie said.

He lifted his neck and saw her. "Oh, hey. I thought you'd be back at the dorm already."

"Not yet. I wanted to see if I could find anything out from my dad or the Premier, but all students have been sent to their rooms." A small chuckle left her as the two neared the Valtic entrance.

"Well, I'm sure Christion will tell you what's going on soon. Think you can meet him tomorrow at your mom's?"

"Yeah, that's not a bad idea. You should come too."

"Really? Are you sure?"

"Yeah, definitely. Plus, I need to teach you how to use your magic. I mean, you can only read so many books. Time to start your training." Rosie smirked as the two headed through the empty library and common room.

As Justin neared the portrait to the natural door, Rosie stopped him. "Wait."

"What's up?" Justin replied, stepping away and moving

back to Rosie.

"I was just thinking, you don't belong in the natural dorm anymore."

Justin chuckled. "Yeah, I guess you're right. Um, how about if I go get some of my stuff and then we can head to the other dorm together?"

"Yeah, I'll wait here." Rosie threw herself on a plush leather couch as Justin went through the portrait hole. In the silence she could think.

She wondered what the attack was about. Why the clan decided to do a drive-by of the school. If it was approved by Raphael, or if Dana decided to take a few others and act in defiance.

"Rosie?" a voice said at the back of the room.

Shooting to her feet and spinning around she found Christion's eyes boring into hers.

"Hey, what's going on?" Rosie asked, nearing him.

He approached her and the two sat down.

"I thought I told you to go to your room." He lifted a brow but cocked a mischievous smile.

"Dad, come on," Rosie said, shaking her head.

"Alright. The situation is growing out of hand."

"What do you mean?"

Taking a seat, Christion continued. "I've been spending time with some of Raphael's followers—clans that are allied with him and under his rule. They want Kingsley out and me in."

"Yeah, that's basically what Raphael told me. What's the Premier's plan? Is there any way this can end peacefully?"

"There's always a chance, but even if Kingsley was willing to step down, I wouldn't want to be the Premier."

"But why? You'd make a great leader. And the fact that you don't want it already says you should have it. You would do what's right for the community as a whole."

"Kingsley does that too."

"Does he?" Rosie asked, folding her arms.

"I like to think so," a third voice said. Rosie sat up and nearing the two was Premier Kingsley. He walked around the couch and sat in an armchair across from both, smiling at Rosie.

Keeping her stance she pressed, "Well, then what else is being done? Tonight could've been a lot worse."

Kingsley nodded and spoke, "We know from inside sources that the attack was isolated. It was a spur of the moment fluke, planned by young members of the clan."

"The same type of kids who want to join the school?"

"Yes. This was an attempt to crash a party., not fight."

"Sure felt like a fight." Rosie rolled her eyes and sat back.

"Emotions heightened at the sight of everyone now controlling their magic. They think they lost and therefore, fought."

"If only they knew," Christion whispered.

"Knew what?" Rosie asked, her interest piquing.

"Christion," Kingsley warned, but Christion ignored him and continued.

"The students and townspeople have their power in check, yes, but there is still a lack of what everyone's overall power could be. The beacon helped with control, but it also supplemented. With the clan channeling that power, they could easily overcome us. Which is why," Christion now turned to Kingsley, "we need to formulate a peace treaty. And fast."

"As I have said, I am trying my best."

"Well try harder," Christion said harshly, now standing.

"What would you suggest I do? Take their demands into actual consideration?"

"If it was between staying in power and saving the community, which is honestly more important?"

"I will not bend to these creatures!" Kingsley bellowed. He stood and paced towards Christion. "Once we answer their demands then they win."

"But no one else gets hurt."

"They win and then they will demand more and if they don't get it then they will go back to their own ways."

"Call a summit," Justin said. At some point during the argument, he had slid back into the room and stood behind the couch where Rosie sat.

The two men turned to Justin and Kingsley raised an eyebrow before saying, "Please, Justin. Elaborate."

"What if we got you, Christion, and Raphael in a room together to talk? No politicking, no B-S. Just an actual sit down with an open discussion about a compromise."

"I doubt the council would go for it," Kingsley spoke softly, yet still mulling over the thought.

"You're the Premier. You can do as you please."

The statement, while true, sent a shiver up Rosie's spine.

"What if it was off the books?" Christion suggested. "Just a late-night catch-up with an old friend?"

"We could meet here," Kingsley said.

"What about tomorrow?"

Kingsley paused for a moment and then looked up at Christion. "Set it up. See if Raphael will even be interested. If so, we will meet in my office tomorrow night."

"I'll go to him now." Christion began to move to the door but paused. He turned and pulled Rosie into a hug.

"Be safe," she said, hugging him a little tighter.

"Always am." He pulled away and winked, then gave Justin a nod and left the room.

"Justin, Rosie, thank you for your input."

"Of course," Justin replied.

Rosie on the other hand chewed her lip but managed to smile.

"I know I don't need to tell the two of you that what was just discussed is completely confidential. Any mention could be considered treason. Yes?"

"We know," Justin said, sitting down next to Rosie.

Rosie also nodded in agreement and studied her hands. She refused to raise her gaze until she heard the door click close.

"That was interesting," Justin said.

Rosie stared at him and nodded.

"What's going through your head right now?" Justin asked.

"A lot."

"Like what? Tell me."

"I just don't know if a sit-down is going to solve anything. I mean, yes, it's a start, but what will be accomplished?"

"I think that is the main point—to start having friendly relations, to stop the attacks and restore power. There just needs to be a jumping off point to the larger stuff."

"Yeah."

"What else? I know there's something else on your mind."

"It's just, my dad."

"You think he should lead?"

Rosie nodded before saying, "I mean, is that crazy? It's

absurd, right?"

"I don't think so. Christion has been around a lot longer than anyone else, at least that we know of in our world. He has proved to be a great leader from what I know of his past and have seen so far, but I don't think now would be the best time for a change in leadership. If there is going to be this major shift in our community. If we are to welcome multiple new species, then the Superiority needs to remain stable."

"I know." She brought her head up and met his eyes. "It makes sense. I agree. I just think, after everything settles, a new Premier or a contender should step up."

"I'm just curious… what don't you like about Premier Kingsley?"

"Nothing. I mean, a few things. I just…" Rosie paused and took a breath, then turned around the room, making sure it was still just the two of them. "I think Premier Kingsley has done a great job for our society. He has protected the supernatural beings and ensured we thrived in a safe environment. That being said, the fact that he has forgotten about others up until now is shocking and it makes me wonder what else he has done in over a century of leadership that is just wrong."

Justin nodded as she spoke and when she finished, he hesitated. "I agree with you, but I also think that while being in power, you must adhere to not just your wants but those of the people you govern."

"Didn't you just tell Premier Kingsley that he was the Premier and could do what he wanted?"

"Sometimes, those in power need an ego stroke to get to the desired outcome."

Rosie let out a laugh and stood. "Come on. I'm done talking

in circles. Let's get to bed."

With Rosie leading, the two entered the witch-wizard dorm and paused in the lobby.

"So, where should I go?" Justin asked, examining the room.

"Use your magic to liquify the glass." She led him over to a mirror in the room and demonstrated how he should place his hands. "The wall will show you your hallway and lead you to your new room."

"Just like that?"

"The school contains so much magic that she is like a person. The school knows what she's doing." Rosie smiled and watched as Justin held his palm up to the mirror. Immediately, the barrier started to wave, and Justin stepped halfway over the threshold.

He held up a hand to wave as he walked through the barrier and Rosie called out, "Tomorrow, your real training starts!"

"Sounds good, teach," he called back. They stood smiling at each other until the wall sealed back to normal.

Chapter Twenty-Five

"Any news?" Justin asked Rosie as they sat in the dining hall eating their lunch.

Scattered students sat across the hall, but since they were the only two with partial schedules, no one else from their group joined them.

"Nothing yet. My mom said that my dad left early the next morning. He left a note saying he would be back in a few days but that was a week ago." Rosie thought about the meeting between Kingsley, Christion, and Raphael constantly. She hoped to get a play-by-play from her father but sure enough, he was sent off on a mission, probably to ease tensions with Raphael and the clan.

"Do you think it worked?"

"It had to. I mean, there haven't been any attacks, no sightings of any other species nearby, and I mean, you feel the power surge, right?"

Justin nodded and stared at his hands before snapping both and forming small flames on his thumbs.

Rosie laughed and shot across the table, blowing the flames out before anyone could see.

"What?" Justin said in a fake innocent tone.

"You know you're not supposed to do that in the dining hall. Magic-free unless otherwise told."

"I know, but I mean, it's so much fun."

Rosie laughed again, nodding in agreement.

"Shoot," Justin said, staring at his watch. "I need to go meet Professor Walker now."

"More lessons?"

"Just a quick one before class." Gathering his things he waved goodbye and headed out. As soon as he was gone another body sat next to Rosie.

"Hey," Riley said. Staring at her, he reached for her hand but then pulled it back into his lap.

"Oh, hey," she replied, turning to him. Since the dance, Rosie had forgiven Riley for his behavior, but still couldn't shake his own unforgiving attitude towards Justin.

"What were you guys chatting about?" Riley asked, rubbing the palms of his hands on his thighs.

"Not much. He had to go to extra lessons with Professor Walker and then just schoolwork."

"Cool."

"Yep."

"Rosie?" Rosie lifted her head and met his gaze before he continued, "Are things going to go back to normal?"

Rosie breathed out. She knew in forgiving Riley she needed to let go of her anger. "Yes." She reached out and grabbed his hand. He smiled and squeezed it in return.

"Hey!" Garrett yelled at the two and he entered the hall and sat down.

"Um, hey. How's it going?" Rosie asked, pulling her hand back so she could eat.

"Uh, great! I mean I feel fantastic, don't you guys?"

Rosie smiled and turned her head to search the hall, which was filling up with more students. "The beacon must be regenerating its power," Rosie said, turning back to Garret.

"Do you think everything is back to normal?" Riley asked Rosie.

"Maybe." As she said it Professor Shay walking across the hall to the head table caught her eye. "Maybe, we'll find out right now." She jerked her head in Professor Shay's direction, and it seemed she wasn't the only one to notice. The entire dining hall settled and awaited the announcement.

"Good afternoon, everyone," Professor Shay started. "I'm sure you all have started to feel more in control of yourselves. I am happy to report that our beacon has been partially restored and we should be able to access our pendants once more!"

Cheers erupted, and Professor Shay raised a hand for the hall to settle again.

"While it is exciting that we have even more power and control of our magic, it is imperative that we do not fall back into old ways. Continue to practice your exercises and charge your talismans and crystals if need be." Professor Shay stepped down and as soon as she did the room erupted into conversations.

"Partially restored? What does that mean?" Garrett asked, leaning in.

"I have no idea," Rosie said before eyeing her watch. "Shoot, I need to go." Snatching up her things she rushed out of the hall and to her next class.

Entering the high school floor, Rosie found Justin and Professor Walker already in the classroom, which looked out to the expansive, bright mountainside.

"Hello, Rosie," Professor Walker said as she entered, and Rosie stepped back in shock as she saw someone else there.

"Mom?" Rosie asked.

"Hey!" Ms. Connors said, standing up from the teacher's desk and rounding it to hug Rosie.

Rosie pulled her in and when they separated, she raised an eyebrow to Professor Walker.

"Ms. Connors is today's lesson."

Rosie's mom leaned against the desk and Rosie sat in the front row next to Justin. She looked at him and he shook his head, not knowing what the lesson was.

"As you both know, it is very unusual to become a true amalgam. Rosie, I don't think you truly are. Especially after learning about your father and the visions you had last year."

"You know? About Christion?"

"Yes, I know all about Mr. Flame and how he is your dad. A vampire-witch. Well, it's no wonder you possess such great power."

Rosie breathed a sigh of relief at her father's true identity still being secret, and eyed her mother, who winked at her.

"We are going to dive deeper into each of your backgrounds and see how and why your magic surfaced."

"And my mom?"

"Since we can hypothesize that your magic is also derived from her family line, I would like us to learn more about her background and if she has any underlying gifts."

"Sounds fun," Ms. Connors said, standing now. "So, examine, prod, ask away!"

Justin turned to Rosie and raised an eyebrow. As if she knew what he was thinking, she nodded her approval for him to inquire further.

"I guess, can we first get you to take the King's Preparatory entrance exam?" Justin asked, then looked over to Professor Walker.

"Excellent thought," Professor Walker said, pulling an already printed examination from her desk. "Ms. Connors, if you could please?" Professor Walker gestured to Rosie's mom to take a seat back at her desk. "The same instructions that I gave your daughter when she took this exam apply now. You have fifteen minutes to complete the exam. No questions will be answered. You can start now."

Ms. Connors immediately began to read and propped the pencil in her hand. Both Rosie and Justin studied Ms. Connors as her eyes darted across the page. She read through the first page and without putting her pencil to paper, she flipped it over and widened her eyes at the last five questions. Immediately, the scratching of graphite sounded, and Ms. Connors' hand flew across the page as she scribbled.

When she finished the back, she looked up at Professor Walker and handed her the paper.

"I couldn't answer the front page but the second, well, that was easy." She smirked at Rosie and Rosie smiled back before staring at Professor Walker.

"Did you know your parents, Ms. Connors?" Professor Walker asked.

"Unfortunately, no. They died when I was just a baby. Car crash I was told. I went to live with a family friend."

"And you didn't have grandparents?" Justin asked.

"No. It was just me and then me and Rosie."

"Mmm," Professor Walker said as she studied the paper further. "You listed that you've had premonitions. Can you describe them further? Tell us when they started?"

Rose Connors shifted uncomfortably in her seat before staring at Rosie. Rosie had never known her mother to have a single magical bone in her body. If she had premonitions, even spoke to the dead, then Rosie knew she needed to learn about her ancestors more.

"Well, I guess to start, um, all my life, whenever I've slept, I've seen some sort of scenario or event. Most don't relate to me. At least, I never recognized anyone until…" Her voice trailed off and her furrowed eyes met Rosie's.

"What, Mom?" Rosie asked.

"Last summer, before you left."

"What about it?"

"You had been with the Zimmers. I was alone and would have these vivid dreams and they would get so intense that I would try to block them out."

Rosie nodded, understanding what her mother meant.

"One night I went to sleep without my usual nightly concoction, and I dreamt of you."

"What happened in your dream?"

"I saw flashes at first. An invitation, the King's Preparatory emblem, then you, in a cave, fighting for your life." At the words, Rosie's mouth dropped, and she sat forward as her mother continued. "I saw you use your magic and a huge blast of light. I woke up screaming and immediately tried to get to you."

"What do you mean?"

"I went to the Zimmers' in the morning, but I didn't knock. I just waited outside for you. I was a coward. I'm so sorry, Rosie." Tears formed in Ms. Connors' eyes, but Rosie nodded for her mother to continue.

"It's okay, Mom. Go on."

With that encouragement, she continued, speaking directly to Rosie, "You walked out and I followed. You went to work, and I saw you were safe, so I went back home. But then, I got the mail. The invitation was there. I stared at it, debating if I should toss it or burn it but couldn't bring myself to do either."

"You wouldn't have been able to," Professor Walker said. "There is an enchantment on the letters so that one way or another they would be received by each recipient."

Ms. Connors nodded and then stared back at Rosie. "I hid it instead and then the next few weeks were a blur, until you visited."

"And I found the invitation," Rosie said, remembering it being under a chair.

Glumly nodding, Ms. Connors' eyes filled with more tears. "I couldn't lose you. I know I had lost you, but I couldn't actually lose you Rosie."

Rosie rushed to her mother, squeezing her in a tight hug. "Mom, it's okay. You weren't you and you were trying to protect me."

"I just couldn't." Quiet sobs streaked Ms. Connors' cheeks.

"Ms. Connors," Justin asked after the two released.

Clearing her throat she turned to Justin. "Yes?"

"During that year, when Rosie was away, did you see anything else related to her?"

"Yes." Clearing her throat again and then shifting towards Justin now, she reached out and grasped his hand. "And you. I'm so sorry for what that man, Egil, did to you."

Justin smiled and kept Ms. Connors' hand in his.

"Did you see everything?" Justin whispered.

"None of it was your fault. You weren't you. If I thought

differently, you wouldn't be allowed within ten miles of my daughter."

They smiled at each other and then their hands released.

"Mom, since breaking the spell, have you had more premonitions?"

"Every night."

"What do you see?"

"It started out as just small things. Dreaming about someone tripping at the general store, seeing your first day going well, but then they evolved. Or I guess devolved."

Rosie raised an eyebrow.

"I began seeing you but older and it was as if it was the past."

"I had those same dreams," Rosie replied. "When I first got here. It was the woman in white."

"Yes, she was wearing a white dress."

"Did you ever see her, um, elsewhere?"

"Like not in a dream? No. Always as I slept."

Professor Walker spoke up now, "After speaking with Rosie on this matter last year, we theorized this woman was an ancestor. Someone tied to you and this area."

"Has she talked to you or told you anything?" Rosie asked.

"No. I've just seen snippets of her life. Her traveling around town, practicing magic, spending time with her daughter."

"Daughter? Did you hear a name?"

"Um, Annabelle, I think."

Rosie searched her mind and pulled forward the memory of her sifting through the boxes in the greenskeeper shed back in Illinois. Before she came to King's Preparatory, before she knew she was a witch, before her life altered completely.

"Mom, your dreams… they're of the first Rose Connors. And you said she was a witch? You could see her practicing magic?"

"Yes, but what does that mean?"

"I'm not sure," Rosie answered.

"I mean, it could…" Justin started before pausing and looking at Rosie.

"What?" Rosie asked, her eyes growing in anticipation.

"I think it means she is the reason you're here. The experiences you are going through now, she also went through. And that by being here, she is trying to tell you something. Both of you—something about your past."

"You think there is a message she is trying to communicate?"

Justin nodded. "She obviously wants you two to know something."

"I'll investigate it more, try to communicate with her," Ms. Connors said, grabbing Rosie's hand and squeezing it.

Rosie smiled and squeezed back. "What about recent events?" she asked now. "Anything on the clan, or attacks on the school, or Kingstown, or the Superiority?"

"I've mostly just seen the past."

"Actually, Ms. Connors," Professor Walker said, "I just got a message from Premier Kingsley." Professor Walker held a previously folded paper in her hand. "He would like to see you in his office."

"Oh," Ms. Connors grimaced then giggled, "wow, I feel like I am back as a student and being summoned to the big bad principal's office."

"What does he want?" Rosie asked, shifting to her mother's side.

"While you three were chatting, I let him know what type of witch your mother is and he is keen to talk to her. He can help you and give you resources to hone in on your power."

"Type of witch? Hone in?" Rosie asked, staring at Professor Walker.

"Please, Rosie. I know you already have an idea of what type she is."

Dropping the act, she gripped her mother's hand and turned to her.

"Mom, you're a seer."

"What's that?" Ms. Connors asked, looking from Rosie to Professor Walker and back again.

"A seer is a powerful witch, but rare. You can—" Rosie said, but Professor Walker cut her off.

"Ms. Connors, don't worry. Premier Kingsley can discuss all of this with you."

"Yes, of course. I should go meet with him." She looked at Rosie. "Don't worry. I will talk to you later honey." Ms. Connors smiled and hugged Rosie before stepping out of the room.

Rosie and Justin packed their bags and as they did so, Professor Walker spoke.

"That was a very insightful lesson. For the next class, please bring a detailed family tree. I think we should further explore each of your backgrounds and see if we can find any other underlying gifts we haven't discovered yet."

"Do you think I could also be from a magical line?" Justin asked, slinging his backpack over his shoulder.

"Justin, I truly believe you are a pure amalgam, but I want to make sure first before we start training you further."

"Could I have a specialized power as an amalgam?"

"No, but that doesn't mean you won't be a powerful wizard."

Justin nodded and allowed Rosie to step in front of him as the two walked from the class.

"What do you think the Premier is going to talk to my mom about?" Rosie asked, nibbling on a nail.

"He probably wants to see how he can use her gift to his advantage."

"What?"

"I'm just being honest. If she is a seer, then she will be very valuable for the Superiority."

"But if he already had negotiations with Raphael, then he shouldn't need her right? I mean, could she be in danger?"

"I think all of us are in some potential danger. But just talk to her tonight. I'm sure she will let you know what's going on."

"Yeah, I guess."

The two bounded up the steps to the next level and entered the specialized floor.

"Woah," Justin murmured at the dimly lit hallway.

"Your eyes will adjust," Rosie said, giggling and pulling open one of the few doors on the floor.

The dark, stuffy room smelled of various flowers, waxes, spices, and stone. Empty tables sat around the two and Rosie began to grab a pot, burner, and measuring cups.

"How can I help?" Justin asked, mimicking her moves.

"Grab a yellow onion skin, three fruit fly wings, a pinch of cayenne, and a cat ear."

Justin chuckled and moved over to the various shelves that covered the classroom, pulling down the needed supplies.

"What's so funny?" Rosie asked, amused at his cocked

smile.

"Nothing. It's just, I never thought I would have to cook something that had cayenne pepper mixed in with a cat's ear."

Rosie laughed, as she now considered every movement in the potion's lab as normal.

Justin laughed with her and once all the ingredients were settled on the table, he awaited further instructions. She began chopping and measuring items when Justin spoke.

"So, what are we making anyways?"

"I mean, I know you just said to wait for tonight, but a little potion to overhear Premier Kingsley's conversation won't hurt, will it?"

"What do you mean?"

"Just that, if we drink this, we can penetrate the wards around his office and find out exactly what the Premier wants with my mom or find out more about the negotiations."

"You really can't wait, can you?" Justin asked, a chuckle escaping him.

"I just hate not knowing."

"I get it. It's part of our nature."

Rosie nodded as she stared down at the boiling mixture. Mixing the ingredients and then straining the liquid into a separate bowl, the two examined the light brown concoction.

"Is it supposed to smell like that?" Justin asked, an eyebrow raising.

"Unfortunately." Rosie grimaced. "Here, come over and put your hands over the pot."

Justin did so and stared at Rosie.

"Okay, now for the potion to do anything, you have to inject magic into it, otherwise we are just two crazy people drinking the most disgusting thing ever."

"Alright, how much magic?" Justin asked.

"For this? Call up a handful."

"And how do I know when enough is enough?"

"It will feel like you are holding a baseball in your palm. Call it to your fingertips and then release it."

Justin nodded and focused on his hands. Small waves of light pooled at his fingertips, and he spread his fingers out further. The sheer, golden light streamed down into the cauldron and then Justin clamped his hands shut.

"Was that good?"

Smiling broadly, Rosie stared at him in amazement. "It was perfect. I can't believe how much control and restraint you already have."

Justin ran a hand through his hair in an attempt to hide his reddening cheeks.

Leaving his side, she grabbed two glasses off a nearby shelf and poured half a cup of the potion into each. "Bottoms up?"

"Wait. Have you tried this before?" Justin asked, gently stopping her hand from letting the liquid slip down her throat.

Pulling the cup away she shook her head, but a smile played at her lips.

"Okay, let me go first at least," Justin bartered.

"What? No way." Rosie began to lift the cup again, but Justin held on to her.

"Please. You are the more experienced witch. If something bad happens then you can fix it or get me to Doctor Geller or Professor Walker for help."

Rosie sat for a minute contemplating the option. On one hand, the potion could work without a hitch and they both could go on their merry way, but on the other, they could go deaf.

"Okay but I'm going to try it at least since I made it. If something were to go wrong and something bad happened to you, I wouldn't forgive myself."

The words left Rosie quickly and Justin smiled.

"You mean that?" he asked.

"Shut up and let me drink this goop." She smiled and plugged her nose. Though she took proper precautions not to taste the mixture, the small lumps that made it past the strainer stuck to her tongue and throat as they passed. Taking a breath after swallowing, the taste set in.

Coughing and gagging as the taste settled in her mouth, Justin's hand rested on her back and a new cup fit into her hand.

"Here drink this," Justin said, indicating to the water he just handed her, but she shook her head.

"I can't. It will dilute the effects." She swallowed a few more times before speaking again. "I'm okay. Let's go."

"Wait, did it work?"

"I don't know yet. We won't know until we leave this room."

"Alright then, lead the way."

Rosie smiled and reached for the doorknob. As she stepped into the hallway, she waited to be blasted with various conversations but all was silent.

"I can't hear anything."

"Is there anyone else on this floor?"

"There should be a moon rituals class and a crystal power class down the hall, and the freshman wolves are meeting in the room across the way."

"Maybe they're spellbound, like the room we were just in?"

"Yeah, I just thought this would break that barrier."

"Did I do my part correctly? Did I put enough of my magic in?"

But Rosie couldn't answer Justin. The thrum of his beating heart and the whooshing of his blood passing through his veins thrummed in her ears and caused her to lose part of her vision.

Chapter Twenty-Six

"Rosie, are you—"

"Shhh!" Rosie commanded, lifting her hands to cover her ears.

Without a word, Justin rushed her from the floor and up to the main level. Turning down the never-ending hallway towards Doctor Geller, Rosie listened in to all she could, but with each new conversation, a piercing pain stabbed behind her eyes.

"Wait," she mustered, clutching her forehead.

"We're almost to Doctor Geller," Justin whispered as low as possible, but Rosie winced at his words.

"Stop, the lobby."

"No, it's not worth it."

"Justin, now," she gritted out, pressing her eyes closed, noise from every direction reverberating in her head.

Huffing a breath, Justin pulled her along the hallway, back towards Kingsley's office.

"Don't breathe so loud," Rosie tried to joke, but she could hear Justin's eyes roll next to her.

The loud creaking of the lobby door echoed and as soon as Rosie entered the lobby, she heard her mother's voice.

"And this new position will keep me here still, right?" Ms. Connors' faint voice asked in the distance.

With one of her hands guiding her around the edge of a couch and Justin holding onto her other arm, Rosie found the cushioned seat and the two sat.

"Can you—" Justin began to ask.

"Shhh. Yes."

"Yes," Kingsley's voice sounded, "you will still be able to stay in Kingstown. You will just record your visions every day and send them into the office where we will be able to review and detail any findings that may be relevant to our community."

"Okay. I think I can do that."

"Good. Now I need to ask, have there been any visions related to the attacks at school or the Superiority? Anything that you can assist our efforts with?"

"Rose," Christion's voice sounded now.

"Dad?" Rosie whispered.

Christion continued, "It is imperative we know if Raphael is planning on double crossing us."

"You're meeting with him?" Rose asked.

"It was, as far as we know, a success," Kingsley said.

"But there are doubts?"

"There are always uncertainties in these matters," Christion responded.

"Raphael agreed that he and his clan and other creatures alike who wish to join the Superiority will do so," Kingsley said.

"Well, that sounds like he got what he wanted then."

"Yes and no. In order to become a member, you must register with the Superiority."

"Again, I'm not seeing an issue."

"Rose," Christion started, "the clan and the species not already included within the Superiority are proud and think us asking them to register with the community isn't for their own benefit."

"Their benefit?"

"They want our protection, but they don't want to contribute to the community," Kingsley said bluntly.

"Also, they weren't happy with the fact that the transition would take place over the span of seven years."

"Seven years? Why so long?" Rose asked.

"To give both communities time to acclimate to the change. We need to prepare for all the new bodies. Ensure there is enough housing, jobs, spaces at the school for the kids, find teachers… It's a long list of things that need to be done before we can properly ingrain everyone."

"Well that just seems silly," Rose scoffed.

"Silly?" Kingsley asked. "How so?"

"Of course there needs to be a period of acclimation and processing, but I don't think seven years is the answer."

"Then what would you do?"

Rosie could hear Kingsley stop pacing and the room stayed still.

"I mean, I would first call a summit. Not just you two and Raphael but call their council and ours. It sounds like Raphael wants to join the Superiority and his only hold up is how it will be perceived by his following. Call the groups together. Discuss the importance of registering."

"And if they refuse?"

"I have no doubt that between the two of you, you can convince them of not only the importance of it but also the solid reasoning behind it."

"These species will feel like they are being tracked."

"Then it would be for their own safety. Isn't that correct, Premier? At least that is what I was told when I joined the Superiority and updated Rosie's forms."

"My forms?" Rosie whispered.

"What forms?" Justin asked.

Rosie shook her head and tuned back into the meeting.

"Yes, we need to know who is in our community so we can properly ensure the safety of every member. It wouldn't be unheard of for our kind to be uncovered and persecuted."

"Seems like we need to stop persecuting each other first," Christion muttered.

"What does that mean?" Kingsley asked, now moving across the room.

"If we included all species in the beginning, we wouldn't be in this current predicament."

"No one knew sasquatches, watchers, and other humanoid creatures had the same intelligence level back then."

"I did."

"And where were you, Christion? I'd love to know."

Silence swept over the room and after what felt like forever Ms. Connors spoke.

"It doesn't matter now. We are where we are. We should focus on bringing those outside the Superiority in and ensuring everyone prospers from the inclusion. Hold a summit. Show the other members of Raphael's group what the Superiority has to offer. Allow them in now. To jobs, to school, to everything. Then, as time passes, more will become available to all."

"But the stress on the community with such an explosive

growth could be detrimental."

"Then make it a year, not seven."

"A year?"

"Yes, but if you want the attacks to stop now, start with including the children in the school."

"Why, Rose?" Christion asked.

"Parents won't want to hurt a community their children are actively involved in."

"Smart," Kingsley muttered, and stalked back to behind his desk and sat down. "And you have had no visions regarding this matter?"

"Not involving attacks or fighting but as we spoke, this plan just felt right. Like I have seen it come to fruition."

There was another pause then Kingsley spoke, "Okay, Christion, inform Raphael there's to be a summit. Explain to him our new plans. He should agree to gather his council once he has heard the more favorable terms."

As Kingsley spoke his voice began to fade until Rosie could only hear Justin's faint breaths beside her.

"Woah," Rosie said, clutching her head.

"Are you okay?" Justin asked.

"What?" she responded, cupping her hand around her ear.

"Is the potion wearing off?"

"Yeah, and you won't believe—" But as she spoke Christion descended from the portrait hole and cocked an eyebrow in her direction.

"Hi, Dad!" Rosie yelled, standing and running to his side.

"What are you up to?" he asked immediately, studying her face.

"Nothing. Just hanging with Justin."

Justin feebly waved at Christion, but his focus stayed

entirely trained on Rosie.

"What did you hear?"

"Hear? What are you talking about?"

"Rosie, your ear has brown goop coming out of it." He lifted his pinky finger and lightly dabbed her cheek where the liquid dripped.

Using the sleeve of her blazer she wiped the potion away but part of it matted into her hair.

"Gross," she whispered, running her fingers through the strands.

"So, tell me."

"Ugh, fine. I know about the summit Mom suggested," Rosie admitted.

"And what do you think?" Christion asked as he led her back to the couch. She sat next to Justin who leaned forward trying to put together what the two discussed.

"I think it's a smart idea. Especially if clan members are hesitant to join the Superiority."

"I think it is a good idea as well. What about letting the children into the school?"

Rosie pictured Dana's face and imagined her strutting around the school as if she owned it. Heat rose to her face, and she shook her head.

"If it helps grow the community and keep violence at bay, then it should happen."

If the school grew in number, how often would she run into Dana? she thought.

"Okay. I am going to reach out to Raphael," Christion said, then he stood up.

"How long will you be gone?"

"Only a few days, but when I'm gone, Rosie, keep an eye

on your mother."

"Of course, but I think she just proved she can handle herself."

"Oh, I know she can," Christion chuckled but continued, "but with this new role she has, a lot of people will want to use her. I need you to make sure she doesn't do anything reckless. She can be too trusting sometimes and if the wrong person convinces her to help them…"

"I understand. I'll make sure to be around for Mom."

"Thank you, sweetie." He engulfed Rosie in a hug and then planted a kiss on the top of her head. Then he smiled and walked out the lobby door.

"Sounds like you heard a lot of interesting news," Justin finally addressed Rosie.

Rosie smirked. "You have no idea."

* * *

"So, what you're saying," Garrett said, "is that the school is about to be filled with banshees, sasquatches, walkers, and other species?"

Rosie nodded her head as the group sat together at lunch.

"How are they going to accommodate everyone?" Eleanor asked.

"El," Riley said, "we go to a magical school. I don't think it will be too hard to fit everyone. Just expand a building here or plop a dorm down there."

"But what about class sizes? I mean there are only, what, thirty teachers? How is everyone going to fit into a classroom? What about the crystal test? Are they all going to do it? Will they bring in any potential protectors or intellects for testing next year? Will—"

"Eleanor," Justin said. "Breathe." The group laughed and Eleanor smiled.

"I think they are forming solutions for everything if the clan agrees to the new terms as we speak," Rosie said.

"Things are definitely going to change around here," Garrett mumbled, popping a fry into his mouth.

"Who knows?" Justin said. "We could learn more than we were aware of. They may have a different way of harnessing their power if they just now stole from the beacon."

"Speaking of which, is that part of their terms? Will they restore power? I know the majority of us have control and there was a power surge, but the little kids don't have a grasp yet. And neither do a handful of folks in town. The Superiority agents are still patrolling to make sure there aren't any more attacks."

"I'm sure that will be stipulated in the agreement," Rosie said. She thought about what she told her friends. She let them know about the likely incoming students and the pending summit, but kept her mother's gift to herself.

Since learning of her mother's visions, Rosie had tried every night to hone in on the power herself, but unlike last year, her nights included dreamless sleep. At least she couldn't remember any dreams if they did come.

"Do we know when the summit is?" Riley asked Rosie, leaning in closer.

"Um, no but I'm sure it's soon. The Premier and from what I heard, Raphael, want to make this transition occur sooner rather than later. Neither wants bloodshed."

"Unlike some of the other clan members, huh?" Garrett snorted before shifting his tone to be serious. "Oh, hey Drew. How's it going?"

"Hey, um, it's good. Um, Rosie? Can I talk to you for a second?"

"Yeah." Rosie stood and walked with Drew to the corner of the dining hall. She turned to her friends who lifted their brows and watched, but she just shrugged and focused her attention. "What's up?"

"My sister contacted me."

"What?" Rosie took a small step back and widened her eyes. "I thought she cut off contact with you?"

"She did, but apparently deep, deep, deep, and I mean really deep down inside her, she still cares."

"Why? What did she say?"

"To get out. To leave."

"What else?"

"That was it. She just said I need to leave King's Preparatory."

"She's planning something?"

"I think so. I'm sure not everyone is happy about the summit occurring in the clan."

"How do you know about that?"

"My mom. She isn't with my dad, and she wasn't allowed to raise us, but she is still a part of the group. Raphael told everyone that there's going to be a summit. The leaders of each species within the clan and their advisors are planning to meet with the Superiority council on Friday."

"But that's only two days away. I figured more planning would have to be done."

"The elders in the group want to see resolution."

"And the younger members?"

"There are a handful who don't want to be dictated by the Superiority."

"But they won't be."

"I'm sure they won't but there are stories that have traveled from mouth to mouth for generations."

"Like what?"

"Being persecuted by those under the Superiority. Being forced by Superiority agents to conform to the life normally led by those members. The Superiority monitoring individual movements and squatch gatherings. The list goes on and on."

"I mean, that could've happened, but I can't believe something like that is going on now."

"Just the fear of not being able to continue with our traditions and rituals is causing an internal revolution to happen. I think Dana was warning me to get out before something drastic happens at the school."

"Like what? Do you have any indication of what or when an attack could take place?"

"Friday. The council and elders are meeting here Friday for the summit."

"No, they are meeting at the Superiority."

"From what my mom said, they want to meet here. To let clan members see the school. To bring along a group of kids to check it out. Then they will continue deliberations."

"Is Dana going to be part of that group?"

"Not that I'm aware of but I bet she has control over some of the kids who are coming. They're going to do something, Rosie."

"Okay, let's get to Professor Shay and let her know."

"That's why I'm telling you. I'm leaving before I am even more shunned. If I go back now, my mom said I can stay with her. I'll be able to still enjoy some semblance of life back home."

"No, Drew, you can't leave. You'll just be back once the groups have come to an agreement."

"But they aren't in agreement yet. And the longer I stay here, the more exiled I become." Drew looked down at his hands then back at Rosie. "I can feel it, you know? I can feel myself slipping away from my people, my home."

Rosie stared at Drew for a moment, then clasped his hands. "Go. Be with your mom."

"Thank you, Rosie. And if it means anything, I hope to see you next year."

Rosie smiled as he walked off and she turned to Riley. He cocked an eyebrow and turned his head to follow Drew then looked back at her. She held up a finger to her friends and then rushed from the dining hall. She wasn't surprised though when stamping feet sounded behind her as she bounded up the stairs.

"Rosie, wait up!" Riley called, and she slowed. He made it to her side and Justin, Eleanor, and Garrett ran behind.

"I have to see if Premier Kingsley is here."

"Why?"

"Because we could all be massacred on Friday."

Chapter Twenty-Seven

As Rosie ascended and faced James Kingsley's portrait face, she stepped forward to move through the veil. But as she did so, her foot and face came into contact with a solid wall.

"Ow," she exclaimed, before losing her focus and falling to the floor.

"You okay?" Justin asked, grasping her under the arm, and gently helping her up.

"Yeah, just, it's locked."

"He must not be there, then," Riley said, stepping to her side and taking her other arm.

"It's never locked, though."

"Can you blame him?" Justin asked as the group sat down on one of the sofas. "I mean, you found the office last year and he probably wants to keep whatever he is planning to discuss at the summit under wraps. Plus, if the summit is happening here, then he really wants to safeguard anything he may have that should be confidential Superiority information."

"Then what do we do now?" Garrett asked, staring at Rosie.

"Your mom," Justin said. "We could tell her. She can contact Premier Kingsley and tell him what's going on."

Rosie swiftly pulled her phone out of her pocket and dialed.

The phone rang but her mom never picked it up and it never went to voicemail.

"Something's wrong."

"What?" Riley asked, moving in.

"My mom's phone. It just kept ringing."

"Okay, don't panic," Eleanor said, trying to reassure Rosie.

"Yeah, it's the middle of the day on a Wednesday," Justin reasoned. "She just started her new position at the Superiority. Is it possible that she had to go in? To sort out paperwork?"

"Yeah," Rosie agreed, nodding as the knot in her chest loosened.

"Why don't we go find Professor Shay. I'm sure she can get a message to Premier Kingsley within the hour. She's got to be in the dining hall."

"Yeah, okay." The group stood and moved back through the school, nearing the dining hall.

"Seriously?" Eleanor asked, spinning in a circle as they now moved back up and through the never-ending hallway. "Why is it so quiet? Where is everyone?"

"I guess everyone is at lunch or in class?" Garrett said, grabbing hold of Eleanor's hand. Rosie stared at her watch and nerves caught at her. It was only two in the afternoon. School was still in session and yet no one could be found.

She started to hustle, her friends following but stopped when down the hallway, a door clicked open. Rosie's head whirled around.

Coming into the stairwell in her high stiletto heels was Professor Walker.

"There you five are!" Putting a finger to her pendant she spoke again, "I've found them."

"What's going on?" Rosie asked, stepping closer to Professor Walker. She couldn't find the Premier, reach her mom, and she needed to get to Professor Shay. A bead of sweat pooled on the side of her forehead but her head cocked.

A coy smirk pulled up on one of the corners of Professor Walker's mouth before saying, "It's time for the next Illumination Games."

***

"But Professor Walker," Rosie protested as the group plopped down on the field next to the school.

The rest of the students from every team sat awaiting instructions, but Rosie couldn't worry about some dumb games.

"Rosie, I've heard what you said. I'm going to alert Premier Kingsley now." She motioned her arm and standing at the far end stood James Kingsley. He stood with about twenty others Rosie didn't recognize.

"Hey! My dad!" Garrett said, standing again.

"You'll have time to visit after the Games, Garrett."

Sitting back on the soft grass, Garrett nodded but kept his eyes over at the group.

As Professor Walker walked towards the adults at the end of the field, Rosie turned to Garrett.

"What is your dad doing here?"

"I don't know."

"Do you know who the others are?"

"Yeah, they're all council members."

"From the Superiority?"

"Mh-hm."

"Well, do you know them?"

"Sort of. My dad represents the wolves, Mr. Lightstrom, Sunnie's dad, represents the fairies, and the rest are selected through their respective groups to make decisions on their behalf."

"Is that Gregor the Great?" Riley asked, sitting forward.

"Who?" Rosie asked.

"One of the greatest protectors. He leads the agent program at the Superiority. I heard he once took down three rogue vamps at once."

"That's nothing," Eleanor chimed in, "I heard he was bitten by a lone wolf during a full moon and willed himself *not* to change."

"That can't be true," Riley said, laughing and shaking his head.

"It is possible," Justin said, "though nearly impossible."

Riley grumbled but turned back to Gregor. To Rosie's surprise, he was twice the size of Manger. *He must be in his thirties*, Rosie thought as she inspected the tattoos that covered his arms and even peeked out the top of his shirt on his neck.

"Those are wards," Justin whispered.

"How can you tell?" Rosie asked, spying the various intertwined designs.

"Superiority agents aren't supposed to have any markings on them unless they are for protection or to assist them in some way."

Rosie continued to scan the group and as members of the council shifted around, her mother came into view.

"Mom!" Rosie exclaimed, standing up.

Her mother spied her and smiled, but then turned her attention back to the other council members.

"What do you think she is doing here? Do you think she saw something?" Rosie asked Justin.

Before Justin could respond though Professor Shay's voice boomed over the group of students.

"Quiet down now." The students settled and directed their attention to Professor Shay who continued, "While the Games are fun, they are meant to keep you on your toes and prepare you for any situation that you may fall into once you've left King's Preparatory. Each team will compete against one another again, but only the Illumination Teams will participate. The rest of the team will watch on. Illumination Teams, sort yourself, come to me, and then we will continue."

"I'll catch you later, Rosie," Riley said, kissing her cheek before walking off.

She was about to call out to him, but Garrett interrupted.

"We're missing Ellie, Frederick, and Cameron," he said as the Valtic team began to gather around.

"Where are they?" Rosie asked, scanning the group.

"Ellie flew off with a colony of bats, Frederick had to go home for a funeral, and Cameron was detained for attacking a wolf."

"Seriously?"

Garrett grimly nodded, but Rosie's eyes widened.

"Reese, Eleanor, and Justin," Rosie called out, "you're on the team. Congrats."

"Wait, really?" Eleanor squealed as she jumped up and down.

"Yes!" Garrett exclaimed. "Okay, now that we have

everyone, let's move!"

The group of Valtics headed towards the other Illumination Teams who stood by Professor Shay, near the council.

"Do we have everyone?" Professor Shay asked, scanning the group. "Perfect. As you can see, on the next peak of the mountain, there is a finish line. You will need to cross over there first to win."

"Easy!" a boy from Surgent yelled, eyeing the finish.

"You would think so," Professor Shay retorted, "but you will first have to enter the dark forest." She waved her arm and then outstretched it, and as she did the ground began to rumble. Thousands of tall, thick trees sprouted up from the ground, creating a dense wood.

Rosie spied the Surgent boy's face and it had fallen.

"Once inside the woods, you will have to face certain obstacles if you wish to emerge on the other side and complete the task at hand."

"What kind of obstacles?" Eleanor asked.

"That's for you to find out." Professor Shay smiled and stepped aside as James Kingsley passed her.

"In the forest are dangers you know of but may have never faced. Using your knowledge, brute force, or gifts, you will need to successfully subdue the threat and continue. Only one person from the team needs to cross the finish line."

"We got this," Garrett whispered to Rosie. She nodded in agreement but stayed focused on Kingsley.

"You would like it to be easy, but let's make it a bit more challenging, shall we?"

Kingsley winked at Professor Shay, and she once again, outstretched her arms. Thick, white fog consumed the forest and as if she controlled time, the sun dipped low, and the moon now shone bright over the group.

"You have five minutes to deliberate strategy," Kingsley said before turning back to the council.

Rosie stepped towards Kingsley, hoping to warn him of what Drew told her, but someone caught her arm and pulled her back into the group.

"Professor Walker is handling it," Garrett said. "Focus."

She nodded and listened.

"With how thick the forest is," Justin said, "we won't be able to see."

"We will have to make our own light then," Garrett responded.

"Nothing too bright though," Rosie added. "We don't know what's in the woods and we don't want anything to focus on us."

Garrett nodded in agreement before looking at his dad and waving.

The athletic build of Mr. Parker shadowed Garrett, and he eyed his son up and down before wiping a speck of dirt off his expensive suit and speaking with another council member.

Garrett faced the group again and Rosie caught Eleanor's eye. She shook her head before focusing back on her boyfriend.

"Okay, Reese, I want you to fly above," Garrett commanded, his voice now stern and lacking any humor he normally had. "Look out for advancing threats. If you see something, dive down."

"Would it be easier if I flew ahead and tried to reach the finish line first?"

"No," Justin blurted out.

"Why not?" Katherine asked, stepping forward. "I mean

why don't I use my speed to try to reach the finish? We can use our abilities, right? So why not try to win as quickly as possible."

"Because that's not what they," Rosie said, eyeing the council, "want. They want to see us use our skills on whatever they've put in there. I bet there are boundaries in place to stop that from happening after we cross the forest threshold." She nodded towards the woods and as if on cue, a glass-shattering scream rippled through the trees, causing them to quake.

"Well, now we know what one of the obstacles is," Justin snorted in disbelief.

"Was that a banshee?" Katherine asked, turning towards the forest, as did every other student.

"Wanna bet what else is out there?" Justin whispered, shaking his head.

"I can't believe they would set this up," Rosie whispered back.

"What?" Garrett whispered, as the rest of the group eyed the forest line, attempting to see what else lay beyond it.

"We are going to face creatures that aren't under the Superiority," Rosie explained.

"What? So like, banshees, sasquatches, watchers, walkers, spirits?" Garrett asked.

"And more, potentially."

"But why?"

"I don't know why, but I do know this plan is going to hurt the Superiority and any chance of peace if word ever gets back to the clan or elders."

Justin shook his head and Rosie furrowed her brows. She turned to the Surgent team and Riley smiled and joked with the other members. She turned back to Justin.

"We need to try to keep as much peace as possible. If something happened to any creature out there and Raphael found out, we could be looking at war. My dad is with them right now. They could kill him for this."

"Maybe they aren't real?" Eleanor said, joining Rosie at the side.

"Huh?"

"Well, Professor Shay made it nighttime, and the fog appeared. What if the creatures are just illusions?"

"I mean, it's possible," Justin answered, and looked at Rosie.

"Still, real or not real, the Superiority is basically asking us to train. To learn to fight these creatures. I won't do it."

"Rosie, come on. The Superiority wouldn't try to force us to fight in a war," Garrett said, eyeing his dad. "They probably just want to test our skills. And who knows? There could be any number of creatures out there. That might have not been a banshee."

"He's got a point, Rosie," Eleanor said, leaning onto Garrett.

Rosie stared back at the council and found her mom's face. She laughed and smiled next to the group. Surely, Rosie thought, her mother would never condone such an activity.

"Okay, we need to stay in a tight group. That way none of us are picked off. Strongest will be at the sides and back. Justin and I will be at the front. When something approaches or Reese alerts us, we can put a barrier around our group. Then we can determine the best way to fight off or outmaneuver whatever we face."

"Sounds like a plan," Justin said, grinning.

"Alright, teams!" Professor Shay started, "You will enter the forest one at a time, starting with the winner from the last challenge all the way to the last place team."

"Okay, not a great start," Garrett said, grinding his teeth. One by one the other teams entered the forest. Ten minutes had passed, and Professor Shay walked up to the Valtic team.

"It's time, Valtics. Luckily, for you, the Astive team is already out of the running." Rosie's eyes widened.

"Is everyone okay?" she asked, but Professor Shay just walked away.

"Let's go guys!" Garrett shouted and the team formed a circle. Justin and Rosie stood at the front, Garrett was slightly behind Rosie, and Eleanor behind Justin. Reese flew up into the air, his cardinal form getting a bird's eye view. The other team members filled in behind and on the sides while Katherine flanked at the back.

The group stepped through the fog and as soon as the barrier was breached, screams of students, snarls of creatures, and the wisping of trees took over the team.

"Woah," Eleanor said, stopping.

"Keep moving," Rosie urged as she stared out in front of her and then looked up to find the red bird flying above. With Reese still surveilling, Rosie focused forward.

"Should we just keep moving straight forward?" Garrett asked, falling into Justin and Rosie's jogging pace.

"Yes," Justin responded. "If we go straight then we should be able to reach the edge of the forest and then can have Katherine book it up the peak to the finish line."

"Awesome, does that sound good to you Kat?" Garrett asked, but no reply came.

Rosie whirled around and sure enough, Katherine was gone.

"Crap, crap, crap, crap," Garrett started to say, turning in a circle.

"Hey, pull it together guys," Justin said, bringing the group closer together. "We can get through this. We just need to stay together."

"Um, where's Madeline?" Eleanor asked as she scanned the group for the wildcat shifter.

"Oh jeez," Garrett whispered under his breath. "Pine, can you transform so you can lead the way with some light?"

"Done!" Pine said, shifting into fairy form.

"We should keep moving," Justin said. "Something is picking us off and if we just stay here, we're sitting ducks."

The group hustled forward, Pine now leading the way. Rosie jumped over fallen trees, squeezed through trunks, and ducked under lashing branches, all while scanning her surroundings and the team of Valtics.

Whooshing out of thin air, Reese plummeted in front of the group, halting all. He turned towards the east, and everyone shifted in that direction, waiting for something to appear.

"Get ready!" Garrett commanded, stepping forward, his canines lengthening and claws sprouting.

"AH!" the group screamed as a body fell out from the thicket of trees and landed in front of them.

"Riley?" Rosie asked, stepping forward and leaning down at his side. Gashes clawed his back and dirt covered him from head to toe.

"Are you okay?" she asked, still at his side.

He began to sit up and stared at Rosie. "I'm okay, I think."

"What got you?" Garrett asked, kneeling.

"Chupacabra."

"Where's the rest of the Surgents?"

"Gone. Taken. I'm not sure."

"Okay, well come with us," Rosie said, pulling him up to

his feet.

"What?" Garrett said. "I mean, Rosie, this is a competition. No offense man."

Riley chuckled. "None taken." He massaged his neck but still stood with them.

"Garrett. Look at him! He's coming with us," Rosie argued as Garrett rolled his eyes.

"Ugh, fine, but you can't cross before us."

"Wasn't planning on it." Riley grasped Rosie's hand, but she pulled it away.

"Sorry, I just need to focus."

"Yeah, of course," Riley responded, his head falling.

The group continued to move forward. Ten minutes of drifting in the fog and Rosie became aware of how still and silent the forest now was. No longer could she hear the screams or snarls from when she first entered. She couldn't even hear tree branches moving or the chirps and buzzing of insects.

"Everyone, stop!" she ordered. As she halted, the air became icy and the sensation of small needles piercing her skin erupted. "Run!"

She jolted forward and heard the sprinting strides of her team close behind.

"What is it?" Eleanor yelled, but as she called out, Rosie turned to the group and pressed her lips closed even further. She widened her eyes to give warning not to speak but it was too late. Eleanor's body had been ripped away and flew up. Everyone stopped and searched for what had grabbed her.

Garrett opened his mouth, but Justin threw a hand over it and shook his head.

Kneeling on the ground Rosie spelled out in the dirt,

Vengeful Spirits. She stared back up at Eleanor, who seemed to be in a state of shock. Suddenly, a piercing scream erupted from her throat and then blood pooled from her mouth.

Her body fell from the air and hit the ground with a loud thud. Running to her side, Rosie could see her ankle had been broken from the fall, but what was worse was that her tongue lay next to her head.

"Stay here," she mouthed to Garrett. He nodded and caressed Eleanor, knowing they wouldn't be bothered as long as they remained silent.

Rosie tipped her head and the rest of the team stood and ran from the small clearing. Once the icy chill dissipated, Rosie stopped to catch her breath. She searched the sky above for Reese but couldn't find the bright red cardinal anywhere.

"Shoot," she muttered, and Justin also noted the shifter's absence.

"We can't be far from the edge," he reassured her, placing a hand on her shoulder.

After catching her breath, Aquamarine started speaking. "What the hell?" she exclaimed, pacing back and forth. "What does the administration, jeez, the Superiority think they're—"

But a giant, hairy body rammed into hers.

Justin, Riley, Rosie, and Pine fell backwards at the incoming force. The snapping of bones jerked Rosie up and Pine, back in his human form, grasped at his back.

"What is it?" Justin yelled, running to his side.

"My wings," he grunted out. "They didn't reset properly."

"Can you run?" Riley asked.

"I think so."

Rosie stayed back as Justin and Riley helped Pine back into his shorts. She searched for Aquamarine, but she had disappeared into the forest with the sasquatch.

As she turned in a circle, she spotted a clearing into the desert, just beyond the tree line.

"The exit's there!" she bellowed and turned to the three, but they were gone.

Had the sasquatch returned and taken them? she wondered. Without any hesitation, she ran towards the desert clearing. The only way she could help her team now was by ending the games.

Lengthening her strides and sprinting past branches that whipped her face and body, she reached out further to safety. A roar sounded behind her. She told herself not to look back, but she couldn't help but jerk her head around.

Stomping only a few yards behind her was a ten-foot-tall brown sasquatch. Its teeth were barred and snarling foam dripped from its mouth.

She refocused on the clearing, but another sound came from behind her. A blood curdling scream echoed and threw her off balance, but she remained standing. The scream echoed again, and Rosie's head felt as if it was going to split. The scream ended and every noise got blocked out.

Warm liquid dripped from her ears, and this time she knew it was from her ear drums bursting and not a potion.

Ten more steps, she thought to herself, and with every step she could sense more and more feet right on her heels. Without being able to worry what else was behind her she shot forward, a hand clawing her back just as she reached the threshold.

Unable to hear her own scream, she shot a blast of

light back, stopping whatever was coming towards her and pushing her into the desert.

Landing on her stomach and face she tumbled and flipped before stopping in front of a patch of jumping chollas.

Laying on her back for only a second, she caught her breath, then jumped to her feet, her hands raised in front of her.

Now under the light of the moon, she searched for anything that could threaten her, but there was nothing. No one. Breathing a sigh of relief, she turned to the peak and threw her hand on a divot in the rocky wall and began climbing.

Scaling its side, she forced her tired, limp arms and legs to push her forward. Grabbing with her left hand at the dirt-covered top of the peak she pulled her body up and spouted a little more magic to shoot her up the rest of the way.

A King's Preparatory flag with the emblem stitched on it sat at the top of a pole and she grasped the skinny rod. At her touch, ruby fireworks shot into the air. She peered below and the trees sank into the ground. In the distance, her classmates appeared on the field, the Valtics on their feet cheering. She then scanned the desert that used to be the forest and found the other Illumination Teams standing, unhurt, alongside others she didn't recognize.

Cheers and chants bombarded her, and she lifted a hand to her ear. The dried blood sat there but her ears didn't hurt, and her hearing returned to normal. A whirling sensation pulled at her waist and suddenly she flew through the air. Panic and shock thrummed through her as she screamed, nearing the rest of the school.

Chapter Twenty-Eight

As she neared the field, her speed slowed, and she was thankfully able to plant her feet on the ground before the invisible loop around her released.

"Congrats!" Ms. Connors said, running and hugging Rosie. Rosie hugged her mother back. Clapping hit her shoulders and she pulled away to see Riley.

"Are you okay?" she asked, examining him. His shirt was still tattered, but the scratches were now nonexistent.

"I'm great! Even though we lost."

Rosie chuckled and she turned to find the rest of her team as Kingsley's voice boomed over the group.

"Congratulations, Valtics!" the Premier announced. "I want to thank all for making these games a special success, especially to our visitors!"

Rosie's head jerked around. She studied the group of individuals behind Kingsley, and stepping to the front was Raphael. Then emerging from behind the rest of the group, were teenagers.

"Our special guests from the Western Clan were gracious enough to accept our invitation to the school so they could see some of the fun extracurriculars we offer here at King's

Preparatory!"

There was a short pause where every King's Preparatory student turned to one another, confusion falling over the group. Professor Shay began to clap enthusiastically, and then every student started. Whoops and hollers bellowed, and Rosie was sure Kingsley or Shay amplified the cheers to impress the visitors.

"Thank you, Premier!" Raphael said, stepping forward and placing a hand on Kingsley's shoulder. His eyes scanned the crowd of cheering students, and then landed on Rosie's still body. He smiled and nodded in her direction before speaking again. "It has been such a treat so far to tour your lovely campus. The children of the clan," he said, and gestured to the group of ten teens standing by, grinning, "are excited to continue learning more about this wonderful campus over the next few days and seeing what the potential future of our two groups melding together would look like."

"They're staying here?" Rosie whispered to her mom, but she hadn't noticed she was now back up by Kingsley.

"Over the next few days, our two communities will gather and form a resolution to join as one!"

More applause erupted over the group. Rosie was sure the students didn't understand what was happening, but rather were just following Professor Shay's lead and the excitement in Kingsley's voice.

"Do you think the rest of the Superiority knows what's going on?" Justin asked, stepping up to Rosie's side.

"I hope so, or the Premier is about to be bombarded with a lot of angry phone calls from parents," Rosie replied.

The group of leaders started to walk, back towards the school, but Professor Shay stood in front of the students.

"Students, please make your way to the dining hall. We will be having a short presentation on what is to come for the next two days and show our guests what King's Preparatory is all about."

Students immediately began to stand and shuffle back towards the school as well, but Rosie stayed put, scanning the group of clan teens.

"No Dana," she stated to Riley and Justin.

"Do you think this is what Drew warned us about?"

"I'm not sure, but I have a feeling Dana would want actual bloodshed."

A girl from the group advanced forward and Rosie immediately lifted a guard for protection.

"Hi!" she exclaimed, her voice sweet and high. "I'm Sedone!" She extended her hand and Rosie continued to stare.

Reaching out to end the awkward exchange, Riley grabbed her hand. "Hi, I'm Riley."

"Nice to meet you Riley," Sedone said, the rest of the group walking to her side. Her eyes turned to Rosie.

"Hi, I'm Rosie and this is Justin."

"Yes! Rosie! We've heard a lot about you."

"Really?" Rosie asked, her eyebrows lifting.

"Yes, Dana had a lot to say about you."

Rosie's stomach sank and she pulled her magic forward, ready for a fight if need be.

"Don't worry," Sedone said, "all of us take what Dana says with a grain of salt. That girl is off her rocker."

The group nodded and chuckled before passing by the three.

"Well, they seem..." Justin started but didn't finish.

"Nice?" Riley said, looking at Rosie.

She continued to stare at the clan teens walking off toward the other students.

"What are you thinking?" Justin asked, turning towards her.

"Just, they're different."

"Is that good?" Riley asked, grabbing her hand and walking forward.

The three walked alongside each other, and Rosie continued to study the teens.

"I mean, they savagely attacked us in the forest, but Sedone seemed genuine in her greeting."

"Plus, they all agreed Dana is nuts," Riley joked.

"Do you think they are manipulating us?" she asked Justin.

Justin eyed Riley and then Rosie. "It's hard to tell," he replied. "They could want to be here. It seems like it is only a small fraction of the clan who doesn't necessarily want to join the Superiority. This group could want a normal high school experience."

"Normal?" Riley snorted, lifting an eyebrow.

"You know what I mean," Justin replied.

The three followed the rest of the school up to the dining hall.

"I'll catch you later?" Riley asked as he separated and moved towards the Surgent table.

She nodded, then pulled out a chair and plopped down next to Justin. Scanning the room for the visitors.

Surprisingly, they sat scattered throughout the room rather than sticking together. The officials from the clan sat at a table near the front stage and Professor Shay stood to address the school.

"Over the next two days, potential students from the Western Clan will be shadowing and touring alongside each of you. Those of you who are guides for our visitors have already been notified and will assist our guests in any way possible."

"Will they join the school right away?" Justin whispered to Rosie.

"The school year is almost over. We only have, what? A few weeks left? I bet they will start next year."

Professor Shay continued, "Students, elders from the clan, and our very own Superiority council members will be around the next few days to observe. You may be pulled aside or even out of class to answer any questions regarding the school, your experiences here, or to report how the tour is going. Please provide honest feedback. It is imperative to our society. Each of you are playing an important role in our future."

Rosie snorted and Raphael's eyes hit hers. She coughed to cover up the laugh, but he and Kingsley eyed her.

"As it is almost three in the afternoon, please go back to your regular class schedule. Guides, have your guest shadow you. Tonight, at six sharp, we will have our official welcome feast!"

The room clamored and excited conversation erupted as students stood. Some groups walked down to classrooms and others back to their dorms or living rooms. Rosie and Justin sat watching the hall clear, and she watched Kingsley also get up.

He started towards her, her mother next to him, and the men and women from the council and clan followed.

"Gentlemen and ladies, I'd like you all to meet two of our

brightest students. Rosie Connors and Justin Fent."

"Connors? She's related to you, Rose?" one of the men asked.

"My daughter." Ms. Connors smiled and stared down at Rosie adoringly.

"Rosie is a witch," Kingsley continued. "Just came into her powers a year ago. They had been trapped within, but she was able to unleash them."

The group turned to one another and nodded and whispered.

"And Justin here," Kingsley continued, "is a true amalgam."

"Really? So young?" a different man exclaimed, stepping forward.

"Fent," Mr. Parker said. "Why does that name sound so familiar?"

Justin cleared his throat before speaking. "I'm friends with Garrett, sir."

Mr. Parker paused but began again, "No, you're the kid who assisted Witam."

"Now, now Joe, the boy wasn't himself," Kingsley said.

Justin's face burned red hot, and his head fell as more hushed conversations erupted. Rosie stared at Garrett's dad, wondering how such a loveable goofball could come from such a callous man.

"His name was Egil," Rosie spat. She placed her hands, which were balled into fists, firmly on the table and continued, "And he lied and manipulated a lot of people to get what he wanted, didn't he? I mean, you as a council approve who is hired at the school, right? Even you couldn't see what he was. Even you, Mr. Parker, were tricked."

Mr. Parker's eyes narrowed, and Rosie maintained eye

contact with the enormous wolf.

"Rosie!" Ms. Connors whisper-shouted at her, but Kingsley clapped a hand on Mr. Parker's back and chuckled.

"She does have a point!" Kingsley laughed, leading Mr. Parker and the rest of the group away. "Why don't we all move up to the conference room to discuss our earlier conversation?"

The leaders walked away, and a soft hand rested on Rosie's shoulder.

"You okay?" Justin asked, now standing up.

Rosie pushed off the table and shook her hands, which throbbed from pressing against the wooden table. She stared at Justin and nodded. "Yeah I'm good, but are you?"

Justin started to laugh.

"What?" Rosie asked, her eyebrows furrowing together.

"Nothing," Justin spurted out.

"No, seriously. What?"

"While I appreciate you standing up to Garrett's dad for me, it might be better not to get on the Alpha's bad side." Justin continued to laugh as he started towards the library.

"Well," Rosie said, starting after him, "I couldn't just let him speak to you like that! I mean, he really should know better."

"They'll never know better. Most men never find the courage to admit when they are wrong. Only the words to blame others."

Rosie thought about the words, and while she agreed with Justin, she couldn't understand how the individuals who were charged with protecting those under the Superiority could hold such narrow-minded views.

The two walked and found their way into the greenhouse library. Sitting with Justin at a table on the second floor of the library, Rosie pulled out her notebook and set up her study station before heading back down to Ms. Pamfet.

"Hi, Rosie," the sweet librarian said.

"Hello," Rosie greeted as she pulled out a folded piece of paper from her pocket.

"Have a list for me today?"

Rosie smiled sheepishly and handed the paper over.

"I'll get these pulled and up to you in a jiff."

"Thank you," Rosie said before returning to her seat.

"What are you researching now?" Justin asked as Rosie scooted her chair back in.

"How do you know I'm not doing schoolwork?"

"Because we have the same schoolwork and I know for a fact you are done with everything."

Rosie chuckled and opened to a fresh page and started scribbling.

"So, I'm in the dark? Okay, I'll have to guess then."

Rosie smirked but continued to write.

"You are researching how to restore the beacon?"

Rosie lifted an eyebrow as she wrote but didn't look up.

"No, that's not it. You've been researching that for months and if the clan joins the Superiority, then the beacon will be restored. Mmm, let's see. You are learning ways to fight sasquatches, in case Dana ends up coming to school."

Rosie snorted but continued with her note taking.

"No, huh? Okay, my final guess. You are trying to harness your mother's gift."

Rosie's head whipped up to find Justin smirking down at his own book.

"How did you..." Rosie started to ask.

"I remember you had those dreams last year and then when

you learned of your mother's gift, I figured you would try to hone in on the ability. So, have you?"

Rosie huffed before staring back at her notes on dream weaving and predicting before muttering, "No."

"Mhm, interesting."

"What is?" Rosie asked, setting her pen down and interlacing her fingers.

"Just," Justin started, "you had the gift—"

"Not really. I mean, I saw the past, but I never saw the future."

"But that is a form of the gift."

"I guess, but I haven't been able to harness that power again."

"And that's what you're trying to learn how to do? With the list of books you just requested from Ms. Pamfet?"

Rosie nodded and turned her head up to Ms. Pamfet, who rolled a cart with six books on it to the table.

"Here you go, Rosie," she said, and Rosie and Justin stood to help unload the thick texts.

"Thank you," Rosie said before sitting back down and pulling the first, *Our Subconscious*, forward.

She turned to the table of contents, but before reading the first topic, Justin started again.

"There may be a faster way to unlock your power."

Rolling her eyes and ignoring Justin, Rosie continued to read. Thankful that no more interruptions came from Justin, Rosie scanned the pages. She committed the words to memory but as she read, the exhaustion from just participating in the games started to weigh on her eyelids. They started to droop, and the sweet call of sleep resonated with her. As her head fell forward a little though, it jostled back up at the sound of books slamming to the floor.

"What?" Rosie asked, searching if the noise came from her table. Both hers and Justin's stacks were still standing. Justin, however, was no longer sitting with her. Turning her head around and scanning the area, he couldn't be found.

Reasoning that he must've gone to find another book when she rested her eyes, she started to read again but didn't manage to get past the first sentence.

Standing up and walking down the stairs, Rosie searched for Justin, Ms. Pamfet—anyone else—but she was alone. Suddenly, an erupting roar rumbled through the library. Stomping feet and snarling barks echoed closer. Rosie sprinted back up the stairs and desperately searched for a place to hide.

Crawling under her table, Rosie held her breath. The splitting of the wooden doors caused Rosie to jump, and she scooted a little closer to the edge so she could see what stood below. Right at the edge, only a few inches from her face, was the top of a sasquatch's head. It didn't face her though. Instead, it stood off against a wolf.

Baring its teeth, the wolf circled closer to the sasquatch, but it expanded its body and readied itself for the wolf's lunge. Sure enough, the wolf leapt forward, its jaws spread wide but the sasquatch engulfed the wolf.

Moving forward more and peering down the side of the edge, Rosie saw what happened. In a bear hug with the sasquatch, the wolf attempted to wriggle free, but the sasquatch squeezed harder and a sharp snap and small whine came from the wolf.

The sasquatch tossed the wolf aside and Rosie stared down at its open, lifeless eyes. Busting into the room were more wolves, followed by shifters and then vampires.

Rosie recognized a few of her classmates and one of the council members who happened to be a vampire. They started to move in on the sasquatch, but behind them other creatures came hurtling down the hall.

Watchers, banshees, and other creatures in the clan advanced.

Rosie stood and yelled, "Behind you!"

Her classmates turned to look but the sasquatch turned to Rosie.

A snarling grin spread on its face and a large, hairy hand reached up, wrapping itself around her leg.

Hitting the ground, Rosie reached out to grab onto something to keep her away from the death grip of the sasquatch, but her body continued to slide across the floor, and then she fell.

Chapter Twenty-Nine

Rosie's head shot up from the book in front of her, a piece of paper sticking to her cheek. She stared at Justin and then stood, examining her surroundings.

"Rosie, you're okay," Justin said, now standing and moving to her side. He assisted her back down and sat in the seat next to her.

"No, there was fighting," she mumbled, rubbing her cheeks and trying to grasp what just happened. "I was dreaming?" she asked Justin, now staring at him.

"You were. You had a vision."

"But, how?"

"Please don't get mad."

"Justin, what happened?" Rosie began to grow hot and turned towards him.

"I thought by leading you through a guided hypnosis I could help unlock your subconscious, and in return, your gift."

"I didn't give you permission!" Rosie said, shooting backwards now crossing her arms.

"I know, I'm sorry, I just thought that if I did this without your knowledge, we would get results."

"Why would you think that?"

"Rosie, you tend to be a little tense. For the hypnosis to work, I needed you to be relaxed, and not knowing what was happening helped. Clearly."

Rosie's anger lingered but the scenes from a moment earlier replayed.

"Woah," Justin whispered, and she refocused on him. "Rosie, I assume you are rewatching what you just saw. Your eyes, they brighten and glow blue when you do."

Rosie furrowed her brows and shook her head. She sat in silence, unsure if she needed to run and tell Kingsley what was going to happen or if she should study her dream more.

"You said you saw fighting, Rosie," Justin said. "What happened?"

She lifted her head and met his gaze. She didn't know what mattered from the dream. Was it the entire scene? The location? The people? Her mind swirled with confusion.

"Just start with what you saw," Justin reassured. "We can dissect the vision later."

Rosie nodded. "I was here. At this table. And there was a rumbling noise and a sasquatch entered and then a wolf. The sasquatch killed the wolf. Then others joined."

"More members of the clan?"

Rosie shook her head. "No, Superiority members. Classmates. They arrived to stop the sasquatch, but it was a trap. They were led away and then surrounded by clan members. I called out to warn them but in doing so I was made known and attacked, and then, then…"

"Then you woke up," Justin said, grabbing her hand. "You're okay now, Rosie. You're safe."

She faced him now. "But if that was a true vision, then that means there is going to be an attack on the Superiority." She stood so fast that her chair flew out and landed on its side. "We have to go see Kingsley," she said, and began to descend the staircase.

"Wait, Rosie," Justin called, but she didn't stop. She shifted between bookshelves and plants, tables and students. Justin reached her side, and they exited the library.

"Do you even know where he is right now?"

"With the other council members."

"Exactly. And your mom. Speaking of which, don't you think you should talk to her about this first? She can help you understand the vision better."

"Justin, there isn't any time."

"I know, and I agree, the Premier should know as soon as possible, but maybe your mom has seen something similar."

"You think she has seen a battle happen? Between the clan and Superiority?"

"Why else is she in attendance at these meetings?"

Rosie thought about her mother. She had just been promoted to her new position within the Superiority. It was supposed to be a remote position, but if she had seen ways to avoid conflict between the two groups, then it made sense for Kingsley to have her around during discussions.

"If she has seen something," Rosie started, "then she also needs to know I have seen fighting."

"So instead of going in, guns blazing, let's pull your mother aside. The group will just think she needs to deal with a family matter. Then you can tell her what you saw, and she can relay it to the Premier."

Rosie nodded in agreement and the two moved through the corridors and hallways, finally reaching the main floor.

"Do you know where the conference room is?" Justin asked Rosie, staring up and down the never-ending hallway.

"No idea." She walked along the hallway, pulling open doors as she went.

"Rosie!" Professor Shay exclaimed as Rosie stared blankly at the headmistress, who was standing extremely close to Professor Manger.

"Um, sorry!" she said, trying to close the door to continue her search, but Professor Shay stopped her.

"What do you think you are doing?"

Rosie pulled the door back open so she couldn't hide behind the wooden slab, and she took a small step in.

"I'm looking for my mom."

"Oh," Professor Shay said, surprised, "well, she is busy right now. With the Premier and party delegates."

"I know, but still. It's important."

Professor Shay sighed, but lifted her wrist and checked her watch.

"I suppose the delegation is due for a short break from their deliberations. Come on."

A short growl escaped Manger's throat, but Professor Shay patted him, and he took a seat, glaring at Rosie.

"Hey, Rosie!" Justin said, entering the room but quickly shifting his feet to allow Professor Shay to pass. "Hi, um."

"Don't worry Mr. Fent. I was just showing Rosie to her mother. Come along."

Justin smiled at Rosie, but she remained focused on explaining the vision.

The two followed Professor Shay through the hallway down to the very end. She knocked on the door and a small, older woman opened it quietly and peered out.

"Could you please retrieve Ms. Connors?" Professor Shay asked the woman, who in turn bowed her head compliantly and stepped back.

With her view of the room clear, Rosie searched it. The dim room, lit by only candles and torches, resembled a cave rather than a traditional conference room. The rocky walls glinted with gold, copper, silver, and platinum, as well as different gems and jewels. Rosie, reaching for her Valtic necklace, wondered if this was where the crystal ball pulled their pendants from. Seated around a long, petrified wood carved table were the same individuals who were present at the Games.

Spying her mother, Rosie stepped forward to draw her attention, but Professor Shay stared down at Rosie and shook her head.

Rosie nodded and stepped back but kept her eyes trained on the woman walking towards her mother. Not even needing to bend over to whisper into her mother's ear, she informed Rosie's mom and she turned to the doorway.

James Kingsley noted the new additions, and over the hushed conversation announced, "Why don't we take a short break?"

Murmurs of agreement sounded, and different members of the group stood to stretch, others walked off to a corner to speak further, and Ms. Connors and Kingsley strolled over to the doorway.

"Mom," Rosie said as she approached.

"Honey, is everything okay?" Rosie eyed Kingsley and then her mom continued, "It's okay. Tell me, what's going on?"

"I had a vision," Rosie blurted, causing both her mother's and the Premier's eyes to widen.

"Why don't we step into the hallway," Kingsley suggested before gesturing out and closing the door behind him. As soon as the door snapped shut, he asked, "What did you see?"

Rosie stared at her mom, but she nodded in encouragement. "The school was attacked. A lot of people are going to die."

"Who attacked?" Ms. Connors asked, stepping closer and grabbing Rosie's hand.

"Clan members. Ones not happy with the resolution."

"How many?" Kingsley asked.

"I'm not sure. It was just one huge sasquatch at first but then students and Superiority members were surrounded. A hundred?"

"Okay, so just a small faction," Kingsley murmured to himself before turning back. "You're sure this was a vision? Not just a dream? The games today could've spurred a vivid dream."

"It was a vision," Justin said. The four stared at him and he continued, "I led her through it. Also, her magic was triggered during the journey."

Kingsley nodded. "Did you recognize anyone?"

"The sasquatch was huge. As tall as the second level of the library. I had never seen the wolf it killed before, but I recognized the vampire council member and a few others, and there was a pack of wolves."

"Okay, and the rest of the fighting clan members?"

"It was a huge group. I couldn't distinguish one from another."

"Alright, Rosie, thank you. Please, both of you, keep this information to yourselves. If there is to be an attack, we don't want the rebels to know that we know."

"Rebels?

"Yes, rebels. There is a small group in the clan fighting this merge, but we will take care of it."

"But are you going to tell the elders? Have them stop it?"

"Rosie," her mother started, "don't worry about what happens next. Just focus on school. We have this handled."

Kingsley nodded and then stepped back into the room.

"I'll talk to you later, honey," Ms. Connors said, kissing Rosie's head before heading back inside.

"Professor Shay," Rosie said, "you're not honestly going to just sit around, are you?"

"Rosie, do you think I would defy the Premier's orders?"

"But—" Justin said.

"Don't worry. I will make sure the school is protected." She winked at the two, closed the door, and started back down the hallway.

"Should we tell anyone, warn them?" Justin asked.

"No, but I think we should just keep an eye on the visiting students and be ready."

"Do you know when it will happen?"

Rosie searched the memory and Justin muttered, "Woah," as her eyes lit up bright blue again.

"The clock in the library," she said, "it was stuck on seven-oh-three."

"Any idea of what day?"

"It has to be today, tomorrow, or Friday. The council members were here, so were Superiority agents. My guess is Friday."

"That would make sense. If an agreement is or isn't made, I suspect some sort of announcement will be made or broadcast by the Premier."

Rosie started speed-walking back down the hallway.

"Wait, Rosie, shouldn't we go back and—"

"Premier Kingsley is aware. My dad isn't. He could stop this. I know it."

Chapter Thirty

Rosie slammed her phone down on her desk before turning it over quickly to ensure she hadn't shattered the face. Sure enough, cracks erupted across the front and Rosie stared at her own reflection behind the broken screen. It had been two days of trying to reach Christion with no response from him.

"Still no word from your dad?" Justin asked, sitting down next to her.

She shook her head glumly but attempted to drop her attitude when Riley and Eleanor, followed by the bulk of their year, walked into the grand lecture hall.

"Any idea why we are meeting in here and not on the combat field?" Riley asked before leaning over and giving Rosie a quick peck on the cheek. He sat on her other side while Eleanor took the seat behind her.

"Not sure," Rosie answered. "Maybe Manger wants us to learn strategy or something else rather than brute force?"

"Oh, I hope so. I'm still sore from yesterday's training," Eleanor said, massaging her arms.

"Or maybe it has to do with our visitors,' Justin said, then indicated with his head the group of clan students heading to the front.

Rosie's head turned up and she found Sedone in the group of clan members. The group walked around ten seats reserved at the front and sat down.

"Let's get started," Professor Manger's authoritative voice sounded, and the room quieted. "For the last couple of days, we have had our guests shadow you and observe you. Now we have been given the opportunity to do the same."

"In a controlled environment of course," a man said from the back of the classroom.

Rosie turned her head and Raphael sat in the back corner, hidden in the dark.

"Of course," Professor Manger grunted. "If one at a time, each of you could come forward and tell us about yourself and your strengths and weaknesses." Professor Manger nodded to a boy who sat at the end.

Standing up, the boy moved to the front of the class. He had to be only five-feet-tall and looked like he should've had a parent with him.

"Hi," he started before clearing his voice and speaking a little louder. "I'm Ron and I'm a sasquatch."

Small chuckles and hushed whispers sounded.

"Silence!" Manger shouted and once the room quieted, Ron continued.

"In my natural form, I am seven-two and can crush a skull with one hand." Rosie surveyed the room and found that most eyes had widened at the spoken fact.

"Good for him," Justin whispered with a chuckle. "He should show off to this bunch."

Rosie nodded in agreement and continued to listen.

"There are various sasquatch colonies located throughout

the world. There are different names for them. Skunk Apes, Yetis, Big Foots, but we are all the same species. A weakness that we have is we can only communicate if we are all in one form or another. If I remained in this state and someone else from my tribe was in their natural state, then we wouldn't be able to speak. In our natural state, we render only grunts and growls, but can speak to each other telepathically."

"Why do you think they are revealing this? Especially if the Premier spoke to them about knowing of an attack?" Justin asked.

"Who knows if the Premier brought it up? I'm sure Raphael approved what they could and couldn't divulge." She peered back around and found Raphael, but turned her head back forward as his eyes had been solely on her.

At the front, Ron now sat down, and a different student came forward.

"Hi, I'm Sheena. I'm a Banshee."

"Do you think every single person down there is a different type of supernatural?" Rosie asked, leaning over to Justin.

He nodded, and Rosie took a deep breath.

The students went down the line. A sasquatch, a banshee, a dark watcher, a walker, a chupacabra, a troll, a goblin, an elf, a wrangler, and then Sedone stood.

"Hi, I'm Sedone. I'm an elemental."

Rosie sat forward and the room burst into murmurs. Even Professor Manger stepped back in surprise.

"What's an elemental?" Riley asked.

But Rosie didn't answer. Both her and Justin leaned further forward in their seats.

"As an elemental," Sedone continued, "I can manipulate earth, air, water, and fire. I am one of only a handful in existence, so we rely on alliances with other species to survive."

"But you are one of the most powerful creatures in existence," Rosie blurted out. Heads turned in her direction and Sedone let a wry smile cross her face.

"If taught properly. Unfortunately, with such a limited number of our kind, no one has been able to reach the final plane."

"The what?" a boy called out.

Sedone continued, "When an elemental becomes complete with their powers, they can be the thing they try to manipulate. Shift themselves into air, fire, earth, or water."

The room broke out into more side conversations and Professor Manger called everyone's attention back.

"Thank you to our guests for providing us with such detail on their species, something we may not have ever gotten. Homework for tonight is to select a creature spoken about today and detail what was discussed. I hope you were taking notes." Manger smirked at the groans before stepping out of the classroom.

"Do you think there are more creatures in the clan? Other than those who were here today?"

"Definitely." Rosie nodded thinking about creatures that couldn't shift to a human state. Centaurs came to her mind. "I think if we don't come to a truce with the clan, we will be up against a lot more creatures than what we saw today."

Suddenly, her phone buzzed in her hand, and she fumbled it before reading the screen.

"Dad?" she asked into the phone.

"Hey kid, how are you?" Christion's voice sounded on the other end.

"Dad, are you okay? I've been trying to reach you. You haven't been at the summit, and I figured you would be involved."

"I'm okay, don't worry. I am involved but just in an out-of-the-picture way."

"But you're safe?"

"Yes, I'm safe."

Rosie's shoulders relaxed and she stared at Riley, Justin, and Eleanor, nodding. The three broke out into a grin and headed out of the class.

"When can I see you?" Rosie asked.

"I'll be back on campus today. I'll find you. But I gotta go." In the background Rosie could hear a commotion and then the line went dead.

"He okay?" Riley asked.

"I think so. He should be here tonight, so I'll catch up with him more then."

Riley nodded and extended an arm around her shoulder.

"Um, Rosie?" Sedone called from behind.

Rosie stopped and turned back. "Hey, Sedone."

"Hi." She nervously looked around the group. "Can we talk? Privately?"

"You can say anything in front of us," Riley said, but Rosie put a hand on his chest.

"Go ahead," she reassured. "I'll meet you guys later."

Searching Sedone up and down one last time, he nodded and followed Eleanor and Justin.

"What's up?" Rosie asked, turning back to Sedone.

"Well, you seem to know about elementals?" she asked, nervously.

"Just what I've read. I was under the impression there

weren't any in existence."

"Yeah, I mean it's close. I'm the last one."

"What?" Rosie said. "But I thought there were a handful? You just said?"

"A lie. It's just me."

"I'm sorry. That must be hard."

"It is. My parents died when I was little, as did my grandparents."

"I'm so sorry. I can't imagine your pain."

Sedone nodded. "Anyway, before they passed, Raphael took us in. Again, we depend on alliances to remain safe. I'm not sure how much you know about our history, but Elementals have been pursued for thousands of years."

"I know. Your power is harnessed and once harnessed, you can be used against the human world."

"There are a lot more natural disasters that aren't as natural as you'd think." Rosie nodded but let her continue. "Raphael seems to think that this alliance with the Superiority will be the best thing for us. We will belong to a larger group and be a part of a society that is dictated by control. We wouldn't need to worry about random attacks or fighting amongst ourselves."

"So, there is disruption within the clan?"

Sedone's face immediately went red and she opened her mouth.

"It's okay," Rosie reassured, "I won't say anything."

Sedone closed her mouth and gave her a grateful smile. "Raphael has done a wonderful thing. Uniting all of us. But the inner dynamics of the group are far more complex than he realized. Within the Superiority, there is a council, a true hierarchy, an order. If you think we would be safer under the protection of the Superiority, then I will do my part to try and bring our community into yours." She nodded and grinned at Rosie, then passed her.

Left in the room alone, Rosie thought about joining the rest of the school for dinner, but instead raced back to her dorm room.

Reaching the knob and pulling the door open, Rosie almost ran right into Olive.

"Woah!" Olive shouted. "What is your deal?"

"Sorry, Olive," Rosie said as she passed her and dove underneath her bed.

"So weird," Olive whispered before clicking the door closed behind her.

Pushing boxes and clothes aside, she dug out the *Being* book. Rosie understood she could wait for Christion for answers, but without knowing when he would be back, she searched the book.

The soft skin pages sailed beneath her fingers as Rosie read. Resting the book open, she held her hands above the book and called for the information she needed. Words shifted on the pages, moving and twisting. Then they peeled from the pages and floated in the air. Once the words were off the page new text appeared.

She shifted her hand across the book and more words shifted off while others were transferred from other pages, leaving all the information Rosie wanted to read. Viewing the next five pages, Rosie now had a full list of all humanoid supernaturals, their powers, weaknesses, and strengths, including Elementals.

Placing her hand on the page, a burning sensation hit her palm and she yelped. She desperately wanted to remove her hand as heat radiated through it, but she kept it as still as possible. The words copied from the book and as if a pointed pen scribbled on her, the words transferred to her skin. Quickly, she eyed a notebook on her desk and willed it forward. It fell next to the *Being* book, and she took one hand and placed it on the bare pages. The words flowed from the pages onto her and then into the notebook.

As soon as the piercing scratching on her skin ceased, she lifted her hands and ripped out the page from her notebook, now stained with the words from the *Being* book. Studying it, she waved the paper with the information and it hid within the sheet so she was left staring at a blank page. She smiled and headed back down to the dining hall.

"You okay?" Justin asked Rosie as she stepped into the lobby of the wizard dorm.

"Oh, you're not at dinner?"

"No, I wanted to make sure you were okay after talking with Sedone."

"Yeah! I'm fine," Rosie said reassuringly. "Turns out, there is a lot more strife within the clan and between the different species than we realize. Sedone told me that she hopes the Superiority will be able to bring order to each tribe, colony, and cluster."

"Wow, really? Do you think the Premier knows? Would Raphael tell him?"

"I'm sure Raphael wouldn't say anything, but through my dad, I expect the Premier is aware."

"Is that for your dad?" Justin asked, pointing to the blank piece of paper.

"More like from my dad." A coy smile turned at her lips and she held up the paper and waved it again. The scribbled list appeared, and Justin read it.

"You think all of these creatures could be included in the clan or at least are allied?"

"Yep, and if they try to attack, we'll know how to stop them."

* * *

Rosie glanced at her watch and bobbed her knee up and down. "It's six-thirty. We should get to the hall before dinner ends."

"Before dinner ends, or in case something happens at seven-oh-three?"

"Both." The two sat in their dorm lobby studying the list and trying to figure out which creatures would be easiest to take down, which they should leave to more experienced Superiority members, and which everyone should avoid completely if present.

"Can your visions of the future be altered or changed if preventative steps are taken?" Justin asked, staring at the daunting notes. He gathered them up and the two started for the dining hall.

Rosie thought for a moment as they walked through the Valtic common room. "I feel like these steps would be punitive though."

"How?"

"Destiny is destiny. Plus, who's to say the steps won't accidentally put the premonition into action rather than if nothing was done? There are too many factors."

"But there has to be a calculation of some sort we can derive to ensure the prevention of deaths."

"It's possible. Something we should talk to my parents about."

Justin nodded and he opened the door for her to step through to enter the dining hall. Clinking of silverware on plates and excited conversation spread across the room.

Sitting down at the Valtic table, Eleanor leaned across the plates and bowls of food and asked, "Where have you guys been? Riley's been worried." She nodded her head in the direction of the Surgent table and Rosie turned.

His eyes were set on hers and they held a mixture of relief and anger. He directed them toward Justin and then back at her and she mouthed, "Don't worry." She started to stand again so she could walk over to him, but Premier Kingsley stood at the front of the room.

"Attention, students," Professor Shay announced over the room, and all heads turned up to the stage.

"Students," Premier Kingsley stated, pacing a moment before holding center stage. Rosie peered behind him, seeing satisfied looks on each of the council members faces and even on most of the elders. She spied Raphael, who also seemed happy.

"There's been a resolution," Rosie whispered to Justin.

He opened his mouth to ask how she knew but the Premier continued.

"Right now, the Superiority is sending out news to every family within our society, whether they are right here, in Kingstown, or on the other side of the world. News of enormous triumph and history."

"Here we go," Justin whispered back.

"As many great conclusions are reached, strife and hardship must come first, but I am pleased to inform everyone here that all other humanoid supernatural creatures throughout the world have been invited to join the Superiority and live within our society."

The room clapped and Rosie eyed Garrett, who smiled at his dad. Unfortunately, his dad didn't acknowledge the gesture.

"Starting next year, children from various creature species and subspecies will join here to learn in harmony and prosperity."

More clapping ensued, and Rosie spotted the handful of clan kids who were clapped on the shoulder and had their hands shaken.

"Further, with this influx of students, we will be opening up a second King's Preparatory."

Rosie's eyes furrowed together. "A second school?" Eleanor asked. "Who will go there?"

The room hushed and Kingsley continued, "Letters will be sent to you and your family with your new school designation."

"I knew it," Justin said, chuckling. Rosie turned to him. "I figured, with all the new students, they would divide everyone up equally. No way Raphael or the elders would have a school just for the clan. They would want all species to mix."

"To ensure their safety," Rosie said.

"Exactly."

Murmurs and questions floated around the hall.

"I don't want to be split up from you guys," Eleanor said, grabbing Garrett's hand and squeezing it.

"Same," he replied, eyeing his dad. "Let me see if I can get some answers about which students will be assigned here."

"Do you have any idea where the second school will be located? Will it still be in Arizona?" Rosie asked Garrett.

"I have to imagine it will be on the opposite side of the country," Justin said, the faces staring at him turning into horrified stares. "I mean, that would make the most sense. They might divide the groups up based on who acclimates best to what type of weather or where people are geographically."

Rosie's head turned to Riley, and he stared at her with concern.

"I'll try to see if I can find out more from my parents too," Rosie said, now searching for her mom at the front.

Ms. Connors sat next to the Premier's empty seat and Rosie searched down the row, spying each member and teacher at the table.

"Any sign of your dad?" Justin asked.

Rosie shook her head but as she did so, a thundering clap echoed through the room and everyone's head turned to the bang of the door where Christion had run in.

Rosie jumped to her feet along with others throughout the room. Screams erupted at Christion's bloody figure running to the stage.

With her feet moving before her mind could register what happened, Rosie reached the stage where Christion sat on the platform, Kingsley and her mother bent at his side.

"What happened, Christion?" Kingsley asked, Raphael now joining the group.

Christion's eyes met Rosie's before he glanced up at Raphael. "It's a faction of the clan." He turned to Kingsley.

"They heard the announcement. Superiority agents showed up to their homes."

"What?" Raphael exclaimed. "You promised there would be no interference on your end when we shared the news."

"I didn't authorize it," Kingsley said, standing to reassure Raphael. Then Kingsley turned to the council members. All searched each other's faces, all except Mr. Parker, who looked at Kingsley with an *I told you so* expression.

"I will pull back our agents at once," a different member said, now standing and dialing a number into his phone.

"It doesn't matter," Christion said. "It could've been you delivering the news personally, Raphael. They still would have attacked."

"Do you know which members?" Raphael asked, now gesturing for the elders to join them."

"The entire dwarf society, a faction of the elves, part of the watchers and spirits, and a handful of sasquatches."

"Is that all?" Ms. Connors asked as she inspected Christion's injuries.

"There could be more but from the rally I overheard happening, that was it."

"Would the other members of the clan, those who want to be a part of the Superiority, fight with us?" Ms. Connors asked Raphael and the elders.

Raphael contemplated a moment and before he could answer, one of the elders spoke.

"We will fight with you." The older man turned to the others. Some started to make calls while others left.

Christion stood, his hand gripping his side and he addressed Raphael. "This is part of the deal, Raphael. If you are with us, you need to tell us now."

Raphael nodded and gathered with the others.

"And the beacon, it's restored?" Christion now asked Kingsley.

"At my announcement, it should've been."

At the statement, Rosie closed her eyes and grounded herself, letting down her magical walls. Waves of power flowed into her and without needing to siphon at all, she drew on the earth's magic. Popping open her eyes, she nodded at Christion, who studied her. She opened her mouth but snapped her head to Professor Shay, who now addressed the school.

"Students, quickly return to your dorms. In ten minutes, they will be secured, and no one will be able to enter or exit. Hasten there now!"

Students clamored throughout the room, racing to their respective team rooms which would spit them out at their dorms. Rosie scanned the crowd. Riley faced her and he tried to push through the swarm of people, but his body was dragged through the Surgent door.

"Rosie," Justin said, moving to her side along with Eleanor and Garrett.

"Come on," Eleanor said, pulling her arm.

"No, wait." She read her watch and sure enough it said seven-oh-two. Her eyes glanced up at the dining hall door and a high-pitched scream reverberated across the dining hall, shaking the glass ceiling and sending her vision into darkness.

Chapter Thirty-One

Along with the few others still in the room, Rosie clutched her ears and bent over. Her mind went blank for a second but as she drew her eyes open, they found a handful of creatures entering the hall.

"Run!" Christion screamed at her, and she turned. As she sprinted to the Valtic door, she peeked behind her.

Eleanor pulled on Garrett while Justin pulled on Eleanor. Ripping her away from Garrett, Justin hauled Eleanor over his shoulder towards Rosie. Behind the two, Garrett ripped through his clothes and into his werewolf form alongside his father.

Widening her eyes, she ran back towards the group, but like Eleanor, Justin grabbed Rosie's waist and threw her over his other shoulder.

"No, wait!" Rosie shouted, but it was drowned out by Eleanor's yells, the growls of creatures preparing to fight, and the slamming of the Valtic library door.

Justin continued to run through the library but halfway through the room he stopped to adjust his grip. Using the second, Rosie popped back to his front, and kneed him. Dropping Eleanor now, Justin stepped back but recovered.

"Rosie, Eleanor, I can't let you go back."

"You can't leave him!" Eleanor shouted, tears streaming down her face.

A thud hit the door, and then another. The three looked back and watched as the wood began to splinter. With the distraction, Rosie tried to slip past Justin, but he blocked both girls.

"Garrett is skilled, he will be okay," Justin reasoned.

"He might!" Rosie yelled. "But his dad won't. I saw him die!"

At her side Eleanor gasped, and beyond the door a howl and then a whine pierced through. Another hard bang against the door creaked the wood open more, and Rosie spied a large, orange eye peering in. Then there was another growl and another bang.

"I have to keep you safe," Justin said, staring back to her. "I made a promise." He drew his hands up in the air and with one, he controlled the two girls, lifting them towards the back of the room. With the other, he slammed bookcases and tables against the weak entry.

As Justin whispered under his breath, Rosie watched magical chains link against the furniture so they would hold in place longer.

"Justin, please! My mom! My dad!"

"Who do you think made me promise to keep you safe, Rosie?"

A banshee scream echoed behind the furniture tower, thankfully dulled by the magic that pulsed in the room.

Running up the stairs with the two, Justin headed for the secret room. As he reached the top of the staircase for the second level, a blast burst from behind him. Dropping both

Eleanor and Rosie, the three skidded across the ground and hit a bookshelf against the wall.

Edging forward, the front of her body stuck to the ground, Rosie peered over the ledge. Sure enough, the top of a sasquatch's head came almost to eye-level. Putting a hand over her mouth, she controlled her breathing.

Shuffling next to her, Justin nudged her, his eyes trained towards the sasquatch. She nodded and he lifted a hand, pooling magic into his palm, and she did the same. The dense balls of magic lifted up and above the creature, but a blast of splintering wood dissipated the magic.

Bursting through the door, Mr. Parker foamed at the mouth, snarling. Rosie and Justin watched on as Mr. Parker flew forward and hit the sasquatch in the gut, knocking it back. The thunderous fall caused books to leave their shelves, hitting Eleanor and bouncing over to Justin and Rosie.

As Rosie tossed a book aside, a crunching of bones echoed below them and a small whimper from a hurt dog sounded. Rosie stood and looked over the edge. Mr. Parker, now tossed off to the side, attempted to drag himself away but the beast moved in.

"NO!" Rosie yelled in a desperate attempt to give Garrett's dad a chance.

The distraction worked and the sasquatch turned to Rosie. A menacing grin spread across its face and with Justin and Eleanor now at her side, the three stepped back as it approached.

"Now what?" Justin asked as the three also noticed the barrage of other creatures pouring into the library.

"Eleanor, run," Rosie said, stepping forward, conjuring a ball of magic, and thrusting it at the creature.

"No way!" Eleanor yelled and before Rosie could stop her, she burst over the railing and kicked the sasquatch across the face as she jumped through the air.

Widening her eyes, Rosie saw what Eleanor couldn't. As her friend flew by the hurt sasquatch, one of its arms reached out to grab her.

"If she is caught, she'll be crushed," Justin said, reading Rosie's mind. Flames erupted from Justin's palms, and he directed the fire forward. Streams of fire scorched the hair of the sasquatch and it growled loudly. It brought its hands away from Eleanor and to the flames engulfing its body and Rosie jumped down.

Eleanor was already at Mr. Parker's side, evaluating his wounds.

"He needs help," she said as Rosie turned her back to them to keep an eye on the sasquatch. It was still attempting to put the flames out, so Rosie searched the room and found her classmates, teachers, and Superiority members dueling with rebel clan members all around her.

"Keep him under the table," she commanded Eleanor. "Stay here and protect him."

Eleanor nodded and surveyed the room. As she did so, Rosie stared back at Justin, who was descending the staircase while fighting off a boy.

The boy opened his mouth to scream but Justin took a ball of magic and covered his mouth with his hand, then sent him over the ledge. The boy who had just fallen sat up, and Rosie saw he meant to scream but his mouth had disappeared. He stood, eyebrows coming together in rage.

Rosie started towards him but the harsh stench of burnt hair hit her nose and she turned backwards to the sasquatch, now badly burned, and madder than ever. As it started to charge her, her heart thrummed harder and a body hit hers, taking her out of the way from being crushed.

At her side now, Justin helped her up while her savior took her other arm and the three prepared for the next charge.

"Dana?" Rosie asked, staring at the girl in shock before returning her gaze to the angry sasquatch.

"Surprised? Me too," Dana said, before running forward and bursting into her own sasquatch form. Her body hit the other sasquatch and the two fell on top of a table, sending it crashing down.

"Come on!" Justin said to Rosie, pulling her hand. At his grasp she felt her magic weave with his and come together. With their free hands, they sent bursts of power at attackers until they stepped back into the dining hall. Justin weaved around broken tables, ripped books, and the broken door. Once across the barrier, the two searched the room as they ran to the stairwell.

A slew of injured bodies lay throughout the room and Rosie searched their faces.

"Justin, they're not here. My parents."

"The Premier isn't either."

"Help," a weak voice said, up by the stage.

Rosie leaped up towards the voice and knelt while Justin kept watch for any attackers. The man, an elder from the clan lay on his back, holding a gushing wound on his stomach.

"Justin!" Rosie called as she put pressure on his wounds.

Justin ran to them as a small dribble of blood dripped from the man's mouth and his eyes sat on Rosie's. He lifted his hand and held her wrist. "Break the stone, break the power."

"The beacon? But our control?" Justin asked, holding his

head up.

"Break the stone, break the power," the man repeated before coughing once and then his eyes went blank.

Justin gently set his head back down and Rosie released her now bloody hands from his stomach.

"Do you think he meant the beacon?" Justin asked, his brows furrowing.

"I don't know what else he could've meant." Rosie stood again and looked up at the ceiling.

Above them, mer-students swam fiercely towards the embankment to help.

"We should find my dad. He'd know for sure."

"Let's go," Justin said, and the two ran across the rest of the hall to the staircase. "Do you think they went up to help?"

"No, they went down. My dad must have tried to get my mom out."

They shuffled down the staircase, checking each level before reaching the very bottom.

"What's here?" Justin asked, touching a doorknob, but like their first day touring the school, his hand instantly pulled back and he shook it.

"Are you okay?"

"Yeah, nothing serious." He shook it one more time before placing his hand back at his side and staring at the door. "I've never been down this far, have you?"

"With Walker, once, but she made me wait here."

"Do you know how to get in?"

"Well, if the beacon is restored then this should be easy." A loud thud echoed up the hallway and the *ching*-ing of a suit of armor rolling down the stairs echoed.

"We should hurry," Justin said, positioning himself a

few steps higher, attempting to see what, if anything, was approaching them.

Rosie nodded and grabbed her Valtic necklace. Carefully, she set the stone in the middle of the doorknob. It clicked into place, as if it belonged in the knob the entire time. She pulled her necklace back on and on its own, the door swung open.

Pushing it further inward, Rosie stared down the black hallway.

"Wow," Justin said before forming a ball of fire in his hand and sending it forward.

The light flew down the seemingly endless hallway. The two stared at one another and Justin gestured her forward.

The two stepped past the doorway and the door clicked closed behind them. Each formed balls of fire and Rosie led the way. Now with more light, the two studied the hallway. Walls of stone, similar to the conference room, surrounded them. Glistening metals and jewels laid in the walls caught their eyes. Rosie's free hand glided across the wall, the roughness somehow soothing her.

"Where do you think this leads?"

"It's one of the many networks that connects the different caves in the mountain range." Rosie remembered the school blueprint she had memorized last year and knew that the tunnel had gone off the blueprint's page.

"Could it be—" Justin started, but angered voices sounded ahead of them.

"It has to be destroyed!" Rosie heard Premier Kingsley exclaim.

"We can't, people will die!" Christion responded, his voice echoing down the hallway. "Your vision, Rose."

"James has a point," Rosie's mom said in a calmer voice. "My vision showed that if we destroy the beacon, then the clan members won't be able to draw their magic from the earth."

"They just transferred the power originally to a different beacon and continued to hone it. They don't have true control of their powers. They will shift into a human state until they can learn to regain their magic and we will of course offer to help them," Kingsley reasoned.

Rosie and Justin continued forward, a gleam of light coming into view.

"If we destroy the beacon now," Christion started, "then we risk hundreds dying by Superiority hands. If agents don't realize what's happening, they will be attacking helpless individuals."

Stepping up to an opening, Rosie's eyes widened at the gigantic cave she stood in. Torches lit the circular room, bouncing light off rubies, sapphires, emeralds, and diamonds sitting unmined in the walls. Surrounding the jewels were the metals which hooked the pendants to each respective gem. Gold, copper, silver, and platinum.

"Rosie," Ms. Connors exclaimed, stepping forward. "What are you doing here?"

"Looking for you. An elder from the clan, he gave us a message." She turned to Justin, and he stepped forward.

"What message?" Christion asked, his eyes hopeful.

"Break the stone, break the power," Rosie stated.

"See!" Kingsley burst out as he moved towards the beacon.

"Wait!" Christion said, also moving to come between Kingsley and the stone. "We need to think logically."

"Christion," Ms. Connors said, "it's time." Her eyes were

flashing blue, but she was consciously in the room still.

Could she have visions and communicate at the same time? Rosie wondered. But before she could understand when her mother had become such a powerful seer, the room shook, sending dust and small rocks falling on them.

"It's time," Kingsley said, moving forward.

"But—" Christion protested.

"Dad," Rosie said, "there are a lot of people up there hurt, some dead. We have to stop this."

"Raphael is on our side, Christion," Ms. Connors pipped. "He agrees with our plan. He is up there and will try to stop innocents from being hurt."

"It is time," Kingsley repeated, now more firmly. Then he nodded to everyone in the room. "I will need everyone's power. Link hands."

Ms. Connors grabbed Kingsley's hand, and Justin hers, and Rosie his. Rosie extended her hand to her father. His eyes pleaded with her, but she knew they couldn't wait any longer. Without his permission, she grasped Christion's hand and nodded to Kingsley.

A force of magic raced through her veins, more power than she had ever felt before. Unable to stop herself, a scream erupted from her mouth. The magic burned her insides and over her own pain and screams she could hear Justin and her mother in agony as well.

Her father's grip on her hand hardened but she continued to squeeze her eyes closed from the pain. Another squeeze forced her eyes open. The crystal in front of them held a bright light inside and from the bottom cracks erupted outwards. Another hand squeeze and she met her father's eyes.

"I'm sorry," he mouthed, and he began to slip his hand away.

"No," Rosie grunted out, but his hand tore back, and he raced from the room.

"Dad!" she screamed, but as she did, the beacon shattered, and a thunderous blast sent the group flying back.

Rosie's back and head slammed against the cave wall, and she crumbled to the floor, the torch flames extinguishing. Her eyes opened and an ache thrummed throughout her body. Sweat dripped from her forehead and she reached her hands out to find someone, anyone, in the pitch-black room.

"Rosie?" her mother's frantic voice called from across the way.

"I'm here," she squeaked out, reaching forward and grabbing a warm arm.

"It's me," Justin said, grabbing her hand back and helping her up.

With a snap of a finger, the room relit, and James Kingsley stood by the center of the room. Scattered across the cave were shards of crystals and near the center more sat next to an empty scorched spot in the earth. Reaching for her chest, Rosie grazed where a tiny shard of the beacon rested in her skin. Her fingers brushed the black stone and as she did the stone settled further. Staring down she tried to inspect the cut but at that angle she needed a mirror to properly inspect it.

Standing up, she groaned as her body ached. At the thought of her pain a swirl of magic swept through her, relieving her. She widened her eyes and stared at Justin, who also seemed to be moving, unscathed. He stepped towards her, but before she could inspect him further for injuries Kingsley spoke.

"Is everyone okay?" he asked, surveying them.

Each nodded, completely healed and confused.

"Good, I am going to check that everything is sorted now." Kingsley moved through the room and paused before eyeing Christion entering the room again. Shaking his head, Kingsley walked by him, quickly moving down the hallway.

Rosie watched him go, then turned her head towards her parents. Her mom sat on the floor still, a gash bleeding from the side of her face. Her father knelt beside her, cupping her chin and examining the cut. Soon enough though, the gash started to heal, and Rosie found the shards of crystals grow underneath her mother's skin as it did.

Still confused, she shook her head and brought her attention to her father.

"Dad, what did you do?" Rosie asked, kicking a few shards away and sitting on the other side of her mom.

"I had to try to stop it. I couldn't let innocents die."

"If we didn't take the source though, more could have. If you would've just held on, not one of us would be hurt. The stone would have disintegrated rather than implode," Rosie tried to reason, but her dad stood.

"How do you know that?" Christion asked, cocking an eyebrow.

Rosie opened her mouth, but she was at a loss for words. She thought about the power surging through her.

"Heal your mother's wound please," he said, not noticing the power they each now had, and started down towards the hallway.

"Wait! Where are you going?" Rosie asked.

"To see where I can help."

Rosie wanted to stop him, but at the same time she wanted him to go.

She watched him disappear down the hallway, and then sat at her mother's side.

"How are you?" Rosie asked as she inspected her mom.

"I'm okay, sweetie. Are you okay? Justin?"

Rosie studied Justin, who shook an elbow out and nodded. "I'm okay, Ms. Connors. Thanks."

"Should we get out of here? See how we can assist?" Ms. Connors asked the other two.

Nodding, the three moved down the hallway with balls of flames leading their way. Reentering the staircase, all was still and silent in the school.

"Think the fighting stopped?" Rosie asked.

"With both the Premier and your father up there, it must have."

"I'll run and check the dining hall," Justin said, hustling up the stairs and entering a doorway off the staircase.

"Mom?" Rosie asked.

"Yes? What is it, sweetie?"

"Do you feel different?"

Her mother paused and she turned to Rosie. "Different in what way?"

"When the Premier destroyed the beacon, did you feel anything other than the burning?"

Her mother nodded her head and examined Rosie. "There was something."

"For me too. I feel stronger. More powerful."

Ms. Connors nodded but swiftly changed the subject. "Are you okay? Do we need to go see the doctor?" Her mother's hand gently wrapped around her shoulder. Rosie shook her head.

"No one is in there," Justin called down, now reentering

the staircase.

Rosie and her mother stared up at him and made their way to his side.

"The lobby?" Rosie suggested and Justin nodded in agreement. The three continued up and just before they could reach the lobby, loud conversations sounded.

Opening the door to the hall, Rosie studied the scene. Hundreds of Superiority agents supervised and detained various supernatural creatures. Some were being led out to the lakeside, others sat and were being questioned, and a few were being treated for their wounds.

"Rosie," Christion said, moving away from Raphael and towards their group.

"Is everyone okay?" Rosie asked, still inspecting the room.

"No casualties," he responded, a small grin on his face.

"Garrett? Mr. Parker?"

"Both are fine. Well, not fine, but they are alive."

Rosie's lungs filled with air as relief flowed through her. "Are they here?" She searched for her friend, but she couldn't find Garrett in the sea of people.

"No, they were transported to the Superiority hospital for treatment. Mr. Parker suffered serious damage to his spine. It's likely he won't ever walk again."

"Does that mean..." Justin started and Christion nodded grimly.

"What?"

Justin turned to Rosie. "Mr. Parker won't be able to shift again. He will remain in his human form and because he was the alpha of his pack..."

"Garrett's now alpha."

"But he's only a teenager," Ms. Connors gasped.

Christion nodded. "Something not that out of the ordinary for wolf packs. He'll be trained on his new duties while remaining in school. Then, when he comes of age, he will officially take over his duties."

"What kind of duties?"

"Rosie! Justin!" a girl yelled across the room.

Dana struggled and fought two Superiority agents who held her arms down and back. As she was led out of the room, she glanced at the two desperately.

"Wait!' Rosie yelled, navigating the room. "She's with us!" Rosie hopped around chairs, and she stared back at her dad as the agents continued to ignore Rosie and take Dana away.

Only after the agents looked to Christion, who nodded his head to release Dana was it done.

"Jeez," Dana muttered, rubbing her upper arms as the agents strolled away.

"You okay?" Rosie asked, not thrilled to see Dana but also not mad.

"Yeah, thanks."

The two stood awkwardly for a moment before Rosie broke the silence.

"So, you reaching out to Drew? It truly was a warning? Not that you were attacking?"

"Obviously. You know I stand with Raphael. Wait? Did you think I was behind this?" A roar of laughter erupted from Dana, and she clutched her side.

"I mean, it's not that outlandish of a thought. You did attack us at our dance," Rosie defended.

"That was just a little fun," Dana said before she moved around the room to check on other clan members.

Rosie shook her head and turned about the room. "Dad?"

Rosie asked under her breath as she searched. She spied him standing with the Premier and Raphael. She moved towards them, but Justin caught her arm.

"Hey, let them talk. They need to after what just happened."

Rosie nodded but kept her eyes trained on them.

"Do you think, now that the two groups are one, plans will still move forward with integrating the school? The town? Everything?" Rosie asked, staring around the room before staring up at Justin. She grazed her fingers over his arm, feeling the shards of rock that lay just below his skin.

Reaching with his own hand, he grasped hers and nodded.

"Rosie, I just wanted to say—"

"Rosie!" Riley called from across the room. Riley grabbed Rosie around the waist and pulled her up and into him. "Are you okay?" His hand grasped the back of her head as he snuggled her closer into his chest.

She breathed in, relieved he wasn't hurt.

"We're okay," Rosie said, pulling back, darting her eyes to Justin and then back to Riley.

Without even looking in Justin's direction, Riley continued. "What happened? Is everything back to normal?"

"I wouldn't phrase it quite like that," Justin said.

Pulling away, Riley scanned both Rosie and Justin. He eyed the shards of the beacon that had implanted within them, his eyes widening. "Do you need to see Doctor Geller?" Holding her hand he moved closer to the door, but Rosie stood in place.

"No, Riley, I'm okay. I think. Everything is as normal as it can be but there is going to be change."

"There's still going to be the integration of the Clan with the Superiority?"

Rosie nodded and said, "Probably, and a second school."

"Do you know anything else? When will all the changes occur?"

"There are two more weeks in the school year," Justin said. "Chances are we'll find out before summer break."

Riley nodded his head before wrapping Rosie in his arms again. "I don't want to be separated from you."

"Me either," she whispered, eyeing Justin as she said it. Quickly though, she found her father walking away with Raphael and the Premier. The three moved to her mother and the group huddled together.

Chapter Thirty-Two

"I'm running for Premier," Christion said at the dinner table, causing both Rosie and her mother to spit their food out and widen their eyes.

During the week since the attack, the two communities had started to form as one. More and more clan members, now Superiority members, had moved into Kingstown and started working either in town, at the Superiority, or at the school. A few students also began to integrate at King's Preparatory.

"Christion?" Rosie's mother said, her eyebrows hitting her hairline. "What are you talking about?"

"With the two societies as one, I think it is time for new leadership."

"But James has been—"

"Kingsley has been in charge long enough. Because of him, there has been discord between creatures, a higher rise in human deaths, and a lack in preparing our youth for the real world." Christion stared at Rosie who still sat shocked.

"Can you even do that?" Ms. Connors asked. "Run against him?"

"There is no official election, but Raphael and I have been

discussing it. Between himself, the elders, and a handful of council members, we can instate a formal election process, which should have been how the Superiority ran in the first place. Just because someone is immortal, doesn't mean they are the best for the job."

"But he has proven himself a great leader, no?" Ms. Connors asked. "I mean, he has been there for me, for Rosie, the entire community. He stopped the fighting last week."

"Yet, he could've hurt many more in the process."

"But he didn't. Christion, I don't think you are seeing things properly."

"I am seeing things clearly for the first time. Rose, I have been alive for centuries. I have sat by, on the outskirts or in the background, manipulating situations, but I can't sit back and do that anymore. Our society needs a dedicated leader. One who won't just think of those who are more magically inclined but of all creatures within their purview."

"Does James know?"

"Not yet. But we are meeting tomorrow morning."

Ms. Connors shook her head and set her fork down. "No."

Rosie and Christion stared at her in wonderment before Christion spoke, "No? What do you mean?"

"No. You're not running for Premier."

"Rose you can't—"

"Can't what? Disagree with you that this is a stupid idea?"

"Rose, you must see that his reign needs to end. And with our society only growing, someone who understands the various workings of each type of creature, their cultures and beliefs, should be in charge. I have that experience. Kingsley, does not."

"Mom, Dad does have a point," Rosie interjected, but then

turned to her father. "But why run now? You didn't want the job before. Why not work with the Premier instead?"

"Because your father no longer has a post at the Superiority or the Premier's ear. Not since he almost sabotaged the end of the attack." Ms. Connors stood and cleared her plate shaking her head.

Christion quickly moved to her side.

"I thought we discussed this. Moved past it." he said, attempting to wrap an arm around her.

"You did. I didn't. You could've killed Rosie by breaking that bond. Don't you see that?" Tears began to fill her eyes and she stared at Rosie, worry furrowing her brows.

Rosie now stood. "Mom, I'm okay. I don't agree with what Dad did, but I understand why he did it."

"You could've died."

"But I didn't," Rosie said, now walking over to her mom and grasping her hands. "We are all okay." She grinned and Rosie eyed her dad who put a hand on her shoulder.

The tears in her mom's eyes then fell and Rosie embraced her. "I can't lose you," Ms. Connors said.

"You won't."

"I can't lose either of you," she then said, staring up at Christion.

"I'm not leaving. And I'm going to make sure you both always stay safe."

"You can't promise that."

"I can. Especially as Premier, I will make it my duty to keep you both safe."

Rosie snorted. "You can't worry about us. You have a lot of others to be thinking about."

"Do I have both of your blessings?" Christion asked, staring mostly at Ms. Connors.

She stared into Christion's eyes and nodded. As she did so he engulfed both of them in a gigantic hug. "Okay, now with your blessing, I need to go coordinate my plans for when I meet with Raphael."

"Why?" Rosie asked, separating herself.

"I have his endorsement for Premier, and he will have mine as Vice Premier."

"There isn't a Vice Premier," Ms. Connors said, raising an eyebrow.

"There will be when I'm in charge." He bent down and kissed both on the head, then left the apartment.

The two sat in silence for a moment, then Rosie spoke, "Are you really on board with Dad trying to become Premier?"

"No. I think he is better suited to the background like he has been, and I think James has done an amazing job and can continue to do so."

"But dad can't?"

"Your father has the relationships and the skills. He has empathy and a good heart. But that's not what makes a politician."

"But shouldn't we want the good guy to win?"

"There's already a good guy in the position. The difference is, James knows how to play the game, knows the difference between what should be done versus what actually can be done, and knows how to best lead those within the Superiority."

"How can you know that?"

"You know my new position with the Superiority. I now work with James daily. By his side. My gift is amplified by him and now with the beacon." Ms. Connors raised her cardigan sleeve and exposed the small fragments of the beacon embedded in her arm. "My power is stronger."

Rosie nodded and grazed the stones. "Are you seeing more?"

"My visions are longer, clearer, and I can call on them if I focus. I can also see into the present and past."

"So, the Premier has you close so he can use you?"

"Not use, Rosie," she said with a laugh. "I am able to assist the Premier in his decision-making by focusing my skill to find actionable and reasonable solutions to Superiority issues."

Rosie repeated her mother's rehearsed answer in her head. "But you could help Dad too. Are you going to help the Premier if there is an official race?"

"I am going to resign from my position if it comes to that. Work in a different department or as a consultant for the Superiority. I won't help either side win or lose."

Rosie nodded and began to pack her things. "I should get back to campus. I have a meeting with Professor Walker tomorrow morning."

"Okay sweetie," Ms. Connors said, pulling Rosie into a hug after she slung her backpack over her shoulder. "Get back carefully and get some rest. I love you."

"Love you too."

* * *

"I'm assuming you know your school placement already?" Professor Walker asked, flipping through the handful of papers on her desk.

"Um," Rosie started, as this was the first thing Professor Walker had said to her since entering the office ten minutes ago. "Here?"

"Yes," she said, pulling a paper from a tall stack, setting it in front of her and then looking up. "You will remain here at King's Preparatory Southwest. You have also been selected as the new Illumination Team captain for Valtic."

"But Garrett…"

"Mr. Parker has many other new responsibilities to look after now and can no longer take on the role as captain."

"But we should at least talk to him about it. Maybe he can—"

"Rosie, this was his decision, not mine."

"Will he be back at school soon?"

"Next year. He is back with his pack now. I know you know how important it is to establish himself as alpha as fast as he can."

"I know. If he doesn't, he could lose his pack."

"Exactly. Now since you will be starting your junior year, you need to know the importance of staying focused on your studies and start thinking about your future."

"But I'm still going to be here for the next four years?"

"You are but during your junior year you will take the Superiority Measurement Standards Exam. Have you heard of it?"

Rosie shook her head no, and she sat forward. "What's the test on?"

"There will be three sections. Two written exams, and a practical exam. The exams are broken up further into different sections. The first exam will test your knowledge of all things supernatural. Qualities, history—you get the picture?"

Rosie nodded, taking a mental note so she could begin studying later.

"Good. The next exam will test you on the general knowledge you should know to live in the human society. Math, science, english, etcetera, plus life skills and knowledge one would know if they were to interact with other humans. This shouldn't be too difficult for you since you grew up in that world." Rosie smiled but allowed Professor Walker to continue. "The final exam is a practical split into two parts. The first will test you on your skills as a witch. You will have to perform a series of spells, rituals, create potions, or possibly do all three depending on your tester. Then, during the second part of the test, you will demonstrate how you would react in a Superiority emergency."

Without thinking Rosie started to laugh. "I'm sorry Professor, but can't we just mark that off as a pass?"

Professor Walker smiled but shook her head. "Unfortunately, we can't but with your experiences you should do fine."

"What's the purpose of this testing?" Rosie asked. "I mean, we go to college here, most of us are likely to end up at the Superiority with jobs, so why do we need to do these standardized tests?"

"To figure out where you should be placed after graduation."

"But don't we have the two post-grad years?"

"No, this will determine your learning track for those years and from there, where you can be placed and what jobs you can hold."

"Wait, I don't get to decide?"

"Rosie, our system works because it has been carefully designed to match individuals with their best path of being successful. I know it is difficult to hear that you may not get the path you originally wanted but the Superiority recognizes you have different wants, and you can apply to outside positions so don't worry. Now, you will be here this summer, correct?"

"Um, yeah, as far as I am aware. I will probably stay with my mom in town."

"Good, because with the new students coming into the school, I will need your help if you're available. You will be compensated for your time and it will look very impressive to Superiority recruiters."

"Whatever you need."

"Great, you and Mr. Fent will be teaching the new students about the human world and topics related to surviving in it."

"Justin is also staying at this location?" Rosie asked, a smile turning up on her lips.

"He will be. And he will remain on campus over the summer."

"Why? He can go home, right?"

"I can't discuss that with you, Rosie. You know that." Rosie nodded and allowed Professor Walker to continue. "I will have you both back here in a weeks to discuss lesson plans and then you will start teaching. Any questions?"

Shaking her head, she stood. "Not right now, but if anything comes to mind, I'll let you know."

"Sounds good, Rosie. Now get to lunch."

Rosie left the office and glided back to the dining hall. As she walked down the stairwell, she passed students she recognized and students who were newly integrated. The idea that she would teach these kids with Justin at her side sent a flurry of butterflies through her stomach.

"Hey," Rosie said as she sat down next to Riley in the dining hall. "Guess what?"

"Mhm?" he replied.

"I get to teach here over the summer. Help the new students and get a leg up on next year's work. Plus, I'll be able to stay with my parents and do some normal family activities and…" Rosie paused.

Sitting still, Riley concentrated on his plate as he pushed his food around.

"What's wrong?" she asked, placing a hand around his arm, pulling him closer so he would look up.

He stared at her and then said, "I won't be here next year."

"What?" She removed her hand and sat back.

"I've been selected to go to the new King's Preparatory Northeast Campus. I leave on the last day of school."

At his words, Rosie's stomach knotted, and a lump caught in her throat.

"No, that's not right. You're staying here."

"I just got done talking to Manger. My mom has taken a position to assist with Superiority-Human Relations at the new school."

"But wouldn't she need to eventually relocate here? Where the headquarters are based?"

"Surprisingly, there's a satellite office in Minnesota. So that's where the school will open, and that's where myself and anyone else on the eastern half of the continent will be. Plus, anyone who is more acclimated to cold weather."

"Let me talk to my mom and my dad. They can probably

do something. I'm sure your mom will understand that you want to stay here."

"It's done, Rosie." He stood and left the table without another word. She watched as he entered the Surgent portrait and disappeared from her view.

"Hey," Eleanor said, taking a seat next to her, "you okay?"

Rosie turned back to the table and found not just Eleanor but also Justin sitting down.

"Hey, um, not really."

"What's going on?" Eleanor asked, furrowing her brows.

"Riley isn't going to be here next year. He is going to the new campus."

"Oh gosh, I'm so sorry Rosie," Eleanor said, putting an arm around her. "I'm sure you guys will be okay. And you'll talk all the time. And I'm sure there is some way the schools will connect. Whether it is through a portal or something."

Rosie thought about the any-portal and nodded. "Yeah, that's true. It's not the end of the world. I know I'll still see him almost every day."

"Exactly! Don't stress. It will all work out."

Rosie nodded and she turned to Justin. "Did you hear the news?"

Justin set his spoon down and lifted an eyebrow. "News?" he asked.

"You and I are teaching here this summer. Professor Walker said you'd be staying?"

Perking up in his seat, a smile played at his lips. "Yeah, I mean I knew I was staying, but awesome. What are we teaching?"

"Creature-Human interactions and human world knowl-edge."

"Sweet, so all the new students?"

"Yes, and hopefully, after living on the cusp of both societies, they already have somewhat of a background in the subject so it shouldn't be too difficult to teach."

"Students," Professor Shay announced, as she gathered the room's attention at the front of the hall. "A formal announcement will be presented to you and your parents in a bit but for those of you here, I just received word that the Premier will be on campus tonight, along with council members and elders. They will be here to answer any questions you or your parents may have regarding your school placement or the integration in general. This will take place after dinner, so if you have any discussion topics for this forum you will be able to present them then." Professor Shay stepped back and normal conversations throughout the room continued.

"That's interesting," Rosie said, eyeing Justin. Before she could continue and he could reply, Eleanor sat up.

"Do you think we'll see Garrett?" She searched Rosie's face.

Giving a small grin back and gently resting a hand on hers, Rosie replied, "I hope so."

Eleanor's eyes lit up and she stood. "I'm going to get ready."

"Ready? What for?" Justin asked, but Eleanor just chuckled and walked off.

"It's a girl thing," Rosie said before pushing her plate aside and picking up her phone.

There hadn't been any news regarding her father's intention to run for Premier through any Superiority presses or independent supernatural news outlets that she could find. She opened her contacts, ready to call her mom for an update when a message from the school set off her phone. The chiming echoed throughout the hall as students opened their own phones to read the message Professor Shay had just told them.

"It's just the announcement about tonight's Q and A," Rosie told Justin as he reached for his own phone.

"Cool, no other news?" he asked, silencing his phone.

"Not that you'll find there."

Raising an eyebrow, Justin replied, "You know something. What's going on?"

Rosie stared at Justin before scanning the dining hall. Students sat scattered throughout and there were only two teachers up at the head table. After determining it was safe to talk, she leaned in.

"My dad has a plan to run for Premier."

"What?" Justin said, surprised.

Rosie nodded her head and turned to look around the room again.

"There isn't an election to become Premier. How is he going to do it?" Justin asked in a low voice.

"I'm not sure of the specifics, but he is going to petition the council and elders. He was supposed to have met with Raphael to coordinate and get his support. He would make Raphael Vice Premier."

Justin sat quietly, staring at his plate, then lifted his head. Seeing past Rosie's shoulder he widened his eyes.

"What?" Rosie asked as she turned her head. Spying over her shoulder, James Kingsley walking across the dining hall with Raphael.

Chapter Thirty-Three

Both the Premier and Raphael stared at Rosie, and she shifted her eyes back to Justin.

"Do you think he…" she asked, pausing before speaking the rest of the question aloud.

"He couldn't have."

"But what if?"

The two stood and began to step away from the table.

"Rosie," Raphael said, feet pausing right behind her.

Turning, Raphael stood near Rosie, a devilish smile playing at his lips.

"Hi," Rosie said, taking a small step to the side. Kingsley was standing near Professor Shay, talking animatedly, before he handed her a stack of documents.

"Oh, don't mind the Premier. He's just planning for tonight's meeting. There are a lot of things to discuss, including a very big announcement." He winked at Rosie and walked back towards Kingsley.

Leaving the dining hall, Rosie and Justin marched up to the hidden room in the Valtic library and sat.

"Do you think my dad is going to be here tonight?" Rosie asked, pulling her phone out.

"Maybe, but why was Raphael here with the Premier? Do you think the Premier found out about your dad's plan?"

"I don't see how." She scrolled her phone before finding Christion's number and calling him.

One ring, two rings, three rings, then three beeps.

"The call failed," she said before retrying. The same thing happened.

"Try your mom," Justin suggested, sitting on one of the tables.

She dialed her mom's number and within one ring her voice sounded on the other end.

"Hi, sweetie. Everything okay?"

"Is Dad with you?" Rosie asked.

"No, I'm at work right now. Why? What's wrong?"

"I just can't get a hold of him."

"Well, don't worry just yet. He's probably prepping his master plans for tonight."

"He is planning to announce his intention to run for Premier tonight?"

"Yes. He was supposed to meet with Raphael and then a few elders and council members throughout the day."

"Raphael is here."

"At the school?"

"Yes, with the Premier."

Only silence came from the other end of the phone before Rosie's mom spoke up. "Rosie, I need you to not do anything rash and not panic."

"What, Mom? What is it?"

"I just tried to search for your dad. With my sight. See what he was doing today, where he was now, and how his announcement goes later."

"And?"

"I couldn't see anything."

"But… What do you mean?"

"I'm unable to draw any visions of your dad."

"Has that happened before? I mean, could you just be tired or aren't able to draw on your ability?"

"Maybe, you're probably right." Hearing a sigh on the other end, Rosie attempted to calm down.

"Tell me he's okay, Mom."

Another silent pause came from Ms. Connors before she replied, "I can't Rosie, but I'm sure he is. We have to believe he is."

"Okay. Love you mom."

"Love you."

Rosie hung up and paced the room. Unsure of what to do next, she sat down and tried calling her dad again.

"Rosie?" Justin said, taking one of her shaking hands.

She allowed him to take her phone and put it on the table before blinking away the tears in her eyes.

"Your dad knows how to disappear. He knows how to conceal himself. Do you think he is doing that now? To protect himself from any ramifications of his plan?"

With logic overcoming her emotions, she nodded. "Yeah, I guess he would."

"And implementing such a plan would be risky, right? So, it makes sense that he is trying to protect you and your mom in any way possible."

She continued to nod, wiping her nose. "Yeah, yeah, okay. Maybe he is just trying to keep a low profile. If the Premier heard about this, he could ask my mom to see what he was up to."

"Exactly. Don't stress out yet. Plus, it sounded like he had already had his conversation with Raphael. Raphael must be playing some sort of game with the Premier until the announcement tonight."

"Right." Rosie continued to calm her breathing. "Okay, so we wait until tonight to find out more. And until then?'

"We relax. We don't have any exams or responsibilities for the rest of the school year. Why don't we get Riley, Eleanor, and whoever else we can find and go on a hike or play a game on the field?"

"Okay, let's do it."

* * *

"Whoooo!" Eleanor yelled as she jumped off the side of the cliff, landing in the aqua blue water below.

"Safe to say she is excited to see Garrett tonight," Rosie said with a chuckle.

"I thought she had to go get ready?" Justin asked, laughing.

"I convinced her that she should let loose before seeing him. That her full-on Eleanor energy might not bode well for his first night back on campus."

"Good call," Justin said. "Well, I'll see you guys down there." Doing a front flip off the cliff, Justin landed in the water below, leaving Rosie and a silent Riley up at the top.

"On your left!" Flynn called, jumping off next, followed by cheers from Gunner and Katherine.

"Seems like others had the same idea to decompress," Rosie said, knocking her shoulder lightly into Riley's.

"Mhm," Riley grunted, sitting on a rock near the edge.

"Come on, Riley. It's not the end of the world. We will still see each other constantly and I can use the any-portal to get to you."

"Yeah," he mumbled, picking a fingernail.

"Seriously?" Rosie yelled, forcing Riley to jerk his head up and in her direction.

"What?" he asked, clipping the end of the word.

"Stop with the attitude. Poor you. You get to be a part of history. Be a part of the first class at a brand new secret magical school. Get to see your mom every day and have her be brought into this world."

"Rosie—"

"No. Stop pouting. We only have a few more days together and I refuse to let you spoil them."

"But—"

"Oh enough!" Rosie grabbed his hand and before he could object, she pulled him to the edge of the cliff and jumped.

The two soared down and allowed the cool, fresh water to envelope them as they shot past the surface. Still hand in hand, Rosie broke upwards and gasped laughing.

Riley burst up and grabbed her under the arms and threw her in the air as he laughed. She landed in the water again and the two continued to splash each other. The childish game fueled the innocent joy and excitement that neither had during the regular school year.

"Truce! Truce!" Riley yelled, swimming towards the shallow end of the water.

"Coward!" Rosie laughed, swimming behind him.

"Having fun?" Eleanor asked as she floated on her back.

"Too much," Rosie chuckled, wading out of the water and

lying on the bank.

"Hey guys!" Justin called from behind the waterfall. "Come check this out!"

The three swam to the waterfall, diving under the hurling water and emerging in the cave on the other side.

"What's up?" Rosie asked, looking around the cave for any indication of why Justin called them over.

"I thought it best to talk behind the splashing of water rather than out in the open."

"Um, okay?" Eleanor asked.

"What's there to discuss?" Riley asked, putting an arm around Rosie as they sat.

"I think we can assume that there will be some upset and discord with the finalization of the integration."

"Sure, some," Rosie agreed.

"And we know that some of us won't be here but will be at the new campus."

"And?" Riley asked, shaking his head in annoyance.

"Well, if we can't use the portal in school, then we should use this one in case we need to meet and strategize."

"What?"

"Or, you two," Justin said, nodding at Rosie and Riley, "can use it to meet up. You know, if you miss each other."

"I'm so confused," Eleanor said, searching the cave for some sort of portal.

"Go ahead," Justin said, his eyes now looking at the bottom of the pool.

Rosie and Riley stared down and a dull shimmering glow lit up from the bottom.

"Come on!" Justin reassured them, diving down first. Right after him, the other three dove. The cave bottom extended and narrowed as Rosie approached the portal opening.

Reaching forward, Justin's hand passed the threshold, and as if someone on the other side had pulled him through, he zoomed across.

The same thing happened to Eleanor and then Riley. Finally, Rosie's own hand crossed to the other side and a sensation of being thrust forward hit her back and she rolled out of the portal and onto the forest ground.

Justin and Riley helped Rosie up, and she stared around at the surrounding trees and then turned to where the portal was.

A tall, thick tree sat before her, an arched hole leading into the hollowed trunk. Stepping forward, she tried to peer inside without crossing the barrier. Darkness was all she could see.

"Call for it," Justin said. She stared at him and then back at the hole. This time she thought of the portal. Its location, the water, the cave, and the waterfall. Then, in the distance within the tree trunk, the portal appeared.

"Cool," Rosie whispered, taking another step forward before her wrist was caught by Justin.

"Not too close. We don't want you to get pulled back home." She smiled and then turned to Riley.

Even though it was summer, and they had emerged from the portal completely dry, the crisp air nibbled at them.

"Justin, how did you do this?" Rosie asked, growing closer to Riley for warmth.

"I know how upset each of you were at being separated, and I just wanted to do something nice. I thought up the idea after we first heard the news that Riley wasn't going to be at our school anymore, so when we broke away to get ready, I searched for a quick solution and found *Introduction to Portals*. It's scary how simple it was to set this up."

"Well, thank you. Seriously," Rosie said before hugging him. Then she looked back at Riley.

"Honestly, thank you, man," Riley said, tilting his head in Justin's direction and smirking.

"Wait, if you knew where to put the portal," Eleanor started, "then do you know where the new school is?"

"I have a vague idea," Justin smirked, and he began to walk from the portal. Riley and Eleanor started to follow but before Rosie stepped away, she turned to see exactly where they were. The hollowed tree sat behind a cluster of other old trees. On the opposite side of the tree was a fallen trunk, surrounded by purple and pink wildflowers. Rosie searched the sky and in the high branches of the trees in that particular area, there were dozens of hawks staring at the group below. Inspecting the beady eyes that followed her movements closer, she stepped towards one of the trees where at least seven hawks were perched.

"Rosie!" Riley called, falling back to her and reaching out with his hand. "Are you coming?"

"Yeah," she said, "just wanted to make sure we would be able to find our way back." She stole one more glance at the hawks and then continued.

The four navigated the cold forest, avoiding sharp twigs and rocks as they were only in their bare feet.

"We will have to have clothes packed and ready at each location," Riley said as he avoided a small thorny bush.

Nodding in agreement, Rosie followed his steps and breathed a sigh of relief when she found Justin and Eleanor's figures stopped at the edge of a clearing.

"What is it?" Rosie asked, staring at Justin.

"There," he said, pointing into the distance.

Rosie searched and searched but all she could see was the bare opening.

"Here," Justin said, first wrapping his hands around her waist and then slightly turning her to the right. Suddenly, coming into view, just beyond the far side of the tree line, were houses built into the trees.

"Treehouses?" Rosie asked, turning back to Justin.

Smiling, as he nodded, the two stared back and further inspected the camouflaged school.

"Wait, I think there are people over there," Rosie said, stepping forward, but as she did a blast of magic flew at them.

Flying backwards, Rosie watched as the two on the other side of the clearing continued to fight.

"Dad!" she screamed, but before she could call out, her body hit a tree trunk and she fell to the ground.

Chapter Thirty-Four

"Everyone okay?" Justin whispered, making his way to Rosie. Riley had landed near her but had missed the tree, and was busy brushing dried leaves and mud from himself.

A whirl of wind hit Rosie's back and a stinging pain radiated through her body.

"Ah," she said, clutching her lower back. Feeling the scrapes and cuts from the rough bark, she winced, hoping the gashes were small.

"You'll be okay," Justin said, eyeing the scrapes, and at his words, the beacon shards in her warmed and her back healed.

With the relief, she stood taller and raced forward. "My dad," Rosie said before dashing back to the clearing.

"Rosie, no!" Riley said, reaching for her but she moved too fast, adrenaline pumping through her.

Blasts of light and fire came from both men. Each trying to kill the other.

"Dad!" Rosie called again and Christion's head swiveled in her direction.

With this distraction, the other man sent a wave of lightning from his palms and hit Christion in the chest.

"NO!" Rosie screamed, forcing her legs to move faster to

her father as he flew backwards and landed on his back.

It's okay, she kept thinking. *He's immortal and he'll get up. He can't die.* But as she drew closer and closer his body remained unmoving.

She turned to the man he had been fighting. He had shoulder-length greasy black hair which barely covered the long scar that ran across his face. His pale, ghoulish complexion forced him to stand out more in the dark green forest and his eyes, rather than burning bright blue, had a swirling black iridescent shine.

Seeing her, he lifted a hand and shot out, but Rosie dodged the short burst of lightning and rolled on the ground. Trying to find the man, Rosie searched the heights of the trees but couldn't find him up high. She then looked at the ground and saw he had been thrown backwards.

"Rosie, run!" Justin said, sending another force of fire in the man's direction.

Rosie couldn't move though. She turned to her father and army-crawled to his body.

"Dad?" she whispered, tears forming as she noticed his eyes remained open and his body was stiff. "Dad?"

"Come on!" Eleanor said, hoisting Rosie up and away.

"No!" she screamed, flailing to break away so she could check on her father again. "Go back!"

"Get her back!" Riley yelled, dodging the black smoke now pooling from the man's hands.

Eleanor hoisted Rosie over her shoulder and ran back through the clearing and to the portal.

Screaming and kicking the entire way, Rosie tried to escape her friend's clutches, but Eleanor was a warrior, a protector, and knew how to restrain Rosie.

As her body cleared the threshold, and her screams were drowned by being in the water, Rosie allowed a full wave of magic to burst from her body. At its release, her and Eleanor shot upwards and landed on the ground in the cave behind the waterfall.

Uncontrollable sobs escaped her, and she couldn't control herself any longer. She hit and punched the dusty rocky floor and allowed the physical pain to enter her. To try and let it take away from the pain of never seeing or talking to her father again.

"Rosie, stop," Eleanor said, holding her arms to her chest and bear-hugging her.

After trying to shake away for a good minute, she leaned into Eleanor and let loose further.

"Rosie," Riley said, emerging from the pool, and taking her off Eleanor and into his arms. "I'm so sorry."

"Where is he?" Rosie asked as she caught her breath and gritted her teeth. She wiped her nose and narrowed her eyes. "Where's that, that… thing?"

"He vanished," Justin said, placing a hand on her shoulder.

"How?" Rosie asked, turning to him.

"I don't know. I've never seen what he did before," Riley said. "There wasn't a portal, and he didn't just evaporate. He pooled dark, black clouds around himself and vanished into the ground."

"What? Was there something under the fog?" Eleanor asked.

"There were hands dragging him down," Justin said.

"Hands?"

Justin nodded. "They grabbed his shins and legs and pulled him down. I think…" Justin paused staring at Rosie. "I think it was a dark demon."

"A demon?" Riley asked.

"Yeah." Justin breathed hard but continued, "I talked with Christion about them. Dark demons."

"Tell me," Rosie said, moving closer to Justin and grabbing his arms. Tears fell from her eyes again and lifting his hand, he caressed her cheek and wiped one away with his thumb.

"Dark demons are otherworldly creatures that are pure evil."

"Like actual demons? From Hell?" Eleanor asked.

Justin nodded all while focusing on Rosie.

"Does that mean there are angels?" Eleanor asked further.

"There's a lot that Christion has seen that no one knows about," Justin said.

"Had," Rosie said. The group stared at her, and she looked around. "Had seen."

"I'm sorry," Riley said, pulling Rosie back into him so her head rested on his chest.

"What else Justin?" she asked.

"Dark demons had been after Christion for decades, centuries. He played death and they wanted his soul. He was able to keep a low profile and stay hidden from them but—"

"But coming back into the Superiority tipped them off?"

"No. That's the thing. There are low-level demons that are just annoying and don't cause real problems or threats. They just mess with people. But there are high level demons, dark demons, like the one we saw, that are called upon to collect bounties. Reapers."

Rosie thought of her father, his lifeless body, and began to cry again. Her body shook and she couldn't catch her breath.

"Let's get her back to campus," Riley said, guiding Rosie up the staircase by the waterfall.

As the four made their way back to campus, Rosie didn't pay attention to her movements. The only thing running through her brain was her father fighting, then dying.

"Did my dad tell you that he could be killed?" Rosie asked Justin.

He nodded. "Since they are from another world—"

"The underworld," Eleanor corrected.

"Yeah, they possess certain magic that isn't available to us. That magic allows them to steal the lives they were promised or that shouldn't still be here."

"Any immortal?" Rosie asked.

"Yes."

"So, they could be after James Kingsley too?"

"It's possible."

"Then we need to get to the Premier," Rosie huffed, moving faster back to the school entrance rather than her dorm.

"No, Rosie, not yet."

"I have to."

"We will," Riley said, pulling her back. "First, let's get you checked out and changed."

Aches began to throb throughout her body, but she tried to call the beacon in her to heal. Nothing happened though, so she reluctantly nodded.

"I'll take her," Eleanor said as the group started to separate.

Entering Eleanor's dorm, she put Rosie in the shower and grabbed her new clothes. The entire time Rosie went from uncontrollable sobbing, to planning what to do next, her compartmentalization not taking proper effect.

Once dressed, Eleanor guided Rosie from the bathroom to a chair. She picked up a brush and weaved it through Rosie's hair.

"I'm so sorry." A gentle hand rested on Rosie's shoulder and Rosie's head fell on her friend's hand.

"I know. Thank you."

Twisting Rosie's hair into braids, Eleanor remained quiet. Putting both hands on Rosie's shoulders, Eleanor squeezed them and threw a sweatshirt over her own head.

"Ready?"

Nodding, Rosie stood and walked to the door. The two girls made their way up to the lobby, meeting Riley and Justin in silence. The four then walked through the school and up into the dining hall.

Buzzing students sat throughout the room but Rosie's eyes scanned it for Kingsley.

"He isn't here," she whispered, walking across the corridor towards the stairwell.

"Where are you going?" Riley asked, matching her pace.

"I need to talk to him."

Riley walked at her side, Justin and Eleanor following.

"Students," Professor Shay announced, gathering the attention of the room. "Please find your seats."

Rosie continued forward but Professor Shay called, "Rosie. Please. We would like to start."

Tears pooling in her eyes, she stared at Professor Shay, hoping she would see she needed to be elsewhere, but with a gesturing hand she indicated Rosie had to stay.

"We'll talk to him after dinner and the Q and A," Justin whispered. Rosie's feet remained planted, but Justin gently placed a hand on her arm and guided her to the closest empty seats.

"Students, parents, teachers, and staff," Professor Shay

started, "as promised we will indulge ourselves in a quick dinner and then be able to have an open discussion with our Premier regarding the new integration and changes taking place at the school. Please, enjoy the dinner and we will get started shortly."

Food began to appear on the long tables, and the clinking of silverware and glasses sounded. Rosie turned her head around the room again, noting a handful of parents sitting next to their children, but there was still no Kingsley.

"Do you think he already knows?" Rosie asked Justin.

"He could, especially if he was monitoring the new school site."

"I can't believe he's gone." Rosie looked at her hands which sat in her lap and watched a tear hit her palm.

A hand rubbed her back and Rosie sat silently thinking about her dad, her mom, and her future.

Picking at a piece of splintered wood on the table, Rosie heard the loud creak of the dining hall door opening over the scattered conversations. She whipped her head around as Kingsley, Raphael, and a handful of others poured into the hall.

"Screw this," Rosie said, standing. She moved towards the group who eyed her suspiciously.

"Rosie?" Kingsley asked as she neared. Tears began to burn her eyes and she worried that she wouldn't be able to speak for fear of releasing the floodgates. "Are you okay?" he asked, nearing her.

"He's dead," she whispered. She stared at Kingsley's face and understanding swept over him.

"Raphael," Kingsley called. Raphael moved to his side. "Christion is dead. Summon the others. As Vice Premier—"

"Vice Premier?" Rosie asked, her head shooting up towards Raphael.

Kingsley raised an eyebrow at Rosie but then continued to Raphael, "You have control of this meeting. I am taking Ms. Connors to my office to speak. Call her mother and send her there as well."

Raphael nodded and turned to the group. After instructing one of the members, he dialed his phone and handed it off, then led everyone up the stage and to the front.

"Hello, everyone," Raphael began, but that was all Rosie heard as she was shepherded out of the dining hall.

The two sat down in the Premier's school office. Kingsley made his way to a small bar cart in the corner of the room and poured a thick brown liquid into one glass and then a self-swirling pink liquid into another.

"Here, drink this. It will calm you down," Kingsley said, handing her the pink drink.

"Loose juice?" Rosie asked, taking a small sip of the sweet drink. Instantly, her shoulders relaxed some and her mind eased.

"I forgot that's what you kids call it," Kingsley said, giving only a sad chuckle before sipping his own drink and sitting down.

"How did it happen?" he asked.

Rosie looked up and stared at the Premier. His hands coiled around his glass but there was a slight shake to them. His green eyes bore into her, expectantly waiting for her answer.

"A dark demon. A reaper."

Drawing his eyes away from Rosie, he stared at a picture on the wall, and his shaking hand brought the glass back up to his mouth. He gulped the last of the liquid and poured himself another glass.

"You're sure?" Kingsley asked, turning back to Rosie. "You saw it?"

She shook her head but answered, "Justin saw. He knew what happened. Christion had spoken to him about the creatures."

Finishing off the drink and refilling his cup again, Kingsley nodded in thought.

"They're the only thing that can kill immortals, right?"

"They are," Kingsley replied, walking to the picture on the wall and studying the desert mountain and cave which sat somewhat hidden behind a hill. "Christion's body?"

"It happened at the new school."

"How did you…" Kingsley began to ask but shook his head. "Never mind. It isn't important. I'm sorry for your loss, Rosie."

A tear rolled down Rosie's cheek and she swiped it away. "Thank you."

"Rosie!" Ms. Connors said as she ran into the office. Rosie's mom engulfed her, and Rosie sat letting the rest of the tears fall as her mother caressed her.

"Are you okay?" her mother asked, stroking her hair and squeezing her.

Unable to speak, she nodded her head against her mother's chest and kept her eyes closed.

"What is it?" Ms. Connors asked, staring at the Premier.

"Rose," Kingsley started. "Have you been able to see Christion at all today?"

"No. Why? What's happened?"

There was a short pause before Kingsley spoke again, "Rose, I'm sorry."

Sucking in a breath, Ms. Connors began to cry and held her daughter tighter.

"What happened? Why couldn't I see him?" she asked between sobs.

"A mythical, otherworldly magic was at play. Your magic might not have been strong enough to penetrate that type of power."

"How could he die?"

"This magic," Kingsley explained, "is the only type of magic that can kill an immortal. Dark demons are of a different realm. The realm of souls. They believe immortals play their master, Death."

"Are you in trouble? Will they come after you?" Ms. Connors asked, pulling away from her daughter and leaning towards Kingsley.

"They may."

"Only if summoned," Rosie whispered, remembering what Justin had said. "They will only come if called. Who knew of my dad's real identity?"

Kingsley's eyes widened but he sat back down. He stared at Rosie's and her mother, who sobbed silently.

"Of course, the three of us knew," Kingsley stated. "And then select members of the Superiority."

"Who? How?"

"I informed select council members in order to make the integration between the communities even more seamless."

"Okay, who else?"

"Members of the clan knew. Raphael and his inner circle."

"So, a lot of people?"

"About twenty?" Kingsley guessed.

"What about anyone with a grudge?"

"Not that I can think of."

Rosie racked her thoughts before quietly speaking, "Well, you have a motive."

Kingsley sat up as he started choking on his drink. After a few coughs he spoke, "Me? What motive could I possibly have?"

"You didn't know about Christion?" Ms. Connors said, wiping her nose.

"Know what?"

"My dad was going to run for Premier."

Kingsley paused and searched both Rosie's and her mother's faces for any sign of deception. He leaned back in his chair and stared down at his desk.

"You really didn't know?" Rosie asked.

Kingsley looked up at Rosie. "I didn't. There was a rumor that someone would try to run for the position now that the integration is underway, but Raphael had the solution of becoming Vice Premier. I thought that would unify us further without causing much disruption."

"Yeah, Raphael was supposed to run with my dad," Rosie said. "Could he have done this?" she asked, sitting forward.

"It doesn't seem likely. It's possible he and your father agreed to different terms. I will speak with him immediately."

Standing up, Kingsley walked back towards the office entry but turned back.

"I am truly sorry for your loss."

He started to head out again, but Rosie stopped him.

"Premier," she said, and waited for him to turn back.

"Yes?"

"If dark demons can kill immortals, what will you do?"

A smirk tilted at the corners of his mouth. "Don't worry

about me." He walked back to the two and put a hand on each of their shoulders. "Stay as long as you'd like and Rose, take as much time as you need to grieve."

Ms. Connors nodded and embraced Rosie as Kingsley left. More sobs sounded from her mother, but Rosie sat with her eyes closed. Imagining what she would do to the person who summoned the dark demon. Thinking about what she would do to the person who killed her father.

Epilogue

Ms. Connors walked away from the settling dirt on the mountainside.

"I'll see you soon?" she asked Rosie as she paused by the pathway.

"Soon," Rosie said, before giving her mother a small hug and separating. Ms. Connors started walking down the rocky path, wiping a single tear from her cheek.

Turning back, Rosie stared at her father's grave. The dark brown dirt sat still as a slow warm wind brushed Rosie's hair up. On the side of the mountain, close to the top, overlooking the vast, lush, beautiful desert, Christion Flare's remains rested. A tall boulder, shaped more like a gravestone, stood at the top of the grave. There were no etchings or words printed on it and it was surrounded by other rocks and plants, but Rosie had the stone memorized.

"Bye, Dad," she whispered, and turned. Only she, her mother, and Justin attended the ceremony.

Kingsley had wanted to throw a grand funeral for all to come and pay their respects, but Rosie wanted to keep her father's identity a secret. She also didn't want to share the grief with anyone else.

"You okay?" Justin asked, stepping forward.

Rosie nodded her head and moved closer to him. In the weeks since her father's death, Riley had gone to his new home, calling and messaging Rosie as much as he could, Kingsley and Raphael implemented new laws and order to the established integrated community, and Rosie's mother worked fourteen-hour days at the Superiority.

"Yeah, I'm okay."

"You sure? I mean I haven't seen you cry since—"

"I said I'm okay." Rosie walked forward, distancing herself before stopping and taking a deep breath. "I'm sorry, it's just… Everything keeps changing."

"I know but I promise, this summer, it won't." He nudged his shoulder against hers, forcing a small smile to cross her lips.

"Just a summer of magic and sleuthing?"

"Exactly."

As the two walked down the mountain and back towards campus, Rosie wove magic between her fingers.

"Are you sure your mom is okay with you staying on campus?"

"She's gone most of the day. It just makes sense for me to be at school instead."

"Good, I want you there." Rosie raised an eyebrow and Justin quickly commented, "I mean, it'll be good since then we can work more on finding out who summoned the dark demon."

Rosie thought about the evil creature who took her father's life and hatred filled her. A hand clasped over hers and Rosie stared down at Justin siphoning magic away from her.

"What are you doing?" Rosie asked, pulling her hand away.

He raised his hands defensively. "It was either I siphoned, or you were going to blow a new cave in the mountain."

Rosie stared at her hands. They were a dull red and heat emanated off them. She shook them at her sides and then stuffed them into her pockets.

"Thanks."

"No problem," Justin said, moving by her side.

With her hands cooling off and the sun starting to set, Rosie looked out over the vast desert. She didn't look at it for its beauty or to admire the colors the sunset cast over the land. Instead, she searched for other creatures. Other witches casting magic or shifters prowling around.

"So, do you have any new leads?" Justin asked as he too stared at the surrounding desert.

"I thought you said we were going to take the day off searching for my father's killer?"

"Well, it seems like you need a pick-me-up."

"I guess I do, huh?" Rosie laughed, staring up at Justin.

The two stood still for only a moment, but in that moment, Justin leaned forward, his mouth inches away from Rosie's lips. His knuckles lifted and grazed her face and Rosie closed her eyes at his touch. She took in his sweet yet musky scent and calming aura. Finally, sensing his presence gone, she opened her eyes and Justin smiled at her.

"So?" he asked, waiting for her reply.

Cocking a grin, she walked ahead of him and spoke. "I have a few ideas."

About the Author

For S.A. Alba, writing a novel had always been a dream and making that dream a reality with her first book, King's Preparatory and the Book of Being, has been a thrilling adventure. S.A. Alba looks to inspire and entertain readers far and wide and hopes others will delve into her other writings as they become available. For more information on the author and upcoming books, please visit bysaalba.com.

To learn more about the magical King's Preparatory world, please visit kingspreparatory.com.